Hazard

Rockliffe Book 5

STELLA RILEY

Copyright © 2018 Stella Riley
All rights reserved.
ISBN-13: 978-1984362063

ISBN-10: 1984362062

Cover by Ana Grigoriu-Voicu, books-design.com

CONTENTS

	Page
Prologue	1
Chapter One	7
Chapter Two	21
Chapter Three	40
Chapter Four	56
Chapter Five	69
Chapter Six	82
Chapter Seven	96
Chapter Eight	114
Chapter Nine	131
Chapter Ten	145
Chapter Eleven	166
Chapter Twelve	184
Chapter Thirteen	199
Chapter Fourteen	214
Chapter Fifteen	228
Chapter Sixteen	240

	Page
Chapter Seventeen	253
Chapter Eighteen	268
Chapter Nineteen	281
Chapter Twenty	296
Chapter Twenty-One	311
Chapter Twenty-Two	327

PROLOGUE

PARIS, 1770

He didn't know how long he'd been lurking in the shrubbery, only that it had been longer than he'd expected. The gathering dusk suggested he'd been there an hour or more – and *still* there was no sign of mademoiselle's maidservant.

How much longer dared he wait? Mother's breathlessness had been acute that morning and they'd run out of the apothecary's tincture; consequently, since his sister couldn't leave Mother alone, he'd promised to buy a bottle on his way home. But if he delayed much longer, the shop might be closed; which left him with a choice between leaving the small favour that had been asked of him undone or staying to complete it.

It had been a peculiar day. Sir Kenneth Forbes-Montague, the English diplomat for whom he worked as an under-secretary had been absent from the office throughout – while from elsewhere in the house had drifted the sounds of turmoil and argument. But it wasn't until he'd arrived at the place in the garden where he usually ate his noon-day meal and found Sir Kenneth's sixteen-year-old step-daughter sobbing into her handkerchief, that his own part in it had begun.

Awkwardly, he'd asked what was wrong.

And she, utterly woebegone but still beautiful, had poured out a confused tale about English half-brothers taking her away and Sir Kenneth being powerless to stop them.

'I don't *know* them. It's been six years since Father died and five since Mama married Papa Ken and took me away from them. Only now Mama is dead and Papa Ken was never made my guardian and the brothers are coming to take me to England and I don't want to *go!*' She'd stopped speaking to stare beseechingly at him. 'Will you take a letter to Monsieur de Chevigny? Please?

You're the only person I can ask - and Philippe will help me. I *know* he will. You'll do that for me, won't you?'

Looking into those tear-drenched eyes, it hadn't occurred to him to refuse. The three hours each week spent teaching her French had become the one source of colour and light in an otherwise grey existence which consisted solely of duty, responsibility and the constant battle to make ends meet. So he'd treasured those hours; not because the girl was beautiful but because she was warm and vibrant; because she laughed and chattered and fed bon-bons to her chaperone, to her poodle and to him. Inevitably, he'd allowed himself to become stupidly fond of her. Not stupid enough to fool himself that anything could ever come of it ... but idiot enough to be flattered when she'd turned to him for help.

So he'd said, 'Of course, Mademoiselle. It will be my pleasure.'

'Thank you. *Thank you!* If you wait near the gate when you are leaving for the day, my maid will bring the letter.' Then, squeezing his hand, she'd added, 'It must be secret, you understand. If anyone finds out --'

'They won't.' He'd smiled reassuringly at her. 'They won't. I promise.'

And that was the reason he was currently hiding among the rhododendrons ... without any idea at all that it was already too late.

* * *

In the three cramped rooms behind the church of St Sulpice, a different sixteen-year-old girl was fighting a battle with fear and helplessness. Mother, who had been ill for over a year, had been struggling for breath since first light ... a struggle which had worsened considerably during the course of the day until, by mid-afternoon, the girl was becoming desperate.

She boiled more water, tossed in the last handful of nettles which the old woman in the rooms below had said was an infallible remedy and tried to raise Mother against the pillows to inhale the vapour. The parsley tea which had been the first thing she'd tried had seemed to help ... but within little more than an hour Mother had been breathing in great, raucous gasps again, her chest heaving with the effort and a bluish shade bracketing her lips. Now, having run out of the tincture and her brother not due home for hours with another bottle, the girl didn't know what else she could do and was beginning to panic.

'Please,' she begged, trying to sound calmer than she felt. '*Maman*, please ... lean forward a little and breathe the steam.' Holding the basin with one hand, she put a cloth over her mother's head to form a tent. 'It will help. There ... just breathe. *Please* breathe.'

But her mother's head flopped back against the pillows, the movement nearly upsetting the bowl. Her struggles for air were becoming shallower, more laboured ... and further apart. The girl set the useless nettle-water on the floor and sat on the side of the bed, staring despairingly into Mother's gaunt face while her mind scurried in a circle that always ended in the same place.

There was no one to help – and even if there had been, she didn't dare leave Mother long enough to fetch them. Neither was there anyone who would go to the apothecary or lend her the money to pay for the tincture. She was alone ... and she had a terrible sense of foreboding.

Holding tight to her mother's hand, she begged, 'Don't die, *Maman*. Please don't. Hold on a little longer ... just a little longer until the medicine comes.'

* * *

In the gardens of the Hôtel Fleurignac, dusk edged towards dark and still there was no sign of the maid. With anxiety clawing at his gut, he reluctantly decided he couldn't wait any longer. He swore silently to himself, recognising that the small, seemingly simple favour he had promised mademoiselle was turning out to be neither small nor simple. And then, from barely a few feet away, came the sound of more than one person pushing their way through the bushes directly towards him. Unease turned abruptly into dire premonition.

Someone was coming and, no matter who it was, it didn't bode -

The thought remained unfinished as two men burst through the foliage around him. A fist took him in the stomach and a foot connected with the back of his knee, sending him to the ground. Confused and hurting, he tried to get a look at his attackers, mentally cursing the gloom. Then an English voice snarled, 'Did you honestly expect to get way with running off with our sister? That she'd be permitted to ruin herself over a poverty-stricken piece of gutter-scum like you? Well? *Did* you?'

Dragging air into his lungs and managing to raise himself on to his knees, he said, 'I don't know what you're talking about.'

'Bloody liar.' A kick sent him sprawling again. 'I've got the letter her maid was bringing to you.' And in a sneering, lovelorn falsetto, '*Beloved – you must come to me or all is lost.* Faugh! And where the hell were you going to take her? Some back-street hovel?'

Nothing about this made sense. Trying to clear the fog in his head, he said, 'The letter isn't for me. I was --'

Another kick, this time hard and vicious against his ribs.

'Of course it's for you! Who else could it be for?'

They were both large, both unpleasant and clearly in no mood to listen to reason but he had to try. 'There must ... there'll be a superscription.'

A hand grasped a fistful of his hair and dragged his head up.

'There isn't. Just a pretty picture of a flower. Now why do you suppose *that* would be?'

It was becoming increasingly difficult to think, let alone speak.

'I – don't know. Perhaps the maid --'

'Oh for Christ's sake!' said a second voice impatiently. 'Why bother talking? Let me just give him a lesson in remembering his place and have done with it.'

'Fine.' The hand transferred its grip to his collar and hauled him to his feet. 'Enjoy yourself.'

After that, the blows came thick and fast, allowing him no opportunity to either defend himself or fight back. Not, he realised dimly, that it would have made much difference. There was blood in his mouth and searing pain everywhere else. His last thought as he fell to the ground again and one last violent kick sent excruciating agony roaring through him was that he wouldn't get to the apothecary now.

* * *

The bells of St Sulpice chimed the hour. It was eight o'clock. Even given the extra time it would take to call at the apothecary's shop three streets away, her brother should have been home an hour ago; an hour during which Mother's breathing had diminished to virtually nothing. There was no sound any more. No raw, desperate rasping as she fought for air; and no movement either beneath the faded pink night-rail.

Where are you? she asked her absent brother. *You can't have forgotten. But why are you so late? You should be here. I need you. Maman needs you. Oh … why don't you come?*

And then, between one minute and the next, she realised that even if her brother walked through the door with the tincture right now, it would be too late.

Maman had given up her unequal struggle … and was gone.

STELLA RILEY

LONDON

Summer, 1777

CHAPTER ONE

'You told me the play here was honest!'

The brash, angry and overly-loud voice sliced through the buzz of convivial conversation and the rattle of dice. At the Hazard table, play paused briefly, a handful of gentlemen stopped speaking and a few heads turned, eyes seeking the voice's owner.

Since it was the height of the evening and the main gaming floor of Sinclairs was at its busiest, only those closest knew who had spoken. But the companion to whom the contemptuous remark had been addressed must have made some quiet reply because the carrying tones, laced with more than a hint of provincial accent, retorted, 'Then you've been hood-winked, John. If the owners of this place knew their business, *he* wouldn't have got through the door!'

This time the words were accompanied by the stab of a furiously pointing finger which caused the men standing nearby to step back. Bit by bit, conversation withered and died, play stopped and everyone looked around to see whom that finger was denouncing; and when they found the answer, the silence in the room became suddenly acute.

Keeping both face and posture under rigid control, the man who was suddenly the unwelcome centre of everyone's attention looked steadily back into the flushed face of his accuser. He was aware that the gentlemen with whom he'd just now been talking had melted from his side and that the centre of the gaming floor had somehow emptied into an airless space. Everyone was waiting with baited breath to see what would happen next ... but since one could not deny an allegation that hadn't yet actually been put into so many words, the only sensible course was to remain silent and hope it never was.

'George.' John Clavering, the fellow's companion and the member who must have had him signed in as a guest, laid a tentative hand on his friend's sleeve. 'He *is* the owner.'

'What?'

'That is Monsieur Delacroix. He owns the club.'

Another silence, this time briefly incredulous until, shaking off the other man's hand, George strode into the centre of the floor saying, 'If that's so, this place is God-damned hell.' He halted some two yards from Aristide and, impaling him on a hard stare, said, 'I remember you. You're the bastard who took more than two thousand off me in Paris three years back.'

There had always been a chance that this might happen; that someone from his less-than-immaculate past might walk into Sinclairs one night and recognise him. For one very good reason, Aristide had no difficulty remembering either this man's name or the occasion to which he referred. Sir George Braxton ... and a more than usually lucrative evening at the Maison Belcourt.

Of course, he thought grimly. *Of all the men I fleeced over the years, it had to be this one, didn't it? Still, he hasn't actually accused me of cheating yet – so perhaps there's a chance of brazening it out if I keep my nerve.*

Allowing a slight frown to crease his brow, he said calmly, 'I'm afraid I have no recollection of ever having met you, sir. Perhaps your name might --'

'Sir George Braxton – as I reckon you know only too well!'

Aristide shook his head half-regretfully.

'I'm sorry ... but no. Perhaps you are confusing me with some other gentleman?'

'I'm damned well not. I don't forget faces. And *you're* no gentleman.'

'That would depend on your definition. But as Mr Clavering has already pointed out, I *am* the owner of this establishment in which you are a guest. And though I accept that losing a large sum is naturally galling, I can't help but observe that it is as easy to lose as to win and --'

'It's easy to lose when you're playing a Captain Sharp,' snarled Braxton. 'And that's what you are. A damned *cheat!*'

A spectral gasp of shock, there and yet not, filtered around the room.

Aristide maintained his outward composure even though he could feel the blood congealing in his veins. He said, 'You are insulting, sir. And, as I have said, mistaken.'

'And *I've* said that I'm not.' An unpleasant smile curled Braxton's mouth. 'You won't talk your way out of this. I'll not have it. And we'll see how many members your club has left by morning, won't we?'

Merde. Aristide cursed mentally. *This is a disaster. I have to get him out of here.*

'If you wish to pursue this misunderstanding, we may do so in my office and allow these other gentlemen,' he made a graceful, sweeping gesture to the room at large, 'to continue enjoying their evening.'

'Oh you'd like that, wouldn't you? A chance to wriggle out of your dirty linen in private. Pity I'm not green enough to let you, ain't it?'

'For the third and final time,' said Aristide quietly, 'you are in error.'

Sir George stepped closer to loom threateningly.

'Are you calling me a liar?'

'Not that I've heard,' remarked Nicholas Wynstanton, strolling with seeming laziness towards the pair. 'He said you were mistaken – which is the kind of thing that might happen to anyone, especially after three years. Happens to *me* between one day and the next.'

There was a faint scattering of laughter, causing Braxton's brow to darken still further.

'To *you*, maybe – but not to me. And not in this case. I remember the occasion well enough. It was at the Maison Belcourt. And I remember *him*. He's a cheat. What's more, he's bloody good at it!'

'That's a very serious allegation,' observed Nicholas. 'Can you prove it?'

Braxton's shoulders stiffened. 'Are *you* calling me a liar as well?'

'Not intentionally.'

'What's that supposed to mean? And who the hell are you anyway?'

'Lord Nicholas is my brother,' came a soft, drawling voice from the doorway to one of the smaller card-rooms. 'As to his meaning … I believe he is merely questioning your *memory*. After all, in a case such as this, he is quite correct in suggesting that an accusation alone is insufficient. Some additional substantiation is also required.'

Braxton stared into cool, night-dark eyes and recognised that, for tonight at least, the game was over. He had only been in London for a short time but the Duke of Rockliffe had been pointed out to him more than once – along with the information that his Grace wasn't a man to trifle with.

Looking back at Aristide, he said harshly, 'I'll find proof. Don't think I won't. I doubt if I'm the only man you've cheated and I'll bet there's some who feel they've lost more than they should at your tables. This doesn't end here. I want my money back – and one way or another, I'll get it.' And turning on his heel, he pushed his way through the silent audience and strode out.

From above, hidden in the shadows of the gallery, Madeleine Delacroix watched the tableau on the gaming floor dissolve into something approaching normality. Play recommenced at the Hazard table and conversations were resumed but from her vantage point she could see the number of dubious glances being cast at her brother.

That was good of Nicholas, she conceded. *But this won't go away – not just like that or even because Rockliffe stepped in, when everyone down there knows* why *he did. Also, if Aristide thinks he can count on Rockliffe standing by him, he'd better think again.*

After that, the evening seemed interminable and it was over two hours before Aristide entered his private office, with both Nicholas and Rockliffe at his heels.

'I thought,' Nicholas was saying to his brother, as they came in, 'that you were returning to the Priors.'

'And so I am,' replied the duke, closing the door behind him and offering Madeleine a slight bow. 'Mademoiselle. Doubtless you witnessed the earlier unpleasantness?'

She nodded, her eyes trained on her brother.

'What are you going to do about it?'

Aristide shrugged wearily and turned to pour brandy for his guests.

'What do you suggest?'

'I've no idea – but you'll have to do something! You heard that man. He wants his money and he's determined to get it.'

'I think,' said Rockliffe thoughtfully, 'that we should perhaps clarify some part of Braxton's accusation.' And when no reply was immediately forthcoming, 'I recommend that you choose your words carefully, Monsieur Delacroix.'

Aristide drained his glass in a single swallow and then said abruptly, 'I played cards with Braxton in Paris. He lost.'

A frown gathered in Nicholas's eyes. He opened his mouth to speak and then thought better of it.

'Very wise,' murmured the duke. 'Do not invite knowledge you may regret.'

'My past is … less than spotless,' admitted Aristide jerkily. 'But my present life is *not*. I do not cheat at cards or anything else. And I take every possible measure to prevent even the merest suspicion of dishonest play at Sinclairs.'

'Good enough,' said Nicholas slowly. 'But what of Braxton? Did he make this accusation at the time?'

'No.'

'Well, that's something I suppose.'

'I didn't play at Belcourt's after that night, so our paths didn't cross again.' Aristide stared down into his empty glass. 'And two months later, I was here in London.'

'*Can* he prove anything?' Madeleine demanded.

'No. That is … I don't think so.'

'He doesn't need to,' said Nicholas reluctantly. 'It's little more than a month since rumour nearly ruined Sebastian Audley, for God's sake! And Braxton's already done enough to cast suspicion on both you and Sinclairs.'

'I'm aware of that.'

Setting down his glass untouched, Rockliffe said, 'You will understand that – given the circumstances – I can do little more than I already have. If asked, I am prepared to endorse the honesty of play in the club. I may even add that I have played cards with you myself from time to time and have no qualms about doing so again. But that, I am afraid, is all.'

'It is more than I would ask, your Grace. And your intervention downstairs was greatly appreciated,' returned Aristide. 'As, of course, was yours, Nicholas.'

'Well, I wasn't about to just stand there while he brought the ceiling down on you, was I?' retorted his lordship.

'No, Nicholas,' said his brother dryly. 'You were about to give that ill-bred fellow an excuse to challenge you – which would not have helped matters in the least. And now I shall take my leave. I wish to set out for Kent first thing in the morning.'

'So you're not going to Sarre's supper party tomorrow evening?'

'Obviously not,' replied Rockliffe. And, with a brief nod for Aristide and a bow for Madeleine, he strolled unhurriedly from the room.

Lord Nicholas eyed Monsieur Delacroix narrowly. He said, 'Now *there's* a thought. You'll be attending Sarre's party, won't you?'

'No,' replied Aristide, with the merest hint of annoyance.

'No? Why not?'

There was a brief, tense silence. Then Madeleine said edgily, 'Just because *I* refused to go, there's no reason why *you* should not.'

Aristide said nothing.

Regarding Madeleine over folded arms, Nicholas said, 'Why won't you go? I'm aware that you and Adrian had some sort of falling-out at one time but you ought to have got over it by now. And even if you haven't, mending matters from tonight is more important. You can say what you like about Adrian but he stands by his friends.'

'I don't question that. And of course he lies so very well, does he not? Even, at times, without opening his mouth.'

Nicholas gave a crack of laughter.

'He'd call that acting, not lying – though it's a fine distinction. But that's beside the point. The important thing is that being seen under Adrian's roof will cast doubt on anything Braxton may say. What's more, nobody will be able to cold-shoulder either of you without looking rag-mannered.'

'And God *forbid*,' said Madeleine acerbically, 'that anyone should so far forget themselves as to be *impolite*.'

Aristide groaned inwardly but before he could speak, Nicholas said bluntly, 'That is actually true. If folk went about saying whatever was in their heads, there'd be blood on the streets.' He paused, holding her gaze and then, when she didn't speak, turned back to Aristide. 'Come to Cork Street tomorrow. You'll probably know nearly everyone there.'

'I'll consider it,' sighed Aristide, '*after* I've spoken to Adrian about tonight and *after* I've made the acquaintance of his wife.'

Nicholas blinked. 'You still haven't met Caroline?'

'No. She arrived three days before Sebastian's wedding and apparently spent every minute making his new house fit to live in.' A gleam of amusement lit Aristide's usually cool eyes. 'As for the six days *since* then, she's insisted that Bertrand join them to manage the Cork Street household while she drags Adrian from one warehouse to another to choose hangings for the newly-renovated north wing at Sarre Park.' The gleam became a smile. 'I gather that has also been a time-consuming task.'

'Which I am sure that Adrian is enjoying immensely,' remarked Madeleine, with acid-tinged pleasure. 'But it's *such a* shame that her ladyship hasn't so far had time to honour Sinclairs with a visit.'

'If that's you deciding to dislike Caroline before you've even laid eyes on her,' returned Nicholas swiftly, 'it's the most stupid attitude I ever heard. Grow up, why don't you?'

Aristide stared … first at Nicholas and then at his sister … and managed, not without difficulty, to remain silent.

Flushing, Madeleine said stiffly, 'You are putting words in my mouth.'

'I don't think so.' He reached for his hat and turned towards the door, then stopped. 'You were considering whether or not to accept my invitation to come driving with me. I'd have thought a week long enough to make up your mind. So what is it to be?'

In the month since she'd insulted him by saying she wouldn't sleep with him when it appeared he'd never had any intention of asking her to do so, she had found herself at a serious disadvantage; and the ultimatum he'd thrown at her eight days ago had brought her face to face with a truth she hadn't wanted to admit even to herself. None of her careful self-discipline … none of the measures she'd taken to protect herself from the kind of heart-break she'd experienced once before had been the least use. When Nicholas had given her the chance to cut him from her life once and for all, she had been unable to do it. And tonight when he had stood at Aristide's shoulder without being asked, something in her chest had cracked wide open.

The flush deepened. He'd told her to choose … and that he wouldn't ask again; so if she said no now, that would be the end of it – which was precisely what she'd kept assuring herself that she wanted. Except that it wasn't what she wanted at all. So she looked up at him and said quietly, 'Yes. If you still wish it, I'll drive with you.'

'Good,' said Nicholas, keeping his tone completely free of the stupid pleasure that was washing through him at this one, really very small victory. 'Tomorrow, then. I'll call for you in Duke Street at three o'clock.' And with a glimmer of his usual grin, 'Don't change your mind.' Then he was gone.

For a full minute after the door closed behind him, there was silence. Finally, Aristide said mildly, 'Dear me. Did my ears deceive me?'

'Don't! Just don't!' warned Madeleine. 'I couldn't very well say no after the way he supported you tonight – but if you insist on discussing it, I *will* change my mind.'

'If you do that, it will be entirely your own decision,' came the cool response. 'However ... let us return to the question of Lady Sarre's supper-party. I'll speak to Adrian in the morning. If, after I've done so, the invitation still stands --'

'Of course it will. He won't want to see Sinclairs ruined any more than you do.'

'Just at present, the club isn't his first priority.'

'The not-quite-new wife? Dear me. He *must* be besotted if the novelty hasn't worn off after nearly six months.'

He shot her an irritable look.

'For the love of God, stop it! You and Adrian were friends once and you could be again if you'd only stop snarling at him.'

'He snarls back,' she grumbled defensively.

'If you sharpen your claws on his wife, he'll do more than snarl.'

'I'd be perfectly happy never to *meet* his unfortunate wife.'

'So I've gathered. But if her invitation is still open, we should accept it. And you will behave. The situation is quite bad enough without you making it worse.'

Madeleine sighed and abruptly capitulated, knowing that her personal feelings were of scant importance under the circumstances.

'I won't make it worse,' she said. And added long-sufferingly, 'I'll smile at the bride and overflow with commonplace inanities. I'll even be civil to Adrian.'

Despite everything, her brother suddenly laughed.

'Don't overdo it. Adrian might faint.'

* * *

'They're at breakfast,' Bertrand informed Aristide when he arrived in Cork Street on the following morning. 'The whole house is in turmoil and there's a dragon upstairs spitting out orders. But *they're* still at breakfast. It's been over an hour now, so one imagines they have finished eating.' A glinting smile dawned. 'Go on in, why don't you?'

If Aristide's mind had not been on other things, he might have recalled Bertrand's particular brand of humour. As it was, he opened the door to the breakfast parlour – and wished he hadn't.

There was an instant of frozen silence. Then the Countess of Sarre scrambled off her husband's lap, scarlet-cheeked with her hair tumbling down her back and hastily tried to re-arrange her bodice. With studied nonchalance, the Earl, *sans* cravat, reached for the buttons of his vest and continued lounging in his seat – a fact which told Aristide something he'd rather not have known.

Keeping his gaze on Adrian to allow her ladyship time to tidy herself, he said, 'My apologies. I should have knocked. I ought also, by now, to know better than trust Bertrand.'

'Someone will murder him one day,' growled Adrian. 'Me, probably.' He shifted uncomfortably. 'Sit down and help yourself to coffee.'

'It will be cold by now,' said Caroline quickly, seizing an excuse to flee the room. 'I'll order a fresh pot.'

'Please don't trouble on my account.' Aristide decided it was probably safe to look in her direction. 'I merely needed to --'

'It's no trouble. None at all.'

Caroline was half-way to the door when Adrian glanced at her and suddenly saw the funny side. Anyone would think he was playing the discovered lover in a bawdy comedy. His voice brimming with laughter, he said, 'Don't run away, darling. It's too late for that and it's not as if we were doing anything married couples aren't allowed to do. So pull the bell and when Bertrand answers it, hit him with that God-awful statue of Minerva.' He stopped, tilted his head slightly and added, 'Meanwhile, allow me to finally introduce my business partner, Monsieur Delacroix. Aristide ... meet the Countess of Sarre. If you promise to forget what you just saw, she'll probably permit you to call her Caroline.'

Stopped in her tracks, Caroline sent her husband a thoroughly exasperated look and then turned, with what dignity she could muster, to the Frenchman. Her immediate impression was of fair hair neatly tied, serious blue eyes and restrained but immaculate tailoring. He also looked either uncomfortable or worried. She couldn't tell which.

But he bowed with perfect correctness and said, 'It is a pleasure to meet you at last, Lady Sarre. Allow me to offer my deepest felicitations on your marriage.'

Caroline curtsied and smiled at him.

'Thank you. I've been hoping to visit Sinclairs but what with one thing and another, there's been no time.'

'I'll take you to the club tomorrow, if you like.' Deciding that he could now rise without risking further embarrassment, Adrian offered his hand to Aristide saying, 'What brings you here so early?'

'There was ... an incident last evening that you should know about.'

This time the note of strain in his voice was very evident and, seeing Adrian frown, Caroline immediately said, 'I'll leave the two of you to talk. And I'll send fresh coffee.'

'There is no need --' began Aristide again.

But he stopped when Caroline shook her head and said, 'I should go anyway. Lady Brassington is helping prepare for this evening since I have no experience in such matters – but I ought to be doing *something*.'

'Will she let you?' asked Adrian with a grin.

'Probably not. Ah – I nearly forgot. She asked if she may bring her widowed god-daughter this evening, so naturally I said yes. And that reminds me.' She looked back at Aristide. 'Adrian says you declined our invitation. It would give us both great pleasure if you and your sister were to reconsider.'

And then she was gone, the door closing softly behind her.

Aristide looked at Adrian and muttered, 'You may feel differently when you've heard what I have to say.'

'As bad as that, is it?'

'Yes. Or it could be.'

'So sit down and tell me.'

Aristide nodded and took a seat at the table. Then, in as few words as possible, he described the events of the previous evening. He had just arrived at the point where Rockliffe had intervened when a tap at the door heralded a housemaid with the coffee. Adrian waited until she was gone and then said dryly, 'It's becoming a shade uncanny just how often Rock is on hand when a *deus ex machina* is needed. I suppose he asked if Braxton's allegations were true?'

'After a fashion. He didn't want to hear me admit to sharping in so many words.'

'No. He wouldn't. But I daresay he put two and two together.' Crossing to the sideboard in search of clean cups, Adrian poured coffee and said, 'What I *don't* understand is why this fellow Braxton is so sure you cheated. I thought you were better than that.'

'I *am* better than that.'

Grinning at the note of affront, Adrian couldn't resist another small jibe.

'Well, something must have given you away. He didn't catch you dealing from the bottom of the pack, did he?'

'No. He did not.' Aristide's tone said that this was just insulting. 'At the time, he had no idea what I was doing or how. He drew his conclusions later.'

'Yet last night,' said Adrian slowly, 'he announced it as a fact. Doesn't that seem odd?'

It didn't seem odd to Aristide and, just for an instant, he was tempted to explain why. Adrian, after all, was the one person with whom he could share the truth of what had happened ... and the one person who would appreciate it. But since the full story wasn't going to help now any more than it would have done last night on the main floor of Sinclairs, he didn't see any point in wasting time discussing it. Consequently, he said a shade impatiently, 'Who knows how the man's mind works – and what does it matter? It doesn't alter the basic problem.'

'No, I suppose not. Truthfully, we always knew something like this might happen and accepted the risk. So now all we can do is deal with it. I don't know Braxton. How likely is he to be believed?'

'Since I don't know anything about him either, I have no idea.'

'Then we'd better find out. I'll send instructions to Henry Lessing and tell him to report to you. In a few days you'll know what Braxton is worth down to the last penny and probably what colour his drawers are as well.'

Aristide stopped stirring cream into his cup and looked up. 'That's all very well but it won't destroy the implication regarding Sinclairs. And Braxton isn't prepared to let it lie. He wants his money back. But I can't pay him because it would amount to an admission of guilt. He also said he'd find proof. If he does that --'

'*If* he does. After three years, I wouldn't have thought his chances very high. But we'll cross that bridge when we come to it. For now, our primary task is finding ways to reduce the damage … and I suggest you begin by attending Caroline's party tonight. Everyone knows I spent years in France and a good many people probably suspect that you and I knew each other before my return. Receiving you socially will reinforce that suspicion, thus casting doubt on Mr Braxton.'

'Sir George Braxton,' corrected Aristide. Then, 'Yes. That's what Nicholas says. And Madeleine.'

'*Madeleine?*' Adrian gave a small, hard laugh. 'I didn't think wild horses could drag her anywhere near me if there was a way to avoid it.'

'She says she'll come. She's even promised to be on her best behaviour.'

'God. *That* will be something to witness.'

Aristide pushed his cup aside and said flatly, 'You know why I refused the invitation when you first offered it. You've barely managed to stay clear of the mire yourself – and for your wife's sake, I'd have thought you'd like to keep it that way. So although I understand the advantages of being seen under your roof, I think her ladyship should know what I've told you and be given the chance to rescind the invitation.'

'She won't do it,' shrugged Adrian. 'Oh – I can tell her, if you like. But it won't change anything. Caroline will ask whether you did what Braxton says you did; then she'll ask whether you're *still* doing it; and after that she'll tell you to present yourself punctually – and probably remind you to bring a clean handkerchief.' He grinned and leaned back in his chair. 'The Vernons are in Hertfordshire and Harry and Nell are on their way to Paris. But the Ingrams will be here, along with the Delahayes, Lord and Lady Amberley and a handful of others you know – possibly even Sebastian and Cassie, if they can bear to get out of bed. Also, the redoubtable Lady Brassington. So will you be joining us – or not?'

There was a long silence. Finally, Aristide said, 'Yes. We'll come. And thank you.'

'Excellent. You've no idea how much I'm looking forward to seeing Madeleine's notion of company manners. And ensuring that she extends them to Caroline.'

CHAPTER TWO

On the following afternoon, Lord Nicholas drew up his carriage before the Delacroix residence, vaulted down to the pavement and tossed a coin to the crossing-sweeper to hold his horses. A brief glance at the house told him that, though only of moderate size, it was well-proportioned and elegant – which didn't surprise him since Aristide had excellent taste.

The fellow who answered the door *looked* like a butler ... if one discounted the breadth of chest and shoulder. Nicholas swallowed a grin and hoped that, in addition to the obvious muscle, the man had more intelligence than Madeleine's guard-dogs at Sinclairs.

'Good afternoon, my lord,' said the butler in perfectly rounded tones. 'If you will follow me to the drawing-room, I shall inform Mademoiselle that you have arrived.'

'There is no need, Minton,' said a cool voice. 'I am here.'

Nicholas turned and looked up to where she stood at the turn of the stairs. She was wearing dove-grey, subtly banded with black and choosing to busy herself with her gloves rather than meet his eyes as she descended the remaining steps.

Ah, he thought. *Invisible wall firmly in place, is it?*

Bowing and resisting the temptation to ask her who'd died, he said pleasantly, 'Good afternoon, Mademoiselle. You are delightfully prompt. But I'd have waited, you know.'

She looked at him then. 'Of course. But we had an appointment. And tardiness is both rude and inefficient.'

An *appointment? Inefficient?* He very nearly laughed. She was trying to put him in his place before they'd even got through the door. Didn't she know she'd have to try a lot harder than that? He said, 'If efficiency is the order of the day, we'd better not waste any more time.' He offered his arm. 'Shall we?'

Aware of how officious she'd sounded and wanting to kick herself, Madeleine cast a suspicious glance at him. Since, however, he didn't look as if he was laughing at her, she allowed him to lead her out to the carriage and help her into it.

Flicking another coin to the urchin who, clearly amazed at this largesse, said, 'Gawd! Thank you, m'lord!', Nicholas set his horses in motion. Madeleine, meanwhile, made her second mistake of the afternoon by opening her mouth without thinking.

'You'd already paid him,' she observed, thus giving away the fact that she'd been watching through the window.

Although his mouth curled a little, Nicholas chose not to remark on this. He merely said, 'A shilling or two is nothing to me but a great deal to him. Neither I nor anyone else can cure London's poverty. But we can all give a little help here and there.'

This time she didn't reply, busy trying not to think what this said about him.

Eventually, after letting the silence linger for a few moments, Nicholas asked how she was enjoying the new house.

'It's well enough.'

'Better, surely, than living in a couple of rooms over Sinclairs?'

'Yes.'

'And very conveniently situated.'

'Very.'

Still determined to be difficult, eh? thought Nicholas. *Well, two can play at that game.*

He drove on to the gates of the park, swung his team through them and turned on to the already busy main thoroughfare. He didn't speak.

At first, Madeleine was glad of the silence but after five minutes, it began to feel uncomfortable. A swift sideways glance told her that Nicholas apparently didn't find it so. She wondered what he was thinking. Then she wondered if he would presently say something excruciatingly awkward that she wouldn't know how to answer. Her fingers tightened on the handle of her parasol and it was suddenly difficult not to fidget. Eventually, unable to bear it any longer, she said baldly, 'Why am I here?'

Nicholas tilted his head to cast her a thoughtful glance.

'An interesting question,' he said. 'Why are *any* of us here?'

'Don't be obtuse. You know what I meant.'

'Not necessarily. You might have wished to discuss philosophy.'

She very nearly ground her teeth.

'Odd as it may seem, I didn't. You invited me to drive with you, I accepted the invitation – and here we are. But if we're going to sit here in silence--'

'Pardon me,' cut in Nicholas smoothly, 'but I had the impression that was what you wanted. Monosyllabic replies don't exactly further the conversation, you know. Or did you expect me to deliver a monologue?'

'Of course not.'

'What, then?' He glanced at her, noting the way one gloved hand was clenched tight in her lap. 'Relax, Madeleine. We can talk or not. It's up to you. Meanwhile, I promise I won't over-turn us.'

'I never thought you would.' She drew a faintly impatient breath and said, 'My lord, I don't recall giving you leave to use my name.'

'I don't recall asking you to. And you can stop my-lording me. My name, as you know very well, is Nicholas.'

'*Lord* Nicholas,' she insisted.

It was his lordship's turn to become exasperated.

'It's only *Lord* Nicholas because my brother is a duke, as was my father before him.'

'And neither of them would approve of you consorting publicly with a female from a gaming house.'

To her surprise, he laughed.

'My father – if he wasn't six feet under and therefore not in a position to say anything – would make the same mistaken assumption you made yourself and congratulate me. God knows he had his fair share of mistresses. It's a mystery to me how he found sufficient time or energy to produce five legitimate offspring – and why after Rock, Lucilla and me and knowing him for the philanderer he was, Mama let him near enough to produce Kitty and Nell. It wasn't as though she was even remotely maternal, after all.'

For a second, this plain speaking caused Madeleine's jaw to drop. Then, recovering herself and returning to the point at issue, she said, 'And his Grace, your brother will be equally complaisant?'

'Rock will leave me to know my own business best,' he replied. And with a quizzical glance, 'Madeleine ... just what are you doing with your parasol?'

'What does it look like?' she snapped, feeling her colour rise. 'I'm protecting my face from the sun.'

'It would be an odd way of doing it even if the sun *wasn't* behind us.'

She set her jaw and said nothing.

'You're hiding,' he said.

'I am doing nothing of the sort!'

'Liar.' The laughter in his voice removed any sting from the word. Bringing his team to a halt, he said, 'It's not working, anyway. Say hello to Charles Fox.'

Managing not to groan, Madeleine altered the angle of her parasol and summoned something resembling a smile. 'Good afternoon, Mr Fox. A pleasant day, is it not?'

'Most pleasant,' he drawled. 'And made even more so by the discovery that you look as radiant by sunshine as by candlelight.' Then, to Nicholas, 'A departure from your usual daytime habits, surely? But of course, one sees why.'

Nicholas grinned back at him. 'What do you know about my habits, Charles – or even daylight, come to that? You rarely stir before dark yourself.'

'I fear that is all too true. But each to their own, you know.' He stepped back and made Madeleine an extravagant bow. 'Such a pleasure, Mademoiselle. Sadly, however, his lordship is holding up the traffic so I shall say *adieu*.'

Laughing a little, Nicholas drove on. 'You see? That wasn't so bad, was it?'

'Mr Fox is a law unto himself,' she muttered. 'As are you.'

'Good Lord! Was that a compliment? No, no. It can't have been!'

'I'm sure you are no stranger to compliments, my lord.'

'Nicholas,' he corrected. 'And they're rarer than you might think. I'd like to say that's because Rock over-shadows me just as he does the rest of the world ... but it wouldn't be true.' He managed a wistful sigh. 'Why, only a few minutes ago, you were hiding behind your parasol rather than be seen in my company.'

'I was *not* hiding,' she hissed through gritted teeth. 'But even if I *had* been, that would not have been the reason.'

'I know it wouldn't.'

Just for a second Madeleine found herself deprived of breath as well as words.

Taking advantage of this, Nicholas said flatly, 'I asked you to come driving with me and after debating the question for an entire week, you finally accepted my invitation. I'll wager peace treaties have been settled quicker. However, since us being seen together is now a *fait accompli*, your reservations on my behalf are pretty pointless, aren't they? So do you think we might just enjoy the sunshine and a conversation that doesn't have you weighing every word to set me at arms' length?'

'I wasn't.'

'Yes. You were. But if you're so worried I'll ask questions you don't want to answer, choose a topic yourself. There must be *something* you consider safe ground.'

She found herself wondering how he had learned to read her so accurately. Then, because he was plainly waiting for her to speak, she cleared her throat and said, 'The difficulty last night with Braxton. I wondered if it might not be solved by Aristide offering to play cards with him again and ... well, letting him win.'

'Absolutely not. When a fellow thinks he's been fleeced, he doesn't chance it happening again. And I imagine ensuring one's opponent wins requires similar skills to ensuring that he *doesn't* ... which involves risks of quite another kind, wouldn't you say?'

'Yes. I suppose so.' Madeleine sighed. 'But Braxton said he'd find proof. How can he do that when it happened three years ago and in Paris, for God's sake?

'I suppose he'll look for other men who've played against Aristide and lost.'

'And if he doesn't find any?'

'Hard to say,' shrugged Nicholas. 'Perhaps he'll give up.' And thought, *Or perhaps he won't. Perhaps he'll search out anybody who's got a grudge against Aristide ... or a couple of men who can be paid to lie.* He tipped his hat to Lady Barclay and Viscountess Hendon, both of whom were taking a good long look at Mademoiselle Delacroix and then tossed a casual greeting to Lord Carlisle as his carriage passed them from the opposite direction. 'Did Aristide speak to Sarre?'

'Yes.'

'And?'

'He said Aristide and I should both attend tonight's party in order to protect the reputation of Sinclairs.'

Her choice of words along with the coolness of her tone wasn't lost on Nicholas. He said shrewdly, 'It's not just the club – and you know it.'

'Perhaps.'

'There's no perhaps about it.' He paused. 'Why don't you like him?'

She stared straight ahead so that he couldn't read her expression.

'Who says I don't?'

'Sarre does. Not that he needed to, since you make it obvious.' He waited and when, once again, she didn't reply, he said, 'All right. Not my business, I suppose. But I hope you're not going to let whatever it is stop you accompanying Aristide this evening.'

'No. I said I would go – and I will.'

'Good. Then I shall see you there.' He gave her a lazy grin. 'And now – solely between you and me, of course – just how good *is* Aristide with cards?'

* * *

That evening, two other ladies sat before their mirrors prior to leaving for Cork Street, each contemplating the evening ahead from differing viewpoints.

In Bruton Place, Cassandra Audley prepared to leave the house for the first time since her wedding ... and realised that she'd be perfectly happy not to do so. For seven halcyon days, the outside world had ceased to exist and neither she nor Sebastian had missed it. They'd roamed their house, laughing and arguing about furniture and hangings they had yet to purchase. They'd chased each other through the empty, echoing rooms, in a series of foolish games that nearly always ended the same way. And Cassie had discovered that her husband had numerous ways of being wicked ... all of which were thoroughly enjoyable.

Tonight was also the first time she'd seen her maid since her wedding night. Now, clad in corset and petticoats, she sat at her dressing-table while, silent but bristling with disapproval, Susan began work on her hair.

'Now there's a pretty picture,' remarked Sebastian from the doorway, 'though I'll admit to recalling ones I liked better.'

Knowing what he meant but hoping that Susan didn't, Cassie said, 'Rubens? Titian?'

'No. Botticelli comes closest to the one I have in mind.' He strolled towards her, teasing yet predatory. 'Perhaps your maid could finish your hair later?'

Susan didn't wait to be told. Slapping down a handful of hairpins, she stalked out.

Sebastian laughed. 'Oh dear. Something I said?'

'She's sulking.' And on a small sigh, 'Truth to tell, I feel a bit like sulking myself. I know we have to go this evening. Adrian is your closest friend, as Caroline is mine and this is their first party. Of *course* we must go. But it just feels a little like ...'

'Letting down the drawbridge?' He stood behind her, his hands resting on her shoulders. 'It needn't be. We don't have to accept other invitations ... and the house isn't fit for visitors yet.'

Cassie brightened. 'That's true. The reception rooms aren't furnished.'

'There's a table in the front drawing-room and that huge chair in the library,' Sebastian reminded her, his voice low and warm. 'Have you forgotten those?'

She hadn't. Neither had she forgotten the use to which they had been put. The recollection sent the now-familiar sensation of liquid heat flooding through her. Knowing it, Sebastian drew her back to lean against him while his fingers skimmed down to trace the rim of her corset. He said consideringly, 'Ah. An obstacle. This may require some ingenuity.'

'Sebastian ... we can't,' said Cassie unevenly. 'We'll be late.'

'So?' One intrepid fingertip slid inside the corset. 'Then by all means, let's be late.'

* * *

In her god-mother's house in Albemarle Street, Genevieve, Lady Westin was looking forward to the evening more than she'd looked forward to anything in a very long time, yet still she scowled at her reflection, deciding that she was heartily sick of black. She'd been swathed in it for ten months, one week and three days ... and all for a husband she had not been sorry to lose.

She'd leapt into marriage with Christopher Westin six months before her eighteenth birthday because she'd thought marriage to anyone at *all* would be better than continuing to live with brothers who planned to sell her to the highest bidder, regardless of whether or not the gentleman in question had a tooth left in his head or was crippled with gout. Young, handsome, charming Kit Westin had seemed the better option by far.

The wedding flowers had scarcely been dead before she'd begun to suspect that she'd made a mistake; but it took a long, miserable year to learn just how big that mistake had been and four more before death set her free – only to plunge her into an immense and wholly unexpected scandal.

Forcing back her thoughts, Genevieve turned as Lady Brassington, her second-cousin and god-mama, appeared in the mirror behind her. She said, 'Thank you for allowing me to accompany you this evening, Cousin Lily. You have no idea how starved I am for company.'

'If I did not understand and sympathise, I wouldn't have asked Caroline if you might attend. For I should not, you know. Even though it is to be a small party without dancing or music, it is not strictly permissible for a widow who has yet to put off her blacks.'

'It's only another six weeks,' said Genevieve persuasively, 'and I have a lovely violet silk that's no more than two years old. Surely no one would object if I --'

'Stop,' said Lady Brassington firmly. 'Thanks to the unfortunate nature of your husband's departure from this world, I doubt there's anyone in society who couldn't tell you the precise date of it. Colours are therefore out of the question. You may just about get away with making an appearance in Cork Street this evening – though I doubt your brother would agree with me. Indeed, I'm fairly sure Kilburn would say you shouldn't be in London *at all*. Have you sent him a note as I asked?'

'Not yet.'

'You *must*! His lordship won't be pleased with either of us anyway – you for coming to town without informing him or me for taking you in. But if he hears it from someone else --'

'I'll do it tomorrow,' promised Genevieve quickly. 'Truly, I will. But if Ralph had ever spent a single night in that dismal house to which Kit's cousin relegated me the instant the funeral was over, he might wonder how I endured it.' She spread beseeching hands. 'I'm nearly twenty-four, Cousin Lily ... and for the last six years, I may as well have been prison. But I'm free now and I intend to enjoy my freedom – regardless of what Ralph or anyone else thinks. I *deserve* it.'

* * *

By a half after ten, all but four of Lady Sarre's guests had arrived and the house in Cork Street buzzed with conversation and laughter – a good deal of it speculation regarding the as yet absent newly-weds. While the ladies maintained that dearest Cassie would absolutely *not* miss Caroline's first party, the gentlemen were divided in their opinions and discreetly wagering a few shillings on whether or not 'dearest Cassie' would succeed in luring Mr Audley out of the bedroom.

Presuming that, like himself, Sarre was more interested in the other absentees, Nicholas strolled over to where his lordship was chatting with the Marquis of Amberley and said bluntly, 'Where the hell has Aristide got to? He ought to be here by now.'

The Marquis grinned. 'What's the matter, Nick? Worried he'll steal your reputation for always being the last to arrive?'

'Or worried that he's changed his mind - or, more likely, let Madeleine change it for him,' suggested Adrian.

Nicholas shook his head. 'She was certain enough this afternoon.'

'This afternoon?'

'Yes. I took her driving in the park.'

Amberley and Sarre exchanged amused glances.

'Progress at last,' remarked Adrian. 'Or was it?'

'Well, it wasn't a disaster, if that's what you mean. We discussed the Braxton affair and – ah.' He stopped and looked at the Marquis. 'You heard about that, I suppose?'

'There was some talk at Whites this morning, yes.'

'And?'

'Aside from Ansford – tedious and predictable as ever – remarking that there is no smoke without fire, the general view was that, while nobody knows Braxton, *everybody* knows Rock can spot a sharp at ten paces. From what I heard, I doubt Aristide need worry overmuch.' Eyes narrowing slightly as he gazed across the room and without waiting for either gentleman to reply, Amberley said quietly, 'Who is the lady in black who has been keeping Rosalind and Althea trapped in conversation for the last ten minutes?'

'Lady Brassington's god-daughter,' sighed Adrian. 'Apparently, she arrived without warning yesterday, so Lady B asked Caroline if she might bring her this evening. We knew she was a widow – but neither of us thought she'd still be in full mourning.'

Nicholas eyed the lady in question. 'Who was the husband?'

'Some fellow named Westin.'

'*Westin?*'

'Yes. I've never heard of him – but I'm gathering that you have?'

'Along with most of London. He was found dead outside a particularly revolting brothel. July of last year, it would have been. You'd remember, Amberley?'

'Indeed. As I recall, he'd been attacked but not robbed – which a lot of people felt told its own story. Not that one can hold that against his unfortunate widow. Except ...' The Marquis hesitated and then went on, 'Didn't Westin marry Kilburn's sister?'

Nicholas nodded but said, 'Half-sister, I think it was.'

Looking from one to the other of them, Adrian said, 'And that is significant because?'

For a few seconds, neither gentleman spoke. But finally Amberley said reluctantly, 'The Harcourt men are an unpleasant lot. Kilburn – the current viscount – has fought four duels. The last time he killed his man and spent the best part of a year in France as a result. Cedric is rumoured to have been trying to recreate the old Hellfire Club. And Bertram is a gamester, a drunk ... and what might politely be called a gigolo.'

'He's a bloody whore,' muttered Nicholas. 'Why dress it up? The widow may be respectable but her brothers aren't and neither was her husband.'

Frowning a little, Adrian said slowly, 'You are saying that she is tarnished by association?'

'Some people will probably look at it that way,' agreed the Marquis.

'I see. Then perhaps, if only for Lady B's sake, we should give her the benefit of the doubt. And meanwhile,' Adrian grinned suddenly, looking beyond them to the doorway, 'you both owe me a guinea. Sebastian and Cassie have arrived.'

Inevitably, half the guests immediately converged on the bridal pair, the gentlemen to shake Mr Audley's hand and the ladies to draw Cassie into a laughing, chattering circle.

Suddenly alone at the edge of the room, Lady Westin pinned a smile on her face and glanced around for someone – *anyone* – she could approach without appearing ill-mannered. Cousin Lily had presented her to a number of people earlier in the evening but most of them appeared to be clustered around the new arrivals. Moreover, she'd become increasingly aware that, despite her best efforts, neither Lady Amberley nor Mistress Ingram had seemed to warm to her. This might have been because she was still in black or, more likely, because she'd been trying too hard. Whatever the reason, although they'd been perfectly polite, it had been the sort of courtesy that suggested they would terminate the conversation as soon as the opportunity presented itself – which it now had. Swallowing hard, Genevieve strolled towards the room where refreshments had been laid out ... and found her path blocked by a slender, sandy-haired fellow who, though he held a tray of wine, neither looked nor behaved like a servant.

'Have some Canary,' invited Bertrand, handing her a glass with a lazy half-smile, 'and study the painting over the fireplace. It is quite horrible.'

And he continued on his way, without waiting for a reply.

Genevieve looked at the painting. It was a still-life featuring a quantity of dead birds, a brace of rabbits and a small deer ... and it was, as the odd French fellow had said, horrible. Genevieve drank her wine and stared at it with dedication for what felt like an eternity until Lady Brassington arrived at her side.

'The evening isn't living up to expectation, is it?' she asked quietly.

'No. Not really.'

Her ladyship sighed. 'I ought not to have brought you. Everyone here must know that neither Cedric nor Bertram are received anywhere and that Kilburn is only tolerated in certain quarters because of the title. As for Westin ...' She stopped, shuddering. 'Eyebrows were bound to be raised even *without* you appearing in widow's weeds. And on top of all that, this evening is partly in honour of the newly-weds.'

'So I see,' said Genevieve listlessly. 'Who are they?'

'Sebastian Audley and Sir Charles Delahaye's daughter, Cassandra. The couple took the *ton* by storm a week ago by getting married at what should have been their betrothal ball. Quite the romance of the Season, as well as being a universally popular match.'

'How delightful for them.' Genevieve stared at the crowd across the room, her eyes focussing for perhaps the fifth time on one particular member of it. She said, 'Who is the tall, dark-haired gentleman in blue?'

Lily Brassington didn't need to look to know the answer.

'Lord Nicholas Wynstanton – the Duke of Rockliffe's brother. Don't even think of it.'

Think of what? wondered Genevieve. *I only want to find out if I still remember how to* talk *to a man. And as far as I can make out, Lord Nicholas is one of only two unmarried gentlemen in the room, the other being Mr Fox with his ridiculous blue wig and fan. But even though I've caught his lordship's eye twice, he's pretending I haven't.*

Perfectly – and a shade irritably – aware that the widow was inviting his attention yet again, Nicholas turned to grin at Sebastian.

'I'd ask how married life was suiting you if it wasn't clearly a silly question,' he said. 'I suppose you *had* to turn up just when I'd put money on the fact that you wouldn't?'

Sebastian took a sip of wine and said carelessly, 'My apologies. We were ... delayed.'

'Yes – and I can guess by what.'

Sebastian didn't reply but the look in his eyes said something along the lines of, *Shut your mouth before I put my fist in it ...* which only increased Nicholas's amusement. Luckily, before he could tease Mr Audley further, the door opened on Monsieur and Mademoiselle Delacroix, causing him to say instead, 'Aristide and Madeleine. And about time, too.'

Watching Adrian welcome them, Nicholas took a moment to notice that Madeleine's sombre garb of the afternoon had been replaced with flamboyant emerald silk. She looked, he thought as he strolled towards her, more stunning than any woman had a right to.

'We were beginning to think you weren't coming,' remarked Adrian as he bowed to Madeleine. 'As it is, you're just in time for supper. Caroline will be delighted.'

'And forgive us for being so late?' queried Aristide. 'It was unavoidable, I'm afraid. Lord Manston suffered a seizure over a game of basset.'

'Good lord!' Nicholas shook hands with Aristide and turned an enquiring gaze upon Madeleine. 'The poor fellow won't die, will he?'

'The doctor says not,' she replied, as if she didn't care either way. Then, resolutely facing Adrian, 'It was good of you to invite us, my lord.'

Laughter danced in the silver-grey eyes.

'Not at all, Mademoiselle. It is our pleasure.'

She met his amusement with a repressive glare. 'Thank you.'

It was perhaps fortunate that Caroline arrived beside them before Adrian could offer any further provocation. Bathing both Monsieur and Mademoiselle Delacroix in a warm smile and reaching out to take Madeleine's unresponsive hands, she said, 'I'm so glad you were able to come this evening, Mademoiselle.

I've been very much looking forward to making your acquaintance.'

'And I, yours,' replied Madeleine, untruthfully. In fact, she was somewhat taken aback. Despite what Nicholas had said, she'd expected Adrian's wife to regard her with reserve, if not actual suspicion and was therefore surprised to be greeted with genuine pleasure. She had also expected a beauty ... and so was equally surprised to find the Countess no more than quietly pretty.

'I'd offer to introduce you to some of our other guests but Adrian says you already know most of them and probably much better than I do,' continued Caroline. 'Also, here is Nicholas waiting to steal you – for which no one could blame him. I really do think *someone* might have told me how very beautiful you are.' Then, in response to something glimpsed across the room, 'Oh dear. Lady B appears to be panicking. Please excuse me.' Upon which note, she moved away leaving Madeleine marooned with Nicholas.

'Lady Brassington,' he said helpfully.

'What?'

'Lady B is Lily Brassington. In case you were wondering.'

'I wasn't. I was wondering if Lady Sarre is always so ... forthright.'

'Yes.' He grinned suddenly. 'She's rather like you – but without the claws.'

'I don't have claws,' snapped Madeleine through clenched teeth.

'Of course you do. But don't worry. Most people are quite used to them now.' And without giving her time to reply, he placed her hand on his sleeve and said, 'Come on. Let's say hello to Cassie.'

Aristide and Adrian, meanwhile, were managing to exchange a few private words.

'Aside from Manston's seizure, how were things at the club this evening?' asked Adrian.

'Normal. The usual faces and no notable exceptions.'

'Well, that's encouraging. There's apparently been some talk about Braxton at Whites but Amberley says that no one made much of it. He doesn't see any cause for concern.'

'Yet,' returned Aristide tautly.

'All right. Yet. But there's no point in worrying about something that may never happen and that you can do absolutely nothing about anyway.'

'Thank you for reminding me of that last fact.'

'Oh – don't be such a pessimist.' Turning to find Bertrand at his elbow with a tray of claret, he took two glasses and, while passing one of them to Aristide, muttered, 'What in God's name are you doing? I'm paying two footmen to do that. So take a glass yourself and get rid of the damned tray, will you?'

'One of the footmen helped himself to a *soupçon* too much of your brandy,' replied Bertrand calmly. 'I have dismissed him.'

'Oh Lord. Does Caroline know?'

'No. She and the dragon are busy saving the lobster patties which have burned.' He gave a sudden sardonic grin. 'The little widow looks disappointed. She has been trying to catch Lord Nicholas's eye all evening and now sees him with Madeleine.'

'So now she knows she was wasting her time.'

'What widow?' asked Aristide without much interest.

'The dark beauty in black,' replied Adrian, moving aside to provide a clearer view of the room. 'Over there, being interrogated by Charles Fox.'

Aristide glanced around … and then became very still. Something coiled in his stomach and his skin felt cold. He thought, *It can't be*. But there was no mistaking that face. Even after all these years, he would have known it anywhere.

Somehow managing to keep his voice perfectly level and even slightly bored, he said, 'Who is she?'

'Lily Brassington's god-daughter and widow of one Lord Westin. Interested?'

The name Westin didn't so much ring a bell as produce a full peal.

'Perhaps.'

'Enough to want an introduction?'

I don't need an introduction, thought Aristide. *I know who she is. Or rather, who she was.* But he shrugged and said, 'Why not?'

'Really?' Adrian stared. He couldn't recall the last time Aristide had shown even the remotest interest in a woman. And if he had liaisons with the less respectable sort of female, he was damned discreet about it. 'Why?'

'No particular reason – though as you said yourself, she's beautiful. And it's curious that a widow, still in mourning and whom you don't know, is here at all. Isn't that sufficient?'

'Just present him, why don't you?' said Bertrand. 'He may stop the poor lady wishing she hadn't come.'

'Then by all means let's rescue her from Charles,' said Adrian negligently. 'He must have found out everything he wants to know by now.'

Since Mr Fox melted away with the slightest of bows and a smooth word of excuse, this assumption appeared to be true. Wondering belatedly if he shouldn't have given Aristide a little more information, Adrian made the introduction and watched the widow dimple and curtsy. There was no denying her beauty, he thought clinically. Ebony hair, long-lashed golden-brown eyes, flawless skin and a body, invitingly curved in all the right places. He couldn't blame Aristide for wanting a closer look. But something about the absence of expression in Aristide's eyes gave him the feeling that there was more to it than that.

Shrugging mentally, he smiled, murmured something about needing a word with Caroline ... and left them together.

Without speaking, Aristide looked steadily into lovely, topaz eyes. The last time he had seen them, they'd been full of despair and drowning in tears; tears which had cost him much more than the price of a handkerchief. He waited.

Genevieve summoned her most dazzling smile and said, 'I am astonished, sir. I hadn't expected to encounter a Frenchman here.'

'No?'

Aristide held her gaze and decided not to help her. So far, she had given no indication that she recognised him. A small knot of something he decided was anger started to burn in his chest but he did his best to ignore it and waited. She would remember. Surely she would?

'No. Are you a visitor to London?' she asked when he said nothing further.

'I live here.' Still nothing. Did she *really* not know him? If that was the case … if she had no recollection of him at all … he had been nothing to her. Less than nothing. The anger burned more fiercely. He stopped ignoring it.

Genevieve was confused. Something was tugging at a distant corner of her memory but it refused to come into focus. More importantly, she didn't understand why the gentleman had requested an introduction if he wasn't going to talk to her. Of course, he'd arrived with the exquisitely-gowned lady currently conversing with the duke's brother and the flushed, laughing bride.

Purely to break the awkward silence, she said, 'Is the lady in green silk your wife, Monsieur?'

'No. She is my sister.'

'Oh. You must forgive me. I have been away from London for some time.' She managed a light-hearted laugh, despite thinking, *Four miserable years, in fact.* 'I am mostly unacquainted with the company this evening. Perhaps your own position is similar?'

Aristide refrained from asking what the hell gave her that idea. With a slight gesture to the room at large, he said, 'Not at all. I know everyone here.'

The repressive tone was beginning to make the conversation a struggle. Cringing inwardly, she heard herself say, 'Lord Sarre is a particular friend of yours?'

'Very much so.'

The burning core inside him was white-hot. She didn't remember; wasn't going to remember; had no bloody idea who he was or what trying to help her had cost him. A beating which had left him bruised, bloody and broken for weeks, unable to work even if he'd still had a job – which of course he didn't because she'd cost him that as well. And finally, his mother. Genevieve Harcourt had robbed him of the chance to say goodbye and had been the cause of Madeleine being alone at their mother's bedside while she breathed her last. All of those things – his whole life collapsed like a house of cards – for trying to help this woman who didn't know him from Adam. Suddenly, he wanted to howl the truth at her; but he wouldn't. He wouldn't because he never acted on impulse and because the easy way wasn't always the best.

Something in that chilly blue gaze made Genevieve increasingly uneasy. She said, 'I'm sorry, Monsieur but … was there something you wished to say to me?'

Aristide took his time about replying; so long that he could see her wondering if he was going to. Then he said slowly, 'No. Quite the reverse, in fact. Perhaps the answer will come to you … or perhaps not. Think about it.'

CHAPTER THREE

Inevitably, the following afternoon brought Genevieve's eldest brother, Viscount Kilburn, down upon her. Equally inevitable was the fact that he was out of temper.

'May one enquire, Genevieve,' he said in his peculiarly soft voice, 'why you decided to quit Shropshire in favour of Albemarle Street without first finding it necessary to apprise me of your intentions?'

She stared at him in silence, hating both the control he had over his temper and the way it always made her nerves tighten. He was tall, well-made and shared her own sable hair and hazel eyes. She supposed some women thought him handsome. Well, of course they did. His numerous *affaires* were a byword – yet he expected *her* to behave with perfect propriety. He was the biggest hypocrite in all creation.

'I'm a widow, Ralph,' she said for what felt like the hundredth time. 'I'm also twenty-three years old. I don't need your permission to visit my god-mother.'

'You are labouring under a misapprehension, my dear. But we will come to that presently. For now, please explain to me how – while still in your period of full mourning – you came to attend a party last evening.'

Genevieve suppressed a groan. How had he found out about that so quickly?

'Lady Sarre invited me to her home. Since there was neither music nor dancing and no more than twenty persons present, it was perfectly proper for me to attend in the company of Cousin Lily.'

'From what I hear,' drawled Viscount Kilburn coolly, 'the Countess of Sarre is the spawn of some northern tradesman who caught an earl thanks to her immense dowry. As to Sarre himself, there are numerous unsavoury whispers about him. You would be well-advised to choose your friends more carefully.'

'Oh of course!' she snapped sarcastically. 'After all, our family is a pattern card of respectability, isn't it? How *are* Cedric and Bertram these days? Still playing in the gutter?'

His jaw tightened, the only visible sign of anger he ever showed.

'You do not need to provoke me, Genevieve. I am already sufficiently displeased. And we will not evade the point.'

'Which is what?'

'Do not be unnecessarily obtuse. You appeared in society despite being unable to put your blacks aside for a further two months. Moreover -'

'Six weeks.' She fixed him with a defiant stare. 'I shall be out of black in exactly six more wretched weeks. I'm not pretending to mourn Kit for a day longer than I must.'

'Moreover,' the viscount continued as if she had not spoken, 'quite aside from Sarre and his ill-bred wife, I am told that one of their guests was a man who runs a gaming-house. May I at least hope that you did not make *his* acquaintance?'

'I've no idea. I met the Marchioness of Amberley and Lady Delahaye – both of whom should meet your standards. And the Duke of Rockliffe's brother was --'

'He is French.'

'What?'

'Aristide Delacroix is French. Perhaps that will help your memory.'

It did. In fact it sent a jolt of something so violent and so unexpected through her that she felt faint. The name Delacroix had meant nothing to her last night and still did not. The name *Aristide*, on the other hand, was a different matter. It fused a number of previously unconnected things, such as the Frenchman's peculiar behaviour and the odd feeling that had plagued her while she'd been with him; the vivid dream about Paris and Papa Ken that had woken her in the early hours of this morning; and now a given name she'd all but forgotten because she'd never used it in its correct form.

'Genevieve? Is something wrong?'

Her brother's voice jerked her back to the present and the need to behave normally so he didn't become suspicious.

'No. I recall some talk about a gaming club and a gentleman being taken ill there – but I wasn't paying much attention. It may have been Whites, for all I know.'

'Sinclairs,' offered Kilburn, more helpfully than he realised.

Genevieve tilted her head and then nodded. 'Why, yes. That might have been it.'

'We progress at last. And did you meet its proprietor?'

'No.' She looked him in the eye, lied and decided to apply a little provocation. 'Why on earth do you care? Don't tell me *you* don't frequent gaming clubs.'

'That is beside the point. And what I most assuredly do *not* do is to fraternise on an equal footing with the grubby little men who own them.'

'Of course you don't. But God knows why you think you can be so high in the instep, Ralph. Your own reputation isn't exactly spotless, is it? As for Cedric and Bertram, I know enough of their doings to be aware that they're a disgrace. Why don't you attend to your own behaviour and theirs before you concern yourself with mine?'

'I have already done so. Our brothers are in Dorset with instructions to stay there.'

'And how long do you expect *that* to last?'

'For as long as neither one of them can afford lodgings of their own in London, since I have forbidden them Kilburn House.' He drew a breath and then loosed it. 'Please stop this, Genevieve. Whether you accept it or not, a lady's reputation is more fragile than a man's and yours is already damaged, thanks to your marriage to Westin.'

'Ah. I wondered when we'd get round to him.'

'You chose him,' he reminded her coldly. 'Had I not been detained abroad at the time, I might have stopped it. Cedric, of course, decided not to. And you were irrevocably set on him, were you not?'

Yes. I was set on him. He was twenty-five years old and good-looking – whereas you'd been trying to thrust me into the arms of Lord Bute or the Earl of Daventry – neither of whom would see sixty again. So I'd have wed the devil himself if it got me out of your clutches. Which, as it turned out, is precisely what I did.

'I didn't know what he was. How could I?'

'True as that is, it doesn't change anything,' said Kilburn wearily. They'd had this conversation before and never to the satisfaction of either of them. 'What matters now is ensuring that your next husband is sufficiently well-placed to rehabilitate you in the eyes of society.'

'My next husband can wait,' she said flatly. 'Once I'm out of black, I plan to enjoy widowhood.'

'That, thanks to your financial situation, may not be possible.'

'What are you talking about?' She frowned at him, half-wary and half-impatient. 'As long as I'm not extravagant, the marriage settlements should meet my needs.'

It was a long time before he replied and during the ensuing silence Genevieve thought she detected a hint of pity mixed with the displeasure in his eyes. *Pity? From Ralph?* Suddenly, she was seriously alarmed.

He said, 'Having been involved in the drawing up of the settlements, Cedric has since had the management of them. I regret to say that his investments on your behalf have proved no more successful than any of the others he has made.'

The pit of Genevieve's stomach fell away.

'The – the money is gone? He's lost it all?'

'Most of it. What is left may yield an income of three or four hundred a year – no more. You might possibly scrape by on that. People do, I believe. You couldn't possibly *live* on it.'

For a moment she had trouble breathing until another thought brought relief washing over her. She said, 'The will. Provision would have been made for me in Kit's will.'

He inclined his head but his expression remained unchanged.

'It was. His will was drawn up along with the marriage settlements at the time of your betrothal.' Kilburn paused. 'Westin's legal and financial affairs existed in the same sorry tangle as the rest of his life. He ought to have updated his will when his father died and he inherited the barony. He didn't ... so it remained the will of Mr Christopher Westin which, in the event of his death, provided a widow's jointure for the support of his wife, Mistress Genevieve Westin. But by the time of Christopher's death, he was no longer *Mr* Westin. He was *Lord* Westin, the third baron.'

Just for an instant, Genevieve found this too ludicrous to credit.

'You're saying Kit's cousin is quibbling over names? Seriously?'

'Not just that. Christopher did not merely inherit a title. House, land and a certain amount of wealth came with it – none of which are referred to in his will. Inevitably, this raises other questions and has thus enabled Jonathan Westin to throw your jointure into the mix. I believe he will eventually have to give way ... but I don't imagine it will happen quickly. And that leaves you once more dependent upon me.'

Genevieve knew exactly what that meant. Nausea clawed at her insides and she said bitterly, 'Hence your determination to see me speedily re-married.'

Kilburn rose and walked away to gaze out of the window.

'It is not solely for my benefit or because, in our family, money is always in short supply. I can house and clothe you but, as you yourself have pointed out, my reputation will not help you socially. The right marriage can. It will give you comfort, security and position. Westin was a bad choice in every respect but you have a second chance. You are still beautiful and of child-bearing age; you are the sister of a viscount and the grand-daughter of an earl. I can think of at least four gentlemen of suitable standing who would almost certainly consider making you an offer.'

'Yes.' She stared at his elegant back and wished she could stick a knife into it. 'I'm sure you can. But tell me something. How long have you known I've been left virtually penniless? And why is this the first I've heard of it?'

'Cedric came to me with the problems surrounding Christopher's will when he finally accepted that he couldn't deal with the matter himself. The fact that his investments had failed came to light at the same time.'

'Which was when, exactly?'

'Three months ago.' He turned to face her. 'I didn't tell you because I hoped to resolve the issue with Jonathan before it became necessary.'

'How considerate. But I'm surprised you've only got four men on your list of prospective bridegrooms. Given three months to plan my future, I'd have thought you might have come up with twice that number. London can't be that short of wealthy old men, can it? Oh – but I'm forgetting. You're probably not considering anyone below your own rank, are you? That would narrow the field a bit.'

'Be careful, Genevieve.' His eyes grew cold. 'You are entitled to your spleen and I am prepared to tolerate a certain amount of it. But don't push me too far.'

She stood up, fists clenched at her side.

'I'm not seventeen any more, Ralph. And I'm no more inclined to let you choose my husband now than I was then. *If* I decide to re-marry, I'll choose him myself.'

'You did that before, did you not?' For the first time, something approaching a smile curled the hard mouth. 'And we both know how well it turned out.' The viscount strolled towards the door, then paused, turning back to her. 'Lord Daventry married Adela Frensham, you know. He made her a widow within the year and left her with a house on South Street, a small estate in Suffolk and an annual income of roughly ten thousand. Her ladyship now enjoys everything that society has to offer, along with the pleasure to be found with an accomplished lover. In all respects but one, her life might have been yours.'

A headache of monumental proportions was brewing in Genevieve's skull and bile lodged in her throat – which was why she missed the trap and said exactly what he wanted her to say. 'All respects but one?'

Kilburn took his time and the half-smile lingered. Finally he said, 'The lover, my dear. Even *my* broad view of morality doesn't extend to incest.'

* * *

In his office in Ryder Street, Aristide spent the morning at his desk with the usual paperwork; tallies of last night's losses to the club, the usual batch of correspondence, invoices from purveyors of food and fine wines, staff wages and a dozen other similar matters. He dealt with about a quarter of it before giving up in disgust at his mind's determination to continually wander back to the previous evening.

It had been a long time since he'd last thought of Genevieve Harcourt. Certainly, he'd never expected to see her again. But the second he *had* seen her, all logical thought processes had been suspended. Just one glimpse had him remembering things he didn't want to remember and feeling things he told himself he *absolutely did not* feel. And beyond all of that was the fact that she hadn't recognised him; that he occupied as little place in her memories of life in Sir Kenneth Forbes-Montague's Paris household as the footman who made up the fires or the maid who dusted her bedchamber. If she'd known – and how could she *not* have done? – that her brothers had beaten him half to death and convinced Sir Kenneth to dismiss him, it plainly meant less to her than the loss of a handkerchief.

The sight of one of the downstairs day-staff hovering outside the open door reminded him that he was expecting the latest in a long line of applicants for the post as his assistant. Thankful to have something else to think about, Aristide emptied his face of emotion and said, 'Yes. Bring Mr Hastings up.'

None of the previous candidates having been suitable, he didn't feel particularly optimistic. Some of them had lacked one or more of the skills he considered necessary – most often education, manners and unassailable discretion. Others thought working in a gaming house would be easy and amusing or that they'd be permitted to play there themselves, mixing with Sinclairs noble patrons. One had even made it clear that he'd be doing Aristide a favour by accepting the position. None of them had been a man Aristide could imagine himself working with on a daily basis and he was starting to wonder if such a person actually existed.

Mr Edward Hastings – a pleasant-faced, serious-looking young man in his middle twenties – entered the room, closed the door behind him and bowed slightly.

'Monsieur Delacroix ... thank you for seeing me.'

Aristide gestured to a chair on the other side of his desk and wondered where the problem would lie this time.

Coming briskly to the point, Mr Hastings told him.

'Sir, you will be expecting references from previous employers but I don't have any. If this is an insurmountable problem, I'll leave without wasting any more of your time.'

Well, thought Aristide, *this is different.*

He picked up the gentleman's letter of application which was one of the best he'd received; elegantly-constructed and blessedly succinct.

'You could have told me that in this.'

'Yes. I should have done. But I hoped that if we met, *you* might let me explain.'

The slight emphasis told Aristide that other prospective employers hadn't done so.

'Very well. I'm listening.'

A hint of colour and an expression of gratitude touched Mr Hastings' face.

'Thank you. It's like this, sir. My current position is the only one I've held since leaving Cambridge. I wish to quit it but my employer is ... making it difficult.'

'He's refusing to give you a character?'

'Yes.'

'Why?'

For the first time, Edward Hastings avoided Aristide's eye.

'I suppose because he is used to me and dislikes change.'

Aristide let silence linger for a few seconds before saying dryly, 'You are asking me to give you a job, despite your lack of references, Mr Hastings. Modesty is all very well but I wouldn't have thought this was the time for it.'

Surprise flickered in the younger man's eyes, followed by a hint of amusement.

'Plainly, then? I've been Lord Leighton's secretary for five years. Amongst other things, I deal with all his lordship's correspondence as well as any business arising from the House. He admits to finding me invaluable ... and is adamant about not letting me go.'

'I think,' said Aristide slowly, 'you're going to have to tell me what I'm missing.'

'Sir?'

'I imagine you live in Lord Leighton's house, are well-paid and find your work stimulating?'

'Yes.'

'In addition, serving as a nobleman's private and political secretary is clearly a better road to advancement than managing a gaming-house.' He waited and when the other man remained silent, said, 'None of this makes sense unless there's something that you haven't you told me. Well?'

Mr Hastings frowned down at his hands, plainly fighting within himself. Finally, on an explosion of breath, he said, 'I wish to get married. In my current situation, I can't.'

'Ah. Lord Leighton won't permit it?'

'Not in a million years.'

'Why not?'

Another inward battle and then, 'Because the lady I wish to marry is his daughter.'

Aristide's eyes widened slightly. Whatever else he'd expected, it wasn't that. But before he could say anything, the floodgates opened on a torrent of words.

'We've been in love for three years – since before Henrietta had her first season. So far she's managed to avoid a betrothal but her parents are becoming impatient and it can't go on indefinitely. They don't know about us, of course. But the situation is hopeless. We can't marry unless I find employment elsewhere and I can't do that if his lordship won't give me a character. The whole thing's a bloody nightmare.' He got up, as if belatedly aware of what he'd said. 'My apologies, Monsieur. I think I'd better go.'

He was half-way to the door when Aristide said pensively, 'I met Mademoiselle Leighton once.'

Mr Hastings turned slowly. 'I know. It was at a supper-party hosted by Lord Harry and Lady Elinor Caversham. Hetty said she enjoyed talking with you.'

'You weren't going to mention that?'

'Would it have made a difference? And anyway, you might not have remembered.'

This time the silence was a long one and during it, Aristide decided to follow his instincts. He said, 'Very well. If you're sure you want to give up any political ambitions you may have had in order to marry Mademoiselle Leighton, I will match your current salary and arrange accommodation.'

Mr Hastings gaped at him. 'Wh-what? You'll give me the position?'

'Yes.'

This time, the young man lost himself in a tangle of half-sentences which, perhaps mercifully, were cut off by a knock at the door.

Sighing, Aristide said, 'Inform Lord Leighton that you will be leaving his employ and let me know when you can start in mine.' A glimmer of humour appeared in his eyes. 'Good luck with that, by the way. And now you may open the door.'

Still faintly stunned, Edward obeyed. The same fellow who'd shown him upstairs earlier peered in and said, 'Beg pardon for interrupting, sir – but you've a visitor. A lady.'

'What?' Aristide's brows snapped together. 'Are you sure?'

'Yes, sir. She's wearing a widow's veil and she's got a maid with her, so she's not a – well, the other sort, if you take my meaning. Sally took her to wait in the blue dining room. We didn't know what else to do with her, sir – being as she wouldn't leave.'

There was a brief silence during which Monsieur Delacroix's face was wiped of all expression. Then, waving the door-keeper away, he impaled Mr Hastings on a very acute stare and said, 'What is the most important requirement in an establishment like this?'

Mr Hastings didn't hesitate. 'Discretion.'

'Quite. Never lose sight of it for a second. And it begins now.'

* * *

While her maid sat on a chair near the door, Genevieve put back her veil and examined the room. The walls were hung with buttermilk-coloured figured silk, the windows curtained in heavy blue velvet and both colours were woven into the rich carpet beneath her feet. The mahogany dining-table was laid for twelve with delicately-patterned china, sparkling crystal and silver cutlery – all of it of the very best quality. At one end of the room a large sideboard held a selection of bottles with yet more glasses and several armchairs were grouped about the fireplace. Everything was elegant yet comfortable and wouldn't have been out of place in any fashionable gentleman's home. She found this unexpected. She also wondered how the man who, seven years ago, had been her step-father's under-secretary had afforded it.

Since she still didn't understand why she hadn't recognised him the previous evening she had no idea how she was going to explain it to him. She only knew she had to try. And because the conversation was unlikely to be easy and because she had other, bigger problems to address, she wanted to get it over with quickly.

The door opened and Monsieur Delacroix stood on the threshold for a long moment, surveying her.

Genevieve looked back, absorbing the long pale blond hair, eyes the blue of a cloudless winter sky and neatly-tailored bones ... things which were disconcertingly both familiar and alien. Then, before she could speak, he took a few steps into the room and greeted her with just five words. 'You should not be here.'

'I know.' Having given her maid instructions to leave them alone, Genevieve waited until the girl had gone before saying simply, 'I needed to speak with you and didn't want to wait. This seemed the only way to do it.'

He remained where he was, his expression unreadable.

'Am I to assume you've recovered your memory?'

'Yes. You'll be thinking I should have known you last night, I suppose.'

You suppose? he thought. But said only, 'It crossed my mind. Why didn't you?'

'I don't know exactly ... except that you look different.'

'Ah. Older, perhaps? Better-fed? Less threadbare?'

'Yes. All of that.' And something more, she realised. He wore an indefinable aura of authority, along with a suspicion of power; both of them worlds away from the young man he'd been in Paris ... and both a more effective disguise than improved physique and fine tailoring. Fleetingly, she wondered if he knew it – and rather suspected that he did. 'I came to apologise.'

'For what, exactly?'

Genevieve blinked. 'For failing to recognise you immediately.'

Her tone clearly said, *What else could it have been?* Aristide considered reminding her and then, once again, decided against it.

When he didn't immediately respond, she hurried to fill the silence before the atmosphere between them could grow any more uncomfortable than it already was. She said, 'You must have thought me very rude – or as self-absorbed and silly as I was at fifteen. I assure you that I'm not. But aside from you looking so different, it was one of those odd moments that come upon one every now and then. The sort when you see a person you didn't expect to see in the very last place you'd expect to see them.'

A little voice in her head said, *Stop talking. It isn't helping. He doesn't look any more pleased to see you now than he did five minutes ago.*

Once again, Aristide let a pause develop, eventually saying, 'So what turned the key?'

She didn't want to tell him that she'd dreamed about Paris ... and that, in the peculiar way of dreams, her meeting with him had somehow become muddled up with it.

'It was your given name. No – I know I never used it.' She'd always called him Monsieur Arry, thinking she was being playfully charming. Now, squirming slightly under an unsmiling gaze, she wasn't sure he'd found it so. 'I was told it earlier today and – and that's when I remembered.'

'Told it by whom?' he asked.

'I – what?'

'With whom have you been discussing me?'

Genevieve swallowed. She hadn't, she realised, wanted to mention Ralph either.

'My brother came to lecture me about attending a party before I'm out of full mourning. He had a great deal to say and – and your name came into it somewhere.'

'I see.' Another inscrutable pause and then, 'But you remind me that I have been remiss in not offering my condolences.'

Her jaw tightened and she stood a little straighter.

'It's of no consequence. I don't pretend to be heart-broken.'

'*Would* it be pretence?'

'Yes – and would fool no-one.' She shrugged. 'I refuse to be branded a hypocrite on top of everything else.'

Reluctantly, Aristide gave her credit for courage – both for refusing to simulate a grief she didn't feel and for choosing to face him. He took a moment to study her while he decided what, if anything, he wanted to say next. The heavy blue-black hair, creamy-pale skin and heart-shaped face were the same ... as were the long-lashed golden-brown eyes, though the woman who looked out of them bore little resemblance to the carefree, laughing girl who'd enchanted him seven years ago. And that girl had been youthfully slender ... not possessed of these new, enticing curves.

He knew as much about the late Lord Westin as the rest of London. He had no wish to know anything more. The widow was beautiful. She always had been. It was an undeniable fact that didn't have to be a problem. But sympathy, if he was stupid enough to let it in, would be.

There were half a dozen questions that might open the locked box of the past but he asked none of them. 'I appreciate both the explanation and your apology but now I think you should go. Unless there was anything else you wished to say?'

'No.' *I just wish you'd smile at me as you used to.* 'Nothing. Except ... from the little I've seen, Sinclairs is beautifully-appointed – this room in particular.'

'Thank you. We aim to please.' He pulled the bell to summon a servant. 'One of my people will show you out the back way so you won't be seen. He will also summon a hackney carriage, if you require it.'

'Thank you.' She gestured to the table with its fully-laid place settings. 'Are you expecting a party this evening?'

They had been. This morning's post had brought him a note of cancellation and a small knot of what he hoped was unnecessary worry.

'I believe so. But the private dining parlours are my sister's province, rather than mine.'

Genevieve's eyes widened.

'Really?' She hesitated 'I didn't meet her last night – although I wanted to. I believe you once told me that we are of an age?'

It was his turn to be surprised. She appeared to remember the oddest things.

'Yes. That is true.' Aristide decided to take a two-fold risk and see what came of it. 'We live in Duke Street. If you leave a card, doubtless Madeleine will be pleased to receive you. Ah – here is Mr Jackson to show you out. Pray excuse me, my lady.'

And with a small, graceful bow, he was gone.

* * *

Later that evening, Genevieve sat in her bedchamber with a glass of claret and gave serious consideration to her future. According to Ralph, she had virtually no money and little chance of acquiring more any time soon; she couldn't remain in Albemarle Street with Cousin Lily indefinitely but would bleed to death sooner than return to the lonely, cheerless dower house in Shropshire or take up residence under her brother's roof; all of which meant that the only other course available was the one Ralph was pressing upon her. Marriage.

In six weeks' time, she could pack away her weeds. With hindsight, she regretted telling Ralph that she wouldn't mourn Kit for a day longer than she had to. Horrid as it was, widow's garb offered protection of a sort. As soon as she went into colours, Ralph would start dangling her in front of the gentlemen on his thrice-blasted list and probably find a dozen ways of forcing her hand. He was good at that. And she wouldn't trust him to choose a lapdog for her, let alone a husband.

She could see only one way out of all this ... but it simply wasn't feasible. How could she find a husband she might actually be able to tolerate inside a mere six weeks? How, indeed, could she hunt for a husband at *all* when she couldn't go into society because she was still in black? She couldn't. It was as simple as that.

Despite the pointlessness of it, she considered the sort of man she'd be looking for. In her position, it would be stupid to expect too much, so ... someone reasonably young and of comfortable means. Most important of all, she wanted to be sure of his character. She'd rushed into marriage with Kit thinking she'd known what she was getting and it had been the worst mistake she'd ever made. She couldn't risk that again.

It took a moment to shove thoughts of Kit out of her head. She never invited them but sometimes they sneaked past her defences and tried to linger.

She half-drained her glass and focused on the problem at hand. Then she shook her head and laughed wryly at herself.

This is stupid. I can't go out in society so I'm not likely to meet any gentlemen at all – never mind managing to charm one into offering me marriage in the next six weeks. The whole idea is ridiculous. Look at last night, for example. There were only three unmarried men at the party. A duke's brother; a Macaroni; and a man who owns a gaming-house.

An exquisitely-furnished, very costly-looking gaming-house.

A gaming-house that must therefore make a great deal of money.

A gaming-house owned by a good-looking man who used to like me and was always unfailingly patient and kind.

Monsieur Arry.

CHAPTER FOUR

Two mornings later over breakfast, Aristide looked across at Madeleine and said, 'Did you discover the reason for Mr Findlay's cancellation the other evening?'

'Yes. He and his brother were summoned to their father's bedside. His lordship thought he was dying – a conviction which comes over him frequently, I gather. His sons, however, have no choice but to heed the call.'

'Good. Nothing to do with Braxton, then.'

'No.' She gestured to the tightly-scripted sheets he'd been reading and said, 'Is that from Henry Lessing?'

'Yes. As ever, he is quite remarkably thorough,' said Aristide, not without a glimmer of amusement. 'But the gist of it all is this. Sir George Braxton is worth about twelve thousand a year, most of that coming from three Staffordshire coal-mines. Four years ago, he also acquired a pottery manufactory in ...' He stopped to glance at the appropriate page. 'Stoke-on-Trent. It was to seek an export market for his fine china that our friend was in Paris when his path crossed mine.'

'And who is he, exactly?'

'In relation to the rest of Sinclairs' membership, you might say he is no one. The knighthood was obtained by his father, along with a small estate – Shenford Hall. Mr Lessing believes that both were purchased.' He looked up at her. 'Surprising the things one can buy, isn't it?'

'Not especially,' said Madeleine cynically. 'Money talks.'

'True.' Laying two of the pages aside, Aristide reached for the last one. 'As one might expect, Braxton isn't a member of Whites or any of the other prestigious clubs but he occasionally plays at the Cocoa-Tree. He has a scattering of what Mr Lessing considers mere acquaintances but only one friend – John Clavering, who brought him to Sinclairs.'

'I take it he won't be doing that again?'

'No. He won't. As for Braxton himself, since making his accusation he has been attempting to ingratiate himself with our existing members – presumably hoping he'll find some support. So far, he hasn't been well-received due to an unfortunate tendency to ruffle feathers. At any rate, the general view is that he is ... how does Mr Lessing put it? Yes, here it is. He's *"an unpleasant, muck-raking mushroom"*.' He dropped the page on top of the others and smiled faintly. 'At the moment, it appears that we may escape repercussions. But Mr Lessing will continue to monitor Sir George's activities – just in case.'

Madeleine eyed him thoughtfully.

'If I were Braxton, I wouldn't be wasting my time with the current members. I'd be seeking out those who've been refused from the outset – or had their membership revoked for some reason. Men who already don't like us very much.'

'Yes. And I daresay he'll get around to that.' Aristide stood up. 'May one ask what the invitation card you are holding has done to earn the dirty looks you've been giving it all the time we've been talking?'

She huffed an impatient breath.

'It's from Lady Delahaye – who I scarcely know – for a picnic at Richmond tomorrow. It would appear that Cassandra Audley asked her to send me a card.'

'And that is bad?'

'No. *That* is perfectly fine.' Madeleine picked up a note and waved it at him. '*This*, on the other hand, is from Lord Nicholas telling – no, *instructing* me, if you please – to send her ladyship an acceptance since he will collect both myself and the Audleys in his carriage at around noon.'

Aristide managed not to laugh but didn't hide his desire to do so.

'A *fait accompli*, then. My compliments to Nicholas.'

'It isn't funny. The man is annoying,' she grumbled. 'As are you, come to that. How come I also have a card from Lady Westin

– someone I have never met but who claims acquaintance with you – asking if I'll permit her to call?'

His amusement faded and he took his time about replying. Finally, he said, 'You will have noticed her at Adrian's party. The lady wearing black.'

'The one Lord Nicholas said was a widow?'

'Yes. But before her marriage, Lady Westin was Genevieve Harcourt. Sir Kenneth Forbes-Montague's step-daughter.'

Madeleine stared at him. 'Was she? Good God!' And then, differently, 'You used to talk about her. You were fond of her, I think.'

Aristide had never revealed precisely what had happened the night he'd crawled home to find their mother dead and Madeleine distraught. He'd let her think he'd been set upon in the street; a random, violent attack of the kind that wasn't at all uncommon in the poorer districts of Paris. He had also let her think that he'd lost his position with Sir Kenneth because he hadn't been fit to be seen for a month and incapable of working for nearly two.

'Seven years ago, she was a moderately bright spot in an otherwise dreary world,' he replied. 'Whether or not you want to know her is up to you. There is no need to receive her because she and I have some prior acquaintance. But there's one thing you might take into account. You often feel an outsider in the world we're beginning to inhabit. So, for other reasons, is she.' He smiled coolly. 'And now I have to go. Mr Hastings gave his resignation in yesterday – so I'm anticipating an angry visit from Lord Leighton.'

* * *

Lord Nicholas was late. Madeleine, already wearing her hat and tutting irritably, used the time to write a note telling Lady Westin that she would be at home the following afternoon. She was just placing it on the hall table when the carriage pulled up outside, so she had the butler open the door and walked through it to stand at the top of the steps. Cassie waved to her. Realising that she probably looked accusing, Madeleine summoned a smile and made her way down to the pavement.

While his lordship descended from the carriage and before he could do more than bid her 'Good afternoon', Mr Audley grinned and said, 'I am to inform you that Nicholas is not responsible for our tardiness, Mademoiselle.'

'Was that an apology?' demanded Nicholas, as he handed Madeleine into the seat beside Cassie. 'It didn't sound like one.'

'He's annoyed,' confided Sebastian. 'And I *do* apologise. We were late.'

'Seems to have become a habit,' muttered Nicholas.

Cassie, pretty and spring-like in pale green tiffany, tilted her lace parasol as if to exclude the gentlemen for the purpose of sharing a secret but without bothering to lower her voice at all, said, 'Nicholas is beginning to resemble Colonel Parker, don't you think?'

The Colonel was a seventy-year-old bachelor who suffered from gout and rarely spoke more than three words at a time. Madeleine appeared to give the matter some thought.

'Not quite yet, perhaps. But it shouldn't be entirely discounted.'

Sebastian laughed.

'I'm sitting right here, you know,' remarked Nicholas. 'And if this is the treatment I get for offering the use of my carriage --'

'Rock's carriage,' murmured Cassie, returning her parasol to its usual angle to smile angelically at him. 'His coat of arms is hard to miss.'

'Rock's brand-new, only just imported from Germany *calèche*,' added Sebastian. 'Generous of him to loan it, in my opinion.'

Nicholas muttered something rude beneath his breath and then said, 'Are the three of you going to snipe at me quite *all* the way to Richmond?'

'I haven't sniped,' objected Madeleine. And to Cassie, 'Have I?'

'No. I don't believe you have.'

'But you will.' Nicholas laughed suddenly. 'And when you do, you'll make these two look like amateurs.'

Thanks to the coachman being able to keep up a smart pace, they arrived no more than ten minutes behind the rest of the party. These, Cassie had told Madeleine, included Lord and Lady Amberley, the Ingrams and a number of young people invited 'to keep my sister from annoying everybody else'. Servants had been sent ahead with everything necessary for the guests' comfort; rugs and chairs already occupied a pleasant semi-shaded location beneath the trees and large hampers of food and drink were currently being unloaded.

A little later, Madeleine sat on a rug by Cassie eating tiny, delicious pastries and sipping cold pale wine while Sebastian lay propped on one elbow at their feet.

'Nearly everyone will be off to the country soon,' said Cassie, examining a dish of strawberries before picking out a particularly juicy-looking one. 'I believe Adrian and Caroline went yesterday and Mama and Papa go at the end of the week.'

'Are you leaving too?'

'No. In a few weeks' time, perhaps – but not yet. Aside from our private rooms, the house is virtually bare.' She slanted a teasing smile at her husband. 'Sebastian is looking forward to shopping for furniture and linens and hangings.'

'Sebastian can't wait,' muttered Mr Audley.

Laughing, Cassie turned to where Lady Amberley and Althea Ingram occupied adjacent chairs, while Nicholas amused himself by teasing the suddenly overly-attentive Marquis.

'Are you going to Hertfordshire, Rosalind?'

'Yes – though we intend to spend a few days with Philip and Isabel on the way.'

Sebastian looked up. 'Has Philip decided what to do about the child?'

Rosalind smiled. 'They are keeping her. As you're aware, Philip had his reservations at first ... but I suspect he's now as besotted with little Alice as Isabel is.'

'He can't be worse than Rock,' remarked Nicholas. 'No one could.' Then, to Lord Amberley, 'The sun is creeping round towards her ladyship. You couldn't just go and move that tree a fraction, could you?'

The Marquis, who had no desire to make everyone privy to the fact that Rosalind was in the early stages of pregnancy, merely gave Nicholas a repressive stare and said, 'You're growing tedious, Nicholas.'

His lordship grinned unrepentantly and might have responded had not Rosalind said pleasantly, 'Nicholas. Go away and find someone else to annoy before I either tip a bowl of blancmange over your head or tell Dominic to toss you in Pen Ponds.'

'Or both,' added the Marquis, quiet but meaningful.

'All right, all right – I'm going!' Nicholas uncoiled and got to his feet, looking suitably aggrieved. 'But I'd like it noted that not a single person has shown me a shred of human kindness today and I'm cut to the quick by it.' Inevitably, this statement was greeted by laughter and groans of spurious sympathy. Ignoring all of it, he held out his hand to Madeleine and said, 'You'll take pity on me, won't you? We'll leave this miserable crew behind us and walk up the hill to take in the view.'

Madeleine hesitated and, beneath the brim of her hat, her face grew warm.

'Never mind about taking pity on *him*, Mademoiselle,' advised Sebastian, smiling. 'Do it as a favour to the rest of us.' And, when she continued to hesitate, added, 'And Nick is right about the view. It's worth seeing.'

What Madeleine saw was that she was being left with little alternative. So she accepted the outstretched hand and rose gracefully to her feet, saying, 'Very well, my lord. Thank you.'

As they strolled away and Nicholas placed her hand on his sleeve, she could feel any number of amused eyes boring into her back. She knew that Sebastian Audley had a wicked sense of humour but suspected that wasn't why he'd applied that hint of subtle pressure.

If Nicholas was aware of any undercurrents, it didn't show.

'Have you been to Richmond before?' he asked. And when she shook her head, said, 'I'll bring you here again another day. We'll go to the village and you can have a Maid of Honour.'

'Not being royalty --,' she began acidly.

But he grinned, shook his head and said, 'It's a sort of cake. For some reason I've not fathomed, Richmond is famous for them.'

Madeleine kept her gaze strictly focussed on the path ahead of them and decided to warn him not to get any ideas he didn't already have.

'Why are you doing this, my lord?'

'Nicholas,' he sighed. 'How many times do I have to say it?'

She ignored this. 'Why?'

'Why are we walking up this hill?'

'Why,' she asked as patiently as she could, 'are we walking together at *all*?'

'You asked me something very like that before – and the answer's much the same as it was then. It's a lovely day to have a pretty woman on one's arm.' He glanced sideways at her but saw only the wide, ribbon-trimmed hat. 'Aren't you enjoying yourself?'

'Yes. But --'

'If you ask me, you use the word *but* far too often. If you stopped suspecting me of cunning stratagems, you wouldn't need it half as much.' Reaching out with his free hand, he lifted the concealing hat-brim and said, 'Haven't you realised yet that I'm not nearly clever – or devious – enough?'

Madeleine batted his hand away and wished she hadn't seen that smile of his. Sooner or later he was going to realise what it did to her – if he hadn't realised it already.

'Next you'll be telling me you're an open book,' she said waspishly.

'Oh – not quite that, I hope.' Laughter ran through his voice. 'An open book wouldn't interest you at all, would it?'

'And I suppose you think you *do* interest me?'

'I think we interest each other equally. The only difference is that you're not ready to admit it.'

'You're mistaken. And even if you were not, what point could there possibly be? You can pretend to be plain, ordinary Nicholas for all you like – but you're not, are you? You're the heir to a dukedom and --'

'For the love of Christ,' he snapped, halting in the lee of a convenient tree and swinging her to face him, 'can we please stop this? If you say it one more time, I swear I'll hurl myself down the nearest well.'

She stared at him, a little pale and for once lost for words.

'You want a point?' he demanded tightly. 'Then let's try this.'

And somehow managing to avoid the damned hat-brim, he hauled her into his arms and kissed her.

Taken completely by surprise, it was several seconds before Madeleine summoned up sufficient presence of mind to shove feebly at his chest. He released her mouth immediately but kept her firmly clamped against his body. Their eyes met and locked.

'What are you doing?' she whispered.

'What does it look like?' demanded Nicholas in the tone of a man goaded beyond endurance. 'I'm kissing you. What's more, I'm going to do it again – more thoroughly this time – and you're going to kiss me back. And when we're done, we'll see if we both liked it.'

Her heart was flapping about in her chest like a trapped bird. She could feel the heat and strength of him right down to her toes. Her arms had some idea of wrapping themselves about his neck. If he didn't let her go soon, she wasn't sure she'd be able to stop them.

Nicholas would have let her go. He was quite, quite sure that he *would* have ... if she'd indicated that she wanted him to. But when he saw the shock and uncertainty in her eyes become something else entirely, he knew he didn't have to. The tension seeped from his muscles, his gaze dropped to her mouth and he settled her more securely into his arms. Then he slid his lips lightly across hers; inviting, seeking permission, tempting her to give it. She answered with a small, sighing breath and her eyes flickered shut. Nicholas decided that was very definitely a yes.

He'd waited months to kiss Madeleine Delacroix so he took his time, wanting to make the most of it since there was no saying when he'd have this chance again. Her mouth was soft and hot and welcoming. She tasted of wine and lemon cakes. And when her hands crept up, first to his shoulders and finally to the nape of his neck, he almost drowned in a wave of exultation.

Madeleine had been kissed before; but not often and never like this. He didn't insist or demand. Instead, he drugged her with a slow sensuality that wrecked her defences and left her weak and stupid ... yet consumed with a knowledge she could neither avoid nor deny. She didn't merely want him. Her feelings went far, far deeper than that; and these moments in his arms with his mouth caressing hers were pure joy.

When he began to doubt his ability to stop his hands going where, at this stage, he knew they shouldn't, Nicholas drew back slowly and with great reluctance. Then, waiting until her eyes opened, he said huskily, 'Well ... as experiments go, I'd say that was pretty conclusive. What do you think?'

As yet, she wasn't sure she was capable of thinking anything. She cleared her throat, took a small step away from him and lifted a slightly unsteady hand to her hat.

'It's still there,' he assured her. 'Though next time perhaps we might dispense with it?'

'There had better not *be* a next time,' she said, refusing to meet his eyes because for possibly the first time in her life she felt shy.

'I knew you'd say something like that. But it might have been worse. You could have said 'won't be' rather than 'better not be' ... so I'll be optimistic.'

If he was truthful with himself, reflected Nicholas, he was several miles ahead of optimistic. She hadn't slapped his face and the confused look in her eyes – which frankly satisfied him no end – suggested that she wasn't going to. But in the next minute or two she was going to say several things he could predict fairly accurately ... so it might not be a bad idea to take the wind out of her sails by getting in first.

Tucking a stray lock of hair under the flower-laden hat, he said, 'In a little while, you're going to say that this was a mistake; that I took ungentlemanly advantage and you shouldn't have let me. You're also going to tell me that, since it didn't mean anything, we should just forget it ever happened.' He paused almost imperceptibly. 'Don't.'

'But --'

'No, Madeleine. It wasn't a mistake and pretending it didn't happen won't change the fact that it did. Whether you like it or not, there is something between us ... and denying its existence won't make it go away.' He smiled a little. 'I'd like to know what that something is and I don't mind being patient. But none of that will matter if you refuse to even think about it.' Another pause; then, when she kept her lips firmly pressed together, 'You didn't ask earlier ... but I, too, will be joining the general exodus from London.'

He watched that take her by surprise, watched her open her mouth on some unguarded remark and then close it again. He waited.

Finally she said politely, 'Of course. Will you stay with friends or perhaps his Grace of Rockliffe?'

You just love hitting me with Rock's title, don't you? he thought, only half amused.

'No. I have a small estate here in Surrey. Rock inherited all the family holdings along with the title. But when I came of age he said I should have something of my own to care for so he gave me my choice of the unentailed properties. I chose Charlecote Park.' He paused, wondering how much to tell her. 'I spend a few weeks there three or four times a year and generally like to be there around harvest time – though that may be problematic this year since Adrian and Caroline are talking about hosting a house-party in early August. However, I'm going down tomorrow and will probably stay until the end of July.'

Six weeks, thought Madeleine. And to conceal the fact that she found the prospect alarmingly bleak, she said, 'I find it hard to imagine you actively involving yourself in harvesting. But perhaps you don't.'

'And perhaps I do,' he retorted. 'If that was a question, ask it.'

'Very well. *Do* you shed your coat and roll up your sleeves?'

'Yes. Anything else you'd like to know before we go back to the others?'

Yes. At least a dozen. 'No.'

'My turn, then – and I'd like a straight answer,' he said, his tone pleasant as ever but unmistakeably firm. 'While I'm away will you promise to consider what I said earlier?'

Madeleine looked at him with misgiving. Everyone thought Lord Nicholas Wynstanton didn't have a serious bone in his body. How did they miss this streak of implacability that rolled over opposition like a mill-stone? Or did he save it just for her?

'Yes or no will do nicely,' he prompted.

'Yes,' she said, on a huff of breath. 'Yes. All right. I'll consider it. But I'm not promising anything more than that.'

'I didn't ask for anything more.' He laid her hand on his sleeve and started back down the hill. Then, with a sudden dazzling grin, 'But I won't say I'm not hoping for it.'

There were so many objections she might have made; so many reasons why the thing he thought possible wasn't possible at all. But he would say none of them mattered. He would never, in a century of arguing, understand that they mattered to her. So she sighed, swallowed and said woodenly, 'We didn't look at the view.'

'We didn't – but fortunately, I've seen it before. All you have to do is add words like 'charming' or remark on how lovely the trees look at this time of year. That sort of thing.' Taking care to keep his voice easy and his tone lightly conversational, he said, 'Now ... I met Henrietta Leighton yesterday. She said Aristide has stolen her father's secretary and that Lord Leighton is hopping mad about it. Hetty, on the other hand, looked positively smug. Do you have any ideas why that might be?'

* * *

Even if she'd wanted to, Madeleine couldn't pretend the kiss hadn't happened. Both it and the sensations it had evoked refused to go away, leaving her tossing and turning through most of the night.

At the age of seventeen, she'd conceived what she now recognised was an adolescent infatuation for a man who didn't want her and it had been painful. Now she had fallen stupidly, helplessly in love with a man who it seemed *did* want her but who she'd told herself over and over again that she couldn't – *shouldn't* – have.

The trouble – or most of it anyway – was that, naturally enough, Nicholas only saw her as she was now. Prosperous thanks to the success of Sinclairs; well-dressed and perfectly presentable. He didn't know what lay under that. There were the years between Father's abandonment and Aristide getting secure employment. The first had happened when she'd been nine; the second not until just after her fourteenth birthday. Five years of dirt and poverty while Aristide took whatever work he could find and Mama's health declined daily; then a brief respite, while Aristide worked for Sir Kenneth Forbes-Montague and she earned a few coins washing dishes in the coffee-house at the end of the street. And then disaster. Mama dead; Aristide beaten half to death, unable to work for weeks and his position gone as a result;

and only Madeleine herself to put food on the table – for which the dish-washing money was woefully inadequate.

She didn't let herself think of the things she'd had to do until Aristide was fit enough to work again. The only thing she *hadn't* done was sell her body – which, though it was a triumph of sorts, didn't take away the stomach-turning disgust of the rest of it.

Or make her suppose, even for a second, that a man of Nicholas Wynstanton's background would find any of it remotely acceptable.

CHAPTER FIVE

On the following morning, whilst pouring the second cup of coffee Aristide habitually took with his breakfast, Madeleine avoided all mention of the previous day's picnic and said, 'Lady Westin is coming for tea this afternoon. Perhaps you might join us.'

He looked up, raising one eyebrow. 'Why?'

'To resume your acquaintance with her?'

He restored his attention to the *Morning Chronicle*.

'I hadn't considered doing so.'

For some reason she couldn't identify, Madeleine didn't believe him.

'Consider it now,' she said, her tone making it more than a suggestion. 'Regardless of anything else, try remembering that she and I have never met. And if you didn't bring her to my attention for reasons of your own, why did I invite her here?'

Aristide folded the newspaper with his customary precision and stood up.

'I did not bring her to your attention. I merely told you that she'd expressed a desire to meet you. I also recall telling you not to do anything on my account. If, after half-an-hour's conversation, you decide to cut the connection – do it.'

Her eyes narrowed. 'You're being unusually difficult.'

'No. I am looking ahead to a busy day. Yesterday, Lord Leighton tossed Edward Hastings out on his ear so today, in addition to all the other matters requiring my attention, I'll be ordering the re-arrangement of your old rooms for his use and beginning his education in the running of the club. If, during the course of the afternoon, I find myself with time hanging heavy on my hands, I may come and drink tea. But don't count on it.'

Aristide quit the room aware that shards of green ice were hitting him squarely between his shoulder-blades. Madeleine watched him go reflecting that men were as stupid as rabbits and about as helpful.

* * *

Because Genevieve wanted to arrive in Duke Street in a carriage like a lady, she had not only to tell Cousin Lily where she was going but also offer some explanation as to why she was going there.

Lady Brassington eyed her thoughtfully.

'You want to meet Madeleine Delacroix because her brother once taught you French?'

'No. Not exactly. But language lessons mean holding conversation. And Monsieur Aristide talked about his sister – mostly because she and I are the same age.' She shrugged. 'It's a courtesy call, really. And I won't invite her here if you'd rather I didn't.'

'Since I suspect this is something else Kilburn would disapprove of, I'd rather not know anything about it at all,' returned her ladyship frankly. 'However, you're welcome to take the carriage. I shall not need it myself.'

During the short ride to Duke Street, Genevieve reminded herself of all the things she mustn't do.

Don't try too hard. Effusiveness makes people suspicious.

Don't show too much interest in Monsieur Delacroix.

Don't lie if you don't have to.

Don't worry about liking her. It's more important that she likes you.

The result was that, by the time she arrived at the door, she was a bundle of nerves.

An extremely muscular butler showed her into a small sitting-room on the first floor where the lovely redhead she'd seen at Lady Sarre's party rose to greet her with a cool smile and a perfect curtsy.

'Lady Westin ... how nice to meet you at last.'

'Thank you, Mademoiselle. It is kind of you to allow me to call.'

'Not at all. The pleasure is mine. Please ... won't you sit? I'll ring for tea.'

Genevieve sank on to an elegant satin-striped sofa and wondered what they were going to talk about once the courtesies were out of the way. Waiting until Madeleine was also seated, she opened her mouth on some trite remark about the weather and instead heard herself say, 'I went to Sinclairs. Did your brother tell you?'

As soon as the words were out, she wondered what had possessed her to say them. But if Mademoiselle Delacroix was shocked – or even surprised – there was no sign of it. She merely said slowly, 'No. No, he didn't.'

'Perhaps he also didn't tell you that, when we met in Cork Street, I didn't immediately recognise him. So later, when I *did*, I realised how rude he must have thought me and I wanted to apologise. The club was the only place I knew I might find him – so I went there.' Genevieve shut her eyes briefly and then said, 'I hadn't meant to tell you any of that.'

'I would imagine not,' agreed Madeleine. 'I suppose Aristide was disapproving?'

'He told me I shouldn't be there – which was true, of course, so I didn't know if he meant me personally or ladies in general.'

'Both perhaps ... but mostly the latter. Establishments like Sinclairs are all-male bastions and the gentleman guard them as jealously as any little boy with his tree-house.'

Genevieve was startled into laughter.

'That's a novel way of looking at it. But the internal workings of *this* tree-house are no mystery to you, are they? I understand that you help with the management of it.'

'I have my own domain. The dining-salons and the exclusive card-room upstairs. But when the club is open, God *forbid* that I should appear on the gaming-floor,' came the sardonic reply. 'Aristide says it is for my own protection. Personally, I suspect that some of the more conventional members might faint at the sight of a female near the Hazard table.'

'Are *no* women permitted, then? Forgive me ... but do not some gaming houses allow gentlemen to ... to bring their ...' She stopped, gesturing vaguely with one hand.

'Their mistresses? Yes. Some do. Sinclairs does not. We aim for respectability; a refined atmosphere, comfortable surroundings and scrupulously honest play.'

'Well, I wouldn't know about the play. But from the little I saw, you appear to have achieved the first two things,' said Genevieve with a smile. 'Monsieur Delacroix received me in one of the dining-rooms. I remarked on how lovely it was and he told me the credit was yours.' She hesitated. 'It was that, as much as anything, that made me want to meet you. If truth be known, I was a little envious.'

'Envious? Of what?'

'Of the kind of relationship with your brother that enables you to work together ... and being able to fill your days with something more interesting than embroidery.'

Madeleine's brows rose a little.

'Surely your marriage must have provided you with similar opportunities?'

'No. It didn't.'

It was fortunate that the tea-tray arrived just then because one couldn't tell a lady one had known for barely ten minutes that Kit would have let the roof fall in before spending money that could be squandered on his horses, at the gaming-tables or on his other nefarious pleasures. In fact, reflected Genevieve, there was very little she could truthfully say about Kit to anyone. London society – or at least, the male half of it – might think it knew everything about Christopher Westin. It didn't.

Madeleine noticed the absence of further details and drew certain conclusions but didn't ask any questions. God knew, there were parts of her own life she wouldn't discuss with anyone; so if Lady Westin's marriage had been flawed, the woman was entitled to keep those flaws to herself. Perhaps, she thought, the two of them had more in common than might have been supposed.

Over tea and cakes, they continued to talk of Madeleine's part in the day-to-day running of Sinclairs and at some point, formal modes of address were abandoned. But when, as was inevitable, the conversation drifted to Paris, Madeleine confined herself to remarking that Aristide had spoken of Genevieve often. And then, in case her ladyship got the wrong idea, added, 'Of course Mama and I understood that a great deal of his work for Sir Kenneth was confidential, so it was natural he could only speak of those parts of it that were not – such as your French lessons.'

Not sure whether to be encouraged or not, Genevieve put this aside and gave a tiny laugh. 'He was very patient but he can't have enjoyed them. I was a bad student, I'm afraid. I teased both Monsieur and the maid who was there to chaperone me; I played with my dog; and I either changed the subject or broke into English at every opportunity. Did he not tell you *that*?'

'He may have done. But since Aristide is generally serious, Mama and I probably took it with a pinch of salt.' Madeleine shrugged. 'It isn't that he lacks a sense of humour, you understand. But he's eternally efficient and doesn't take his responsibilities lightly.'

'An admirable quality – and not as common as one might wish.' Genevieve decided that this was her opportunity to supply a few grains of information that might filter their way through to Monsieur Delacroix. She said wistfully, 'I didn't want to leave Paris. I was happy there but, not being my legal guardian, my step-father hadn't the authority to keep me after Mama died and my eldest brother decided it was time I returned to England.' She paused, smiling wryly. 'I was sixteen – so it seemed like the end of the world.'

'You are not fond of your brothers?'

'Not at all. The younger ones are wastrels. And Ralph – Viscount Kilburn, that is – is set on controlling my life. He is annoyed that I've come to London before my year of mourning is over and even *more* annoyed that I committed the gross impropriety of attending Lady Sarre's party. But --'

She broke off abruptly as the door opened and Aristide strolled in.

He hadn't intended to come. He'd spent half the day telling himself that he wouldn't; that he had far too much to do and that it would, in any case, be a mistake. He'd told himself all manner of sensible things, Aristide reflected irritably ... and yet here he was.

Lady Westin turned slightly pink and then her face broke into a luminous smile – as if his unexpected arrival had made her day perfect. It was a smile which slid through every nerve and muscle in his chest, leaving a trail of heat behind it. There was no reason for her to glow at him like that so he knew he shouldn't trust it. The trouble was, it felt good. He was alarmed by just *how* good. He shouldn't have come. He wished he hadn't. He'd known, hadn't he, that – even without that smile – one look at her was all it took to make his blood run faster?

Madeleine, typically, didn't look surprised to see him. She merely waited until he had bowed over her ladyship's hand and asked if he would like some tea.

'No, thank you.' Looking directly into the familiar topaz eyes, he said, 'I believe I was less than gracious at our last meeting, my lady. I was concerned for your reputation, of course ... but it might have been better expressed.'

'Not at all, sir.' She continued to beam at him. 'I understood perfectly.'

He needed to stop her looking at him like that before he made a fool of himself. Turning away, he said coolly, 'Excellent. So you will not be visiting Sinclairs again?'

'No.' The glow in her eyes faded a little. 'Of course not.'

Frowning, Madeleine said, 'There was no need to say that, Aristide. Genevieve is perfectly well-aware of the rules.'

'And now I know that. Certainty is always preferable to assumptions, don't you think?'

What Genevieve thought was that there was anger under that superficially pleasant tone but she didn't know why. She also sensed that he wished one of them elsewhere – probably her. Her enjoyment of the afternoon dimmed and she said, 'You're right of course. But I generally avoid making the same mistake twice.'

'Yes,' agreed Aristide, trapping her gaze with his own. 'So do I.'

Aware of an odd undercurrent she couldn't interpret, Madeleine decided it was time to change the subject. She said, 'I take it that your day was less hectic than you anticipated, Aristide. Or is Mr Hastings already hard at work?'

'He is indeed.'

Three supremely unhelpful words. Madeleine felt like throwing something at him for once again obliging her to fill the silence.

'Forgive us, Genevieve. Mr Hastings is Aristide's new assistant – and since the search to find him has been a long one, we are hoping he'll prove equal to the task.'

Feeling every bit as awkward as she sensed Monsieur Delacroix intended her to do, Genevieve said, 'Yes. I imagine finding the right person was difficult, though I daresay there was no shortage of applicants.' Neither expecting nor waiting for a response, she stood up and shook out her skirts. 'I should go. This has been most enjoyable, Madeleine – so much so that I've quite forgotten the time and stayed much longer than I should have done.'

Madeleine also rose and pulled the bell to summon the butler.

'In my opinion, the rule about how long a visit may last is nonsensical.'

'It is, isn't it? But so are many of the other social conventions,' replied Genevieve dryly. Then, diffidently, 'May I ... would it be an imposition if I were to call again?'

'Not at all.' Surprised to find that she meant it, Madeleine said, 'Please do.'

The butler arrived; Aristide unlocked his jaws sufficiently to say all the proper things; and Genevieve took her leave. The instant the door closed behind her, Madeleine impaled her brother on an irritable stare and said, 'Have you mislaid your manners?'

'I don't believe so.' He took an apricot tart from the tray and bit into it. 'I was civil.'

'Barely.' She stalked across the room in a swish of taffeta and swung back to face him. 'What is going on, Aristide? Seven years ago you were fond of that woman. I *know* you were. Now, for no reason that I can see, you're behaving as if you either don't trust her or have some grudge against her. Which is it?'

Aristide studied what remained of the tart.

'Neither. You are imagining things.'

'I'm not. I know when you're deliberately setting out to discomfort someone. I've seen you do it enough times.' She stopped, examining the little she knew. 'Are you just piqued because she didn't immediately recognise you the other evening?'

'Piqued?' He seemed to consider it whilst thinking, *Piqued doesn't begin to describe it*. 'No. Surprised, perhaps — but no more than that.'

'Then why behave as you did? Apart from that not-quite-an-apology when you walked in, you could barely bring yourself to look at her.'

Aristide sighed, finished off the tart and dusted sugar from his fingers. He said softly, 'Leave it, Madeleine.' And when she showed signs of arguing, 'Leave it — or I'll ask a few questions of my own. About yesterday's picnic, for example ... on the subject of which you have so far been strangely reticent.' He watched her colour rise and saw her swallow whatever she'd been about to say. 'Thank you. Since you're determined to discuss Lady Westin, perhaps we might start with whether or not you liked her.'

She shrugged. 'Better than I expected to.'

'What does that mean?'

'Truthfully? I felt sorry for her. She neither likes nor trusts her brothers ... and I had the feeling that there was something wrong with her marriage.'

'Yes. It would be surprising if there had not been.'

She stared at him. 'Why do you say that? Did you know her husband?'

'I knew *of* him. For a few weeks after he died Christopher Westin was even more popular with the scandal rags than Sebastian Audley. And the main floor of the club was awash with talk.'

Madeleine sat down. 'I didn't hear any of it.'

'Nor, I imagine, did many other ladies. The gentlemen were careful about that ... at the time, anyway.'

'Tell me.'

'Are you sure you want to know? It isn't pretty.'

The green gaze became positively withering. 'Don't treat me like a child.'

'Well then ... from what I could gather there had been rumours about Westin for years, virtually all of them concerned with his sexual preferences. It was said, for example, that his father had tried to squash the talk by giving Westin a choice between marriage and losing his allowance. He chose marriage but didn't change his ways so the rumours persisted. However, they didn't *fully* surface until he was found battered to death a few yards from a particular sort of brothel on the same night that it had half-burned down. The general view at the time seemed to be that both the brothel and Westin as its customer had crossed a line with the wrong people.'

'What sort of brothel?' asked Madeleine flatly. 'Children?'

'No – or not specifically, though I don't doubt that went on as well.' He looked her in the eye and said, 'It was a house of procurement. Customers stated their preference and the management provided it – one way or another. Westin's taste ran to young girls; if the gossip is to be believed, twelve or thirteen-year-old virgins.'

'*Morceau de merde,*' she muttered, disgusted but not shocked. Life in the Saint Severin district didn't leave one any illusions about the depths of human depravity. 'So he was paying a Madam to ... what? Snatch innocent girls off the street?'

'That is what everyone thought. And it effectively damned him. Even if he'd survived the attack, he would have had to flee the country before somebody stuck a knife in his back one dark night.' Aristide's mouth curled a little. 'After all, no gentleman was going to offer him pistols at dawn, were they? One doesn't give vermin a chance to fight back. One exterminates it.'

Madeleine was silent for a long time. Finally she said, 'Did you know Genevieve was his wife?'

'Not until Adrian introduced me to her.'

'It's hard to imagine what knowing such a thing about one's husband would be like,' she mused. 'Unless he kept that part of his life hidden and she *didn't* know. Some gentlemen manage to do that, don't they?'

'They do ... but I suspect you're asking the wrong question,' replied Aristide expressionlessly. 'I think the real question is less what he did outside his home, than how he behaved *in* it.'

She stood up, eyes cold and voice even colder.

'If you think *that* ... why in God's name couldn't you have been a bit kinder?'

'It appears I can leave you to be kind enough for both of us,' replied Aristide, rising from his chair. 'For myself, I'll wait until I know the cost of it.'

* * *

Two days later in a coffee-house on the Strand, Sir George Braxton stared moodily across the table at Mr Clavering and said, 'I haven't found a single fellow who plays at that damned club who'll talk to me. Not one. Treat me as if I'm nothing, they do.'

'They want to keep their memberships. Then again, it's known that Delacroix is uncommon friendly with the Earl of Sarre – not to mention Amberley and Rockliffe playing at Sinclairs regularly.' Mr Clavering smiled apologetically. 'Don't want to offend, George, but none of 'em know you at all.'

'Oh you don't need to tell me. I know all about titled gents and their friends. Stick together like glue, don't they? Nose in the air and no need to give the time of day to anybody who didn't go to the right school.'

'Way of the world, old fellow,' agreed Mr Clavering. And then, 'Perhaps you should give it up. If Delacroix *did* cheat and there's any evidence of it, it would be in Paris – not here. Seems to me you're not going to get anywhere. Waste of energy, really.'

'Nobody fleeces me and gets away with it,' Braxton growled.

'But --'

'No! And there's no *if* about it. He cheated.'

'What makes you so sure?'

'I'd been winning. For three nights in a row, I'd been winning,' growled Sir George. 'Then that bugger turned up and cleaned me out in the space of a few hours. He took me for over two thousand guineas – and there's no way he could've done it *without* cheating. I'm having my money back and there's an end of it.'

Mr Clavering sighed. The truth was that he didn't like Sir George very much and this obsession with Aristide Delacroix threatened to become unpleasant. Really, had it not been that George had money and, just at present, he himself didn't, he'd have already distanced himself from the fellow. Fortunately, he had that morning received an invitation to a house-party in Keynsham which meant that, in another week or so, he could wave goodbye to George and be living rent-free at Cousin Malcolm's expense.

He said, 'I don't see how you're to do it. If Sinclairs was a hell, you might stand some chance – but it ain't. Never been so much as a whisper against it. And with the likes of Rockliffe playing there --'

'Oh for Christ's sake! I'm sick of hearing about bloody Rockliffe. And according to you, he's left town, hasn't he?'

'Yes. And that's another thing that won't improve your chances. It's the middle of June now. In another month, everybody who's anybody will have gone to the country. Nobody stays in London through August. So if you're going to get any information at all, you'll have to do it while there's still somebody left to talk to.'

George brooded on this for a moment. Finally, he said, 'There'll be men who applied for membership and got turned down, won't there? And maybe others ... members who got thrown out for one reason or another? Seems to me I'd do better talking to them. But how do I find 'em? Who'd know stuff like that? Somebody must. There's always some fellow who knows everything; somebody who collects gossip just for the fun of it.'

This, thought Mr Clavering, was going from bad to worse.

'There's Charles Fox,' he said reluctantly. 'But he won't talk to you.'

'Why not?' Then, irritably, 'No. Don't say it. I can guess. Who else?'

'Viscount Ansford ... but you'd have to be desperate. He never sticks to the point and that lisp of his is maddening.'

'What about them as work in the club?'

Mr Clavering considered this and then shook his head. 'I doubt you'll get a word out of any of them. Being close-mouthed will be part of what Delacroix pays them for.'

'What if I pay 'em better?'

'Offer to buy information? I suppose you could try that and hope they know something useful but --' He stopped, frowning, and then said slowly, 'Delacroix has just taken on an assistant; a young man named Hastings. One wouldn't normally hear something like that – but Hastings was apparently Lord Leighton's secretary for years until he just up and left to take a position at Sinclairs. Leighton is mad as fire about it and was shooting his mouth off at Whites yesterday until he realised what a cake he was making of himself. Then he tried implying there was something shady about Hastings but had enough sense to stop short of actually *accusing* him of anything.'

'Gentleman's scruples again, most like,' grunted Braxton. 'Still ... it might mean this Hastings fellow would be open to a bribe.'

'It might,' agreed Mr Clavering dubiously. 'But you'd need to be very careful how you went about it.'

'Why?'

'Hastings is a younger son with no prospects but what he can make for himself. But he comes of a good family. More importantly, his uncle is Viscount Grassmere.'

'So?'

Mr Clavering drew a long breath and then loosed it.

'Lady Grassmere is the Duke of Rockliffe's sister.'

Sir George smashed his fist into the table with a force that made the crockery jump.

'Bloody buggering hell,' he said.

CHAPTER SIX

Genevieve went over and over that brief meeting with Aristide Delacroix and still could not understand where she was going wrong. She'd apologised for not immediately recognising him; she'd promised not to invade his precious club again; and she'd spent a perfectly innocent hour in his home at the invitation of his sister. What was there in any of that to cause him to turn into a block of ice the second he laid eyes on her?

Seven years ago, he'd liked her. Hadn't he? Yes, she was sure he had – or as sure as one could be. And, as far as he was concerned, she was still the same person she had been then. A little older and her body was … different. But the other changes weren't ones that anyone could see. They were all hidden deep inside her where no one would ever find them.

A second visit from Ralph began by raising her spirits only to dash them again.

'I shall be out of town from time to time over the next few weeks,' he informed her, appearing not to notice how her face brightened at the prospect. 'Aunt Sarah informs me that Grandfather's health has deteriorated to the point where she feels I should be in attendance.'

Their paternal grandparent was the Earl of Sherbourne and when he died, the title would go to Ralph. Genevieve rather thought that the possibility of this happening soon – Grandfather must be nearly ninety after all – explained a few things. She said, 'Is that what this recent obsession with respectability is all about? Not just the prospect of inheriting the earldom but the hope that good behaviour will persuade Grandpapa to leave you some money along with it?' She smiled at him. 'Oh dear. I fear you may have begun that a little late. As I understand it, he can't abide you – or Cedric and Bertram, either.'

'However true that may be, I am persuaded that he will do what is right for the title,' replied Ralph, his tone soft as ever but unmistakeably repressive. 'But that is not what I wished to discuss with you. Since it is likely I will be away a good deal, you may reside with Lady Brassington until your year is up. After that you will remove to Curzon Street.'

'No, Ralph. I don't think I will.'

'Please don't argue, Genevieve. You need an address in a good part of town and a female companion but can afford neither. I, on the other hand, can supply both at no additional cost.'

'A *companion*?' she echoed incredulously. 'That's ridiculous! I'm a --'

'Widow. Yes, I believe I am tolerably aware of that fact. But you cannot have people suppose that you may be ... enjoying your freedom ... in the manner of certain other young widows. Consequently --'

'Like Adela Daventry, you mean?'

His eyes narrowed slightly but he continued as if she hadn't spoken. 'Consequently, I have invited Cousin Marjorie to pay an extended visit. Needless to say, she was delighted to accept.' He paused and then added negligently, 'Of course, if Grandfather shuffles off his mortal coil, things must necessarily change.'

Since it wasn't hard to guess what this meant, Genevieve stared at him, aghast.

'*More* black? No. I won't. I only ever met Grandpapa four times in my life!'

'Be that as it may, he is your paternal grandfather and, as such, entitled to respect.'

'That's easy for you to say. All *you* have to do is don a black arm-band.'

'And take up residence at Gardington.' He smiled coldly. 'As will you. And now I'm afraid that you must excuse me. I have another appointment.'

Lost for words and stomach churning, she watched him go – plainly confident that he'd mapped out her future to his satisfaction

Later, Genevieve sat before her mirror and thought, *Cousin Marjorie, for God's sake. She'll have me knitting socks for the poor while she reads out loud from a book of sermons. And trapped at Gardington with Ralph — and probably Cedric and Bertram as well? It doesn't bear thinking about.*

But where was the alternative?

She'd hoped that it might lie with Aristide Delacroix but that wasn't looking very likely. The man she remembered had possessed warmth and kindness. The man she had encountered three times during the last week exhibited little of either … so even if she managed to engineer further meetings, would he be any better than a husband of Ralph's choosing? Was she, in fact, clutching at straws?

Genevieve sighed. Since, for the time being and with the possible exception of a stroll in the park, she was forbidden the kind of society where she would encounter any gentlemen at all, it was probably worth attempting just one more meeting with Monsieur Delacroix. Then, if he was no less intimidating than he'd been so far, there was nothing to be gained by attempting to further the acquaintance.

This was all very well, she reflected restlessly, but it still left the problem of how that meeting was to be arranged. It was too soon to call on Madeleine again unless she was invited; she couldn't go to Sinclairs; and if there were other places where Aristide might regularly be found, she had no idea what they were.

Really, she thought wearily, the whole idea had been doomed from the start.

* * *

At his desk in the club, Aristide finished writing a note to Sebastian Audley — the only gentleman of his acquaintance left in town who might be able to offer him the advice he needed. Then he tossed down his quill and called to his assistant in the next room.

'Edward.'

Mr Hastings appeared in the doorway. 'Sir?'

'You are humming. Again.'

'I beg your pardon, sir – I wasn't aware of it. Shall I close the door?'

'That may become necessary. Is there some reason for this morning's increased *joie de vivre*? I do not suppose your work is responsible for it.'

'Actually, I believe I'm now thoroughly conversant with the accounts system,' came the cheerful reply. 'And there are a number of small improvements which might be made – with your permission, of course.'

'Make them.' It had taken Aristide less than a day to understand why Lord Leighton had not wanted to lose his secretary. Mr Hastings was hard-working and efficient. He also had a mind like a razor. 'Will that stop the humming?'

Edward grinned. 'I can't guarantee it, sir. Mr Jenkins has told me of a suite of rooms currently available in the building where he himself lodges. If they prove both suitable and affordable, Henrietta and I may be able to marry sooner than we'd hoped.'

'You haven't seen these rooms?'

'Not yet. There's been no opportunity.'

'Then allow me to give you one. Jenkins and one of his assistants will be banking the takings from the last two evenings. Since the bank will need to recognise you in the future, go with them – after which, you can view the lodgings.'

Taken by surprise, Edward opened his mouth, closed it again and finally managed to say, 'Sir – that's extremely good of you.'

'I know. But an hour without musical accompaniment makes it worthwhile.'

Edward left the room laughing and disappeared in search of Mr Jenkins.

Aristide leaned back in his chair, stared at the wall and acknowledged the fact that his lack of concentration had nothing to do with Edward's perpetual humming.

He was beginning to wonder if he'd made a mistaken assumption with regard to Genevieve Westin – or even two. Perhaps she *didn't* know what his promise to deliver her letter had led to. It wasn't hard to believe that her brothers might have failed to admit they'd done their damnedest to knock the stuffing out of him. The thornier issue was why she hadn't countered the lies they had told Sir Kenneth and which had been responsible for his dismissal. Even if the brothers had whisked her back to England the very next day, surely Genevieve and her step-father had corresponded? There had been a strong bond between them which he didn't think would be completely severed by the English Channel. And if they had exchanged letters, his own name and the reason Sir Kenneth had dispensed with his services would have appeared on those pages somewhere. Or so he had thought. But what if she really had known nothing about that night … and still did not?

The trouble was that he was becoming increasingly aware that he *wanted* his suspicions to have been unjust; wanted her to be innocent of all of it … wanted also to believe that the glow of pleasure in her eyes when she looked at him had been genuine. He remembered the lovely, laughing girl she had been; warm, generous and full of joy, without an ounce of artifice in her. And now he saw the beautiful, desirable woman that girl had become … and the combination of the two was playing merry hell with both his mind and his body.

Unable to sit still any longer, Aristide left his desk and crossed to the window with its uninspiring view of Ryder Street. He was making this into a problem when it needn't be one. The solution was simple. Stop condemning her unheard and ask the question.

What do you remember of the day your brothers came?

He didn't think the girl he'd known would lie … and was reasonably certain he'd know if she did. All he had to do was create an opportunity for a private conversation which surely couldn't be so very difficult. He could try to do it this afternoon. The sun was shining; perfect weather for a stroll in the park. And if he could give his assistant an hour off, he could do as much for himself. All he had to do, therefore, was walk round to Albemarle Street and hope to find Genevieve at home.

Spinning on his heel, he snatched up his gloves and hat and walked out of Sinclairs before he could think better of it.

* * *

It was Lady Brassington's turn to host the meeting of the Ladies' Benevolent Society. This comprised some dozen well-meaning ladies who raised modest sums for deserving causes – the current one being an orphanage in Blackfriars. Genevieve would have been quite happy to serve the ladies their tea and sit quietly in a corner. As gently as she could, Cousin Lily explained why this wouldn't be a good idea.

'Due to space and cost, the orphanage can only keep the children until they reach the age of twelve. The Society's main concern at present is what happens to them after that – specifically the girls.' She stopped, spreading her hands helplessly. 'I'm so sorry, Genevieve. But it's the same story with every lady of my acquaintance. No one can help wondering if – if you *knew*.'

Genevieve stared at her, aghast.

'About Kit? I didn't. I swear I didn't!'

'I know that. And perhaps in time others will know it too. But for now --'

'It's worse than that, isn't it?' She was suddenly icy cold. 'They think I knew what he was doing and – and didn't care. That I *condoned* it by silence and inactivity.'

Lady Brassington reached out to squeeze her hands.

'Don't lose heart, dear. It will pass. But for now it would be best if you avoided situations in which you might be snubbed.'

While Cousin Lily's guests arrived and made their way up to the drawing room, Genevieve hid in the small rarely-used downstairs parlour, a copy of *Pamela* open but unread in her lap. Thoughts jostled each other inside her head, none of them helpful.

It isn't fair, was the first and most persistent of them. *I knew how Kit was with me but I didn't know the rest of it until everyone else did. How could I? After the first year, I was hardly ever in London. And even if I'd known – what does anyone think I could have done to stop it?* And then, a little later, *Cousin Lily thinks it will get better. But what if it doesn't? What if no one will ever receive me?* A small, slightly hysterical laugh shook her. *That will ruin Ralph's plans, won't it? There won't be a respectable man anywhere who will take me – which would suit me very well indeed if I hadn't been left penniless.*

Misery and anger welled up until she felt she was suffocating. Snatching up a shawl and bonnet and mumbling an excuse to the startled footman who opened the front door for her, she fled the house.

* * *

Aristide arrived in Albemarle Street a short time later; and because Lady Brassington's butler was still above stairs attending to her ladyship's guests, the door was opened by the same footman who had witnessed Genevieve's flight.

'Lady Westin is not at home, sir,' he said correctly. And then, because her young ladyship had seemed mortal upset and because, despite being foreign, the fellow who'd come calling looked like a gentleman, he added, 'Went out not ten minutes ago to get some air, she said.' And staring woodenly at a point just past Aristide's shoulder, 'I reckon if you was to head in the direction of Berkeley Square, you might come up with her.'

Knowing as well as the footman did that none of this information should have been forthcoming, Aristide nodded his thanks and slid a coin into the young man's hand.

Half-hidden by shade and black garments, he eventually spotted Genevieve on a bench in an unobtrusive corner of Berkeley Square gardens. Her hands were clenched tight in her lap and her head was bent over them as if she was deep in thought. Consequently, she was unaware of his approach until he arrived beside her and said, 'Good afternoon, my lady.'

She started, lifted her face to his and looked even more startled.

'Monsieur Delacroix? What are you doing here?' And coming hurriedly to her feet, 'I'm sorry. That was rude – but you took me by surprise.'

'For which I apologise,' he replied. 'As to how I found you ... I called in Albemarle Street. The footman suggested you might be here.'

'You – you came to see *me*?' She sounded wholly incredulous. 'Why?'

'To hold a conversation I've been avoiding.' He surveyed her clinically, thinking she looked as if she had a very bad headache. 'But there is no real urgency, so if now is not a good time, it will wait until another day.'

Genevieve shook her head and managed a smile.

'Now will do well enough. And if you can send my thoughts in a direction other than the one they're currently taking, I'll be grateful.'

Aristide doubted that. He also realised that, whatever ailed her, it wasn't a headache. But he said merely, 'Well, then. Shall we walk?'

She nodded and took the arm he offered. It was a few moments before he spoke but eventually he said, 'I'd like you to cast your mind back to Paris. In particular, to the day your brothers arrived to take you away.'

She very nearly groaned. 'What about it?'

'Earlier that day, you planned to seek help from Philippe de Chevigny. Do you recall that?'

'Yes.' Some colour filtered back into her cheeks and she said dryly, 'I *was* going to ask Philippe to rescue me – hard though it is to believe I was ever stupid enough to imagine he either could or would. But as things turned out, it was too late anyway. My brothers --'

'-- arrived sooner than expected. Yes. But you had already written a letter to him.'

'Had I?'

'You don't recall it?'

He watched her trying to push whatever had upset her earlier to the back of her mind and focus on what he was asking.

'I don't know. It's hard to remember details because I was completely hysterical through most of it.' She glanced up at him, frowning a little. 'This is important?'

'Somewhat, yes.'

'Very well. Let me think. Ralph – my eldest brother – was brow-beating Papa Ken; the other two were somewhere around, though I didn't see them until much later; and … yes. At some point in the afternoon, my maid disappeared.' Without warning, she stopped walking, took a short, hard breath and stared at him. 'Oh God! Of course. How could I forget that? I sent Amelie to you with a letter because you'd promised to take it to Philippe.'

'Yes.' Aristide debated how much to tell her and decided that it might as well be the truth; or some of it, anyway. 'She never reached me. Two of your brothers waylaid her.'

All expression drained from her face. 'Cedric and Bertram?'

'I imagine so. They seized the letter and made her tell them where she was taking it. Then they came to me.' He paused. 'They assumed – or *chose* to assume – it had been written to me.'

'*What*?' She gaped at him. 'No! They can't have done! I wrote to Philippe. I --'

'You wrote a letter without a superscription to someone you hailed as your "beloved". There was nothing to indicate that person was not I.'

Her hands crept to her mouth. 'What did they do?'

He stared silently into her eyes.

'You really don't know?'

'No!' She stopped, suddenly seeing how similar this was to her earlier conversation with Cousin Lily. Her hands dropped to her sides and the air froze in her lungs. Was there anyone who *didn't* think her a cold, deceitful bitch? Fighting to keep her voice level, she said dully, 'But you thought I did, didn't you? They did something awful and you thought I knew about it and didn't care. That's it, isn't it?'

'It is ... how it looked, yes.'

'How it *looked*. Of course. So tell me. You may as well. I already know they are capable of anything. When they were younger, they enjoyed beating up watchmen and crossing sweepers.' She stopped, piecing together what he'd told her. 'Did ... did they hurt you?'

'Yes.'

She sucked in a painful breath, wanting but not daring to ask how *badly* they had hurt him. 'I'm sorry. I had no idea.'

He didn't say whether or not he believed her and nothing shifted in that cool, blue gaze; yet some premonition told Genevieve the worst was yet to come. Not sure she could bear any more, she took a couple of rapid steps along the path before turning back to him. Then, her voice flat and somewhere beyond hopeless, she said, 'That's not all, is it? There's something *else* you think I must have known. What?'

'Sir Kenneth never told you?'

'Told me *what*, for heaven's sake? He didn't have chance to tell me *anything*! Ralph bundled me into a carriage and set off for Calais that same evening. Papa Ken and I barely had a chance to say goodbye.'

'But you must have corresponded with him since then.'

'No. Oh – I wrote to him scores of times. But I never had a reply. Not one. And eventually I realised Ralph was making sure I never would.' She looked back with weary bitterness. 'You won't believe it – but the level of my ignorance about my own life is truly astounding. So let us have this over with, please. What else am I supposed to have known?'

'Your brothers convinced Sir Kenneth that I had been making improper advances with the intention of seducing you,' said Aristide with less expression than if they'd been discussing the weather. 'Needless to say, I was dismissed.'

It was the final blow in what had been a catastrophe of a day. Feeling utterly sick, Genevieve walked on to the next bench, sat down and put her head in her hands. It was a long time before she looked up and when she did, it was to find Monsieur Delacroix sitting beside her. He said, 'I'm sorry. In time, you will perhaps appreciate why I had to ask.'

'I appreciate that *now*,' she said bitterly, 'and wish others would do as much. But that is another matter entirely. All I can say is that I didn't know any of this and am sorry for it.'

'None of it was your fault.'

'None of it was yours, either. I asked you to help me, you said you would ... and this is what came of it. Your life and probably your sister's life, too, were destroyed for a time because I asked a favour of you. Apologising won't put that right. Nothing will.'

'I'm not seeking reparation. Just the truth.'

'And now you have it – or as much of it as I can give you.' Genevieve stood up, struck by another thought. 'Does your sister know what happened and – and what you believed was my part in it?'

'No. At the time, I had compelling reasons for not telling her and later, doing so would have served no purpose.' Aristide also rose and, deciding against bringing the death of his mother into it, said impassively, 'Since that hasn't changed, I would prefer you didn't make her privy to this conversation.'

'Oh - you can rely on that. If Madeleine knew what you've been thinking, she wouldn't come within ten feet of me.' Walking onwards so he couldn't see her face, Genevieve said abruptly, 'Does she know about my late husband? Do you?'

Aristide fell into step with her along the path. 'Yes.'

She shot a surprised sideways glance at him. 'Yet Madeleine still invited me to your home? And you didn't object?'

'Madeleine is her own mistress. And Lord Westin's sins were his own.'

Genevieve nodded but said nothing because of the sudden lump forming in her throat. He couldn't know what those few words meant to her and she couldn't tell him. Somehow, she couldn't bear him to know that, to everyone else, she was a pariah.

After a while, Aristide said quietly, 'Why did you marry him?'

'*Why?*' She laughed then, albeit unsteadily. 'Knowing what you do of my brothers, why do you think?'

* * *

Entering the house and learning that Cousin Lily's guests were still there, Genevieve crept silently up to her bedchamber and locked the door. Then she crawled on to the bed, curled up into a small, miserable ball and finally let the tears come. Leaving the isolation of Shropshire where neighbours neither called nor issued invitations, she'd thought everything would be better in London only to find that it was far worse. She felt as if she'd stumbled into an empty black tunnel from which there was no way out.

The tears she had stopped shedding years ago could have filled an ocean and it was tempting to let them all flow now but she wouldn't because tears never mended anything. So after a little while, she sat up, pushed her hair out of her face, blew her nose ... and found that, lost amidst the darkness inside her, there *was* one tiny glimmer of light.

Aristide Delacroix had sought her out. He'd *asked*, instead of continuing to assume the worst – which was more than the ladies of society were prepared to do – and he'd listened to her answers without apparent condemnation. Neither did he blame her for Kit's transgressions. Indeed, by the time he'd escorted her to Cousin Lily's door, he'd seemed much less cold towards her.

Perhaps ... but she stopped that notion before it could form. She was incapable of rational thought. And the one thing the last four years had taught her was not to rely on hope.

* * *

Once more back at his desk, Aristide contemplated what he'd learned. He didn't believe she'd lied. Her reactions had been natural and everything she'd said, plausible. Oddly, the near-silent walk back to Albemarle Street had seemed almost companionable. He wondered about that ... but refused to dwell on the effect she continued to have on his body because wanting her wasn't sensible. She wasn't mistress material and even if he was contemplating marriage – which he wasn't – he suspected that Viscount Kilburn would sooner see her dead at his feet than wedded to a man who owned a gaming-house. On the other hand, from things she'd said it was easy to guess that word of Westin's perversions had somehow reached the ladies of society and left them unwilling to receive his widow. And that, reflected Aristide, deserved further investigation.

Half an hour later, Mr Hastings walked in looking a little grim. Shutting the door, he said, 'Sir ... there's something you need to hear.'

Aristide waved him into a chair. 'Yes?'

'After we visited the bank, Mr Jenkins returned here while I went to inspect the lodgings. As soon as I was alone --'

'Are the rooms suitable?'

'Oh – yes, sir. Very much so. I've asked the agent to hold them for me.'

'Good. Now ... what happened after you and Mr Jenkins parted company?'

'A man approached and handed me this letter.' Edward passed it over the desk. 'You can see why I find it worrying. Aside from anything else, the fellow must have been --'

Aristide held up a hand to stem the flow. 'In a moment.'

Mr Hastings, the note said.

Young men can always use some extra money. If you're interested in earning a nice bit of the ready, come to the Black Pig on Fleet Street tomorrow night at nine. Somebody will meet you there.

Naturally enough, it wasn't signed.

Aristide looked up. 'I imagine you were about to say that whoever gave you this had been following you since you left the club. I'm a trifle concerned that Mr Jenkins wasn't aware of that. However ... what other conclusions do you draw?'

'They wouldn't make an approach like this to Mr Jenkins but they know I'm new here. Too new to be loyal and maybe even a bit greedy? They'll know money was being taken to the bank – but if that's what they're interested in, they'll also know there's no set pattern to when it is done. Day and time are constantly changed – I asked Mr Jenkins about that. So if it *is* the money they want, they need inside information and think I can supply it.' He stopped, frowning. 'Or perhaps it isn't about money at all.'

Aristide leaned back in his chair and waited.

Edward glanced around at the locked, solidly-built cabinets that flanked two of the walls. 'I don't know what is in your files. But I'd guess that some of the information you hold would be extremely valuable ... to the right person.'

'Bravo,' said Aristide softly. Then, 'Tell me about the man who gave you the letter.'

'Average-looking in every respect and dressed like an upper servant ... and he had a strong provincial accent.' Edward's shrug suggested that he was annoyed with himself. 'I'm sorry. It wasn't one I'm familiar with so I can't place it.'

It's possible I could, thought Aristide. Every instinct was shouting the name Braxton at him but he knew it wouldn't do to jump to conclusions. He said, 'It would be helpful to know exactly what these secretive gentlemen want. How would you feel about a little undercover work?'

'I thought you'd never ask, sir,' grinned Mr Hastings.

CHAPTER SEVEN

Madeleine had forbidden herself to think about Nicholas and for the first week of his absence she managed to stop him creeping slyly into her head more than five or six times a day. By the second week, however, it was becoming more difficult – a situation not helped by the fact that, with so many members of the *ton* leaving for their country estates, the private dining-salons at the club were growing less busy by the day. The result of this was that when, as so often happened, she found herself at a loose end, she took to prowling around Aristide's office and annoying him by tidying things he didn't want tidied. Edward Hastings was generally in the next room, still working long after Aristide had told him to stop for the day.

Madeleine sauntered past her brother's desk, one hand reaching for a pile of letters.

'Please don't touch those,' said Aristide without glancing up. 'In fact, don't touch anything at all.'

She gave a huff of irritation and wandered off to rearrange a row of books in order of size. One of the thicker ones flopped over on its side with a thwack. Aristide muttered something under his breath ... which was when Madeleine realised that the neighbouring room was unusually silent. It was amazing how quickly one became accustomed to that faint undercurrent of sound. She said, 'Edward isn't humming.'

'Edward isn't there.'

'Oh?' She turned, looking surprised. 'You haven't sent him downstairs for the first time without you, surely?'

'No.'

'So where is he?'

Giving up all hope of getting any work done, Aristide tossed down his quill and glanced at the clock. 'Right now he's sitting in a tavern with a mug of ale, waiting for some fellow to come and offer him a bribe.'

She stared at him. '*What* did you say?'

Aristide explained; and as he did so Madeleine's expression turned to one of mingled incredulity and disapproval. Finally, she said, 'You have sent that unfortunate young man off alone to meet God alone knows what kind of ruffian ... without a thought about what might happen to him after he's said no. Are you *completely* addled?'

'First of all, that "unfortunate young man" as you call him is as clever as a cart-load of monkeys and twice as quick. Just wait until you see what he's doing to the accounts system. Secondly, he would be doing this whether I'd asked him to or not. And finally, he is not on his own. Jenkins hired two men from outside the club to keep an eye on him while he's in the tavern and escort him back here afterwards. Satisfied?'

'Oh. Yes. I suppose.' She changed tack. 'And when exactly were you going to tell me about this?'

'When I knew whether or not it amounted to anything – which, with luck, will be later tonight.' He stood up. 'I'm going downstairs. If you've nothing better to do than aggravate me, I suggest you go home and write a letter to Lord Nicholas. It might stop you moping and improve your temper.'

'I am not moping,' said Madeleine through her teeth. 'I am not out of temper. And I am most certainly *not* writing to Lord Nicholas.'

'As you wish,' shrugged Aristide. And over his shoulder as he crossed to the door, 'Then send a note to Lady Westin, asking her to go shopping or join you for tea – or whatever it is ladies do. I suspect she'd be grateful.'

'*Wait a moment!*' she snapped.

He turned, sighing faintly. 'Well?'

'A few days ago you hadn't a kind word for her and now *this*? Why?'

Since he wasn't going to admit having met Genevieve, Aristide looked his sister in the eye and lied. 'From snatches of talk downstairs, it appears that society is turning its back on her – which means she presumably has very few friends. Just at present, you are similarly bereft so I thought you might be company for each other. But the choice is yours.' Upon which note, he walked out.

The main gaming floor was moderately busy but by no means crowded which meant that, aside from getting away from Madeleine and killing time until Mr Hastings returned from Fleet Street, Aristide had no real need to be there. Then Sebastian Audley strode up to him and said, 'Aristide – forgive me. The house is in turmoil with furniture and God knows what being delivered every hour of the day and my desk is vanishing under an ever-increasing stack of bills. Somehow your note got mixed up with them.'

Aristide smiled, signalled a footman to bring wine, and led the way to one of the small card-rooms. 'Your lady wife has been shopping?'

'*We* have been shopping,' corrected Sebastian. 'And it goes like this. Let's say we are looking for a sofa. Cassandra finds one she likes in the first shop we visit. When asked for my opinion, I do what any sensible fellow would and agree that I like it, too. But of course, we don't buy it.'

'You don't?'

'No. Instead, we spend the rest of the day looking at countless *other* sofas in case, somewhere in London, there should be one we like better. Then, when we are quite sure there isn't, we go back and buy the first one we saw.' Sebastian gave a sudden laugh. 'And it's more fun than it sounds. I always enjoy teasing Cassandra – and this gives so much scope.' He dropped into a chair and waited for the footman to set down his tray and leave. 'So ... your note said you wanted advice of some kind. How may I help?'

'Lord Pennington is drastically reducing his stables.'

Sebastian accepted the glass he was offered and sat down. 'Run aground, has he?'

'If he has, he didn't do it here,' said Aristide, taking a chair on the other side of the table. 'I've been thinking it was time I acquired a conveyance of some kind and have hinted to his lordship that I may be interested in buying. But I know little of carriages and nothing whatsoever about horseflesh, so I need the opinion of someone who does.'

'I've never met Pennington or seen his cattle but I'll be happy to come with you to look at them,' replied Mr Audley. 'As for the carriage ... what style of thing do you want?'

'The sort that comes with a coachman.'

'So Madeleine also has the use of it?'

'There is that,' agreed Aristide. 'But mostly because I can't drive.'

'You could learn.'

'At present, I don't have the time. I've taken on an assistant but he hasn't been here long enough to be fully conversant with the running of the club. When he is ... well, we'll see. But for now, I want a carriage suitable for general use and equipped with a driver.'

'If Pennington is getting rid of his vehicles, a coachman and groom are likely to be out of work – in which case you can probably acquire both together. Make an appointment with his lordship and let me know,' said Sebastian. 'Looking at horses will make a pleasant change from looking at china and silverware. And damned great plants in pots.'

'Plants?' queried Aristide.

'For the hall.' Sebastian shook his head, laughter once more brimming in his eyes. 'It's empty and unwelcoming, you see. But apparently giant ferns in tubs will change that.'

*　*　*

It wasn't until Mr Audley had left that a nod from Mr Jenkins told Aristide that Edward was safely back in the building and sent him up to his office, devoutly hoping that Madeleine wasn't lying in wait.

She wasn't. Waving Edward into a chair and pouring two small glasses of brandy, he said briskly, 'Well?'

'It was the same man who gave me the note – and as far as I could tell, he was alone.' Edward nursed the glass in his hands but made no move to drink. 'He introduced himself as Jones. I may have rolled my eyes when he said that because he added Obadiah to it – as if that made it any better. Then, presumably on the assumption that since I'd turned up to the meeting I must therefore be amenable to betraying my position here, he offered me fifty guineas for the right information.'

'Which was?'

'Not anything we'd thought it might be.' He took a sip of brandy and then met his employer's impenetrable gaze. 'Whoever Obadiah works for isn't interested in simple robbery or anything contained in the files you keep on the members. He wants to know about you personally, sir.'

'Ah.' Aristide merely nodded.

'You don't seem surprised.'

'I'm not. What is he hoping you'll find out for him?'

'Well, that's where it got faintly ridiculous. Obadiah clearly knows exactly what information he's looking for but hasn't the least idea how to go about getting it. He also appears to think you leave confidential papers lying around for anyone to find. Cutting a long story short, he asked me to dig into your own financial records – taking particular interest in any large sums you may have received in the year before you arrived in London and opened Sinclairs.' Edward paused. 'You still don't look surprised.'

'I'm still not. What else?'

'I told him it was impossible; that I don't have access to that kind of information – a situation I don't see changing. Obadiah decided all *that* meant was that I wanted more money, so he increased his offer to seventy-five and started asking about gossip amongst the staff here. Does anyone speak of disputes between yourself and club members? Have there been any accusations of dishonest play at the tables? Did I know of any gentlemen who harbour resentment at having their membership cancelled? That sort of thing.'

'And you said?'

'Sinclairs' employees don't gossip and I've only been here a week. So how the hell – pardon me, sir, but I allowed myself a touch of impatience at that stage – how the *hell* could I possibly answer any of those questions?' Edward grinned. 'Poor Obadiah was so downcast that I dropped a hint about possibly being more helpful when I've been here a little longer. That cheered him up. It also gives you options if you don't want the door slammed shut before you've had a chance to find out who he's working for.'

'Let us hope that won't be necessary,' remarked Aristide calmly. Then, 'I don't suppose greater exposure to the man's accent helped you to identify it?'

'No, sir. I'm sorry. I'm not even sure I can reproduce it.' He thought for a moment. 'It sounds something like "Oi ave ta say Mister Aistings as yoom proving a big disappointment. Yoom as iggorant as a bleeding sheep."' He stopped, shaking his head. 'No. That's not quite it. But it's the best I can do.'

Aristide drained his glass and stood up.

'It's good enough. Thank you, Edward. I take it you had no problems?'

'You made sure I wouldn't, didn't you, sir? I noticed the two fellows Mr Jenkins had watching me right away. So when they followed me out of the tavern, I sent one of them to follow Obadiah instead.'

'Did you indeed?' Aristide realised he shouldn't have been surprised. 'And?'

'And he went to The Bell on Ludgate Hill. It's one of the larger coaching-inns, so we can assume his employer has taken rooms there.' Edward hesitated briefly and then said, 'I think you know who he is, sir.'

'I think so, too.' Aristide took a thoughtful sip of brandy. 'Has anyone mentioned the name George Braxton to you?'

'No. What I told Obadiah was true. Your people don't gossip.'

'I'm glad to hear it. A fortnight ago, Sir George accused me of cheating at cards. Since he did so publicly on the main gaming floor, every member present and a good proportion of the staff heard him. He claims I took a large sum from him and has demanded I pay it back.' Aristide smiled aridly. 'You look shocked, Edward.'

'Not shocked, sir – appalled.'

'Thank you. I have been waiting for him to translate words into action. Now he's done so, I can take some action of my own that I hope will deter any further efforts.'

Frowning back at him, Edward said, 'Am I allowed to ask what you intend to do?'

'Yes.' Aristide drained his glass and stood up. 'I shall place the matter in the capable hands of Mr Henry Lessing, man-of-law. And if *he* can't persuade Sir George that, with nothing but his own suspicions to go on, he's embarking on a forlorn hope, no one can.'

* * *

Monsieur Delacroix purchased a sleek, glossy town-carriage from Lord Pennington, along with a pair of matched greys which Mr Audley said he'd have happily bought himself had he been in the market for horseflesh. Lord Pennington's coachman and head groom were easily persuaded to change employers and undertook to arrange stabling in the mews at the rear of Ryder Street. And when all transactions had been successfully concluded, Sebastian grinned at Aristide and said, 'Have you told Madeleine about this yet?'

'No. In general, I find a *fait accompli* works best.'

Inevitably, Madeleine took the news of her brother's latest acquisition with acid-tinged resignation. 'First a house and now a carriage. What next? Visiting-cards and snuff boxes for you and a little black page for me?'

'No snuff boxes or pages ... but visiting-cards, perhaps,' he replied absently, whilst scanning the letter in his hand. He had given Madeleine the gist of Edward's meeting in the tavern and his own with Henry Lessing. Now, smiling faintly, he handed her the sheet of paper, saying, 'A copy of the letter Sir George Braxton will be receiving at some time today. I do believe Mr Lessing has outdone himself.'

She read the letter and then read it again. Finally, she looked up … and laughed.

* * *

In his rooms at Bellsavage Yard, Sir George didn't laugh. He crumpled Mr Lessing's missive in his hand and scowled at his manservant.

'What the hell did you tell that Hastings fellow?'

'Only what you told me to,' replied Mr Stebbins, alias Obadiah Jones. 'I was careful.'

'Not careful enough if this damned lawyer can write informing me that his client's employees are scrupulously loyal and …' Braxton unscrewed the paper to remind himself of its contents, '… and suggesting that I *"desist from further pointless excursions into this field or risk legal action being taken against you"*. Bah!' He hurled the letter into the fireplace. 'Hastings went straight back and told the Frenchman everything. If they know it was me who sent you, you must've been bloody clumsy.'

'Well, I wasn't,' insisted Mr Stebbins sulkily. 'I never even give Hastings me own name, never mind yourn.'

Braxton's frown deepened. 'Did anybody follow you back here?'

Mr Stebbins hadn't previously considered this possibility but knew his best course was a positive denial. 'No. 'Course not. I'm not a bleeding idiot.'

'Mind your mouth!' snapped Braxton. And then, 'Oh – get out. Clear off and do something useful so I can think.'

'Do what?' asked Stebbins.

'Your job, man! You're a bloody valet, ain't you? Go and do some bloody valeting.'

When Mr Stebbins had slunk away, George got up and poured a glass of gin. He took a hefty, invigorating swallow and thought back on the politely threatening letter from Delacroix's lawyer.

There was more in it than he'd told Stebbins. Mr Henry sodding Lessing hadn't confined himself to warnings about bribery. He'd also included a more serious charge.

"Further attempts to damage the integrity of either my client or his business through false testimony obtained from persons who have neither met Monsieur Delacroix nor visited his club will, if they continue, result in a lawsuit for slander."

George downed the remainder of his gin and managed not to hurl the glass at the wall. He couldn't risk a lawsuit. His name would be in the newspapers, his business would suffer and the whole mess could drag on for months, costing a small fortune. But he wasn't going to give up. Delacroix had cheated him out of a great deal of money and, come hell or high water, he was going to have it back. He just had to find a different way of going about it. Stebbins was useless and his so-called friend, John Clavering, had gone off to a house-party in Somerset. He needed better tools. And there was a fellow downstairs in the tap-room who he was pretty sure could help him find them.

* * *

Although she didn't say as much to Aristide, Madeleine was rather pleased they now owned a carriage and wasted no time in inviting Lady Westin to join her for an afternoon drive in Green Park. The gleaming vehicle behind its sleek pair of grey horses drew up in Duke Street at precisely the time she had ordered; the smartly-clad coachman touched his whip respectfully to his hat; and the young groom bounded down to open the door for her. It was perfect in every respect but one. Her brother, suspiciously elegant in charcoal brocade over an embroidered dove-grey vest, was sitting in it.

Aristide smiled provokingly as she took her place opposite him in the forward-facing seat and said, 'Stealing my new toy before I've had a chance to play with it myself?'

Madeleine ignored this. 'How did you know?'

'That you were taking the carriage out? Higgins told me. He didn't want me to send for him myself, only to discover that he was otherwise engaged.'

She directed a baleful stare at the coachman's back. 'How efficient of him.'

'My thoughts precisely.'

'Your other thought being to invite yourself to join me.'

'Did I need an invitation? And I assumed there would be room ... unless you've offered places to half a dozen other hopeful gentlemen?'

'Don't be ridiculous! I asked Genevieve Westin – which is why, in case you haven't noticed, we're heading for Albemarle Street.'

Aristide said nothing. Higgins had told him that, too. Higgins, it appeared, was busy checking the parameters of his employment – which was turning out to be quite useful. It was the prospect of seeing Genevieve rather than that of trying out his so-called 'new toy' that had persuaded him to leave his desk in the middle of the afternoon.

As the carriage drew up outside Lady Brassington's house, Madeleine hissed, 'If you're not going to be pleasant to her, get out and walk home.'

Aristide merely lifted one brow and descended to the pavement as Genevieve emerged at the top of the steps. He watched the surprise in her face be replaced with the same dazzling smile he'd seen before; the smile that wrenched something inside his chest. But he merely bowed, offered his hand and murmured, 'I hope your ladyship finds my presence less unwelcome than Madeleine does. I believe she is wishing me at the devil.'

'Oh – surely not!' She laughed up at Madeleine. 'It's very kind of Monsieur Delacroix to accompany us.'

'Kindness has nothing to do with it. He's here out of sheer, male possessiveness.'

'Untrue.' Aristide handed Genevieve up beside his sister. 'Madeleine merely feels that one of us should have a nose permanently to the grindstone – usually me.'

Genevieve looked from one to the other of them. Her relationship with own brothers had never included verbal sparring that wasn't barbed. However, something told her that theirs was very different so she said helpfully, 'If you were enjoying an argument, please don't stop on my account. A carriage ride on such a lovely day is a rare treat for me – so I'll be quite content to close my ears and sit quietly.'

'A fair offer – but quite unnecessary,' replied Aristide blandly, taking his seat and signalling Higgins to drive on. 'I never argue.' And before Madeleine could object to this remark, 'Do you remain in London through the summer, my lady, or will you be retreating to the country?'

'London,' said Genevieve positively. 'Cousin Lily does not leave town herself and has said I am welcome to remain with her. Also, in four weeks' time, I can put aside my black – which means having some new clothes made.' She cast an openly envious glance over Madeleine's pale green figured silk. 'Is it true that Maison Phanie is the most fashionable *modiste* at present?'

'Yes. Phanie's gowns are exquisite,' agreed Madeleine, 'but shockingly expensive.'

'Ah. Of course.' Her eyes clouded a little. 'I should have expected that.'

'Quite. Fortunately, one can do just as well outside Bond Street. If you wish, I will introduce you to my own dressmaker – a very talented Frenchwoman. I don't think you would be disappointed.'

'I'm sure I wouldn't. The gown you are wearing is lovely.'

Content to sit back and let them discuss fashion, Aristide watched Genevieve without, he hoped, appearing to do so. Beneath her hat, the ebony hair gleamed blue in the sun and against the black moiré gown her skin appeared very white. He took his time, enjoying the inviting softness of her lower lip and the slenderness of her throat; then he lingered in pleasant contemplation of the full curve of her breasts and the shadowed hollow between them, revealed by the sweeping neckline of her gown. It was but a short step from there to begin mentally removing her clothes ... at which point he hauled his unruly thoughts back under control before he found himself in difficulties.

Merde, he thought grimly. *Out of all the women in the world, why in God's name do I have to want this one? It is extremely ... inconvenient.*

Realising that Madeleine was looking at him, her gaze expressionless yet somehow knowing, he turned away to acknowledge a greeting from one of Sinclairs' more recent members, whose name he ought to be able to remember but couldn't.

Inconvenient? It's a damned catastrophe. She is stealing my wits.

It was perhaps fortunate that Madeleine decided to include him in the conversation. She said, 'Genevieve was asking if you know Lord Sarre merely as a member of the club and I explained that we have been acquainted with him since we lived in Paris. But I can't remember how you first met him.'

'Over a card table,' replied Aristide unexpansively. 'Of course, he wasn't an earl then. In fact, it was some time before I knew he would become one.'

'Really?' Genevieve looked intrigued. 'He'd never told you?'

'No – but our friendship survived it. And the patronage of Adrian and his friends has helped make Sinclairs the success it now is.'

'Is it true that Sinclairs is as popular as Whites?'

'Not quite,' smiled Madeleine. 'To rival Whites properly, we would need to open earlier in the day – for breakfast and the newspapers and so on.'

'And do you plan to do that?' She looked at Aristide, her eyes bright with interest.

He shook his head, wondering where this whole conversation was going. Was she trying to find out what the club was worth ... or whether he was received socially by other titled gentlemen? Or both?

'That would require more space than we currently have. And at present I'm not inclined to move to larger premises.'

He waited to find out what she'd say next; but before she could say anything at all, Madeleine, direct as ever, asked the question that was in his own mind.

'Why do you find the club so interesting?'

'Because it's a hidden world only gentlemen are allowed to enter,' came the prompt reply. '*Any* lady would be intrigued. Am I really the first one to admit it?'

Deciding to take this at face value for the time being, Aristide said with a smile, 'She has you there, Madeleine.'

Genevieve's eyes widened. 'What does that mean?'

'It means,' sighed Madeleine, 'that recently a group of ladies begged for – and were given – a private tour. It's not the kind of thing one would wish to become a habit. But the Duke of Rockliffe's sister isn't a lady who makes it easy to say no.'

'Oh. Yes ... I can see that might be awkward.'

'Not in the way you're thinking,' came the dry response. 'Lady Elinor argues and cajoles until she flattens opposition out like pastry.' And then, deftly changing the subject, 'Do you see the lady over there in turquoise organdie? *That* is one of Phanie's gowns.'

A little later, as they left the park, Genevieve accepted Madeleine's invitation to tea. Back in Duke Street, Aristide told Higgins to return the carriage to the mews and excused himself from the ladies on the pretext of looking through the morning's correspondence. He had spent the previous night at Sinclairs – something he still did occasionally – and which today had proved useful since it had enabled him to change his dress prior to the afternoon's outing. He rather hoped Madeleine hadn't realised that.

The letters proved largely insignificant but he took his time reading them and scribbled a few notes to give to Edward later. Then he watched the clock and killed time with a small glass of sherry until he reasoned that Genevieve would be ready to leave. He knew he was being foolish. Foolish and self-indulgent. But that knowledge wasn't sufficient to stop him grasping an opportunity to spend a few minutes alone with her in the hope of discovering whether her interest in him was limited to his income and connections ... or something more personal.

He timed his return to the drawing-room perfectly. Genevieve was just replacing her hat. He offered to escort her the short distance back to Albemarle Street and waited while she and Madeleine made plans to visit the dressmaker and said their goodbyes. Then, avoiding his sister's eye, he led Genevieve from the room and shut the door behind them.

Once outside in the street with her hand on Monsieur Delacroix's arm, Genevieve recognised that if she wanted to engage his interest, now might be her best – or possibly her only – opportunity. However, there were two problems with this. One was the difficulty of how to give the right signals without being too obvious about it; the other, the more complex matter of whether she wanted to do it at *all*.

It ought to be simple. She could spend the rest of her days dependent on Ralph – which was unthinkable – or she could marry. Ralph thought he could find an eligible *parti* for her but Genevieve doubted if he yet knew that no one would receive her and didn't want a husband of his choosing anyway. Indeed, if she was completely honest with herself, she didn't *really* want a husband at all. And that, of course, was the crux of the matter.

The thought of marrying again made her insides feel cold and shaky and no matter how many times she told herself that it wouldn't – *couldn't* – be like before, the feeling persisted. She believed she could contemplate it with Aristide Delacroix better than with any other man – which was just as well, since he was the only likely prospect. But even then she had to cling to just three words ... *He's not Kit. He's not Kit* ... in order to stop herself giving way to panic.

Regardless of this, time was not on her side. In less than a month, she would be out of mourning ... unless Grandfather died and she was plunged immediately back into it and dragged off to the earldom's principal estate at Gardington. Now, while Ralph was out of town, was probably the best chance she would get to take control of her own destiny. And so, stiffening her spine and telling herself not to be a ninny, she said, 'Thank you for this afternoon. It's been a long time since I enjoyed myself so much.'

'I imagine a year of mourning passes very slowly.'

'Without the support of family or friends it becomes interminable,' she replied truthfully. 'And I suppose it is also more bearable if one is genuinely grieving.'

Aristide glanced down at her. 'But you were not.' It wasn't a question.

'No.' Her steps slowed and she stared down at the pavement. 'You asked why I married him and I cited my brothers. That is only part of it. I was seventeen and no less silly than the girl you knew; the one who played with her dog instead of concentrating on her French lessons. Christopher Westin was young, good-looking and heir to a title. I saw those things and I thought I knew him.' She paused and then added flatly, 'I didn't. Within six months, our marriage was a debacle. But even so, I had no idea about his – his other activities until the scandal burst like a thundercloud when he was killed.'

He frowned slightly. 'Why are you telling me this?'

'I *wouldn't* be if you and I didn't have a prior acquaintance,' she shrugged. 'As it is, I didn't want you to think me completely heartless. I didn't wish Kit dead – but even though widowhood has brought none of the benefits I'd hoped for, it's a relief to be free of him.'

Aristide noted the complete absence of detail and considered enquiring further. Instead, he said, 'A perfectly natural feeling for which no one can blame you.'

'Thank you.' She experienced a moment of temptation; of wanting to tell him that she'd been left virtually penniless and that society had turned its back her. But she repressed it, refusing to use pity as a weapon. So she summoned a bright smile and said, 'That's enough of melancholy. The day is too fine for it and it's spoiling my pleasure in renewing our acquaintance.'

'*Is* it a pleasure?'

'Now we've cleared away the ghosts of seven years ago, yes,' she assured him, wishing that she could read his expression and wondering if he'd always been as inscrutable as he was now. Then managing a mischievous laugh, 'I'll even admit to regretting I didn't pay closer attention to your lessons. I still speak French extremely badly, you know.'

He smiled a little. 'You could practise with Madeleine.'

'I daren't! I imagine my accent alone would be enough to make her cover her ears.' Genevieve took a short, bracing breath and glanced up at him between her lashes. 'Perhaps, since you already know the worst, I might practise with you instead?'

Even though Aristide recognised it for what it was, the flirtatious glance did its work, producing a vivid image of things he'd enjoy practising with her. He said, 'And would I find you a more diligent student now?'

Somehow, the very blandness of his tone suggested an underlying meaning which, though she didn't understand it, still caused her colour to rise. 'Yes.'

'You seem very sure.'

'Well, I'm no longer a flighty child, am I?'

'That is very true. Quite the staid and sober widow,' he said gravely. 'Almost middle-aged, in fact.'

'*Middle-aged?*' she gasped. 'I'm twenty-three – the same age as your sister!'

'Ah yes. So you are. I must have forgotten.'

And that was when she saw it; a glint of something suspiciously like laughter, lurking behind the usually cool blue eyes. Genevieve came to an abrupt halt and said, 'Monsieur Delacroix ... are you *teasing* me?'

'Did you think me incapable of it?'

'No. That is ... perhaps.' She peeped up at him, gave an odd little laugh and said, 'You are generally very serious. But if you were not, you wouldn't have made such a success of your life. Many gentlemen – my brothers included – begin with a whole battery of advantages but achieve nothing. I think Madeleine is very fortunate.'

Aristide shrugged this aside. 'She and I have built Sinclairs together.'

'I know. And I envy her that, as well.'

They were almost at Lady Brassington's door. Feeling suddenly panicky, Genevieve blurted out the first thing that came into her head. 'You didn't say whether or not you are willing to help improve my French.'

Looking unruffled as ever and keeping his inevitable reflections to himself, Aristide appeared to consider it. 'My willingness is not the issue. Opportunity is.'

'Oh.' Her heart sank. *He's saying no. Of course he is.* 'Naturally, Sinclairs takes up a great deal of your time.'

'A great deal, yes,' he agreed. And thought, *Very well, madam. Let us find out where all the charm and compliments and smiles have been leading. Let's see what you'll do with an opportunity if I offer it.* 'But not quite all of it.'

Her eyes flew to meet his before turning away just as quickly. Managing to sound demure but inwardly cringing, Genevieve said softly, 'In that case ... opportunity can always be found, can it not?'

'Where there's a will, there's a way, in fact.'

'Yes.' She wanted to shake him. He was going to make her say it, wasn't he? 'Perhaps ... perhaps we might repeat this afternoon on some future occasion.'

He knew it was time to relent but the temptation to know if she really was pursuing him was irresistible. 'With Madeleine?'

Genevieve turned and looked directly into his eyes.

'Or not,' she murmured.

He let the silence linger while he told himself not to be stupid. Then, ignoring his own good advice, he said, 'Or not. Shall we say Friday?'

Friday was three days away. Another half a week gone from what she had come to think of as her window of escape. Why could he not have said tomorrow?

'That would be delightful,' she said, smiling brightly at him. 'I shall look forward to it.'

As they parted company at Lady Brassington's door, neither of them noticed the man watching them from the corner of Stafford Street. There was, of course, no reason why they should.

CHAPTER EIGHT

In Surrey, Lord Nicholas Wynstanton toured his estate both on foot and on horseback. He spent hours with his steward, discussing improvements; he passed the time of day with his tenants; he visited and was visited by his neighbours; he entered enthusiastically into plans for the traditional Midsummer Eve Festival. And he found he enjoyed everything about it – from an afternoon spent learning to plough a field to an evening in the village tavern – even more than he usually did.

He wondered if that was a sign of increased maturity or something else altogether. He suspected the latter. Certainly, he caught himself looking at the house and grounds with new eyes and, as often as not, imagining Madeleine there. He thought she'd like the place. It was neither overly large nor particularly grand but it was comfortable and had an air of welcome about it. He thought he would find it no hardship to spend the bulk of the year here rather than in London ... though Madeleine might feel differently, her acquaintance with country living being virtually non-existent.

Sometimes he wondered exactly *when* he'd fallen in love with her but he never found an answer; and he frequently wondered *why* – then laughed at himself for doing so. He loved her claws and prickles and frequent sarcasm every bit as much as he was struck dumb by her beauty. She wasn't like any other woman he'd ever met ... and she both dazzled and challenged him. Yet somehow, oddly, he'd never doubted that he would win her in the end.

He also wondered if she'd recognised his intentions yet. She ought to have done. He'd told her, in no uncertain terms, that he wasn't about to offer her a *carte blanche* and he'd started paying her the kind of attentions that spelled courtship. By now, any other female would be waiting for a proposal and becoming impatient that it was taking him so long to come to the point. But then, no other female he knew deliberately surrounded herself with an invisible thicket of thorns and a big 'Keep Out' notice for good measure. What was needed, therefore, was for the word 'marriage' to creep into Madeleine's head often enough for her to become used to the idea ... because until that happened, going down on one knee was going to lead to a flat refusal which would reduce his options to nil.

Lastly, he wondered if she thought of him at all; and if she did, whether she missed him. He would have come to Charlecote anyway. He always did at this time of year. But this visit carried an ulterior motive. He needed to know how she truly felt about him. More to the point, he needed Madeleine to know it, too.

People said that absence made the heart grow fonder. Nicholas was pinning some of his hopes on that being true.

* * *

He would have been immensely encouraged had he known that, as the days went by and despite her good intentions, Madeleine thought about him more often than she wanted to – and cursed him for it. She was beginning to discover that his absence was more distracting than his presence, if such a thing was possible. Life seemed to have lost some of its flavour. The sun shone a little less brightly; evenings at Sinclairs fell flat; and a ravishing new gown had no point at all. Nicholas Wynstanton had turned her life inside out and calmly ridden off to the country, leaving her thoroughly unsettled.

She shouldn't have let him kiss her. She'd known since the night he'd swept into Aristide's office and put out the fire started by Marcus Sheringham that his body communicated with hers in a way that had nothing to do with words. Kissing him had been the second-most asinine thing she could have done because it made her think of the *most* asinine. The eventuality she'd always assured herself was impossible ... and which Nicholas had agreed was never going to happen.

She'd told him she wouldn't be his mistress and he'd retorted that she wouldn't be asked. That ought to have been the end of it. It *had* been the end of it ... until she'd finally been forced to admit to herself exactly how she felt about him. He was warmth and laughter and unexpected sweetness; he was so beautiful that his smile sometimes made her forget to breathe; and his kiss had been a pure invitation to sin.

She wouldn't, of course. But that was no longer a matter of pride or morality or self-respect. It was because an *affaire* was, by its very nature, temporary. And she knew that the pain of losing him would be worse than that of never having him at all. So there would be no *affaire* and no dalliance either; as for marriage – if that *was* the direction his mind was taking – it was out of the question. She would fit into his world about as well as a rook in a dovecote ... and the thought of trying terrified her. It simply would not do.

But none of her internal strictures stopped her wishing or filled what felt like a gaping hole in her chest. And then the letter came and made it all worse.

She had not expected to hear from him; indeed she had been quite convinced that she would not. She doubted fashionable gentlemen wrote letters if they didn't have to ... and she had told herself over and over again that, regardless of what he had said on the day of the picnic, once he was away from her it would be case of 'out of sight, out of mind'. The letter, however, announced in no uncertain terms that it wasn't.

Not that it was a love letter. Far from it. He had covered two tightly-scripted pages with his daily activities, mingled with the goings-on in the village and a good many completely absurd observations.

He had been allowed to handle a plough and had turned over half a field in only *twice* as long as Mr Hinkley would have taken to do the whole of it. A scruffy and extremely ugly dog to which he had been misguided enough to toss the remains of a pork chop at the village inn had fallen in love with his boots and, much to the disgust of his valet, had taken up residence in his bedchamber so it could sleep on them. The Midsummer Fiasco (nobody had called it a Festival since he'd misnamed it by mistake three summers ago) had been a roaring success. After the children had finished dancing, the maypole had looked very pretty despite being a mass of tangles; the men had enjoyed the wrestling, the shot-putting and, most of all, the tug-of-war in which Nicholas had ended ignominiously on his rear in what was surely the only damp patch of ground to be found *anywhere.* The ladies had made him sample a seemingly endless variety of home-made pies, cakes and jam – before waiting, just as they did every year, for him to declare the winners in each category. And Nicholas, just as *he* did every year, awarded rosettes to everybody amidst a chorus of laughter, groans and accusations of cowardice.

The letter was so very like Nicholas – even though the activities spoken of in it were not – that Madeleine couldn't help laughing. She was still smiling when she reached the last few and by now completely unexpected words.

You'd like it here, Madeleine. Certainly, I'd like seeing you here. Next summer, perhaps?

And that was when she had to press her hands over her eyes to stop them filling with hot, stupid tears.

* * *

Genevieve discovered that three days could feel like an eternity.

She accompanied Madeleine to the *modiste* in Gower Street and recklessly ordered two gowns which, even at Céleste's very reasonable prices, she was unlikely to be able to pay for. Still, the rose-coloured grosgrain taffeta and the gold-and-green striped polonaise couldn't help but lift her mood. Then a note from Ralph sent her thoughts scurrying like mice in a cage.

Though Grandfather had rallied a little, the doctor said the end could not be far off.

This being so, Ralph wrote, *I shall remain here which means there is little point in your removing to Kilburn House. Neither, since you are still mourning Westin, need you attend Grandfather's funeral – though Cedric and Bertram will naturally do so. But afterwards, you should prepare to join me here at*

Gardington without delay. A further mourning period, though unfortunate, is unavoidable – but I think we may regard six months as sufficient.

Genevieve stared at the letter and felt sick.

Another six months in black ... at Gardington ... with Ralph and Cedric and Bertram and probably Cousin Marjorie, as well? I can't. I just can't.

And though she despised herself for it, she set about working out how to wring an offer of marriage from Aristide Delacroix.

Given the time available, there were few viable options.

She began by considering a conversation she'd overheard years ago at the first ball she'd ever attended. One young lady had been boasting to another that a hitherto dilatory viscount had finally been brought to the point by the simple expedient of letting him kiss her and making sure he was seen doing it.

Genevieve gave a sour laugh. Well, that wasn't going to work. Nobody would give a fig if the owner of Sinclairs was caught kissing Christopher Westin's widow. The gentlemen would shrug and the ladies would say that such behaviour was to be expected since Lady Westin's reputation was already past saving.

Next, she explored the notion of throwing herself on Aristide's mercy; of telling him the whole truth and begging him to help her. If he still harboured any kindness for her, she supposed that this *might* work – although the notion of weeping on his shoulder made something inside her shrivel. True, she was destitute, almost friendless and desperate enough to try manipulating a man into marrying her ... but she'd like to retain some small shred of pride. And then there was the possibility that, after what had happened last time she'd sought his aid, he might laugh in her face and walk away.

Which leaves what? she wondered despondently. Charm, she supposed; all those little flirtatious tricks that had come so easily to her at the age of seventeen but which now seemed beyond her. She sat before her mirror and stared at the woman who looked back at her. A pale, heart-shaped face; wide hazel eyes full of ghosts; and well-shaped lips set in a tight line. Was that woman still beautiful? Once upon a time, she'd been told that she was; more recently, she'd been told ... things she didn't want to remember. Did Aristide Delacroix find her attractive? Sometimes she'd thought she glimpsed a gleam of appreciation in his eyes but it had always disappeared before she could be sure. If he admired her – even just a little bit – there might be some hope. If not, she was doomed.

At some point in the early hours of the morning, she awoke with a hammering heart and a wild notion thundering through her head. Genevieve hugged her knees and rested her brow against them while she fought waves of hysterical laughter and muttered, *It was a dream. Just a dream, thank God. Otherwise I'd believe I was mad.*

Friday dawned, bringing blue skies and sunshine. Reluctantly because it couldn't be helped, Genevieve told Cousin Lily her plans for the afternoon ... or some of them, anyway.

Lady Brassington looked at her from beneath raised brows.

'You are going driving with Monsieur Delacroix? Why?'

'He invited me.'

'Well, obviously. But really, Genevieve – the man owns a *gaming-house.*'

'A very *respectable* gaming-house,' countered Genevieve. 'You said so yourself. Monsieur Delacroix and his sister are perfectly genteel. And unlike everyone else in London, they don't blame me for Kit's sins.'

'I can see how that might be appealing. But --'

'Have you actually *met* him?'

'No.' Her ladyship sighed. 'And you're quite right. I should do so before judging him purely because he works for a living. Goodness knows, I do as much myself when I guide girls through the social maze. Very well. Tell Soames to show Monsieur Delacroix up when he arrives.'

'Thank you,' said Genevieve. And thought, *I have to do this. If I'm hoping to lure him into offering marriage – and God knows I* can't see any alternative – I can't afford to lose Cousin Lily because of it. But how Aristide will feel about being inspected as a suitable escort, I can't imagine.

Inevitably, what Aristide thought was hidden behind his usual reserve. He bowed over Lady Brassington's hand and thanked her for receiving him.

Lady B noted the good manners, the unruffled manner and the understated elegance of his midnight-blue coat. Smiling slightly and whilst exchanging the usual courtesies, she thought, *Ah. Impeccably-behaved and really rather good-looking. It is a pity about his occupation, though. But for that, he might have suited Genevieve rather well.*

Once outside and in the carriage, Genevieve said awkwardly, 'Cousin Lily worries about incurring Ralph's displeasure. That is why she felt duty-bound to meet you. It wasn't ...' She tailed off, searching for the right words.

'It wasn't that I'm a gaming-house proprietor?' he suggested helpfully.

'Heavens, no!' she lied, a little too quickly. 'Not at all.'

'Then her ladyship is to be complimented on her egalitarian views,' came the bland reply. 'But if both she and you have been wondering about my social standing, allow me to clarify it. More than half the titled gentlemen in London are members of Sinclairs, where they are happy to take a glass of wine with me or join me at the card-table. By contrast, those who might welcome me to their home can be counted on one hand. Does that help?'

'It – it's the way of the world. The rules and double-standards of polite society are legion. And I don't suppose the gentlemen who wouldn't invite you to dine would ask their doctor or their estate-steward either, would they?'

His mouth curled a little. 'No. I don't imagine they would.'

'And just now – as you've probably guessed – thanks to my late husband, I'm even less welcome in the *beau monde* than you are,' she said rapidly before her courage failed. 'Aside from Cousin Lily, you and Madeleine are the only people who have not tarred me with Kit's wrong-doings. That may not be any great matter to *you* but it means a good deal to *me*.'

He smiled at her then, the open, unexpectedly attractive smile that she hadn't seen for seven years, and said, 'Perhaps you should try to say that again in French. That *is* why you've come driving with me, is it not?'

Genevieve felt her cheeks grow hot but decided that being ladylike and coy wasn't going to advance her cause. She said, 'N-not entirely.'

'No?'

'No.' She managed to peep up at him through her lashes. 'Not at all, in fact.'

When he did not immediately respond, her nerves tightened. But finally he said, 'Good. It is too fine a day for lessons ... and I'm sure there are other, more interesting things, we might talk about.'

True as this probably was, Genevieve couldn't think of any of them. Fortunately, while she was still searching for a suitably promising topic, Aristide said softly, 'Not that it doesn't become you ... but for how much longer are you condemned to wear black?'

'Three weeks.' And then, before she could stop herself, 'Three weeks, if I'm lucky. A further six months if I'm not.'

He frowned. 'Why the latter?'

'My paternal grandfather is not expected to live much longer. I scarcely know him but when he dies, Ralph will become the Earl of Sherbourne – and if I am still dependent upon him, he will insist I live at the Dorset estate and observe all the proper conventions.'

'You can't continue to reside with Lady Brassington?'

She shook her head. 'I can't remain a charge on Cousin Lily's purse.'

'Then perhaps a home of your own?'

'Not at present. There are certain ... complications.' She managed a bright, would-be-careless smile. 'Everything will be resolved, of course, but it is taking longer than expected – which temporarily leaves living under Ralph's roof my only option.'

Although he gave no sign of it, Aristide now understood her situation a good deal more clearly than she had probably intended. Westin had apparently left his widow virtually destitute – though how that could have happened, even temporarily, was inexplicable. Lily Brassington sponsored girls from dubious backgrounds for a fee – which meant she was by no means well-off either. And Viscount Kilburn – soon to be Earl of Sherbourne – was using the purse-strings to make the sister who disliked him dance to his tune. All this, combined with society's disapproval, put Genevieve Westin in a far from enviable position, from which, if Aristide was not much mistaken, she was looking to escape. The only question, therefore, was how she hoped to do it.

Since it was too early for the fashionable throng, Hyde Park was reasonably quiet and the coach bowled along the main thoroughfare at a moderate speed. Aware that she hadn't so far done much to charm or invite and conscious of the ears of both coachman and groom, Genevieve wondered how to improve the situation.

Slanting a smile at Aristide, she said, 'I am always a little surprised that everyone flees London during the summer. The park is looking quite lovely today – although it is very hot. And black is not a *cool* colour.'

'Then let us seek some shade.' Dutifully taking the hint and instructing Higgins to turn on to one of the tree-lined smaller tracks, he thought, *This will be interesting. Does she want shade or privacy? And if it's the latter – why?* He bit back a smile. *I doubt she has seduction in mind – though if she does, I may find saying no a problem.*

'Oh this is so much better,' sighed Genevieve, furling her parasol and setting it aside to lay a hand on his sleeve. 'Thank you.'

Aristide found himself drowning in fathomless golden-brown eyes while in receipt of a dazzlingly grateful smile. Just for a second, his brain turned to syrup. Then he recovered himself and, choosing to be unhelpful, said, 'If this weather continues, London will soon feel stifling and you will yearn for the breezes and shady avenues of the country.'

'Perhaps. But not in any part of it that I can think of.' She hoped he hadn't noticed the faint quaver in her voice, produced by thoughts of Shropshire or the fact that the hand still lying on his arm was clenched tight. Forcing her fingers to relax, she slowly withdrew them. Then, striving to regain some lightness, she said, 'I suppose it is difficult for you and Madeleine to leave town – unless you close the club. Do you?'

'No. So far, neither of us has taken any leave of absence – though when Mr Hastings has settled into his position, it may be possible.'

'You are pleased with him?'

'Delighted. He is exceptionally intelligent and ruthlessly efficient,' agreed Aristide. And with something approaching a smile, added, 'Of course, there's always a flaw. He hums.'

Genevieve blinked. 'Hums? When he is working? Why?'

'Because he's in love,' came the dry response. Then, 'Are *you* fond of the works of Herr Handel, Lady Westin? I'm finding they --'

'Don't call me that!' The words burst out almost before she'd thought them. 'Please don't. I hate it. Can't you call me Genevieve, as Madeleine does?'

He surveyed her silently for a moment.

'Genevieve, then. If you insist.'

The way he said her name – pronouncing it in the French manner – set off a ripple of something she didn't recognise behind her moiré bodice and made her pause to swallow hard before saying, 'I do. Yes. Thank you.'

He wondered if she knew that tension was rolling off her in waves. Plainly, there was something she wanted to say to him; equally plainly, she was incapable of saying it – which might be for the best because she was almost certainly going to ask him for help. Aside from money, he couldn't imagine what she thought he could do for her; and if she imagined he'd agree to hide her from her brothers, she must have windmills in her head.

But sitting beside him, she seemed small and fragile; as if, behind that sunburst smile – the smile which he was beginning to suspect was merely a distracting mask – there was nothing but darkness. And so, though he knew he would probably regret it, he decided to give her an opportunity to say what was on her mind.

He said, 'Would you care to leave the carriage and walk for a time?'

Relief and gratitude warmed her skin.

'Oh yes. Yes, please. That would be lovely.'

Aristide repressed a sigh and ordered Higgins to pull up. Two minutes later, Genevieve was strolling at his side, her hand tucked securely through his arm. They walked in silence until, gazing at the trees arching over their heads, she said, 'I wonder why everyone stays by the Serpentine or on the main thoroughfare when there are areas like this? Not the horses and carriages, of course – but those who come to walk. We have it completely to ourselves, do we not?'

Wishing he wasn't only too aware of that fact, Aristide said, 'That is your answer. The fashionable throng comes to see and be seen. A spot like this wouldn't do at all.'

This was not encouraging but she persevered.

'No. I suppose not. But *I* like it.' She smiled up at him and risked pressing a little closer to his side. Surely *that* would be hint enough? 'And I'm so glad to have met you again. Indeed, I haven't been as happy as this since I left Paris.'

He inclined his head. 'That is very gratifying but I fear you flatter me.'

'Not at all.' Genevieve stopped walking, thus forcing him to do the same. 'I enjoyed those hours with you when I was a girl – even though I refused to pay proper attention. And s-spending time with you now is an even greater pleasure.'

This time he said nothing, merely holding her gaze with a steady one of his own. He didn't look charmed. He *certainly* didn't look as if he wanted to sweep her into his arms. He looked, she realised, as if he was waiting. That didn't bode well.

Aristide knew that if he didn't let his gaze stray to her mouth – or anything below it – he could resist the temptation she was very obviously offering. Then, deciding that this had gone on quite long enough, he said coolly, 'My lady ... Genevieve ... if there is something you wish to say to me or some question you wish to ask, perhaps now would be the time.'

The pit of her stomach fell away. 'I don't know what you mean.'

He detached her hand from his arm and took a step back.

'I'm mistaken?'

'Yes.'

'Then I apologise.' Not believing her for an instant, he turned slightly, gesturing back the way they had come. 'I had the idea you wanted privacy. Since you don't, shall we return to the carriage?'

'No! I ...' She stopped, a knot of panic in her throat and her ability to think seemingly locked in ice. 'No. Not yet – please. I hoped ... I w-wanted ...'

Aristide waited and when she showed no sign of continuing, said, 'Wanted what?'

Genevieve opened her mouth to say one thing and heard something completely different come out of it. 'To ask if you'd consider m-marrying me.'

They were the words that had woken her at three in the morning. As soon as they were spoken, she clapped her hands over her mouth and stared at him, aghast. What she saw in his eyes didn't help. For a handful of heartbeats, he looked beyond shocked. Then, his face emptying of any expression at all, he said softly, 'Would you care to repeat that?'

She let her hands fall away from her face and turned away.

'No. I shouldn't have said it the first time. I d-didn't mean to. I don't know why ... I'm so sorry. Please forget it.'

There was another long, seemingly airless silence.

'So you *don't* want me to marry you?' And when she didn't reply, 'Either you do or you don't. A remark like that doesn't come from nowhere.'

Genevieve let her shoulders slump and, deciding that the pit she had dug for herself couldn't get any deeper, said haltingly, 'I – I had thought of it, yes – though I never meant to – to actually *say* it. And I know it was stupid. You can't possibly want to marry me.'

'It's certainly true the idea had never occurred to me,' he agreed dryly.

'No. Of course not.'

'So what made it occur to *you*? Not the concept of marriage – I believe I can work that out for myself. But why me?'

She drew a long unsteady breath and, summoning every ounce of courage she possessed, turned back to meet his eyes.

'Because, if I'm to marry again, I'd rather it was you than anyone else.'

Aristide believed her – and not purely because of the curl of warmth that settled, uninvited, in his chest. She both sounded and looked defeated; as if there was nothing left except the truth. On the other hand, he wasn't naïve enough to believe it was her *only* reason – but then, he already knew what most of those other reasons were. Penury; her brothers; the cold shoulder of society; and lack of other options.

He said, 'You're flattering me again. But let us bypass that for a moment. Is there some reason for haste?'

'If I'm to have any shred of choice, yes.' Genevieve shut her eyes for a moment, trying to block out the intimidating aura of authority which surrounded him. Why she'd ever thought for a moment that Aristide Delacroix might be manipulated, she couldn't imagine. 'There is no point to this. I spoke without thinking. And as I said, I know you can't wish to marry me.'

Actually, now his initial shock was over, he could think of two reasons why he *might* – neither of which he was prepared to share with Genevieve. So he said slowly, 'Tell me why I should consider it.'

Her eyes widened and her breath seemed to falter. Then, shaking her head, she said bitterly, 'Haven't I humiliated myself enough?'

'You think I'm taunting you? That, no matter what you say, I won't listen?' He shook his head slightly. 'If you believe that, how can you suppose I'd be an even remotely acceptable husband?'

She stared at him uncertainly. Could he *really* be willing to consider marrying her? Nothing in his face provided an answer ... but if there was even the remotest chance that he might, she had to take it. And she'd been subjected to worse forms of humiliation than this.

She said hesitantly, 'Although I can't bring money to a marriage immediately, there are funds owing to me which --'

'Forget the money,' he cut in decisively. 'Tell me why I should marry *you* ... or better yet, why we should marry each other.'

'I – I'm the granddaughter of an earl --'

'And soon to be the sister of one. My congratulations.'

Her hands were gripping each other so tightly that her bones ached. What did he want from her? What could she say that might convince him?

'I believe we know each other better than many couples do on their wedding day ... and I think we c-could find contentment together. I believe that you are honourable and – and kind. And a man I may trust.'

He nodded. 'Go on.'

'I'd do my best to be a good wife to you. And I'd try very hard to make you happy – truly, I would.'

Another nod. 'How?'

'I – I'm sorry?'

Having got over his sheer incredulity, Aristide discovered that, against all expectation, he was actually beginning to enjoy himself. Allowing a note of interest to enter his voice, he said, 'How do you propose to make me happy?'

Genevieve licked her lips. 'I – I don't quite know. I suppose I would have to learn. Discover your likes and dislikes … and so on.'

'Ah. You mean how I take my coffee and which is my favourite pudding and whether or not I appreciate conversation over the breakfast table?'

Feeling on much safer ground, she nodded decisively. 'Yes. All of those things.'

'And what pleases me in the bedroom?' he asked blandly.

Her eyes filled with panic and some of the colour drained from her face.

For a second or two she stared mutely at him while summoning the only words which ever helped. *He's not Kit. He's not Kit.* Then, pulling herself together, she managed to say, 'Y-yes. That too.'

'I see. Well, that all sounds very comprehensive and business-like.' Aristide moved unhurriedly towards her. 'So in order to reach a decision, all that remains is to sample the wares.'

'*What?*'

'Perhaps that wasn't the best way of putting it,' he murmured, sliding one hand around her waist and setting the other to her jaw. 'Forgive me. But if we don't enjoy kissing each other, there isn't much hope for anything else, is there?' And he brought his mouth to hers.

Genevieve went completely rigid – less out of fear than because she had no idea what to do. Kit hadn't liked kissing, so he'd never done it. Truth be told, after the first year of marriage, his physical attentions had thankfully become a rare occurrence and he'd satisfied himself instead with his arsenal of insults.

Although Aristide didn't release her, her instinctive reaction caused him to raise his head and look down, an almost imperceptible frown lurking behind his eyes.

'If you don't want this, you have only to say so and we'll think no more about it.'

And that was when she realised that she *did* want it; that it felt good to be held, to have a warm body close to her own and a strong arm bracketing her waist. So good, in fact, that she felt tears stinging her eyes. Tentatively lifting her hands to his shoulders, she whispered, 'I want to ... I've just forgotten how.'

The frown became a smile, almost blinding in its intensity.

'Then allow me to remind you, *chérie*.' And he kissed her.

Her mouth was soft and sweet, shy and woefully uncertain. Somewhere in the recesses of his mind, Aristide recognised that Genevieve Westin hadn't *forgotten* how to kiss; she'd never known. It was a realisation that, even if he hadn't already made his decision, would have brought him to the same conclusion now. Dismissing that until later, he concentrated on the enjoyment of teaching her ... and suspected, when her hands crept, inch by inch, around his neck, that she wasn't averse to learning.

By the time he released her, Genevieve felt as if the world had turned on its axis. She had known on some level that all men could not be like Kit ... but this was the first time she'd had any inkling of just how great the differences might be. The discovery left her confused and temporarily dumbstruck.

Seeing it, Aristide filled the silence for her.

'And so, Genevieve ... do you still wish me to marry you?'

Unable to trust either her own voice or the possibility that he meant it, she nodded.

'In that case,' he said, rather as if she'd offered him a slice of cake, 'I accept.'

Hope, incredulity, joy and terror, chased each other across her face and eventually she managed to say, 'I'm sorry. I can't ... do you really mean it?'

'I really mean it,' he agreed gravely. 'Am I right in assuming that you wish to do this quickly and without your family's knowledge?'

'Yes. Is that possible?'

'Probably.' He laid her hand on his arm and led her back towards the coach. 'When I have worked out precisely how, I will let you know. Meanwhile ... I'd advise complete discretion. And that, I'm afraid, should include Lady Brassington.'

CHAPTER NINE

Until he had decided what, if anything, to tell Madeleine, Aristide avoided her by spending the evening on the main gaming floor. But though he managed to maintain his usual manner, his thoughts were teaming with the ramifications surrounding the promise he'd made that afternoon.

Since the day he'd arrived in London full of plans for Sinclairs, he'd stopped taking unnecessary risks ... but agreeing to marry Genevieve Westin had been the equivalent of staking every penny he possessed on one throw of the dice at the Hazard table. He *ought* to be already regretting it and looking for a way out. So why wasn't he? When Adrian had said he was eloping with Caroline Maitland, Aristide had called him an idiot; and how, exactly, was what *he* was planning to do any different? And yet somehow it was. Because of the two reasons he would continue to keep to himself, he wasn't experiencing even the slightest flicker of doubt.

The first of those reasons was simple. He might not be in love with Genevieve Westin but her body called to his in a way no other woman's had ever done – and marriage was the only way in which he could have it.

The second reason was that her brothers would hate it. Kilburn, particularly, would be incensed to learn that his sister had thrown herself away on a man who ran a gaming club; incensed but, once the marriage became public knowledge, unable to do anything about it. Aristide was no longer the impoverished under-secretary he'd been in Paris; he had money, power of a sort and a handful of influential friends – all of which meant that Kilburn couldn't touch him. It was odd, reflected Aristide, how satisfying the prospect of having a little of his own back in respect of the three Harcourt men suddenly felt. He hadn't thought in terms of revenge for a very long time; not since those days when he'd been too battered and broken even to attend his mother's funeral.

He'd thought of it then, of course. Incapable of any other activity and with the full consequences of that bloody night boiling inside his head, contemplating vengeance was all he had. Afterwards, however, the struggle of everyday life ... of keeping Madeleine and himself from starvation ... had left neither room nor energy for pointless emotions. And gradually, as the years went by, he'd forgotten he'd ever felt them.

Until today; today, when Genevieve had unwittingly offered him a legal, bloodless way to have some measure of retribution.

Kilburn, reflected Aristide, *is going to grind his teeth into dust – even before he finds out that his new brother-in-law is the same man he sent his brothers to pulverize back in Paris. Really, it is quite perfect.*

Putting these thoughts to one side, Aristide began considering how the actual wedding was to be managed. He had no intention of wasting weeks travelling to Scotland and back and he suspected that he'd find obtaining a special licence a good deal more difficult than Adrian had done – all of which left banns. This meant a three or four week delay but he wasn't averse to that. It allowed for the setting in place of other, practical arrangements; and it gave Genevieve the chance to change her mind, if she chose to do so.

It was at this point that it occurred to Aristide that he knew a man whose current position was virtually identical to his own. A glance at his pocket-watch told him that Madeleine should, by now, have gone home to Duke Street. Smiling to himself, he took the stairs to his office.

Edward was still there, surrounded by a heap of members' personal files. Looking up as Aristide walked in, he said, 'This is incredible, sir. How do you *discover* all this stuff? And do the members have any idea that you have it?'

'The method varies. As for the members ... I doubt it. But when a gentleman is racking up substantial debts to the house, it is useful to know something of his other obligations and general circumstances.'

'Such as whose wife he's currently sleeping with?'

'Sometimes.' Aristide sat down and regarded the younger man thoughtfully. 'Have you looked at Lord Leighton's file yet?'

Edward coloured faintly. 'I've ... glanced at it.'

'And?'

'And I've learned that he keeps a mistress in Chelsea, along with the two children he has by her,' he admitted flatly and not without a hint of disgust. 'I had no idea, of course – and am pretty sure Hetty doesn't either. And no – I won't be enlightening her.'

'I never supposed you would.' Aristide toyed idly with a quill. 'However, speaking of Mademoiselle Leighton ... how do your plans progress?'

'Slowly. I've taken a lease on the lodgings I told you of and have begun making them more comfortable – but I won't remove there until Hetty and I are married.'

'Which will be when?'

'Soon, I hope. The problem is that banns will have to be read and so I need a church where no one in the congregation will recognise Hetty's name.' He shrugged. 'That part wasn't so difficult – there are dozens of churches in London. But some vicars insist that the betrothed couple must be resident in their parish or be present in church when the banns are called – or both – which is a problem.'

'Yes.' All of this, Aristide could see was going to apply to himself and Genevieve. 'Have you solved it?'

'I believe so. St Paul's, Covent Garden. Parts of it have been closed off prior to massive renovations but the Reverend Martin is continuing to conduct Sunday services from a side-chapel.' Edward grinned suddenly. 'And he's the sort who, for the right inducement, would bury your grandmother with no questions asked.'

'That's convenient. Worrying, perhaps – but convenient.'

'My thoughts exactly. Truth to tell, I suspect that if one paid him enough, he'd get round the business of banns completely.

But when this is done, Hetty and I will have enough hurdles ahead of us without facing questions of legality.'

Ah. Another very good point, thought Aristide. He crossed to the dresser and poured two glasses of wine. Then, handing one of them to Mr Hastings, he said, 'Do you know, Edward ... I don't think I pay you enough.'

Edward laughed. 'As you very well know, you pay me more than adequately, sir.'

'Yes. But you have just saved me an inordinate amount of trouble.'

'I have?'

'Yes.' Returning to his seat, Aristide sent his assistant a companionable smile and said, 'If I pay all the ancillary costs, including bribing the Reverend Martin ... how would you and your bride-to-be feel about a double wedding?'

* * *

In Albemarle Street, Genevieve hovered between dizzying relief and occasional bouts of terror. Relief that, against all expectation, her future was no longer quite so bleak; terror about everything else.

What if there was some unforeseen difficulty that made a wedding impossible? What if Aristide changed his mind? What if Ralph returned to London unexpectedly? What if someone – anyone – found out before the wedding took place? And what if, after it, Aristide regretted the choice he'd made? Of all those possibilities, Genevieve didn't know which one she feared the most.

For three days, she heard nothing. Then a note from Madeleine invited her for tea ... and was followed within hours by a terse one from Aristide.

I have said nothing to Madeleine as yet. If you can't dissemble successfully, make an excuse. Meet me at three in the afternoon on Thursday in Berkeley Square gardens and I will inform you what arrangements have been made.

Well. That removed one worry – possibly, two. He hadn't changed his mind and had made some moves towards organising their wedding. Feeling cautiously optimistic, Genevieve decided she *could* risk taking tea with Madeleine. As long as Aristide's name didn't feature in their conversation, all would be well.

As it turned out, Madeleine was uncharacteristically distracted, her gaze constantly drawn to the huge vase of apricot roses occupying a table by the window. Eventually, Genevieve couldn't prevent herself saying, 'The flowers are lovely. From an admirer, perhaps? I imagine you have a number of them.'

'Not that I'm aware of.' Madeleine stared moodily into her cup and then added abruptly, 'They're from Lord Nicholas Wynstanton.'

'The Duke of Rockliffe's brother?'

'The very one.'

'Oh. You don't like him?'

'Whether or not I like him isn't the point.'

'Then what is?'

'He doesn't take no for an answer.'

'He doesn't? Well, though I'm not acquainted with his lordship, I have *seen* him.' Genevieve shook her head, laughing a little. 'And I wouldn't have thought any right-minded female would *want* to say no.'

'Perhaps not. But sometimes it's the only possible answer.'

The amusement faded from Genevieve's face and she said gently, 'I'm sorry. You're fond of him, aren't you?'

The green eyes rose sharply. 'What makes you think that?'

'If you weren't, sending him away wouldn't be difficult. But I won't pry – and we can change the subject. Or, if it would help, you could tell me about it. I promise on my honour that nothing you say will go any further.'

There was a long silence. Finally, Madeleine nodded and said baldly, 'I love him. And just at present, he thinks that he loves me. He doesn't. He's just a typical man – wanting what he can't have.'

'Are you sure about that?'

'No. Not really. But whether I'm right or not doesn't matter. What *does* matter is that the chasm between us is unbridgeable and that sooner or later Nicholas is going to have to recognise it.' Madeleine set down her cup with a clatter and clenched one hand hard over the other. 'The longer that takes, the more painful the situation becomes. And I'm so very, very tired of pushing him away.'

'Then perhaps you should stop,' suggested Genevieve.

'No. That is the very worst thing I could do.' Madeleine straightened her shoulders and summoned a smile. 'But that is quite enough of that. Has Céleste summoned you for a fitting yet? If so, we could go together.'

* * *

On the following afternoon, Genevieve set off for Berkeley Square and found Monsieur Delacroix on the same bench where they'd met before. He stood as she approached and bowed slightly. Glancing into his face, Genevieve found the light blue eyes fixed steadily upon her own and looked swiftly away again, feeling awkward.

She said, 'I half-thought you might change your mind.'

'No. Have you changed yours?'

'No.'

'Good.'

'Is it?'

'Since the banns will be called for the first time on Sunday, yes.'

'Banns?' Her nerves jerked painfully. Banns meant a delay of three weeks and she might not have that long. 'Oh. I thought ...' She stopped and tried again. 'Are there not places where one can be married immediately?'

'Not any longer and certainly not legally,' replied Aristide. 'Also, had they still existed, I imagine Viscount Kilburn could overset a Fleet wedding in a heartbeat – even supposing you had no objection to being married in a prison.'

'In a *prison*?' she echoed horrified. 'Do people do that?'

'They used to. We, however, will be wed respectably at St Paul's in Covent Garden, three weeks on Friday.' He smiled. 'Don't mistake me. I find your eagerness charming. But do you think you can be patient until then?'

Genevieve opened her mouth, closed it again and then said bluntly, 'What shall I do if Ralph appears?'

'You will send me word. For now, let us hope that he won't.' He gestured to the bench. 'There are other things we need to discuss ... so will you sit?'

She did so, taking her time over the absorbing task of arranging her skirts suitably.

Aristide waited and, when she neither spoke nor even looked at him, said, 'Do you recall me telling you that my assistant, Mr Hastings, is hoping to marry soon?'

She looked up then, frowning a little. 'I don't think so. But why are you --?'

'I'm telling you because the lady he wishes to marry is the daughter of Lord Leighton. And Lord Leighton is Edward's former employer.' He paused, raising one eyebrow. 'You will perhaps notice the similarity to our own situation.'

Genevieve stared at him, her eyes widening.

'His lordship won't give his permission?'

'Since that was a foregone conclusion,' replied Aristide dryly, 'his lordship hasn't been asked. Consequently, Edward has been busy finding a secure yet legal way of marrying Henrietta without her father's knowledge – and, being Edward, has done it with his usual thoroughness.'

'It's more difficult than one would think?'

'There are pitfalls,' he agreed ... and proceeded to explain them. Then, at the end, he said, 'So you see, Edward has saved me a great deal of time and effort – as a result of which, I have suggested something you may feel I ought to have consulted you about beforehand.'

Noticing that he didn't look particularly apologetic, Genevieve said warily, 'What?'

'A double wedding.'

'*What?*'

'It is a solution that benefits all four of us,' replied Aristide calmly, 'so I hope you don't mind too much.'

'Since you have already done it, that hardly matters, does it?'

'*Do* you mind?'

She drew a long breath and then loosed it. 'No.'

'Excellent. Then we'll be married on the eighteenth of July – which is perfect timing, since I leave for Kent a week later and it will be best if you come with me.'

Genevieve's head was starting to spin. 'Kent? Why?'

'A house-party at the home of the Earl and Countess of Sarre.' Aristide smiled suddenly. 'If you are visiting Madeleine's *modiste* again, you may wish to order more clothes. And before you say you can't afford them, remember that by the time the bills arrive you will be my wife.'

Colour crept along her cheekbones and she said, 'Oh. That is ... I hadn't expected ... that's generous of you.'

'Not especially.' He fell silent for a few moments and stared across the gardens while she recovered her composure. Then, 'What did you and Madeleine talk of yesterday?'

'Not you.'

'I gathered that when she didn't scowl at me over breakfast.' He glanced sideways at her and said, 'Ah. Confidences?' And without waiting for her to reply, 'I'm not asking you to share them. I'm merely thankful that Madeleine has finally talked to *someone* about Nicholas Wynstanton. The situation has been brewing for far too long.'

Genevieve took her time considering how best to reply. Eventually she said cautiously, 'What makes you think we spoke of Lord Nicholas?'

'The roses,' he said succinctly, 'and the note that came with them which probably referred to Lady Sarre's forthcoming house-party – and about which Madeleine would argue till Christmas, were there still any point in doing so. Such arguments, I should warn you, are an almost daily occurrence. However, if you can encourage Madeleine to talk about Nicholas, you will be doing her a favour.' He rose and offered her his hand. 'And speaking of favours, I think I know someone who could make it easier for you and I – and also Edward and Henrietta – to meet more easily.' He smiled again. 'But for now, I'll escort you to the end of Albemarle Street. I think it's about to rain.'

* * *

The shabbily-dressed man followed them at a discreet distance. He watched them part and leaned against a wall, nonchalantly scratching, until the female entered the house where she lived. Then, expecting the French fellow to go either to the fancy gaming-club or his home, he nearly lost him when, instead of heading towards St James', he turned back on himself and crossed into Bruton Street. Muttering irritably under his breath, the shabby man followed. He muttered at much greater length when his quarry disappeared into a house on Bruton Place and remained there for the best part of an hour – during which the heavens opened.

* * *

Sebastian met Aristide in the hall – a corner of which now resembled a small palm-grove – and cheerfully brushed aside his apologies for arriving without warning. Then, on the point of sending a footman to inform his wife they had a visitor, he said instead, 'Unless it was me you particularly wished to see?'

'Both of you – if it isn't too much of an imposition.'

'Nothing of the sort. Speaking for myself, I'm happy to be rescued from the serious question of which painting should go where in the dining-room. So come upstairs and have tea – or something stronger, if you prefer.'

The drawing-room was hung with pale green silk and furnished with three sofas. Raising an eyebrow and gesturing towards them, Aristide said, 'A decision was reached, then?'

'Eventually – though it was touch-and-go. We sat on the floor for a week.'

'We did no such thing,' said Cassie, entering in time to hear this remark. And holding out her hand with a sunny smile, 'Monsieur Delacroix – how nice.'

'Mistress Audley.' He bowed. 'It's good of you to receive me.'

'Nonsense. It's a pleasure.' She chose a chair near the hearth and waved him towards one of the sofas. 'How is Madeleine?'

'She is well, thank you.'

'Then perhaps she might like to join me for a drive or perhaps a little shopping?'

'I'm sure she'd be delighted.'

'Good. I'll send her a note. Meanwhile, what may we do for you?'

Aristide glanced from Cassie to Sebastian. He said, 'I am hoping you might help with something which concerns others as well as myself. But I must ask for complete discretion.'

Sebastian's brows rose a little. 'You have it.'

'Of course,' nodded Cassie.

'Thank you. I know you're both acquainted with Henrietta Leighton. What you may *not* know is that she is betrothed to my new assistant.'

There was a brief, startled silence. Then Sebastian said, 'Your new assistant who was formerly Lord Leighton's secretary?'

'Edward Hastings, yes. The attachment is of a long-standing nature and --'

'So *that* explains why Henrietta spent her last two seasons lurking in corners!' exclaimed Cassie. 'And now, she and Mr Hastings need to marry in secret?'

'Yes. They --'

'Then three cheers for Henrietta!'

'I entirely agree, love,' laughed Sebastian, sitting on the arm of her chair to slide a hand round her shoulders. 'But perhaps we should let Aristide finish?'

She folded her hands in her lap and nodded, her face bright with pleasure.

It wasn't hard, thought Aristide, to see what had captivated Mr Audley.

'Arrangements for their wedding are in hand but it is difficult for them to meet ... so I wondered if you would mind being Mistress Leighton's alibi. It would only be for the next three weeks and she would not need to actually *be* with you ... merely to be able to say that she *had* been.'

'I don't know why she didn't ask me herself,' said Cassie. 'She must know I'd help. In fact, it would be best if they kept the deception as small as possible by meeting here. You wouldn't mind, would you, Sebastian?'

'Not in the least.' Mr Audley's dark blue gaze rested meditatively at Aristide. 'But where do you fit into this? Correct me if I'm wrong, but I thought you implied some personal involvement?'

'I did.' Aristide expelled a long breath and, looking squarely back at Sebastian, said, 'In most respects, Edward's current situation is a mirror-image of my own.'

Cassie stared at him. '*You're* getting married as well?'

'Yes.'

'More significantly,' said Sebastian slowly, 'you're doing it secretly. Why?'

'The lady's family wouldn't approve.'

'Because you are joint-owner of Sinclairs?'

Aristide nodded. Then, realising what Sebastian had said, 'Ah. Adrian told you?'

'He did.'

Cassie let this piece of startling information sail over her head and said instead, 'This all sounds very romantic. Who is she?'

'She's a widow. Unless you met her at Adrian's supper-party, I doubt if --'

'Lady Brassington's god-daughter?' cut in Cassie. 'The beautiful brunette?'

'Yes. *Did* you meet her?'

'No. Who is she?'

'As I said, a widow – and only recently returned to London.'

'Stop hedging, Aristide,' grinned Sebastian. 'Who *is* she?'

'Lady Westin,' came the reluctant reply. 'Formerly, Genevieve Harcourt. Her eldest brother is Viscount Kilburn.'

Mr Audley shook his head. 'Kilburn? Never met him.'

'*I* have,' said Cassie, 'though not more than once or twice because few hostesses receive him.' Her brow creased as she tried to recall why this was. 'Yes. It's something to do with duelling. I think he killed someone.'

'Charming fellow,' muttered Sebastian. 'Just the sort anyone would want as a brother-in-law. But at least it explains the need for secrecy. How long have you known the lady?'

'Three weeks but --'

'Three *weeks*?' echoed Cassie.

'In recent terms, yes. But I knew her in Paris when I was her step-father's secretary.' His eyes on Sebastian, Aristide said, 'Her late husband was Christopher, Lord Westin. I'd expected you to have heard of him. Every other man I know has.'

Sebastian shook his head. 'You forget – I've only been back in England since March. And if Westin was scandal-sheet fodder, I never read the things – being so popular with them myself. What is he credited with?'

With an almost imperceptible glance in Cassie's direction, Aristide rose to take his leave. 'Let's just say that Genevieve is well rid of him and leave it at that. I should go.'

'Not just yet – you'll get soaked.' Sebastian's tone was unusually firm. 'So while we wait for the rain to ease, you and I will go to the library ... where I will pour you a glass of Canary and you will tell me what is unfit for Cassandra's ears.'

Cassie laughed up at him. 'Really, Sebastian ... you might as well let me hear it. You'll tell me yourself later anyway.'

'I doubt that,' muttered Aristide under his breath. And aloud, 'May I tell Edward that Henrietta can expect to hear from you?'

'Please do – and you may say the same to Lady Westin.' She beamed at him. 'This is quite exciting. What does Madeleine think?'

Aristide managed not to groan. 'Madeleine doesn't know. Yet.'

'You'd better get round to telling her, then,' advised Sebastian, shepherding him to the door. 'Unless I'm mistaken, a *fait accompli* isn't going to serve you on this occasion.'

* * *

By the time the blasted Frenchman left the house on Bruton Place, the rain had stopped but the man watching from across the street was drenched. Moodily cursing to himself, he dripped and squelched back to the Bell Tavern to make his report. The powerful and extremely unpleasant individual to whom he made it – and who, in turn, reported to the fellow who paid both of them – eyed him sourly and said, 'You took your bleeding time, Weasel. Where the hell you been till now?'

Weasel sneezed, wiped his nose on his sleeve and thought, *Standing under a sodding tree, getting sodding soaked – that's where.* But he didn't say it because it wasn't the kind of thing anybody in their right mind said to Cross who, as everybody knew, was an arsenal of concealed weapons.

Instead, in as few words as possible, he recited the meagre details of the Frenchman's day, finishing with, 'If'n you ask me, 'e's having a fumble wiv that gentry-mort on Albemarle. Can't blame 'im for that cos she's a tasty piece. But I don't see as any of this 'elps.'

'No,' agreed Cross. 'You wouldn't. Which is why nobody pays you to think.'

* * *

Since putting it off wouldn't make it any better, Aristide broke the news of his impending nuptials to Madeleine the following morning. For a long time, she stared at him as if she thought she'd misheard. Then she said, 'Why?'

'She's a beautiful woman.'

'She is – but that's not it. A fortnight ago you wouldn't have trusted her to count the change in your pocket and now you're going to *marry* her? I'll ask again. Why?'

Briefly, Aristide wondered what she'd say if he told her that marriage had been Genevieve's idea … then discarded the notion. He said, 'I have my reasons.'

'Which you are not going to explain?'

'No.' He tossed his napkin down and stood up. 'Aside from the suddenness of it, do you have any particular objection? It was my impression that you liked Genevieve.'

'I like her well enough. I just wasn't expecting to have her as a sister.' Madeleine also rose from the table. 'And if we're to talk of objections, you'll get plenty of those from her brothers. From what she's said, I imagine that Lord Kilburn will do his damnedest to stop it.'

'Lord Kilburn – like most other people – will know nothing about it until it's too late.'

'And you think that will be the end of the matter? It won't. He'll be furious.'

Aristide strolled to the door and then looked back, his expression benign.

'Yes. He will, won't he?'

And was gone before Madeleine could ask why he thought this desirable.

CHAPTER TEN

The next two weeks sped by and, thanks to Cassandra Audley, more pleasantly than the betrothed couples had dared expect.

Since Madeleine knew better than to try altering her brother's mind once it was made up, she didn't voice any of her questions or concerns to Genevieve and confined herself to wishing them both happy. And if Genevieve detected a certain degree of reserve in her future sister's manner, she pretended not to notice it in case details which Aristide had withheld – such as it having been *she* who proposed to *him* – came to light.

For the rest, a small group – sometimes including Madeleine and sometimes not – met two or three times a week in Bruton Place. Cassandra and Henrietta had merely to resume their long-standing friendship and Mr Hastings was soon on the best of terms with Mr Audley. It was all rather convivial and almost family-like. And it became more so when Mr Audley volunteered to stand up for both grooms at the ceremony.

Genevieve swiftly realised that the only time she ever saw Monsieur Delacroix was at Bruton Place and then, never in private. It was as if, having agreed to marry her and set the arrangements in place, he had little or no interest in furthering their acquaintance … or, she thought with a flicker of anxiety, in her. Of course, it might merely be that he was keeping his distance in order not to raise Cousin Lily's suspicions; but if it *was* that, she wished he would say so.

However, there were other compensations and the one that surprised Genevieve most was Cassandra Audley's warm and unquestioning acceptance of her. Hadn't anyone *told* her that Lady Westin wasn't welcome in polite society? And if they had, why didn't she appear to mind or ever make any reference to it?

It was Lady Brassington who, on learning that Genevieve had been invited to Bruton Place, solved the mystery by saying, 'Make a friend of Cassie Audley. You couldn't have a better one. She's good-hearted, by no means stupid and universally popular. If *she* stands beside you, only the most spiteful will turn their backs.'

Five days before the wedding, four ladies converged on Madame Céleste's premises in Gower Street to give their opinions on two bridal gowns. Whilst waiting for Henrietta and Genevieve to appear in their finery, Cassie said, 'I wish you'd told me about Céleste before, Madeleine. Having seen your own gowns, I knew she was good. What I *didn't* know was that her charges are little more than half those of Phanie.'

Madeleine's brows rose. 'I didn't think expense was an issue.'

'It isn't – but that's not the point.' Cassie grinned and held out a pair of pattern-cards along with two swatches of silk. 'I'm going to order both of these and hope to have them in time for Caroline's house-party. What do you think?'

'The embroidered blue is pretty ... but don't have the lilac stripe.'

'A bit insipid? Yes.' Picking up some different samples, Cassie said casually, 'Sarre Park should be fun. I don't know exactly who is invited but I imagine we can expect the usual set. Not Nell and Harry, of course, but Lord and Lady Amberley and the Ingrams; Rock and Adeline, since they live so close by ... and Nicholas. I considered asking Caroline to invite Henrietta and Edward – once they're married, naturally – but I realised that, with you and Aristide being out of London yourselves, Mr Hastings will be needed at Sinclairs.'

There was a brief silence during which Cassie held her breath.

'I'm not going,' said Madeleine expressionlessly.

Cassie looked at her and stopped pretending disinterest. 'Why not?'

'I've too much to do here.'

'Really? With half the *ton* out of town?'

Madeleine shrugged and said nothing.

Setting her selections aside, Cassie crossed to sit beside the other woman and said, 'It's no business of mine so you can snub me if you like. But I've known Nicholas a long time ... and the lady who wins his heart will be fortunate. There. I felt that needed saying.' She patted Madeleine's hand and moved away again. 'Now ... what do you think of the jade watered taffeta? Better?'

Madeleine kept her eyes fixed on her lap. 'Has he said anything to you?'

'Nicholas? No. Nor to anyone else as far as --' She stopped as Henrietta and Genevieve appeared simultaneously from their respective fitting rooms. And then, 'Oh! You both look beautiful – do they not, Madeleine? Aristide and Edward will be totally *bouleversé*.'

* * *

Madeleine thought long and hard about what Cassandra had said – knowing that it was both true and well-meant. She had put off replying to Nicholas's letter because she didn't know what to say; but when he had sent the flowers, common courtesy dictated that she had to at least thank him. So she'd responded in what she hoped was a similar vein to his own letter but avoided all mention of the Sarre Park house-party. She told herself, as she had told Aristide and Cassandra, that she had no intention of attending it; she also told herself that this was a fact best not mentioned to Nicholas until it was too late for him to do anything about it. What she did *not* acknowledge was a sly, persistent whisper which said, *Perhaps I could go. Just for a day or two?*

* * *

On the evening before their weddings, Aristide ordered Edward out of the office at five o'clock, told him to gather everything he needed for the following day, then bore him off to Duke Street to dine and spend the night. Edward, his nerves beginning to fray, pushed food around his plate and looked enviously at his employer.

Finally, he said, 'How can you be so *calm*, sir? What if something goes wrong?'

'Such as what?'

'Such as the ladies being prevented from getting to the church. Or the vicar refusing to conduct the ceremony. Or Hetty's father rushing in to stop it. Or --'

'Or the church being struck by lightning?' suggested Aristide.

'Oh God,' groaned Edward, aghast. 'Is a storm expected?'

'I was joking! Nothing will go wrong. The ladies will be collected by Mr Audley precisely as planned ... and since Lord Leighton hasn't got wind of our intentions these last three weeks, he's unlikely to do so before tomorrow afternoon.' Aristide pushed the wine decanter in the younger man's direction and added, 'Take a drink and calm down, Edward. Or if you must worry yourself into a fit, concentrate less on *getting* married than *being* married. Because by this time tomorrow, your Henrietta will be Mistress Hastings ... and if husbands everywhere are to be believed, that is the seriously frightening bit.'

'*Men,*' said Madeleine, rising from her chair in apparent disgust. 'If *you* think marriage is frightening, spare a thought for your poor brides. *They* are the ones who are going to have to put up with you, after all.' Her smile was so unexpected and dazzling that Mr Hastings blinked. 'Don't sit up too late – and do not overdo the port. If you both turn up bleary-eyed and the worse for wear tomorrow, the biggest risk will be that Henrietta and Genevieve will change their minds.'

* * *

In Albemarle Street, Genevieve was fighting the temptation to tell Cousin Lily everything and beg her to come to the wedding. She wanted so very badly to have someone of her own there and wondered if, right now, Henrietta was feeling the same. But Henrietta was marrying the man she loved and who loved her in return. *She,* on the other hand, was marrying a man she'd proposed to because she was desperate and who had accepted that proposal for reasons she couldn't begin to guess. Genevieve realised that she ought to be worried ... and in some ways, she was. But much as she wanted Cousin Lily's support, she knew it would be unfair to ask for it. Ralph was going to be incandescent when he found out. And Cousin Lily's best defence would be complete ignorance.

After much soul-searching, she settled for writing a letter which explained everything and which would doubtless be found when she didn't return home tomorrow. This was the occasion of a few tears but Genevieve brushed them away and made herself persevere. Then she turned her attention to the things she would be leaving behind and the question of whether or not she had missed something essential.

Her wedding gown waited for her in Bruton Place and she had managed, bit by bit and with Cassie's help, to remove a few of her most essential belongings. Transferring clothing, however, had been almost impossible. Consequently, she'd had no option but to order two additional new gowns from Céleste, everything required to go beneath them ... and night-gowns that had made Henrietta blush but which Cassie had approved with a brisk nod and the words, 'Yes. Exactly right.'

Genevieve stared at the row of gloomy black gowns in the closet. She would never, she decided, wear any of them again. The anniversary of Kit's death was the day after tomorrow ... but tomorrow was her wedding-day and she would not spend even a *moment* of it as Lord Westin's widow. Ruthlessly shoving aside all the hated black, she found the only coloured gown she had brought with her from Shropshire; the lovely violet silk which had always been her favourite. She would begin her wedding day in that – and hang what anybody thought. If one was going to make a fresh start, she told herself mutinously, one should be thorough about it.

※ ※ ※

There had been a slight skirmish between Cassie and Madeleine over the location of the wedding-breakfast which Cassie had eventually won by saying flatly, 'No, Madeleine. If it is held at Sinclairs, you will be over-seeing everything and worrying that something has been forgotten. What you will *not* be doing is simply enjoying your brother's wedding day. So you will allow

Sebastian and me the pleasure of hosting it for you – and that, I'm sorry to say, is quite final.'

Although not best-pleased, Madeleine had capitulated and turned her attention to a different way of contributing to the occasion. The result was that, on the morning of his wedding, Aristide arrived at the breakfast table to find a note saying, *I have taken the carriage but will return it in ample time to take you to Covent Garden.* And, in a scribbled postscript, *Do* not *tell Edward. He will panic.*

By the time Madeleine arrived in Bruton Place, the morning's initial turmoil was gradually settling into something approaching calm. She found Cassandra, elegant in pale blue tiffany over an embroidered underskirt, issuing the butler with last-minute instructions and, glancing around her, said, 'It all looks lovely, Cassie.'

'Thank you. I *hope* I've thought of everything – or that Cook has. This is our very first party and I want it to be perfect.' She took in the fact that Madeleine's hair was escaping its pins and flower-petals and bits of leaf had adhered themselves to her gown. 'But what have *you* been doing? Gardening?'

'Something like that. How are the brides?'

Dismissing the butler, Cassie turned to lead the way upstairs, saying, 'Calmer, Sebastian assures me, than the grooms will be.'

'Aristide is as calm as the proverbial mill-pond.'

'And Edward?'

'Verging on derangement.'

'Oh dear,' laughed Cassie. And opening a door, 'We have over an hour, so you need not hurry. Your gown is here and there should be hot water. If my maid has done all she can for the brides – they are in the next room, by the way – I'll send her to you.'

Cassie found Susan setting cream roses into Genevieve's night-dark hair while, on the other side of the room, Henrietta's nut-brown locks were woven with pale-pink. Both ladies wore loose robes over their under-dresses and both were laughing.

Smiling at them, Cassie said, 'Madeleine has arrived. I suspect she's been doing something with flowers.'

'And our gentlemen?' asked Henrietta.

'Not as relaxed as you two, I'll wager,' replied Cassie, deciding that the truth wasn't what either lady wanted to hear. 'Well done, Susan. If you've finished here, Mademoiselle Delacroix would appreciate your help. She's way behind the rest of us.'

Susan sniffed, curtsied and left without a word.

'She's feeling put-upon,' sighed Cassie. 'Sometimes there's no pleasing her. She's either burdened with over-work or hurt because I don't need her.'

'She's a very good maid, though,' offered Genevieve judicially.

'She is,' nodded Cassie. And then, with a gurgle of laughter, 'It's just that, at times, Sebastian is a better one.' And when the others stared at her, 'Don't look so shocked. I wouldn't be surprised if Aristide and Edward aren't similarly adept.'

* * *

Since Mr Hastings was growing increasingly twitchy, Aristide called for the carriage half an hour earlier than was necessary and prepared to kick his heels in the dismal church. What he saw as they walked through the door, therefore, took him completely by surprise. There were bowls of flowers everywhere. Creamy-white roses mingled with purple campanula and pale pink sweet-peas, above tumbling greenery; and the scent was intoxicating.

Looking around, Edward said, 'Where did all this come from?'

'Madeleine,' replied Aristide, smiling a little. 'She's outdone herself, I think.'

'She has indeed. Hetty will love it.' He sat down in the nearest pew. 'What time is it?'

'Five minutes later than the last time you asked. Remind me to buy you a watch. We can call it a wedding-gift.'

Edward nodded, barely hearing him. 'Where's the vicar? And Sebastian? Shouldn't he be here by now?'

'No,' sighed Aristide patiently. 'He's bringing the ladies, if you recall. And tradition dictates that brides are always late.'

'*Late?* Why?'

'Either to inflict further torture or to see if we'll wait. I don't know.'

Edward rose and paced restlessly down the aisle.

'What if Sebastian forgets the rings?'

'He won't.'

'Or mixes them up.'

'He won't. Edward … if you have any regard for my sanity, can you please stop imagining every possible calamity?'

'I can't help it.'

'Try.'

Edward swung round to face him. 'Aren't you even *remotely* nervous?'

'No,' said Aristide. And thought, *But I'm beginning to wonder if this isn't going to turn out to be the single most stupid mistake of my life. I don't love Genevieve and she doesn't love me. In truth, we barely even know each other. Does this marriage stand any kind of chance?* Pushing the pointless reflections to one side, he said, 'I shall be as relieved as you to have this over with. I just don't find anticipating catastrophe helpful.'

Mr Hastings relapsed into blessed silence and sat tugging at his cravat. In due course, the Reverend Martin wandered in from the vestry. His shoes squeaked and his surplice was creased. Aristide sighed again.

A carriage drew up outside, causing Edward to shoot to his feet. Then Mr Audley walked in grinning, and said, 'All set, gentlemen?'

Aristide merely nodded. Inevitably, Edward asked if Sebastian had the rings.

'One in each pocket,' came the suitably grave reply. And to the Reverend Martin, 'Too much trouble to summon an organist, was it?'

'He is severely troubled with the gout,' returned the vicar repressively. 'If the brides are here, perhaps we can begin?'

'By all means,' agreed Aristide

'Thank God,' muttered Edward, staring fixedly at the door.

Beside him, Aristide also waited for the first glimpse of his bride. He had no idea what to expect and or how he might feel. She'd look beautiful, of course; she always did, even in funereal black. Would today be any different? Would he react differently? He didn't know.

Followed by Cassandra, Henrietta was the first to appear, radiant in rose-coloured taffeta and soft Mechlin lace. Edward promptly stopped breathing ... then his face split into a huge smile and all his tension fell away.

Waiting for his first glimpse of his wife-to-be, Aristide caught only a flash of moss-coloured skirts as Madeleine apparently stooped to alter the fall of Genevieve's gown. Then Henrietta moved to Edward's side ... and he saw her.

Gone was every vestige of widowhood and instead walked a vision in pale gold net, over darker gold silk; a vision with roses in her hair and in her cheeks, a soft, sweet smile trembling on her lips and eyes that seemed to be seeking his approval. Aristide hadn't known how he'd feel and just for an instant it seemed that he wasn't going to feel anything at all. Then, without warning, all that utterly desirable loveliness hit him like a punch in the stomach.

Holy Mother of God, he thought helplessly. *What was I thinking?*

'Dearly beloved,' began Reverend Martin briskly, barely waiting for Aristide to take Genevieve's hand, 'we are gathered here together in the sight of God ...'

The service proceeded at unprecedented speed. Had anyone known of an impediment, they were not given time to say so. What *did* bring the reverend skidding to an unexpected halt was, 'Who giveth this woman – these *women* – to be married to these men?'

There was a sudden deathly hush as he glared at each of the brides in turn, while Edward turned panic-stricken eyes on Aristide. Then, temporarily deserting his role as groomsman to step nobly into the breach, Sebastian said cheerfully, 'I do.'

'You?' snapped the vicar, plainly disapproving. 'What – both of them?'

'Of course both of them,' agreed Mr Audley. And with a grin, 'Do go on, sir – before you lose your momentum.'

After that and in no time at all, it seemed, the deed was done. Edward Gareth Hastings was joined in marriage with Henrietta Mary Leighton; and Genevieve Louise Westin was united with Aristide Valéry Delacroix. Blinking away a tear, Cassie saw laughter flaring in her husband's eyes and, knowing why, had to suppress a smile of her own.

Reverend Martin, meanwhile, sprinted for the finish line.

'For as much as Edward and Henrietta and Aristide and Genevieve have consented together in holy wedlock and have witnessed the same before God and have pledged their troth to each other by the giving and receiving of a ring and by joining of hands ... I pronounce that you be men and wives together, in the name of the Father, Son and Holy Ghost. Amen.' He snapped his prayer-book shut with a flourish and added, 'You may kiss your brides – then to the vestry, ladies and gentlemen.'

Aristide merely brushed Genevieve's mouth with his. Edward showed every sign of wanting to make a thorough job of it.

The reverend tutted. 'The vestry, sirs. To the vestry – if you *please.*'

'Did you pay extra for speed?' murmured Sebastian to Aristide. 'Or does doing it in half the usual time come at a discount?'

Aristide gave him a look which suggested he save the jokes for later. Sebastian grinned, tucked Cassandra's hand in his arm and swept her in the wake of the vicar. Ten minutes later, they were all outside in the churchyard.

'Well,' said Mr Hastings. 'That was fun. I know everyone said it would be over in a blink but I didn't think it was meant literally.'

'To the carriages, ladies and gentlemen,' declaimed Sebastian. 'To the carriages, if you *please*.'

Leaving Edward and Henrietta to travel back with the Audleys, Aristide settled Genevieve and Madeleine in his own carriage. Although he was aware that he ought to say something to his bride, he had no idea what. So as Higgins set the horses in motion, he settled for the ultimate banality.

'You look beautiful, Genevieve.'

An odd quivery feeling had taken up residence inside Genevieve's gold bodice. Sliding her fingers into his, she looked directly into his eyes and said meaningfully, '*Thank* you.'

He smiled slightly and shook his head. Then, to his sister, 'And thank *you*, Madeleine. The flowers were lovely. Were you up at the crack of dawn?'

'Almost. But it was worth it, I think.'

'*You* did that?' asked Genevieve, awed. 'It must have taken hours! But it was a truly lovely idea – and such a very kind thought. I – I hadn't expected flowers.'

It started to dawn on Aristide that she never expected very much at all – and that consequently every little kindness meant a great deal. It wasn't a comfortable thought. Unfortunately, it was one to which he was going to have to give some consideration. Later.

Once everyone was assembled in Bruton Place and holding a glass of champagne, Sebastian said, 'Unless anyone objects, I suggest we omit the usual speeches. However, I would like to propose a toast to the newly-wedded couples. Monsieur and Madame Delacroix ... and Mr and Mistress Hastings. Your health – and may you be as happy as Cassandra and me.' He waited until everyone had drunk and then added wickedly, 'But *Valéry*, Aristide? Really?'

There was a scattering of laughter into which Aristide said, 'The reverend could have swallowed *that* with my very good wishes.'

Laughter became the keynote of the afternoon as more wine was drunk and everyone sampled the myriad delicacies laid out on the long buffet table. Glowing with happiness, Henrietta clung to Edward's arm, while he looked back at her as if nothing and no-one else existed in the entire universe. Genevieve tried not to envy them and sternly reminded herself that she had been given much more than she could possibly have hoped for only a few short weeks ago. It was both unreasonable and ungrateful to wish that Aristide could be just a *little* less self-contained than usual. But she would make him happy, she vowed silently. She *would*. He wasn't ever going to regret today – not if she could prevent it.

A couple of hours later, Mr and Mistress Hastings departed for their new home amidst a welter of kissing, handshakes and good wishes. Sebastian murmured something in Edward's ear that made him flush … and then they were gone, plainly eager to be alone with one another.

Aristide accepted another glass of wine. Across the room he could hear Cassie persuading Madeleine to stay the night so that he and Genevieve might have the house to themselves … and Genevieve, pink with embarrassment, protesting that it really wasn't necessary and Duke Street was Madeleine's *home*. Madeleine, however, solved the question by saying calmly, 'Thank you, Cassie – but I shall spend the night at Sinclairs. The senior staff are fully capable but I prefer to be on hand in the event of any problem.'

A further half-hour went by. And then, just as Aristide was on the point of suggesting that he and Genevieve also take their leave, a massive thundering at the front door made everyone jump.

'What on *earth* …?' exclaimed Cassie, rising.

Although he said nothing, Sebastian also came to his feet. A few moments later, a tap at the door heralded the butler who said stiffly, 'Your pardon, sir – but Lord Leighton desires a word with Mistress Audley. He is most ... insistent.'

'Ah. I suppose we should have expected this,' said Sebastian resignedly. 'Thank you, Markham. Put him in the library, would you? I'll be there directly.'

The butler bowed and withdrew.

Crossing to her husband's side, Cassie said, 'I'll come with you.'

'No. You won't.'

'But it's me he's asking for.'

'And he'll make do with me,' said Sebastian firmly. 'If Henrietta left a note and he's just seen it, he'll be in a rare temper. So you, my love, will stay here with the other ladies and leave him to me.' He took a couple of steps and then stopped, looking back at Aristide. '*You'd* better come, though. Otherwise, Leighton will be off to create a scene at Sinclairs and when he doesn't find either you or Edward there, he'll be in Duke Street ruining your wedding-night.'

'Why,' asked Aristide a shade irritably, once they had left the room, 'is everyone so concerned about my wedding-night?'

'Not yours – Genevieve's,' said Sebastian. Then, 'How much shall we tell Leighton?'

'Very little he doesn't already know.'

'That's what I thought.'

They found Lord Leighton pacing back and forth before the empty hearth, his complexion almost purple with barely-suppressed fury. The second the door opened, he swung round and, fixing Aristide with a wild stare, said, 'You! I might have bloody known it!'

'Good evening, my lord,' said Sebastian. 'What may I do for you?'

'You can tell me where my daughter is!'

'I'm afraid not. I can merely assure you that she isn't here.'

'Then send for your wife, damn it!'

'My wife has guests. And --'

'Your wife is a meddlesome chit and my daughter has been living in her pocket for weeks, having her head filled with God knows what. Get her in here, Audley. *Now!*'

'No. Anything you wish to say to Cassandra can be said to me.' Mr Audley's voice was level but brooked no argument. 'Though if you continue to speak of her in that way, I'll have my butler show you out. Well?'

Leighton's eyes narrowed.

'You knew what she was doing, didn't you? *Christ*. Up to your neck in it alongside her, I daresay. *Him*,' a vicious jab of his finger pointed in Aristide's direction, 'I could believe. But *you*? Helping a gently-bred girl run off with an unprincipled, slippery man like Edward Hastings? You deserve to be thrashed, sir!'

'This is the last time I'll remind you that you are under my roof,' replied Sebastian. 'Moderate your tone or leave. But let us be very clear on one point. Mr Hastings is none of the things you just called him and he has not 'run off' with your daughter. He married her, very properly and before witnesses, this afternoon.'

Lord Leighton's mouth opened but no sound came out. Finally, he managed to rasp, 'Married? Already? No. It's not possible.'

'It is. The ceremony took place at St Paul's, Covent Garden – should you wish to consult the records.' Frowning slightly, Sebastian said, 'Since Henrietta presumably left a note, surely you knew they were to be married immediately?'

'No. She said ... she said she was going to Hastings and they'd be married. I thought – I thought there was time to stop it.' His lordship's gaze sharpened again as a new possibility struck him. 'Where are they? So long as the marriage is unconsummated, it can be overturned. So where are they?'

'As I've already told you, I don't know.'

'You're lying.'

'No,' said Sebastian frigidly, 'I'm not. And you, my lord, are leaving.'

Lord Leighton swung round on Aristide.

'Not until I know where my daughter is.'

'You'll be waiting a while, then,' replied Aristide, 'since I've no intention of telling you.'

'Why you insolent ...' Fists clenched, his lordship took a step in Aristide's direction only to come to an abrupt halt when Mr Audley's hand closed hard on his wrist.

'Control your temper or I'll toss you into the street myself,' snapped Sebastian, releasing him. 'This is your last chance, my lord. If you want answers, I suggest you stop shouting and listen. Well?'

His lordship managed a surly nod. 'But I'll not tolerate any bloody excuses.'

'Since the situation is of your own making, I have none to offer,' remarked Aristide coolly. 'Refusing Edward a character so that he couldn't leave your employ was a mistake. It made *me* his last resort; and because he couldn't hand over the usual references, I insisted on knowing why. Everything else stems from that.'

A fresh tide of apoplectic colour washed over Leighton's face and he said, 'I'll see you ruined for this.'

'No. You won't.' It was Sebastian who spoke. 'If you are wise, you'll make the best of a bad job and --' His words were cut off by the pealing of the doorbell, followed by more thunderous knocking. 'Oh for God's sake – what now?'

Ignoring this, his lordship advanced on Aristide. '*Where are they?*'

'Not here. Not at Sinclairs. And not at my house in Duke Street.'

'Then where, man? It's the very least you owe me.'

'To the best of my knowledge, I owe you nothing, sir.'

Once again, Markham appeared in the doorway, this time looking grim.

'The Earl of Sherbourne is here, sir. He *also* asks for Mistress Audley.'

'Sherbourne?' echoed Sebastian. 'I don't --'

'Kilburn,' said Aristide flatly. 'The grandfather must have died. It was expected.'

For a long moment, the two of them simply stared at each other while Lord Leighton growled, '*Kilburn?* If *that's* the sort of company you keep, Audley --'

'Go *home*,' said Sebastian, his patience exhausted. And to Aristide, 'Clearly, Henrietta wasn't the *only* one who left a letter. But I'll have Markham deny him, if you wish.'

'No. He has to be faced some time – unless you'd rather it didn't happen here?'

'Don't be an ass.' He turned back to the butler. 'Show him up, Markham – but take your time about it. And send someone to tell my wife to remain in the drawing-room with the other ladies. She is *on no account* to join me here. Is that clear?'

'Perfectly clear, sir.'

'What the hell is going on?' demanded Lord Leighton. 'My daughter is more important than whatever Kilburn wants – so he can bloody well wait.'

'He could – but he won't,' sighed Sebastian. 'Just go, my lord. You'll get no satisfaction here no matter how many times you ask the same questions. So you may as well go home to your wife.' And then, as the newest visitor strode in, leaving Markham hovering helplessly in the doorway, 'Too late.'

The new earl's eyes swept the room, passed over Aristide without pausing and came to rest on Sebastian. 'Audley?'

Sebastian nodded. 'Sherbourne. I believe condolences are in order.'

'My grandfather, yes. And I must return immediately to Dorset for the funeral. So I apologise for the intrusion but you will understand that my business is urgent. I would, however, prefer to conduct it in private.'

'If you can persuade Lord Leighton to leave, be my guest. I've been trying to send him home for the last quarter of an hour.'

Neither lord appeared to appreciate this remark. Leighton spluttered incoherently and Sherbourne said, 'Then you will permit me to speak with your wife.'

'No. I won't.' Sebastian looked back over folded arms. 'Let's get to the point, shall we? You are looking for your sister and think my wife will help --'

'What?' interrupted Lord Leighton. 'Looking for your *sister*?' The earl glanced dismissively at him.

'Yes – though I fail to see what concern that may be of yours.'

'Oh Lord Leighton is looking for his daughter,' said Sebastian, unable to help himself. 'It seems a lot of female relatives have gone missing today. However, it would be helpful to know what the note Lady Westin left actually said.'

The hazel eyes narrowed – the only sign that Sherbourne was in a blistering temper. Arriving in Albemarle Street without prior warning and becoming acutely suspicious when Lily Brassington refused to receive him, he'd had to force his way in only to discover that Genevieve wasn't there. It had then taken the best part of half an hour to learn that she *might* be with Cassandra Audley ... and a further ten minutes to browbeat her ladyship into producing Genevieve's letter.

'Since you clearly know more about this unfortunate matter than I'd anticipated, it began, *By the time you read this, I shall be married*,' he said frigidly. 'Am I to understand that this was not merely a cliché but the literal truth?'

'Yes. Exactly that.' It was Aristide who spoke.

'I see.' The earl looked down his magnificently aquiline nose. 'And you are?'

You don't recognise me, do you? thought Aristide. *My face means nothing because you never saw it. But my name should mean something.*

'Aristide Delacroix.'

There was a sudden catastrophic silence that even Lord Leighton had the sense not to break. Aristide waited, holding the other man's gaze. It seemed that his name did mean something. The question, however, was what.

Finally, his voice dangerously soft, Sherbourne said, 'Of course. The gaming-house keeper my stupidly indiscriminate sister has chosen as her second *mésalliance*. How kind of you to save me the trouble of looking for you.'

* * *

In the drawing-room, news of Sherbourne's arrival brought Genevieve to her feet looking panic-stricken. 'Oh God! How did he find out so quickly?'

'Lord Sherbourne?' asked Cassie, baffled. 'I don't --'

'It's my brother. *Kilburn!* Grandfather must be dead.' She pressed a hand to her mouth and then said breathlessly, 'If Cousin Lily showed him my letter ... he knows. He knows I married Aristide. And now they're in the same room.'

'Is that so terrible?' asked Madeleine. 'It is inevitable they would meet sooner or later, is it not?'

'You don't understand. Ralph is dangerous. He's fought four duels and the last time, the other man *died*.'

'Well, he's hardly likely to challenge Aristide, is he?' said Cassie calmly. 'And though he may not be pleased about your marriage --'

'Not pleased? He'll be *livid*.'

'Then he'll have to get over it. He can shout and bluster all he likes but --'

Genevieve gave a small, hysterical laugh.

'Ralph doesn't shout or bluster. He – he has a way of m-making one say exactly the wrong thing.' She stiffened her spine. 'I'll have to speak with him.'

'No.' Cassie's tone was very firm and she stood up. '*I'll* go.'

Madeleine said quietly, 'Is that wise? If he insults you, Mr Audley will take it amiss.'

'If he insults me, *I'll* take it amiss,' retorted Cassie. 'And if anyone is thinking of throwing down a gauntlet – or whatever gentlemen do these days – they can think again.'

* * *

In the library, meanwhile, the air was thick with tension as Aristide and Sherbourne stared each other down. Realising that Leighton's presence could only make a bad situation worse, Sebastian took his arm in a firm grip and marched him to the door, saying, 'Time to go, sir. As you can see, you are very much in the way. Markham – his lordship is leaving.'

With a muffled curse and a filthy look in Mr Audley's direction, Lord Leighton stamped off in the butler's wake. Aristide, meanwhile, continued to wonder why Sherbourne showed no sign of recognition other than the obvious.

'Finally,' breathed Sebastian. 'I thought he was here for the night. And now, gentlemen, perhaps you will sit down and discuss the situation rationally.'

'By all means,' nodded Aristide, his eyes never leaving the earl's face.

'No. I want to see Genevieve. One presumes that, since *you* are here, so is she.'

'Do you not think,' asked Sebastian in the hope of diffusing the situation, 'that might not be better postponed? I realise that you are shocked --'

'I am not shocked, Mr Audley. I am not even particularly surprised – this not being the first time Genevieve has hurled herself into matrimony with indecent haste.' The quality of Sherbourne's gaze as it lingered on Aristide grew deliberately derisive. 'Westin was bad enough ... but *this*? This abomination beggars belief.'

'Genevieve does not agree with you,' remarked Aristide.

'Spare me some touching story of a love-match,' drawled Sherbourne. 'I know perfectly well why she married you.'

'So do I – which makes your presence here rather ludicrous, doesn't it?'

The merest hint of colour crept across the earl's high cheekbones.

'I wish to speak with my sister. Now. If this exceedingly furtive wedding only occurred today, the situation is still salvageable – unless, of course, Genevieve used the oldest trick in the book and you fell for it.'

'Trick?' asked Aristide, knowing perfectly well what Sherbourne meant but wondering if he'd actually say it. 'I don't follow.'

'Are you really that naïve? I can't help wondering if she slept with you in order to get a marriage proposal which might not otherwise have been forthcoming by telling you she's with child. Did she?'

Sebastian's jaw hardened but he kept his mouth shut.

Aristide took a step towards the earl and, in a tone of pure disgust, said, 'No. She didn't. And you might remember that this is your *sister* you are insulting.'

'I had not thought it possible to insult *either* of you,' replied the earl cuttingly. 'You are an ill-bred tradesman and my sister is completely lacking in either social or moral judgement.'

'I'm so sorry,' said Cassie, not sounding sorry at all and immediately drawing three pairs of male eyes, one of which she was careful to avoid, 'but Genevieve has asked me to convey her regrets, my lord. However, I'll deliver your felicitations to her, if you wish.'

'I most assuredly do *not* wish.'

'No. She said you wouldn't – though I hoped she was mistaken.'

A glimmer of appreciation crept into Sebastian's eyes but he said nothing and wondered if the Valkyrie was about to make an appearance.

Lord Sherbourne subjected her to a long, hard stare and then said, 'I understand that it was *you* who fostered this wholly unsuitable match.'

'Not at all. Genevieve and Aristide agreed to marry without any help from me. As to its unsuitability ... that is a matter of opinion. And the only opinion of any consequence, is theirs.'

'You are very forthright, madam.'

'When the occasion demands it.' Although Cassie smiled, her eyes held a martial gleam. 'Misunderstandings occur so very easily, do they not?'

'You may be assured that you have made your position abundantly plain.'

'I am so glad.' She waited, the words *Was there anything else?* as clear as if she'd actually spoken them.

Just for a moment, Sebastian thought Sherbourne was going to take up the challenge. Then, turning his gaze back to Aristide, he said coldly, 'I see I am wasting my time. You should be aware, however, that this is far from over.'

'Naturally. You will wish to discuss the usual marriage settlements – as will I. Please make an appointment with my assistant at Sinclairs at any time you may find convenient.'

'My convenience,' came the icily furious response, 'will be best served by visiting you at your home tomorrow morning.'

Aristide shook his head. 'That would be a further waste of time, my lord. Until I am sure that *my wife* is happy to receive you, my servants will have orders not to admit you.'

And that was when Cassie saw something in the depths of those green-gold eyes that told her Genevieve hadn't been exaggerating. The Earl of Sherbourne was indeed a thoroughly unpleasant and possibly even dangerous man.

CHAPTER ELEVEN

Inevitably, it was nearly an hour after Lord Sherbourne stalked out of Bruton Place before the party split up; and, during it, Aristide noticed – as, he was sure did everyone else – that it was Cassie's reassurances Genevieve sought and Cassie's hand she held while she received them. He felt slightly aggrieved by this, even though he knew he had no right to. Thus far, after all, he hadn't exactly opened his arms to her, had he?

Having left Madeleine at Sinclairs, he led his bride into her new home and immediately issued his butler with firm instructions.

'If the Earl of Sherbourne calls, he is not to be admitted under any circumstances whatsoever until I decide otherwise. He will not be surprised but that may not stop him trying. Please make the situation clear to the rest of the household, Minton.'

'Certainly, sir. I shall attend to it forthwith.'

'Please do.' Aristide looked at Genevieve. 'This is what you'd prefer?'

She nodded but said incredulously, 'You told Ralph you'd forbid him the house?'

'Amongst other things.' He led her up the stairs and into a bedchamber with an adjoining dressing and sitting-room and, glancing around, said, 'I hope you will find everything you need. But if not or you require the assistance of a maid, please ring. Will half an hour be sufficient?'

'Yes.' Genevieve swallowed, as a different source of anxiety slammed through her body. 'Quite sufficient.'

'Then I'll see you presently.'

The second he was on the other side of the door, he felt like banging his head against the wall. If he carried on like this, it was small wonder she didn't seek comfort from him. And how the hell did he manage to sound so chilly when anticipation of the night to come was burning like an inferno inside him?

The trouble was that he shut off his feelings from everyone – even, to a degree, Madeleine – although it would be fair to say that, except when she was angry, Madeleine did precisely the same. But how had it happened? How, when for years they'd only had each other, had they managed to create this empty space between them? And how, assuming he *wanted* to, was he going to achieve something different with the woman he'd just married? One thing was clear. If he didn't stop behaving as if he had the emotional capacity of an automaton, another chasm was about to open up at his feet.

Genevieve had to summon a maid to help with her laces. Since her hands were becoming unsteadier by the minute, she suspected she'd have had to do so even if they hadn't been impossible to reach. And by the time the girl left her, the tremors had set up an unpleasant churning in her stomach.

She stared at her reflection. Even worn with its matching wrapper, the new nightgown was not far short of transparent. Genevieve pulled her loosened hair forward over her shoulders. That helped but not enough. He was going to see her. He was going to look at her and ...

Stop it. Stop. He isn't Kit. He is not *Kit. He's* not. *Other men aren't like Kit. He isn't. It will be all right. But ... but what if it isn't?*

There had to be other things she could do; and flying round the room, she did them. Then she sat in a chair near but not too close to the small fire and tried to look relaxed.

Clad in a dark blue silk dressing-robe and having tapped politely at the door, Aristide entered the room only to stop dead on the threshold, halted by the gloom and the scent of recently extinguished candles. This might have boded well if she hadn't been sitting bolt upright in an armchair. And as his eyes became accustomed to the shadowy light, other things became apparent; the agitated rise and fall of her breathing, the death-grip her hands had on one another and the fact that, over her night-rail and wrapper, she appeared to be huddled in the shawl Cassie

Audley had lent her for the ride home. In short, she looked terrified.

Well. So much for the wedding-night everyone had been worrying about. He suspected it wasn't going to happen. He also suspected he knew *why* it wasn't. When he'd said he would marry her, he had known that five years of marriage to a man like Westin would have left some residue. He'd known, accepted it and been prepared to deal with it. He just hadn't expected it to be so soon. Hindsight, unhelpful as ever, suggested that he should have done; that this was precisely the moment when the first problems were going to surface. Certainly, it wasn't difficult to work out what was going on in her head right now. But if he said what he thought, it would only reinforce her belief that it was true ... which meant he had somehow to make *her* say it.

Shutting the door, he took the chair facing hers and said quietly, 'This feels unnatural and rather awkward, doesn't it?'

'A little, yes.'

'Is that what is making you anxious?'

'No. I mean, I'm not anxious. Not at all.'

'Clearly, that isn't true. But if you tell me what is wrong, I'll try to make it right.'

'There's nothing wrong – really.' Genevieve summoned her best smile. 'I --'

'Don't.' Aristide lifted one staying hand. 'Please stop doing that.'

'Doing what?'

'Trying to blind me with that particular smile in the hope I won't see past it.'

Alarm of a different sort flickered through her. 'I wasn't.'

'You were.' He kept his tone pleasant but firm. 'It's the veil you hide behind when there's something you don't want anyone to see. And though I'll concede that it was very effective at first, it no longer works with me so I'd appreciate it if you stopped doing it.' He paused. 'What are you afraid of, Genevieve? Me?'

'No! No, of course not. How could I be?'

'That's good. So is it the prospect of lying with me?'

'No,' she said quickly. And then, half-despairingly, 'Well ... perhaps, a bit. But it isn't that. Not really. Or not in the way you mean it.'

He leaned back, keeping his expression neutral.

'That sounds promising ... if a little confusing. Would you like to elaborate? You can say anything to me, you know. I can promise I won't be angry.'

'I know.' Her throat felt thick. 'I know you won't. I just can't ... I can't say it.'

'That bad, is it?' He waited and when she nodded, said 'Let's try this, then. When I asked you why you wanted to marry me rather than some other man, you said it was because you trusted me. Did you mean it?'

'Yes.' It was no more than a whisper.

'So trust me now.' He felt that he was groping in the dark, quite literally. The words hovering on his tongue might either make her spit out the poison or swallow it. 'Trust me now ... and tell me why you don't want me to look at you.'

Horrified, her eyes flew to his face. 'I – why do you think that?'

'The fact that we're sitting in the near-dark is a reasonable clue. Or do I have it wrong? Is it that *you* would rather not have to look at *me*?'

'D-Don't be absurd.'

'That's a relief.' He smiled at her. 'I don't mind the dark, though I'd like to see you better. But I'll settle for understanding why you don't want me to.'

He could see her struggling; both wanting to say it and *not* wanting to. He waited.

Eventually, she drew a long, unsteady breath and, closing her eyes, said, 'I'm afraid that ... that you won't l-like what you see.'

'Really?' He affected a surprise he didn't feel. 'Why?'

Another monumental struggle, eyes still tightly shut. Then, 'Kit said ... he said I was ... that my b-body was ugly. Undesirable. Even d-disgusting.'

And there it was ... exactly what he'd suspected. Pushing down a tide of anger and wondering why somebody hadn't battered Westin to death sooner, Aristide went to perch on the arm of her chair and lifted one of her hands to his lips.

'He lied, *chérie*. He lied. But thank you for having the courage to tell me.'

Though she gripped his fingers and opened her eyes, she still refused to look at him.

He said softly, 'Did he say these things often?'

'Yes.' *And worse*, she thought. *Other things too awful to repeat*. 'Often enough, anyway, after I ... after ...' She stopped, leaving her free hand to finish the sentence by sweeping over her bosom.

Molten lava flooded Aristide's veins and he barely stopped himself saying, *Can I do that?* Instead, managing by some miracle to sound perfectly composed, he said, 'After your body developed? Yes. And you believed him?'

'N-not to begin with. But later ... yes.' She managed a shrug. 'When you are told a thing over and over ... when there is no-one to tell you it isn't true ... then you believe it.'

There was a great deal more here that merited investigation but now was the time for trying to undo a little of the damage, if that was even possible. He said, 'I want you to listen to me – and excuse my bluntness. Your late husband's taste in female flesh ran to very young, undeveloped girls. You know this, don't you?'

'I – I know it *now*. I didn't then.'

God damn his soul to hell, thought Aristide. But said, 'Most men, myself included, find that both sickening and incomprehensible. But it is why Westin would have found you, or any other lovely, adult woman, undesirable. The flaw was in him – not you. Any normal man would find you beautiful and want you very much indeed. *I* certainly do.'

She stared at him as if he'd told her the sun shone at night. 'Oh. You do?'

'Yes.' Aristide released her hand and returned to his own chair, a hint of wryness curling his mouth. 'I didn't agree to marry you for any of the reasons you gave me, Genevieve. I agreed because I wanted to take you to bed.' He waited for the words to sink in, then added, 'I still do ... though I suspect I should wait a while.'

It was a long time before she spoke. But finally, she said, 'Why?'

Just one syllable ... but it produced another surge of hot, aching hunger.

'Why wait? Partly to give you time to believe what I've just said. But mostly because I imagine your sexual encounters with Westin have left you reluctant to repeat the experience.' He hesitated then decided he had no choice but to ask. 'Did he hurt you?'

'Every time.' Her voice was so low he could barely hear it. 'Mercifully, once he began to find my body offensive, it didn't happen often. But when it did, I thought ... I started to think he hurt me deliberately.'

Oh I'm sure he did, thought Aristide grimly. *When the bastard couldn't find a twelve-year-old to rape, forcing his wife was the next best thing.*

A voice at the back of his mind whispered that offering her time might not be the best solution; that showing her how different it could be was possibly the better answer. So he said slowly, 'I'd ask you to forget him, except that I know you can't just yet. But one thing I can promise you. It will not be like that with me.'

'I know,' said Genevieve, caught unawares by the odd pulse of heat his words produced but knowing, at some fundamental level, that it was significant. 'That is – I believe you.'

'Good.' Aristide stood up. If he was going to leave, it would be as well to do it before his body defeated his will-power. 'I'm glad. And now I should let you sleep.'

'No.' The instinctive denial startled her even more than it did him. 'Don't go. Not ... not unless you want to.'

He took a second to control his breathing. 'I don't. But the choice is yours.'

'Then stay. Please. And show me. Show me that it needn't be ugly.'

He remained silent and motionless for so long, she steeled herself for a refusal. But he didn't refuse. Instead, a slow and very different smile dawned; an intensely masculine smile, full of confidence and a promise of something that made her nerves tingle. He said, 'Yes. If you're quite sure ... I can do that. Actually, I think I can do rather better.'

Rising, he held out his hand and, when she put hers in it, drew her to her feet. 'But we must start at the beginning.' Very gently, he teased the fingers of her other hand away from Cassie's shawl. 'And that means this.'

Sucking in a breath, Genevieve allowed him to slide it away and drop it at her feet. Feeling instantly naked, she shut her eyes.

'Don't.' Aristide's hand cupped her cheek. 'Look at me. There is no one else in this room. Just you and me – so open your eyes and tell me what you see.'

'You,' she said, obeying him reluctantly. 'Looking at me.'

'Yes.' His gaze feasted on the creamy skin of her *décolletage* and the lovely curves and shadows hinted at below the sheer fabric. 'Looking at you ... and enjoying it immensely. Although the view would be greatly improved either by the addition of a couple of candles or the removal of your robe. Do you think I might be allowed one of those?'

Genevieve hesitated, wanting to refuse but knowing she couldn't.

She said, '*Just* the robe?'

'Just the robe,' he agreed, edging it from her shoulders so that it floated down to join the shawl on the carpet.

Aristide immediately had to remind himself to breathe. Even in the dim, shadowy light, the nightgown concealed virtually nothing ... and everything it revealed was beautiful. He trailed the back of his curved knuckles along her throat and on down one bare arm to lace his fingers with hers and draw her against him. Then, taking an iron grip on his self-control, he kissed her.

For a moment, Genevieve stiffened, unsure what to do and afraid of making a mistake. But gradually the warmth of his body and the teasing temptation of his mouth drew forth an instinctive response and she freed her hand from his in order to slide both palms up to his shoulders and on to the hair, still neatly tied at his nape. His reply was a small rumble of encouragement and he drew her even closer; close enough for her to feel the erratic beating of his heart. And that was when she finally believed what he had been trying to tell her.

He wanted her. He *really* wanted her. But he would do nothing she didn't want, too.

And that changed everything. Suddenly all the unexpected pulses and brief flares of heat coalesced into something powerful which brought a flood of sensation. She met his mouth with willing, if inexpert, gladness and, freeing the fair hair from its ribbon, drove her fingers through it.

Aristide's hands skimmed the line of her back and then, because the silky shift was no adequate substitute for soft flesh, he charted a course beneath it to slide his palm over and around one lovely naked breast. Then, when she quivered in response, he let his thumb caress its peak. This time Genevieve gasped and shuddered against him, which came close to completely melting his brain and made it necessary to be still for a moment.

Stepping back slightly and lifting his head to look into her eyes, he said unevenly, 'The bed is just over there, where it's even darker than here. If we can reach it, perhaps you'll let me remove the nightgown? Pretty as I'm sure it is, it can't compete with your skin.' And when she hesitated, 'Would it help if I went first?'

Genevieve's breath caught. 'It ... might.'

'Then let's find out.' He untied the sash of his robe and shrugged it off. 'You may look, if you wish. I'm not shy.'

She looked and forgot her own near-nakedness for the few seconds it took him to draw her towards the bed. She barely had time to think that he wasn't shy because he had nothing to be ashamed of ... and then he loosed the ribbons of her nightgown and let it fall. She tensed involuntarily and he said, 'No – don't think. It's just me, remember. Nobody else. And the sad truth is that I can barely see you anyway.' He pulled her into his arms, holding her securely against the length of his body and murmured huskily, 'But I can feel you. And that is almost as good.'

Genevieve could feel him too and her breathing simply stopped for a moment, lost and forgotten in the explosion of pleasure as his skin met hers.

'Yes,' she whispered against his jaw. 'Yes. It's ... better than good.'

'I'm glad you think so.' There was a wholly unexpected note of laughter in his voice. 'And I presume that by now you've noticed that, when I said I wanted you, I wasn't lying.'

'Yes.' The evidence of it was hot and hard against her stomach. 'I ... I want you, too.'

'No, *chérie*. As yet, you are merely ... interested. But give me time.' And without warning, he tumbled them both on to the bed, rolling her over him to the centre of it. 'This is only the beginning.'

After that, sensation was piled on sensation as he slowly teased and caressed and tormented his way about her body with his lips and tongue and hands. To Genevieve's astonishment, he touched and explored as if he would be happy to do so for hours; as if he received as much pleasure as he gave. From time to time, he murmured to her in French, his voice low and seductive; and though she didn't understand the words, his tone expressed appreciation and encouragement when, shyly at first, she embarked on her own voyage of discovery.

By concentrating on and treasuring Genevieve's every tremor of response, Aristide managed to keep a leash on his own desire. But when she was clinging to him, half-sobbing his name, her touch less tentative, he knew that he could take what he wanted. Not letting his gaze leave her face, he joined their bodies with one long, fluid motion and was rewarded with an expression of surprise which melted almost immediately into a mixture of wonder and delight. Doubting that her relief could in any way rival his own, he managed a smile and said, 'Yes. And it gets better. Come with me and you'll see.'

* * *

Genevieve woke slowly. Ghostly pre-dawn light was creeping in through a chink in the curtains. A hard, warm body was pressed against her back and one arm lay across her ribs, its fingers lightly curled around her breast. She luxuriated in the feeling, a bubble of happiness growing inside her; a happiness not only due to her new husband's expert love-making but to the patience and understanding that had preceded it.

Aristide, she thought, wonderingly. *Aristide.*

And tumbled headfirst into love.

* * *

By the time Aristide awoke it was full daylight and the clock in the hall was chiming eight. Genevieve was curled into his side, her head on his shoulder and one hand lying lax on his chest. She was fast asleep. He smiled, half-considered waking her and decided against it. He rarely rose before nine – late nights at Sinclairs being unconducive to early mornings – so he could lie for a little while yet.

Since, however, he was wide awake, he shoved his free hand under his head and stared up at the ruby silk tester, thinking about the night before. Though there were still problems to be faced, last night had drastically reduced one of them. The sex had been surprisingly good and would get even better, once the last of

Westin's filth had been consigned to the gutter where it belonged. He tilted his head to look at Genevieve. Even flushed, rumpled and sleeping, she was still beautiful. And that body ... well. Using his foot, he tugged the sheet down a few inches in order to enjoy the parts of her that he'd so far become familiar with only by touch ... and immediately parts of his own anatomy started getting ideas. Reluctantly, he restored his attention to the canopy.

However, if his marriage wasn't going to be any hardship in the bedroom, things outside it wouldn't be as pleasant – though he couldn't deny that he was looking forward to Sherbourne's impotent fury, first at the marriage itself and then at being asked what settlement he would make on his sister. Not that Aristide intended to rely on that. If the earl refused to cooperate – or even if he didn't – he planned to make provision for Genevieve himself. If someone shoved a knife between his ribs one dark night – which, though unlikely, couldn't be discounted when men owed one large sums of money – his wife wasn't going to be left existing on other people's charity. She would have a home of her own and an income. He should probably also consider the possibility of children ... and then, with a frisson of shock, *Children? Me – a father? God!* He wasn't sure if the prospect was exciting or terrifying. Either way, he needed to visit Henry Lessing without delay and set all the various wheels in motion.

When, after half an hour, Genevieve was still asleep, he slid his arm gently from beneath her and got up. Although he employed a valet to care for his clothes, the man's duties didn't include shaving and dressing him ... and forty minutes later, he was sitting down at the breakfast table with a pot of extremely strong coffee and the *Morning Chronicle*. He eyed the newspaper thoughtfully. He probably ought to put a notice of his marriage in it. Perhaps, he thought with a glimmer of humour, Edward would like a notice of his own put alongside it.

* * *

The sound of rattling china and aroma of chocolate was what finally brought Genevieve into the land of the living. She sat up and realised that she was alone in the bed while the maid who'd helped her last night stood grinning down on her.

'Morning, Miss — ma'am, I should say.' The girl bobbed a brisk curtsy. 'Sir said not to wake you but I fought you might be ready for some chocolate — so I brung it.'

'Yes. Thank you.' Realising that she was naked, Genevieve clutched at the sheet with one hand and reached for the cup with the other. 'I'm sorry. I don't remember your name.'

'Becky. I'm Miss Madlin's maid but I'm to 'elp you till you get a girl of your own. I've unpacked all your fings and put everyfing away. Lovely gowns you got, Miss — even if there ain't many of 'em. Still I reckon you and Miss Madlin'll enjoy a bit of shopping.'

Genevieve vaguely remembered that Becky had also talked non-stop the previous evening and with an accent unusual in upper servants. Managing to get a word in and blushing a little, she said, 'Where is m-my husband?'

'Sir's at breakfast, Miss.' The girl beamed at her. 'If'n you want to join 'im, I can 'ave you ready in a trice. Won't be no trouble. You just finish your chocolate and tell me what to lay out. That striped one, maybe. I'll bet that looks a treat on you. What do you fink?'

'Yes. The stripe will be fine,' replied Genevieve, fighting a desire to giggle.

If not quite in a trice but actually not so very much later, Genevieve had been laced into the green-and-gold polonaise and Becky had twisted her hair up into a simple but surprisingly becoming style. She said, 'Thank you. That's lovely.'

'Pleasure, Miss. Ma'am. Sorry. I 'spect I'll get used to it. Now ... Sir should still be 'ere. He don't usually go to the club much afore eleven. Patrick'll tell you. He always knows where Sir is.'

Patrick turned out to be a very large footman, currently engaged in clock-winding. Smiling broadly at her, he said, 'Good day to you, ma'am. It's grand to see you – and aren't I the lucky one, meeting you before most of the others? Now, Mr Minton will likely have my head on a plate for asking ... but if you've a minute spare later, would you maybe pop down to the kitchen and take a dish of tea with us? Mrs Constantine – she being the cook, ma'am – would be over the moon.'

Although she couldn't help smiling, Genevieve stared at him in awed fascination. Did *all* Aristide and Madeleine's employees chatter as if they were old friends? It was bizarre. She said, 'Please tell Mrs Constantine and the other servants that I look forward to meeting them and I will *certainly* join them for tea later today. But for now, I --'

'Course, ma'am. You'll be looking for Himself – and won't Sir be delighted to see you?' He led her towards the breakfast-room and, bending his head, lowered his voice to say confidentially. 'Miss Madeleine's back from Sinclairs and they're having the usual barney about Kent. It's been going on a week, so it has.'

Across the breakfast table, brother and sister were eyeing each other with unconcealed irritation but as soon as Genevieve appeared, Aristide rose, saying smoothly, 'Good morning. You slept well, I think.'

'Yes. Thank you.' Sensing an innuendo and feeling her cheeks grow hot again, she turned quickly to Madeleine and said the first thing that came into her head. 'Your maid thinks I need more clothes.'

'Ah.' Madeleine sighed. 'I should have warned you. Becky chatters like a magpie.'

'She does – but it was good of you to share her.' Seeing Aristide had pulled out a chair for her, she sat down and smiled shyly up at him. 'I accepted an invitation to drink tea in the kitchen. I hope that was right?'

'Since this is your home now,' he replied, crossing to the covered dishes and putting a little from each on to a plate, 'you must do exactly as you wish. But meeting all the servants at once over tea is probably a good idea – otherwise they may decide to use their ingenuity. And you wouldn't want that.'

His tone was sardonic but not without a hint of humour so Genevieve said cautiously, 'Judging by Becky and the footman I just met, your staff seem very ... friendly.'

'What you mean,' observed Madeleine, 'is that they aren't typical. And you are right. They're not. But they are unswervingly loyal and generally good at their work – though I've often wished that, when required to escort me outside the house, Patrick could do it without holding a conversation. However, he is vastly preferable to the pair I have to deal with at Sinclairs – both of whom are stupid as sheep.'

'They don't have a monopoly on stupidity,' murmured Aristide, setting the plate before Genevieve. 'You don't have to eat it all – but I imagine you are hungry.'

There it is again, thought Genevieve; *a perfectly innocent tone with something quite different lurking beneath it. And judging by the look on her face, Madeleine knows it too.*

'Thank you. But you don't have to serve me, you know.'

'No? And you a bride of less than a day?' he asked. Then, to his sister, 'And now, if you don't mind, we will finish what we were discussing earlier. Caroline's house-party begins in six days' time and, though you continually tell me you will not go, you still have not told *her* that. I shall be writing to tell Adrian of my changed circumstances today and must – since you can't seem to do it – also apprise him of your intentions. So what am I to say?'

Madeleine's expression did not change but Genevieve detected some inner conflict. Finally, however, she said, 'Say no. You can tell him that I am remaining in town because it is too soon to leave Mr Hastings bearing sole responsibility for Sinclairs and --'

'We both know Edward is more than capable of managing without us for a few days.'

'*We* do – Adrian doesn't.'

'He doesn't need to. He'll know that's not your real reason. No – don't worry. I'm fully aware there's nothing to be gained by dragging Nicholas Wynstanton into this. But what I was about to tell you is that I had a letter from Rockliffe this morning. At some point during the course of the party at Sarre Park, his Grace plans to hold a private race meeting at Wynstanton Priors and he has asked me to run the book. It would be helpful if you were present to lend a hand with that.'

She gave him an acid-edged smile and threw his earlier words back at him.

'We both know you are more than capable of managing --'

'Thank you.' Aristide rose. 'I take it that this is your last word? Much though I wish you would change your mind, I have to admit being thoroughly tired of the arguments.'

'Since you are not alone in that, consider them over.'

'As you wish.' He turned back to Genevieve, saying, 'Minton is anxious for a word, so I should see him now. Meanwhile, if you want to make your peace with Lady Brassington, I suggest you invite her here. Normally you would be free to go wherever you wish but I'd prefer you took a few precautions until I have a clearer understanding of Sherbourne's whereabouts and state of mind. I told him to make an appointment to see me at Sinclairs but I doubt he will. He may even have gone back to Dorset since, according to the newspaper, the late earl's funeral is to take place next week.'

'And if we wished to do any shopping?' asked Madeleine.

'Take Patrick. He should be sufficient protection. While Sherbourne can probably walk into Lady Brassington's house with impunity, he can't storm into a modiste's shop without looking ridiculous.' He lifted one of Genevieve's hands and dropped a careless kiss on her wrist. 'I'm sorry. You'll have to excuse me today. After Minton, I need to call on my man-of-law and then there are a few matters to discuss with Edward. But I will see you at dinner.'

Madeleine watched him go and then turned an astringent gaze on Genevieve.

'And if you are thinking he isn't *always* like that – don't. He is. Fortunately, revenge is easy. While you finish your breakfast, I'll order the carriage and tell Patrick to be ready to go out. Then off to Céleste's to spend some of your husband's money.' She grinned suddenly. 'I assume you don't plan to plunge back into mourning for your grandfather?'

Genevieve swallowed a mouthful of egg. 'You assume rightly. I don't.'

* * *

Unlike his assorted underlings, Minton was a man of few words. Coming directly to the point, he said, 'I have recently begun suspecting that either you are being followed or this house is being watched, sir. A non-descript fellow in a misshapen hat. Not wishing to bring it to your attention until I was certain, I set Stephen the task of observation. We are now convinced that it is *your* comings and goings that are of particular interest. When you leave, so does the hat. I thought you would wish to know ... and perhaps issue instructions?'

Now what? thought Aristide wearily. But said, 'To be clear, this began some days ago? It is nothing to do with yesterday's wedding?'

'No, sir. I first became aware of it around the middle of last week.'

'I see. And is this fellow outside now?'

'I suspect so. If you are going out this morning, we will soon know.'

'I'm going to an office off Chancery Lane and then to Sinclairs.'

'Then you will need the carriage, sir.'

'You'd better make it a hackney, Minton. I rather think the ladies may have plans for the carriage – a penalty of married life which I fear may become all too frequent.'

'Indeed, sir. And may I say that the staff and I wish to offer you and your lady our most hearty felicitations?'

'Thank you. Please help yourself to the wine-cellar so that everyone can celebrate this evening. And now … I'll need that hackney in half an hour or so. But first I need to write a letter to Lord Sarre which should be despatched without delay.'

'Certainly, sir. Will there be anything else?'

'Probably,' muttered Aristide. 'I just haven't thought what it is yet.'

* * *

In The Bell on Ludgate Hill, the man known as Cross looked at Sir George Braxton and said, 'He got married yesterday. To the bit of fluff he's been seeing on Albemarle – who it turns out is Westin's widow. Not as that matters. Point is, we're looking at a brick wall. There ain't no point in watching the Frenchie's every move so we know what he has for breakfast and every time he farts.' He didn't bother to admit that bloody Weasel had let himself get spotted and been chased half-way to Holborn by a footman he claimed was the size of a barn door. The likes of Weasel came five to the groat, after all, so the silly sod could be replaced easily enough; but Cross didn't see the point of replacing him at all. 'None of that's going to get you your money back.'

Sir George glowered. 'If that's the case, what am I paying you for?'

'Knowing what's possible and what ain't.'

The truth was that Cross was bored. If there had been another job on offer, he'd have taken it a week ago. The only thing that made this one bearable was that the bumpkin was paying well over the odds for what was merely surveillance. Any street-rat would have done it for a quarter of the price. But if the bumpkin still thought to get his money, it was time for him to be a bit more adventurous.

'And what *is* possible?' asked Braxton tetchily. He didn't like Cross any more than Cross liked him. He also had the uncomfortable feeling that getting on the fellow's bad side wouldn't turn out well. On one occasion, he'd thought he'd seen a knife-handle sticking out of his cuff. 'Something must be, for God's sake.'

'Well, let's see. No matter how hard we look, we ain't managed to find any dirt on him; not me in my world nor you, grubbing round the shirt-tails of his. If he's a sharper, I ain't heard hide nor hair of it and nobody but you is saying it. As for that club of his, it's sewn up tight as a tick. No getting in there without being caught and nobody on the inside whose palm we can grease. As for daylight robbery on banking day, even if I'd be daft enough to *do* it – which I won't since I don't want the Redbreasts after me – it'd take a miracle since there's no knowing when the ready will be coming through the door. Now unless you got any ideas you ain't shared with me yet, I don't reckon you got too many options left. Fact is, I can only think of one that'll get you the result you want. But it's risky and will take some arranging – so it'll cost extra.'

'Considering what I've paid you already, it had better come with a bloody guarantee!'

'Nearest thing you'll get to one,' shrugged Cross.

'So?'

'So … if you can't get the actual money, you take something else.'

'Such as what?'

Bloody buggering hell, thought Cross. *I hate working with amateurs.*

'Something he'll pay any amount for so long as he gets it back in one piece. Think what I told you earlier … and use your imagination. Or do I have to draw you a bleeding picture?'

CHAPTER TWELVE

In the five days before they left for Sarre Park, Genevieve learned her husband's daily routine and, from his servants, things about his character she had never suspected. She did not, however, get to know Aristide better from her own perspective because the only time she saw him was at breakfast and dinner when Madeleine was always present ... and late at night when he came to her bed; and the last of these had little to do with conversation.

She didn't mind this. There were years ahead in which to establish greater closeness and she knew he didn't love her – though she couldn't help hoping that one day he might. As for the hours in his arms ... she wouldn't have exchanged those for anything in the world because, in them, he gave her much more than physical pleasure. He gradually restored her confidence in herself as a woman ... and he allowed her the illusion, during those moments of exquisite intimacy, that he was truly hers and hers alone.

What she learned in the servants' hall astounded her. The first thing was that they were a peculiar mixture; some were what, elsewhere, might be considered unemployable and nearly all had a dark, even heart-wrenching, history. But they had one thing in common. They had each been plucked from the gutter – in some cases, even worse than that – by Aristide or Madeleine. And the result was that, from the butler down to the ten-year-old scullery-maid, every one of them would walk through fire for Sir and Miss.

When asked about this, Madeleine merely shrugged and said, 'Aristide and I have also known bad times. Not all such times are deserved.'

It was one of those occasions when Genevieve noticed that her sister-in-law was growing increasingly uncommunicative and suspected she knew why. Laying a hand on Madeleine's arm, she said softly, 'If you have changed your mind about Kent --'

'I haven't. And I would prefer not to discuss it.'
And that, of course, was that.

Lady Brassington called in Duke Street. She berated Genevieve soundly for her secrecy, bemoaned the disastrous timing of Sherbourne's arrival and finally hugged her, saying, 'Be happy, my dear – I hope that this time you may be. Since he proposed and married you so swiftly, it is clear that Monsieur Delacroix loves you very much.'

Smiling uncomfortably Genevieve let the misconception stand by asking if Cousin Lily had any message she would like given to Lady Sarre.

The last of the gowns she had ordered before her marriage finally arrived from Céleste. Fortunately, two of these were suitable for evening parties and so, despite Madeleine's urging, Genevieve had steadfastly refused to spend any more of Aristide's money since he had already been more than generous. What she thought but did *not* say was that she didn't want her husband to wonder if she'd married him for his money; not now and not ever. So she bought no gowns ... but allowed herself to be tempted by two new hats.

Aristide, meanwhile, sent notices of his and Edward's nuptials to the *Morning Chronicle* and spent two gruelling sessions with Henry Lessing, at the end of which he was satisfied that both his wife and any future progeny would be well provided-for. He also arranged for Genevieve to receive a quarterly allowance, shrugged philosophically when Minton apologised for Stephen's failure to apprehend the fellow in the hat and spent every available minute with Edward, ensuring that the young man knew everything he needed to know in order to temporarily occupy Aristide's own position.

Through all of this, Aristide was aware that, outside the bedroom, he was keeping his bride at a distance. The knowledge made him faintly uneasy ... but not uneasy enough to do anything about it, even if he'd had the time – which, just at present, he didn't. And anyway, the pleasures of the bedroom were all he had been either looking for or expecting of his marriage, weren't they?

On the day before he was due to depart for Kent, he and Edward went over numerous small details that seemed to have been overlooked and at the end of it, Aristide said, 'I've every confidence in you, Edward. But if the unforeseen arises, seek advice from Jenkins, Cameron or Madeleine. One of them should know the answer.'

Mr Hastings nodded and then said hesitantly, 'May I ask you something, sir?'

'Of course.'

'Hetty has hopes of eventually achieving a rapprochement with her parents but says her life is different now and she wants it to remain so. But she has time on her hands and energy to spare and has heard that there is a possibility of Mademoiselle employing an assistant. So she wonders if she might be considered for the position.' He shifted in his chair, looking slightly uncomfortable. 'If I thought she couldn't do it, I wouldn't have mentioned it. But I think she'd be good at it.'

'I'm not the one you need to convince. Also, I have been urging Madeleine to engage an assistant for months, for all the good that has done. However, there's no harm in trying – though I'd advise you to pick your moment carefully.' Aristide rose, stretched his cramped muscles and went to pour two well-earned glasses of wine. 'For what it's worth, you can count on my support.'

'Thank you, sir. I'm obliged to you.'

'If you succeed in persuading Madeleine to take Henrietta on, the obligation will be on my part,' came the arid reply. 'And really, Edward ... after all our recent shared tribulations I think it's time you started using my given name. Don't you?'

* * *

Having said goodbye to a tight-lipped Madeleine, Aristide and Genevieve set off for Kent in their own carriage while, behind them, a hired vehicle bore their luggage and Aristide's valet. On learning that the journey would take some four hours, Genevieve looked forward to having her husband to herself for such an unprecedented length of time. Aristide merely wondered what they were going to find to talk about – and took the precaution of putting a book in his pocket.

Within ten minutes, he realised she wasn't going to let him read it.

She began by asking who else, to his knowledge, had been invited to Sarre Park. Then she wanted to know which of them he was already acquainted with. And finally she said, 'I met Lady Sarre only briefly and exchanged barely two words with the earl. I realise that he is a particular friend of yours, of course, and that he would never offer you any discourtesy ... but I can't help wondering if perhaps he and the countess are not *entirely* happy about including me in their party.'

Faint though it was, Aristide caught the note of anxiety.

'Why do you think they might not be?'

'Well, they don't know me ... but I imagine they *do* know about Kit. And in London, the ladies wouldn't receive me because they thought *I* must have known, too.'

'Cassie Audley received you.'

Her face brightened. 'Oh yes. But Cassie isn't like those other ladies. She was even kind enough to say I might share her maid while we are at Sarre Park.'

Although he noted a point worth questioning, Aristide chose not to digress. He said, 'Yes, Cassie *is* kind. She's also Lady Sarre's closest friend – and became so before Caroline married an earl and was still the grand-daughter of a cloth manufacturer from Halifax. As for Adrian, he isn't merely my very good friend. He's also part-owner of Sinclairs and therefore my business-partner.'

Genevieve stared at him. 'Oh.'

'Quite. I trust I may rely on you to keep that information to yourself?'

'Yes. Of course.'

'Good. My point is that Adrian and Caroline are no more typical of society than is Cassie Audley – or Sebastian, come to that. Though they would accept you for my sake, they'll accept you for your own if you give them the chance.'

That sounded as if it might be a compliment; as if there were things he liked about her other than her body – though God knew, that was more than enough to be grateful for.

'Thank you for telling me. The prospect of meeting a duke and a marquis as well as your friends was making me a little nervous.'

'I know.' Aristide leaned back and surveyed her with an expression which, as usual, defied interpretation. 'Why haven't you found a maid of your own?'

'There hasn't been sufficient time.'

'And that would also account for you not ordering more clothes, no doubt?'

'Partly. But I already have sufficient, you know – and it seemed foolish to buy more evening gowns just for these two weeks.' She smiled shyly. 'You have already been so very generous that I didn't want to present you with yet *more* bills.'

Aristide suddenly felt unreasonably annoyed.

'I believe I already told you that money is not an issue. Also, you do not need to come to me for every penny. You have an allowance of your own to spend as you choose. Mr Lessing did communicate this fact to you, did he not?'

'Yes.' She flushed and looked worried. 'He did. But I wasn't sure I understood correctly. The – the amount seemed very large and Mr Lessing said that it was merely for the quarter, so I thought there must be an error and it would be best to wait until I was sure.'

If possible, he felt even more annoyed. The quarterly figure he and Henry Lessing had decided upon was no more than Madeleine received. And hadn't that bastard Westin given her money of her own? Or her brothers? Had she always been forced to go cap in hand for every bloody hairpin?

'And you didn't think to ask me about it?' he demanded irritably.

'When?' she asked. 'When was I supposed to ask you anything? This is the first private conversation we've had since our wedding night.'

Against all logic, he felt a sudden desire to laugh. She might as well have slapped him. Perhaps, in a sense, she had done. Certainly he was fully aware that he'd stepped blithely into a pit of his own making. He said, 'You should have left me a note. Madeleine and Edward do it all the time.' And quickly, before she could say what he knew she must be thinking, 'I know – I know. My wife shouldn't have to communicate with me by letter. As for the money, there's no mistake. The amount is quite right and yours to do with as you will – but does *not* include paying your maid, when you have one. That responsibility is part of the household expenditure and, as such, belongs to me.'

'Oh. That is … well. Thank you.' She looked thoughtful and then said quietly, 'Perhaps you might have explained all this to me yourself rather than leave it to Mr Lessing?'

'Yes. You're right. I should have done.'

Aristide drew a long, silent breath. He shouldn't have snapped at her and the least she deserved was to understand that his annoyance hadn't been with her. He said, 'I wanted you to have funds at your own disposal so that you wouldn't feel obliged to explain your expenditure to me. I would find that as uncomfortable as you would.' He fell silent for a moment and then, as if unaware that he did it, reached out and folded her hand in his. 'There's something else. You told me that money owing to you from your marriage to Westin was being withheld. I've instructed Lessing to open proceedings with both your brother and the current Lord Westin with the aim of discovering precisely where the problem lies – or whether, indeed, there is one.' A hint of laughter lit his eyes. 'If you end up an obscenely rich woman as a result, you can make *me* an allowance.'

* * *

They arrived at Sarre Park at a little after four in the afternoon to find the earl strolling down the steps to greet them.

'Well, you've certainly created a stir,' said Adrian, gripping Aristide's hand. 'Of course, Sebastian has already given us some of the details but the ladies are still agog for more.' He bowed over Genevieve's hand. 'Welcome to Sarre Park, Madame Delacroix.' And with a sudden grin, added, 'Caroline is going to be furious with me.'

'She is? I mean – thank you, my lord. You're very kind.'

'Adrian, you wretch!' Lady Sarre scowled down on her husband from the doorway. 'You did that on purpose.'

'I did not. I'd just finished the note to Henshaw when Bertrand happened to mention that he thought he heard a carriage. What was I supposed to do? Hide?'

'No.' Caroline descended to the gravel in a swish of ice blue satin. 'You were supposed to ask Bertrand to find me – which is what he *did* do but without any mention of notes.' She extended a hand to Aristide but, instead of letting him bow, reached up to kiss his cheek and then turned immediately to startle Genevieve with a brief hug, before linking an arm through hers and drawing her up to the house. 'Welcome, Madame – and please accept our felicitations. We were about to have tea on the terrace but it can wait until you have settled in.' She beckoned the housekeeper. 'Monsieur and Madame Delacroix, Betsy. I believe we agreed on the rooms near Mr and Mistress Audley, since the ladies are to share a maid.'

'Yes, my lady. The rose suite.' Betsy curtsied. 'If you'd like to follow me, ma'am?'

Genevieve glanced around for Aristide – who instead of following her, was listening to something the earl was saying. Then the countess squeezed her hand and said, 'Go with Mrs Holt. I promise I won't let Adrian keep Aristide long.'

Seeing no help for it, Genevieve smiled weakly and followed the housekeeper.

As soon as she was out of earshot, Caroline said bluntly, 'The two of you can talk later. For now, I think your wife will feel more comfortable if you are with her, Aristide.'

He nodded but before he could move away, Adrian said, 'Shyness – or nerves?'

'The latter. London cold shouldered her for being Westin's widow and she's afraid of receiving the same treatment here. I have told her this will not happen ... but she remains unconvinced.'

A militant gleam lit Caroline's eyes.

'Is it not enough that she was *married* to that awful man?' she demanded. And in response to Aristide's look of surprise, 'Yes – of course Adrian has told me about him and I can't imagine what living with him must have been like.'

'She hasn't said much about it. But reading between the lines, I find I despise Westin a little more each day – something I would not have believed possible.'

Caroline watched him go and then, looking up at her husband, said thoughtfully, 'You know him better than anyone. Does he love her?'

'I know him better than anyone,' agreed Adrian, 'and I have absolutely no idea.'

* * *

Having managed to track his wife to the correct room, Aristide found himself greeted with a barrage of over-enthusiastic chatter. He listened without interrupting until she finally paused for breath, then said, 'Yes. The rooms and the views from them are lovely ... but since everyone is waiting for their tea, perhaps we should go down?'

'Yes. Yes, of course. Mrs Holt said not all the guests have arrived yet. Did Lord Sarre tell you which ones are already here?'

'I didn't ask.' He offered her his arm. 'Shall we go and find out?'

'Yes.' Genevieve didn't move.

'Today?' suggested Aristide, mildly.

She nodded, laid her hand on his sleeve and hauled in a long, bracing breath.

With a faint but not unsympathetic smile, Aristide drew her towards the door, saying, 'It's tea on the terrace – not a firing-squad at dawn.' Then, recalling what Adrian had said, added, 'Sebastian is here, which means Cassie is too. Ah. That's better. *Now* can we go?'

Below in the hall, they encountered Bertrand Didier who shook Aristide's hand, clapped him on the shoulder and greeted him in French. Aristide responded in the same language and then, switching to English, made the necessary introduction.

Bertrand grinned. 'But yes. The lovely lady with a passion for art. *Bienvenue*, Madame.'

'*Merci, monsieur*,' said Genevieve smiling back at him. 'It *was* a horrible picture.'

'It was.' He waved a hand towards an open door and continued on his way. 'The cakes are that way and they are especially good today. Aristide ... *mes plus sincères felicitations – chien chanceaux!*'

Genevieve strove to translate and for the most part failed.

'Did he ... did he just call you a *dog*?' she asked uncertainly.

'If that was the only word you understood, my lessons were a waste of time.'

'*Did* he?'

'Yes – but a very lucky one. It was a compliment, though not to me.'

She blushed and laughed. 'He is very foolish – but amusing.'

'That is one way of putting it.'

'What does he do? I mean ... what is his position in the household?'

'His position is that of Adrian's oldest friend. As to what he *does* ... Bertrand has numerous talents, most prominent among them being an annoying sense of humour. You might bear that in mind.' He led her out on to the terrace. 'And here we are.'

Genevieve glanced around and was relieved to find there were fewer people present than she'd anticipated – though one of them was a lady she thought might not welcome her. Fortunately, however, the first to notice her was Cassie who immediately set aside her tea-cup in order to embrace her.

'Genevieve! At last.' Then, with resignation, 'Madeleine wouldn't change her mind?'

'No – though we both tried to persuade her.'

'Madeleine,' remarked Adrian calmly, 'has made obstinacy an art-form.'

'But no doubt she has her reasons,' said Caroline. 'Aristide, you know everyone, so you won't mind if I ignore you. Madame ... you know Cassie and Sebastian and you'll remember Lady Amberley, from our party in Cork Street. This is her sister-in-law, Isabel Vernon.'

Genevieve curtsied to both ladies, remembered that the Marchioness couldn't see her, and belatedly took the hand that was being offered. Isabel Vernon, meanwhile, smiled warmly and said, 'Our husbands are over there on the lawn, attempting to tire out Rosalind's son and my little girl.' She gave a gurgle of laughter. 'I don't think either of their valets are going to be pleased with them.'

'Why?' asked Rosalind. 'What are they doing?'

'Lying on the grass with the children bouncing up and down on top of them. Their coats are likely to be ruined.'

'A bagatelle,' said Sebastian sauntering over to hand Genevieve a cup of tea. 'The pair of them are having more fun than the children, if you ask me.'

'Go and join in, if you wish,' grinned Caroline. And once more to Genevieve, 'Althea Ingram is finding travelling a trial just at present, so Jack has sent his regrets. But Rock and Adeline should be with us tomorrow.'

'And Nicholas?' asked Aristide.

'Nick has been delayed,' said Adrian. 'He sent a note – something about a fire. Doubtless he'll explain when he gets here, though he said that might not be for a few days.'

'It must be quite serious if it is keeping him in Surrey,' remarked Cassie, drawing Genevieve into the chair beside her own. Then, lowering her voice, 'And speaking of serious matters ... has your objectionable brother tried to visit you?'

'No. He's gone to Dorset for Grandfather's funeral.' A sudden sparkle lit Genevieve's eyes. 'And Aristide told the servants that he is not to be admitted under any circumstances.'

'Yes. He told Sherbourne to his face that he'd do that. But the absolute *best* bit was when he told him to make an appointment with Edward. The look on his lordship's face was utterly priceless.'

Under cover of a conversation with Adrian and Sebastian, Aristide observed his wife. It was interesting. She'd begun to respond to Caroline's easy, open manner but had instantly retreated into her shell when presented to Lady Amberley, as if expecting a rebuff. But with Cassie Audley? When she was with Cassie he caught glimpses of the girl she had been; happy, confident and a little mischievous. He wondered how long he would have to wait before she felt secure enough to be that girl with him. As yet, the only time she let her guard down completely was in bed ... and *there* she was everything he could want; responsive, increasingly passionate and breathtakingly beautiful.

The only woman here who could rival her for looks was the marchioness. Aristide decided, with what he was quite sure was clinical detachment, that Genevieve was the lovelier of the two. He looked at the perfect heart-shaped face and dark-fringed topaz eyes ... and from there it was a short step to the curve of her throat, a slow glide over the swell of her breasts and on to the slender waist. A curl of lust stirred and for once he didn't tamp it down. A man was entitled to want his own wife, after all. He was just wondering how much longer the tea-drinking would last when he saw Amberley and Philip making their way back up to the terrace and realised that it would be a while yet.

Having deposited the children in their respective mamas' laps, two extremely dishevelled gentlemen made their bows to Genevieve before shaking Aristide by the hand and offering cheerful congratulations. Philip Vernon, as usual, could not leave it at that and added, 'Adrian said she was a beauty, Aristide – but God, she's something else, isn't she?' And with a grin, 'What on earth does she see in you?'

'You'd have to ask her,' came the unruffled reply. 'Modesty forbids me to boast.'

Philip laughed. 'Well, I wish you both happy.'

From her perch on Isabel's lap, little Alice had been staring fixedly at Genevieve. Finally, clutching the last of the strawberry tarts, she slid to the ground and approached.

'Pretty,' she said approvingly.

'Thank you,' smiled Genevieve, reaching out a hand to brush one strawberry-blonde curl from the child's face. 'You are very pretty, too. What is your name?'

'Alice. What's yours?'

'Genevieve.'

'Genevieve.'

Alice nodded and, having apparently made a decision, began the laborious process of clambering on to her new friend's knee. Genevieve was just reaching out to help her when Isabel said quickly, 'No, Alice – don't do that!' And Genevieve snatched her hand back as if burned, murmuring raggedly, 'I'm sorry – of course she mustn't – go to your Mama, darling.'

Just for a second before she conquered it, hurt was written large on her face and everyone saw it. His mouth setting like a steel trap and before anyone else could react, Aristide stalked to her side and laid his hand on her shoulder. She looked up at him and whispered, 'I didn't th-think. I'm sorry.'

'You have nothing to be sorry about,' he said firmly. '*Nothing*.'

Meanwhile, Isabel was on her feet looking utterly aghast.

'Please don't apologise, Madame,' she said rapidly. 'It is I who should do that. It was only that her fingers are covered in jam and I didn't want her to spoil your gown. Of *course* you may hold her, if you wish. I meant nothing else – truly.' She glanced around, as if seeking help. 'Indeed, I don't know what else I *could* have meant.'

Caroline knew and she acted without hesitation. Swooping on the child and twirling her around to banish the little girl's worried expression, she plopped her on Genevieve's lap, saying breezily, 'Jam on one's gown isn't too bad. But don't, as I did yesterday, let her get it in your hair. That *really* isn't funny.'

There was a small ripple of laughter and the moment passed. Aristide remained where he was, feeling some of the tension ease from Genevieve's shoulders and watching her concentrating on Alice so that she didn't have to look at anyone else. Then, meeting Isabel's concerned gaze, he said, 'It's all right. Merely a … misunderstanding.'

Isabel nodded and sat down again. And joining Caroline in the breach, Lord Amberley said, 'So … what's all this about Rock holding a race-meeting? And why wasn't I told?'

* * *

A little later, alone in their rooms, Genevieve looked up at her husband and said miserably, 'That was so stupid of me. But just for a moment, I thought …'

'I know. And you weren't stupid.' *You were sliced to the bone by the idea a mother didn't think you fit to touch her child.* 'But it was a mistake.'

'Yes. *My* mistake. Isabel Vernon didn't know about me or – or Kit, did she? But now someone is going to have to tell her.'

'Whereupon she will feel worse than you do.' He had discovered, during the course of the day, that distraction worked best and in a short while he intended to distract her quite thoroughly. But there was something else that needed to be said first. 'Isabel and Philip aren't the child's natural parents. Did you guess that? Alice is an orphan who came to Isabel's attention about two months ago in unpleasant circumstances that far too many people in London know about. But Isabel has insisted on keeping her, nonetheless. That ought to tell you a great deal about her. Does it?'

'Yes.' Her face had lightened a little. 'You're saying she's kind.'

'I'm also saying she isn't bound by what society thinks. You have Cassie and Caroline on your side, *ma chère*. After today, I believe you may also count on Isabel.' He let her think about that for a moment and then added, 'And there is me.'

'I know.' Genevieve wondered how to explain what having him instantly at her side in that painful moment had meant to her; what *he* meant to her. But she had a feeling she might cry if she tried, so she settled for, 'You stood by me even though you knew I'd misunderstood, didn't you?'

It suddenly struck Aristide that he hadn't cared about that. He'd just seen her face and responded instinctively. But since admitting that might lead him into deeper waters than he was prepared for, he turned the question to his advantage. 'Good behaviour usually earns a reward, does it not? And aside from anything else, I have been forced to drink *tea*.' He paused, looking mildly pained. 'Have you any idea how much I abhor tea?'

She shook her head, a smile quivering at the edge of her lips. 'Do you?'

'It is an abomination.' Aristide shed his coat and dropped it on a chair. 'As an Englishwoman, you will not understand this.'

'Not really.'

'Nor that the excessive amount of time wasted drinking it might be more enjoyably spent?' His cravat followed the coat and very, very slowly he set to work on the buttons of his vest, holding her gaze with an intense, heavy-lidded one of his own. 'Much more enjoyably, in fact.'

That look, coupled with the slow passage of his hands shortened Genevieve's breathing and caused involuntary responses in her body. She said weakly, 'Aristide ... it's daylight.'

'Yes. So it is.' He reached the final button, shrugged the vest from his shoulders and advanced on her. 'And thank God for it. Not that I'm complaining ... I'm as fond as the next man of letting my hands discover lovely secrets in the dark. But lovemaking is about more than that, you know.'

'It – it is?'

He had an arm about her waist and was trailing his mouth down her neck while his fingers started unhurriedly unlacing her gown.

'Yes.' Giving her a lazy, predatory smile and abandoning the laces for a moment, his fingers rose to caress her temple. 'It is also about what goes on in here. And for that, we need to look as well as to feel. We have been married a week and I've yet to see how my beautiful wife looks when I am possessing her.' Watching the pulse hammering in her throat, he resumed his assault on her laces. 'I have been imagining doing so for the last hour or more. So ... may I?'

Fire licking her veins, Genevieve swallowed and nodded. 'Yes. Please.'

CHAPTER THIRTEEN

Although Madeleine tried to keep busy, there simply wasn't enough to do and too many hours in the day to do it. As for the nights, when she tossed and turned and awoke feeling wretched, she started to dread them.

Everything Aristide had said about Edward was depressingly true. He managed Sinclairs as if he'd been doing it for years and, with so few guests in the dining-rooms, didn't need her at all. This rankled – and probably would have done so even if her temper *hadn't* been constantly balanced on a knife-edge. Consequently, when on the second day of Aristide's absence Edward politely asked that, if and when she decided to engage an assistant, she would consider Henrietta, she nearly bit his head off.

'Does it *look* as if I need an assistant? Do I appear over-worked and unable to cope?'

'No. But --'

'No. I do not,' she snapped. 'So does that not suggest to your needle-sharp intellect that raising the issue at this time is utterly asinine?'

'Actually, it doesn't,' replied Edward coolly. 'My needle-sharp intellect suggests that now, while we are not busy, would be the ideal time for you to train someone.'

Madeleine glared at him, further infuriated by the knowledge that he was right.

'When I feel a need for your opinion, I will ask for it.'

That's just as well, he thought, *because my opinion is that you should have gone to bloody Kent, instead of staying here to set the entire staff on edge.*

'Then there's no more to be said – which is fortunate because I'm due downstairs. Mr Cameron asked if he could have a word.'

And he walked out, leaving Madeleine scowling at his retreating back – fully aware from whom he'd learned that particular escape tactic and wanting to throw something.

Thoroughly disgusted with herself, she sat down at Aristide's desk and dropped her head in her hands. She had always prided herself on doing whatever had to be done – no matter how difficult. But *this*? This was tearing her in two. She knew you couldn't have everything you wanted – so this was just one more disappointment, wasn't it? She could get over Nicholas Wynstanton. All it took was some self-discipline and determination. But she couldn't find either of those things while she felt as if something was clawing at her insides. And in those last moments before Aristide had left, it had taken every ounce of will-power she possessed not to cry out, 'Stop. Wait. I've changed my mind. I'll come.'

Think of something else – anything else. Aristide and Genevieve, for example. How had that happened – and so fast? Aristide never acted on impulse. He calculated angles, lined up facts and did nothing until he could predict the result – a habit she had frequently found annoying. But in this one thing, a matter which was going to affect the rest of his life, he had apparently plunged in without a backward glance. Why? Someone who didn't know him would assume he'd fallen head over ears in love. Madeleine knew better. Her brother wasn't the least little bit in love. The idea was actually laughable. He was as coolly detached as ever ... which made his marriage inexplicable.

She let herself wonder how the newly-wedded pair had been received in Kent and then immediately regretted it when it set her thoughts back on the treadmill.

What was Nicholas doing? What had he thought when he found out she'd refused to join the party? Had he been disappointed? Hurt? Angry? Had he finally decided that she wasn't worth his time and washed his hands of her? And, worst of all, what would she do if he walked through the door right now?

Madeleine pressed the heels of her hands over her eyes. The possibility that she might have hurt him lay like acid in her throat but what other choice was there? Aristide had been free to marry a woman upon whom society had turned a cold shoulder because, aside from a few close friends, he didn't give a snap of his fingers what anyone else thought. Lord Nicholas Wynstanton, though he hadn't realised it yet, didn't have the same luxury.

And crying over the whole sorry mess wasn't going to change anything.

* * *

As it happened, Lord Nicholas was still in Surrey. However, the Sarre Park party had been augmented by the Duke and Duchess of Rockliffe, along with Lady Vanessa Jane.

Genevieve's initial impression of the duke was that he was probably the most intimidating gentleman she had ever met. Tall, elegant and exceptionally good-looking, his mere presence had a quality which Genevieve found unnerving. All this changed, however, on the day after his arrival. Caroline had organised a picnic by the lake from which everyone had eventually drifted back towards the house. Most guests chose to linger on the terrace for a while but Rosalind, Isabel and the duchess took two very tired children and one peacefully sleeping baby directly to the nursery.

Having ordered tea, Caroline gathered Cassie and Genevieve around a table to discuss the organisation of the party for the estate families to be held the following week, while, a short distance away, three gentlemen indulged in desultory conversation.

It began with Rockliffe saying quietly, 'I have been meaning to ask, Aristide ... has the Braxton situation created any problems?'

'Nothing we couldn't deal with,' came the unexpansive reply. 'Perhaps we should discuss the race-meeting, your Grace? Keeping the book will present no problem at all. But how large an affair are you expecting?'

'Moderately large, I believe.' Lazy humour glinted in the dark Wynstanton eyes. 'Several of my neighbours will compete and those who do not will be there as spectators. As for the gentlemen entering a horse, I daresay we may include you, Adrian?'

'Oh yes. You may *definitely* include me. Sebastian, too. For the rest, Philip has asked for the loan of a horse and Amberley has sent for one from his own stables. We won't know about Nicholas until he gets here – but I'd be surprised if he chose to sit on the side-lines.'

'So would I,' agreed the duke pensively. 'One might even predict which of his horses he will ride ... but there is always the hope he'll choose more wisely.'

Adrian laughed. But Aristide who, typically, had noticed an omission, said, 'And will *you* be entering, your Grace?'

'Oh yes. That is certainly my intention.'

No longer laughing, Adrian shot Rockliffe a suspicious glance.

'And might one predict which horse *you* will be riding?'

'I would imagine that you might be able to hazard a guess, yes.'

'Which would account for those of your neighbours choosing not to compete?'

'That is a distinct possibility.'

Adrian leaned back in his chair and stared forebodingly at Aristide.

'He's going to ride The Trojan. So unless Amberley's horse is something out of the common way, we'll have to pin our hopes on that mad beast of Sebastian's – which has taken longer than you'd think necessary to prove his potency with my --'

His last words were drowned in a rapidly approaching series of ear-splitting wails.

'Oh dear,' murmured Rockliffe, coming unhurriedly to his feet just as Adeline erupted on to the terrace. 'Vanessa is awake.'

'A fact of which the whole of Sandwich is probably aware,' she said aridly. And holding out the screaming bundle, 'Take her. She's all yours.'

The duke accepted his small daughter, settled her deftly in the crook of his arm and began chatting to her. Almost instantly, the deafening cries began to subside. Everyone stared. Adeline looked about her, shrugged and said, 'My apologies. But when she's like this, Tracy is the only one who can quiet her. I used to think she just didn't like me. Then I realised that she's a born flirt and simply prefers gentlemen.'

'But not *any* gentleman, my love,' remarked Rockliffe in the same, soothing tone he was using to the baby. 'We can test it, if you wish. Who will volunteer? Adrian?'

'Thank you – but no. I am only now getting my hearing back.'

'Ah well. Aristide, then.' And without further ado, the duke placed his now gently hiccupping child in Monsieur Delacroix's startled arms.

Feeling ridiculous and never having held an infant in his life before, Aristide peered cautiously down and met a pair of accusing blue eyes. A tiny mouth puckered before opening on what he had no doubt would be another scream. He braced himself. Then Genevieve sank down at his side in a pool of amber taffeta, leaned over the baby and said softly, 'Oh! Isn't she beautiful?'

Aristide didn't particularly think so but wasn't prepared to dispute the matter with the child's besotted father a mere three steps away. He muttered, 'She's going to scream. Perhaps you should take her.'

'No, no.' She immediately stood up and backed off a step. 'But you might try rocking her a little ... and talking to her, as his Grace did.'

'About what?'

'Anything. She's a *baby*, Aristide. She doesn't care what you say, only how you say it.'

So with the utmost reluctance, Aristide began explaining the rules of piquet – in French. For perhaps half a minute, Vanessa appeared to be listening with rapt attention. Then she made a thoroughly indignant sound ... and howled.

Laughing, Adrian said, 'Well, that proves Rock's point fairly conclusively, Adeline. Only Papa will do.'

'That is *not* a comfort,' she complained. And as the noise escalated, 'Tracy, will you please take her back before she deafens poor Monsieur Delacroix?'

Good-humouredly, the duke retrieved his daughter, quieted her with no more than a soft, 'Shh now,' and then smiled invitingly at Genevieve. 'Your turn, I believe.'

Another step backwards, shaking her head. 'That's very kind, your Grace but I couldn't.'

'Why not? You want to, don't you?'

'I – yes. But --' And had to stop speaking when Rockliffe laid the child in her arms.

He said placidly, 'She enjoys a little intelligent conversation. And I find walking more effective than rocking. Take a brief turn in the garden with her, if you wish.' And when she continued to hesitate, 'Perhaps if I were to accompany you?'

Everyone's eyes were upon her; and a man – even a duke – who could calm a squalling infant couldn't be as intimidating as she'd first thought. Genevieve nodded and walked at his side down into the formal garden.

For a little while, Rockliffe didn't speak. He merely watched her smiling down at the baby, his own gaze thoughtful. Then he said, 'Don't forget about the conversation. And don't worry about feeling ridiculous. I never do.'

Genevieve turned towards him, her eyes filling with surprised laughter. Then, returning her attention to Vanessa Jane, she said seriously, 'Do you know how pretty you are? Yes. Of course you do because I expect your Papa tells you every day. You are a very lucky little girl, you know – just like a princess in a story. Well, you won't know that until you are old enough for your Mama to read you fairy-tales.' Vanessa was still quiet and Genevieve was vaguely aware that the duke had fallen a few paces behind. Lowering her voice still further, she went on. 'In those stories, the princess *always* marries a handsome prince and lives happily-ever-after. It's a rule. There's even *one* tale about a princess who kisses a frog and *he* turns into prince! What do you think of that?

But the trouble with stories is that ordinary little girls grow up waiting for their own fairy-tale to come true ... and no one warns them that in the *real* world, if frogs can turn into princes, princes can turn into toads.' Her voice trembled just a little. 'Now *your* Papa will recognise the toads right away and toss them back in the pond. But even so, you need to know that the happy-ever-after rule is only for beautiful story-book princesses – not the real-life ones.'

Casually closing the distance between them and settling his face, which had grown rather tight, into its usual enigmatic expression, Rockliffe said, 'Well done. You appear to have put her to sleep.'

'She was probably bored.'

He smiled faintly. 'Even so. I am guessing you want children?'

'Oh yes.' She nearly added *more than anything*; and then realised that what she actually wanted more than anything was that, before she and Aristide had children together, he would begin to love her ... just the tiniest bit. 'One day, I hope.'

'Even though you don't believe in happy endings.'

Genevieve flushed. 'You were listening?'

'Intently.' He waited and then, 'Well?'

'I ... used to. Once upon a time.'

'And now?'

She glanced across to where Aristide sat and turned back to the duke, smiling.

'I'm beginning to think that perhaps ... I may do so again.'

The silence on the terrace reached epic proportions until, watching the pair turn back, Caroline said admiringly, 'Genevieve certainly has a knack with children, doesn't she?'

And Aristide, who could guess what everyone was thinking, said, 'So it would seem. But just in case anyone is wondering ... allow me to point out that Genevieve and I did *not* marry because she is *enceinte*.'

* * *

Two days later, Lord Nicholas arrived. Having been admitted by Bertrand and directed to the library, Nicholas strolled in on Lord Sarre and said, 'I nearly wreck my carriage getting here and there's not a soul to welcome me except Bertrand – and he just waved me in here. Where *is* everyone?'

'Out enjoying themselves. Most of them have given you up for lost.' Adrian rose from behind his desk to offer his hand. 'What took you so long?'

'Being a good and virtuous landlord.' He dropped into an armchair and said, 'Adrian, my throat's full of dust and --' He stopped as a glass was put in his hand. 'Ah. Excellent.' He half-drained it in one swallow. 'The village tavern caught fire and the smithy next to it.'

'It must have been one hell of a fire if it's taken till now to put it out.'

'Don't be an idiot. The problem was that the inn is the only one for five miles and the village needs a smithy – so something had to be done.' Nicholas shrugged. 'It just took longer than expected.'

Adrian leaned against the desk. He said, 'What did you do?'

'I gave the inn-keeper and the smith a pair of empty cottages on the part of the estate nearest the village, so they can continue to trade. In the case of the tavern, that meant sending in carpenters and God knows what to make it suitable. And it took a county-wide search to replace tools the smith deemed damaged beyond repair – not to mention finding a way of transporting his bloody anvil.' Despite the laughter in his eyes, Nicholas managed to sound aggrieved. 'I've been working my fingers to the bone and consoling myself with the thought that my friends must be waiting with open arms ... and what do I find? I find my so-called friends are a shallow lot who are quite happy to enjoy themselves without me.'

'Look on the bright side,' grinned Adrian. 'At least we're still here. Another twenty-four hours and everybody would have been at Wynstanton Priors for Rock's race.'

'*What?* That's not until the end of the month.'

'It *is* the end of the month, Nick. The meeting is the day after tomorrow.'

Nicholas let his head drop back against the chair and cursed under his breath. Then, drawing a breath of resignation, he said, 'Ah well. It's not a complete disaster. I had my groom take Harfleur directly to the Priors, rather than bring him here and face another thirty miles. He should be there by now.'

'That was a good idea.'

'I have them sometimes. So ... where is everyone?'

'Amberley has taken his horse out for some exercise down on the bay; Caroline is meeting with some of the tenants about next week's children's party; and Rock, Philip, Sebastian and Aristide have taken all the other ladies to Sandwich for a stroll around the town and luncheon at the Old New Inn.' He glanced at the clock and went to pull the bell. 'They ought to be back in an hour or so – which gives you time to bathe and eat.'

'Good.' Nicholas finished his wine and stood up. 'I'm famished.'

'Remembering your last visit, Betsy will have assumed that,' came the dry response. And when the housekeeper arrived, 'Lord Nicholas has finally deigned to join us, Betsy. Take him away, will you?'

'Certainly, my lord.' And to Nicholas, 'I've had your baggage sent up and a bath is being prepared. You will also find a tray which should sustain your lordship until dinner.'

'You're a treasure, Betsy.' Nicholas slid an arm about her waist and planted a kiss on her cheek. 'Pack your bags and come and look after me instead.'

'It's Mrs Holt to you, young man.' The severe tone was belied by the twinkle in her eyes. 'And I've a feeling you would be more trouble than I get in this house. Now ... come with me, if you please.'

It was only after they'd left the room and he'd stopped laughing that Adrian recalled a couple of things he really ought to have warned Nicholas about. Then, with a shrug, thought, *Too late now. I'll take care of it later.*

* * *

The first person Nicholas encountered on stepping out of his room was Mr Audley who said, 'Well – finally. We thought you'd got lost.'

'Lost? Me? Never! I've been busy, that's all.'

'So I've heard.' Glancing about him to make sure they couldn't be overheard, Sebastian said, 'Adrian asked me to tell you something he meant to mention earlier. Were you aware that Aristide got married a couple of weeks ago?'

'*Married?* No. God – that happened damned fast, didn't it? Unless he's been courting some female for months and none of us knew about it. Was he?'

'No. It was fast and it was secret. In fact, until it was done, the only ones who knew about it were Cassie and me. But right now the point is that they're here together so --'

'I think I'd worked that out. So who is she?'

'Her name is Genevieve and she's the widow of a fellow named Westin who --'

'*Westin!*' snapped Nicholas. 'Are you joking?'

'No. I understand he was a particularly nasty piece of work but --'

'That's putting it mildly. He was the scum of the earth.'

'Yes. But that isn't Genevieve's fault and --'

'No – though the family she comes from isn't much better.'

'Nick, will you please stop interrupting and listen?' demanded Sebastian firmly. 'This is exactly why Adrian wanted you to know before you went downstairs. Whatever may think, she's Aristide's wife – and he's not the only one who won't thank you for snubbing her. Cassandra likes her and so does Caroline. So do I, for that matter. And you will, too, if you forget about Westin and Sherbourne and just accept her for who she is.'

'Sherbourne?' queried Nicholas, not really attending.

'The unpleasant gentleman who used to be Kilburn.'

The dark gaze sharpened. 'You've met him?'

'Once. I'll be perfectly happy not to further the acquaintance.'

There was a brief silence. Finally Nicholas said, 'You're right, of course. Nothing I know is the girl's fault. I'll be civil.'

'You'd have been that anyway but made it plain that's all it was. She's had a difficult time and it has left her thin-skinned. So the slightest hint of a rebuff and --'

'Yes, yes – I take your point. But what the hell was Aristide *thinking*? Does he love her?'

'This is Aristide we're talking about, Nick. How would anyone ever know? But for what it's worth, Cassandra is convinced that Genevieve's thoroughly smitten ... so, whether it's mutual or not, he must be doing *something* right.'

* * *

The rest of the company welcomed Lord Nicholas with a good many teasing remarks about both his heroics in Surrey and his eleventh-hour arrival. And before he had managed to do more than greet Caroline properly, he found himself being introduced to Madame Delacroix ... by, of all people, his own brother.

'You will doubtless have been as surprised as the rest of us by Aristide's happy news,' said Rockliffe, drawing Genevieve a little away from Aristide's side, 'but can doubtless see the reason for it. Madame Delacroix ... allow me to present my brother, Nicholas. You need pay him very little mind, my dear. No one else does.'

Nicholas saw the dazzling smile. He also saw the anxiety lurking in those remarkable amber eyes and thought helplessly, *God damn it. Do Adrian and Sebastian think I'm blind, stupid and go around kicking puppies?* But he grinned, bowed over her hand and said, 'A pleasure, Madame. And don't listen to Rock. He's just jealous of my superior looks and charm – always has been.' Then, into the ensuing ripple of laughter, 'My congratulations, Aristide. Rushed the lady to the altar before I got the chance to cut you out, did you?'

'That was naturally my worst fear,' agreed Aristide. And to Genevieve, 'In a moment, he may allow you to speak. Meanwhile, take every word with a large helping of salt.'

She laughed. 'But it was a lovely thing to say – and very kind.'

'Thank you, Madame. It's pleasant to be appreciated occasionally.' Then, to his brother, 'I sent Harfleur to the Priors, by the way. I take it that was all right?'

'Perfectly.' Rockliffe flicked open an emerald-studded box. 'But Harfleur? Really?'

'I knew you'd expect me to choose Pol de Léon ... which is why I didn't.'

'I suppose,' remarked Aristide, as the duke drifted away, 'your stables also contain an Agincourt and a Crécy?'

'They do, as it happens.' Not surprised that a Frenchman would grasp the fact he named his horses after English victories in the Hundred Years War, Nicholas was more interested in searching the room for one particular face. When he failed to find it, he said, 'Aristide? Where's Madeleine?'

'She isn't here.'

Nicholas's expression tightened and he was suddenly very still. 'Why not?'

'You know she never explains herself.' Keeping Genevieve's hand on his arm, Aristide drew his lordship to one side. 'You also know she has the stubbornness of a mule.'

'Yes. But she ... I thought we had an agreement. And there wasn't a single hint of this in her letter,' he said bitterly. 'She let me go on expecting to find her here.'

'I think she was in two minds right up to the last minute,' offered Genevieve. 'In fact, I think she may still be in two minds now.'

'Why do you say that? Has she confided in you?'

She hesitated but only for a moment.

'If she had, it would be wrong of me to break her confidence, wouldn't it?'

He groaned. 'Yes. I suppose so. Does she know she's driving me demented? Or no. I don't suppose you can tell me that either. Forgive me. I need a drink.'

Aristide watched him walk away and then looked down into his wife's eyes.

'*Did* Madeleine confide in you?'

'A little. But I can't tell you either,' she said unhappily. 'I'm sorry – but I promised.'

'Then let's try this. She's in love with him but is convinced it will all end in tears. She believes she's not good enough and that Rockliffe will not only think the same but also act on it; and she's decided that, if she's noble and sends Nicholas away, he'll get over it in a heartbeat.' He continued to hold her gaze. 'You needn't comment. Just tell me this. Given what you know of those involved, if Madeleine *were* to think all that, would she be right?'

'No. I don't believe so. But nothing would persuade her to come with us even though I was sure she wanted to. And … it is her decision, isn't it?'

'I imagine Nicholas feels entitled to some say in it,' remarked Aristide dryly. 'Unfortunately, he can't very well go riding *ventre à terre* to London before the race – though it wouldn't surprise me if he did so after it.'

'And carry Madeleine off over his saddle-bow like a hero in a story?'

'Not if he expects to come out of it with all his limbs intact.'

'You are being absurd again.'

'I am never in the least absurd.'

Genevieve hesitated and then said, 'So you won't laugh if I ask you something?'

'I can't promise. But it seems unlikely.'

'You said you needed Madeleine to help at the race-meeting. Since she isn't here, I wondered … well, I wondered if *I* might do instead.' She caught a flicker of something in his eyes and added rapidly, 'You'd have to tell me what to do, of course and I realise that might be tiresome. So if you'd rather find someone else, I won't mind. It was only an idea.'

'And a very generous offer,' said Aristide. 'I was merely surprised. Wouldn't you enjoy it all very much better with the other ladies, sipping champagne and cheering on the gentleman of your choice, rather than sitting beside me getting ink on your fingers?'

'No. Not at all. I'd much rather be with you! Helping, I mean.'

The suspicion that it wasn't what she meant at all and that she'd mind very much indeed if he refused, caused something to turn over in his chest. But keeping a guard on both face and voice, he said, 'Then thank you. I accept. But if it isn't as much fun as think or you grow bored, you must tell me and --'

'I won't be bored, I promise.' She glowed with pleasure. 'What will I be doing?'

'I'll explain properly tomorrow. But in essence, while I am recording wagers in the book, you will write tickets for those making them. It isn't at all exciting, I'm afraid.'

'That is just *your* opinion,' she announced. 'I'll let you know *mine* afterwards.'

The nose-in-the-air tone was so unlike her that Aristide couldn't help laughing. He said humbly, 'Yes, ma'am. I'll look forward to hearing it.'

* * *

Nicholas spent what ought to have been a pleasant evening but wasn't. He had eaten an excellent dinner in congenial company; he'd played a hand of cards with Lord Amberley and chatted with Adrian and Sebastian over a bottle of extremely good port. And all the time something inside him had been threatening to boil over.

He'd never felt like this about a woman before. There had been mistresses, though not many – and light-hearted flirtations with girls of his own class. But none of it had *meant* anything. This ... this all-consuming passion for Madeleine Delacroix was something else. He didn't understand it and he *certainly* didn't know how to deal with it, though he was determined to do so. But why, in the name of God, did he have to feel this way about the most difficult, stubborn female in all creation?

He realised that he was furious with her. In Richmond Park, he'd all but declared himself and shown her that there was something powerful between them. And she'd promised, hadn't she? She'd promised to use the time of his absence to consider what he'd said to her. And this was her answer? Ducking the issue so she could say no *without* saying no? Well, if that *was* her answer – and this would be the very last chance she'd ever get to turn him away – she could damned well do him the courtesy of saying it to his face.

Staring grimly into the dark outside his bedchamber window, he tried to think. What he wanted to do was go down to the stables, saddle one of Adrian's horses, then ride, hell for leather to London and shake some sense into her. But he couldn't ... and probably shouldn't. Aside from the fact that careering through the dark on horseback was as good a way as any of breaking one's neck, he owed his brother a little more loyalty than to leave before the thrice-blasted race. And, in any case, he'd better not come face to face with Madeleine before his temper had cooled.

Temper. Something else he wasn't familiar with. But he could feel it well enough now, clawing away at his insides as it struggled to get out. He leaned his forearm against the window embrasure and dropped his brow against it. Sleep wasn't going to come ... and going downstairs to get drunk was out of the question if he didn't want to be driving thirty miles tomorrow with a hangover. So all that was left was to make a plan; and that wasn't going to take long, since there was really only one thing to be done if he didn't want to end up a gibbering idiot.

CHAPTER FOURTEEN

'Unless things change, there is to be only one race,' said Aristide. 'All wagers are recorded in the ledger and to avoid later confusion, you write a ticket for each bet. Money does not change hands until afterwards, when the losers pay up and the winners collect, according to my calculations based on the ledger.'

Genevieve faced him across the carriage, her face alight with anticipation.

'Tell me properly about the tickets and what must be on them.'

'In general, you'll write one ticket for each bet. Many of them will be Lord A wagering against Lord B that Horse C will beat Horse D. So you write down the names of the gentlemen, the names of the horses, the amounts of money involved and where they're saying the horse will finish. Most wagers are usually on first place but when the winner is considered a certainty, some gentlemen choose to bet on what will come in second. If the same person is making several bets, they can all be written on the same ticket.' A small smile emerged. 'Don't worry. I'll be there, should you get in difficulties.'

'I'm not worried. I'm looking forward to it.' What she was principally looking forward to was a whole afternoon at her husband's side ... but she was also determined to do her job efficiently so that he would be pleased with her. 'You keep saying 'he'. It's a private meeting on the duke's estate, so do the ladies not wager?'

'I imagine most of them will – though they'll send gentlemen to place their bets.'

She nodded. 'And will we see anything of the race?'

'I won't know that until later today. His Grace has a purpose-built track and various temporary pavilions will have been erected around it; places for the ladies to sit in comfort, others where refreshments may be served ... and somewhere for you and I to work.'

'And who --?'

'Stop.' He held up one hand and the smile grew. 'All your other questions – of which, I am sure there are many – can wait. I've some of my own, if you don't mind.'

'You do?' Genevieve looked surprised. 'I mean – no, of course I don't mind.'

Aristide rather thought she might when she heard what he was going to say. In truth, what he *really* wanted to know was what she'd been saying to Rockliffe's baby daughter that had brought such an odd expression to the duke's face; but since he couldn't think of an adequate reason for asking, the question felt awkward and intrusive ... so he substituted another which, though equally difficult, at least had a point.

'I would like you to tell me about your marriage to Westin. Just ordinary things,' he added quickly, seeing the brightness drain from her face, 'such as where you lived for most of the year and whether he remained there with you. Nothing you'd rather not talk about.'

'I'd rather not talk about him at all,' she replied, staring out of the window. 'But if you must know, we scarcely lived together after the first year. Once his father had died, I was confined permanently to the estate in Shropshire, while Kit spent virtually all of his time in London. He rarely visited more than five times a year and never stayed longer than a fortnight – usually less. But that was a blessing, since he couldn't *look* at me without saying how repulsively f-fat I was.'

'I see.' Aristide took a moment to swallow his anger. Try as he would, he still couldn't fathom what motivated men like Westin but was inclined to wonder if a lack of confidence in their own masculinity had something to do with it. 'Did you like Shropshire?'

'No. I hated it. Kit ignored all the neighbouring families, so they ignored us. Nobody called or invited me to call on them. The only faces I ever saw were those of the servants or tenants. And the tenants – few of whom had a roof that didn't leak or windows that weren't rotten – expected me to help them and didn't understand why I couldn't.'

'There wasn't any money?'

'Not for the estate or anything that ought to have mattered. But there was plenty for horses and gaming and – and other amusements.'

Aristide hardly dared ask, rather suspecting he knew the answer. 'And you?'

'I was allowed a new gown when he was bringing friends for the shooting and didn't want them to think his wife shabby,' she said bitterly. Then, looking him in the eye, 'Perhaps that helps you understand why I – why I thought the allowance *you* make me had to be a mistake. Kit wasn't like you, Aristide ... and I don't mean just in the b-bedroom. He was rude, mean-spirited and – and vicious. I despised him.' Abruptly, she turned back to the window. 'And now can we please stop talking about him? It makes me feel sick.'

'I'm sorry. I didn't ask out of a desire to pry or to upset you.'

'I know that. You asked because you think he's still in my head.'

'And is he?' Aristide asked gently.

'Rarely. You are banishing him quite effectively.'

Although her words startled him, they also brought an unexpected surge of warmth. He said, 'Thank you. I'd be pleased to think so.'

Genevieve merely nodded and changed the subject. 'How much further is it?'

'Nearly another hour, I should think.'

'As much as that? But the two estates are both in Kent, aren't they?'

'Kent is a very large county and Sarre Park is at one of its extremities.' He contemplated her profile. 'Would you like to stop for a little while?'

This time he got a smile. '*Could* we?'

'Of course, if you wish.' He opened the grille and shouted an order for Higgins to pull up at the next inn. 'Another half hour won't matter. And with the cavalcade both in front of and behind us, the local villagers must think it is a royal progress.'

The Rose was a small, modest place with a comfortable parlour and a merry-eyed landlady. She brought tea, ale and slices of cake so large they made Genevieve giggle and insist that Aristide ate some because *she* certainly couldn't and the landlady would be offended if neither of them did. Aristide did his best but told her that if they had to stop again for him to be ill, it would be entirely her fault. They were just about to get back into the carriage when the boy who had helped Higgins water the horses ran over to them clutching something to his chest.

'Wait, m'lady!' he called, rushing across the yard. 'Won't take but a minute.'

Genevieve hesitated. When it was too late, Aristide was to realise that sometimes two seconds was all it took. These, as he was about to discover, were those seconds. In the space of them, he saw his wife holding a small bundle of largely white fur ... and fall instantly in love with it. He groaned inwardly.

'Oh!' said Genevieve with delight, as the small creature wriggled in her hands and tried to find a finger to bite. 'Oh Aristide – look!'

'Charming,' he said, taking the puppy from her and handing it back to its owner. 'But we need to drive on.'

'Please, m'lady!' The boy promptly passed the animal back to Genevieve who cuddled it close and let it lick her chin. 'Will you take her? Please? She's the last. I got places for all t'others but nobody wants a bitch and Father says if she don't go today, he'll drown her and there ain't nobody else to ask. Please! She won't be no trouble – honest.'

Big, amber eyes pleaded with Aristide for a mere instant before the lashes veiled them and she said quietly, 'No. Of course not. We can't arrive at Wynstanton Priors with a dog.'

'No, we can't.' But even as he said the words, there was an unpleasant sinking sensation inside him and all he could think was, *She hasn't asked. And no matter how badly she wants to, she won't. She only ever asked for one thing; marriage. And since then, she's neither asked for nor expected anything. Not once. She's even reluctant to spend that damned allowance. And now this. I could promise to buy her a dog when we get home – but that won't help. Because though she'll never say a word about it, from the moment we leave here, she'll be imagining that scrap of fur being drowned in a bucket. Merde.*

He looked at the boy. 'Is your Father here?' And receiving a nod, 'Fetch him.'

Genevieve looked at him with the tiniest flicker of hope but said nothing.

A moment later, the boy's father trod across the yard, clutching his hat.

'If the lad's been bothering you, m'lord --'

'He hasn't.' Aristide produced two guineas and held them up. 'Will this be sufficient for you to keep the dog, fed and well-treated for two more days?'

The man gaped at him. 'Aye, m'lord!'

'Then do so.' The coins changed hands. 'We will be travelling back this way the day after tomorrow and will collect it then.' Taking the puppy from Genevieve and handing it back to the boy, he added, 'And bathe it. My wife wants the dog – not its infestation of fleas.'

Finding herself back in the carriage without any recollection of getting there, Genevieve hauled in a long breath and said uncertainly, 'I may keep her?'

'Yes.' He kept his tone curt, willing her not to cry. 'You wanted her, didn't you?'

She nodded, unshed tears turning her smile into sunshine through rain. 'I haven't had a dog of my own since Paris and I – I've missed it. Thank you. That was so kind and you needn't have done it and – oh, *thank* you.'

Had it not been for their previous conversation, Aristide might have said, *It's two guineas-worth of mongrel pup, Genevieve. Do you think you might try not to be so damned grateful all the time?*

As it was, he found himself wondering whether her gratitude for every tiny kindness was painful because it told him how long she'd existed without any kindness at all ... or because it made him uncomfortably aware that he gave her nothing except that which gave him something in return.

Still unsure what the answer was, he said stiffly, 'You don't need to thank me. But in future, if there is something you want, don't be afraid to ask.' And with a dry smile, 'I doubt you will ever be particularly demanding. And there is pleasure in giving as well as receiving.'

* * *

The day of the race-meeting dawned bright, sunny and with the promise of heat. The duke's servants spent the morning running hither and thither making the final preparations, a universal air of excitement among them because his Grace had given the entire household permission to watch the race themselves. Below stairs, Mr Symonds, the butler was also running a betting book so that everyone from himself down to the scullery-maid could wager a few precious pennies of their own.

Isabel and Rosalind had shown surprise upon learning that Madame Delacroix would be assisting her husband. Cassie and Caroline had merely exchanged knowing smiles.

After agonies of indecision, Genevieve chose a gown of primrose flowered silk, trimmed in all the right places with a double row of embroidered daisies. Having asked Susan to dress her hair simply, she put on a wide-brimmed straw hat decked with yellow roses ... and tried not to let her excitement show too much.

She found Aristide in the hall with Rockliffe, while outside on the steps a group of gentlemen, all dressed for riding, argued good-naturedly with each other. The duke also wore riding apparel; snowy-white linen, an exquisitely-fitting black coat and gleaming boots. Aristide, by contrast, wore a well-cut coat of gun-metal brocade, against which his hair gleamed even brighter than usual. Genevieve drank in the sight of him. There were at least four exceptionally handsome men present; Rockliffe, Lord Nicholas, the Marquis of Amberley and Mr Audley. She saw none of them.

'Twice round the course gives a distance of precisely eight furlongs,' the duke was saying. 'But with twelve competitors, I am inclined to run two heats of six apiece, followed by a decider. I apologise for the additional work ... but I prefer to avoid accidents.'

'It is of no consequence,' shrugged Aristide. And, holding out a hand to Genevieve to indicate that she should join them, 'I have an excellent assistant.'

'And charming company,' murmured Rockliffe with a glinting smile. 'But since she will be working all afternoon, why don't you take her to see the track and fortify her with a glass of champagne? Also, don't forget to engage her for the first dance this evening – otherwise, from what I saw last night, I fear Mr Overbury may cut you out.' He bowed slightly. 'And now, pray excuse me. I see Nicholas waiting for a word.'

Nicholas, under-slept and tense, looked his brother in the eye and said baldly, 'I'm sorry, Rock – but I'll need to leave after the race.'

'I thought you might,' agreed the duke imperturbably. 'But not *directly* after the race, Nicholas – since a few more hours will make no difference whatsoever.'

Having long-since given up being surprised by Rockliffe's omniscience, Nicholas said, 'You know where I'm going? And why?'

'I have a shrewd suspicion.'

'And that's all you have to say about it?'

'Why? Did you expect something more? Disapproval, perhaps?'

Nicholas dragged a hand over his face and tried, with his usual lack of success, to read his brother's expression. '*Do* you disapprove?'

'Would it make any difference if I did?'

'No.'

'I did not think so.'

'Oh for God's sake, Rock – if you've anything at *all* to say, spit it out.'

The duke sighed. 'Very well. If you insist. I am not averse to the lady for any of the reasons you – or she – may think. I am even prepared to give her credit for not grabbing an extremely eligible gentleman with both hands. I do not, however, care to see you dancing quite so readily to a tune that may or may not stop at the altar – if that *is* where you're hoping to lead her. No, please don't say anything. I know you disagree so let us leave it at that. Walk with me to the stables. I need your help to resolve a small dilemma.'

'What?' Shoving his hands in his pockets, Nicholas fell into step.

'As you're aware, I'm riding The Trojan in the second heat – which I have hopes that he will win, thus earning a place in the final. However, although I am more than happy for my horse to win outright, I would prefer not to be in the saddle should he do so on *this* occasion. Winning one's own race is just a trifle tactless, don't you think?'

'You're saying,' said Nicholas slowly, the bleakness gradually fading from his eyes, 'that if The Trojan makes it into the final, you want *me* to ride him?'

'That is what I was attempting to suggest, yes.'

'And win?'

'I would certainly hope so.'

Nicholas opened his mouth, shut it again and then said, 'But what if Harfleur gets to the decider as well?'

'Against Fleetwood's chestnut and that massive brute of Sebastian's? He won't.' The duke slanted a brief glance at his brother. 'I thought you wanted to ride The Trojan?'

'I do. God knows, I've asked you often enough.'

'And now I am giving you the chance. Of course, if I lose the heat --'

'You'd better not,' cut in Nicholas with a sudden grin. 'Dangling a carrot like that only to take it away? You'd damned well better not!'

* * *

In the hour before the race was due to start, the area around the track gradually filled up with the duke's guests. Parasols twirled and ribbons drifted in the breeze. Ladies in bright silks strolled around arm in arm before finding places in the shade of the pavilion; and gentlemen studying the list of runners and riders chalked up on a large board argued amicably with each other.

Bright-eyed with excitement, Genevieve sat beside Aristide beneath a gaily-striped awning and sharpened her quill in readiness.

Acutely conscious of both her elusive scent and the pretty picture she made beneath that flower-trimmed hat, Aristide strove to concentrate on the task in hand whilst wondering how he'd ever imagined that life after marriage would go on much the same as life before it. His awareness of his wife increased with every passing day and not merely when she was within touching distance. He'd developed a habit of watching her across a room and thinking about her when she wasn't there. Inevitably, although he puzzled over *how* this was happening, he avoided the more alarming question of *why* it was. Whatever the reason, it was disconcerting.

With an effort, he dragged his attention back to the forthcoming race.

Rockliffe riding The Trojan; Lord Sarre, Argan; Mr Audley, Anubis; Lord Nicholas, Harfleur; Lord Amberley, Zephyrus; Philip Vernon, Dark Star; six names he knew and a further six he didn't.

Sebastian, Nicholas and Philip to ride in the first heat; Amberley, Adrian and Rockliffe, in the second.

Interesting, thought Aristide, trying not to notice the admiring looks being cast at his wife by the half dozen young gentlemen who were supposedly debating where to put their money. Recalling the duke's parting shot, he turned to her and said, 'If you haven't already promised the first dance elsewhere ... may I claim it?'

Her smile was so radiant it scorched him and from several feet away he heard a number of indrawn breaths.

'Yes, please. I haven't danced in – oh, such a long time. I just hope I remember the steps and don't tread on your feet.'

'If you do, the fault will most probably be mine,' he said, making an attempt at gallantry. Then, 'Ready? Here come our first customers.'

And after that, there was scarcely any time to talk at all.

It swiftly became plain that, amongst the gentlemen, there were three strong favourites. The Trojan, Anubis and Lord Fleetwood's horse, Warrior. Less interested in the horses than their handsome riders, ladies were divided between Lord Amberley, Lord Nicholas and Mr Audley. Adeline, Caroline, Cassie, Rosalind and Isabel, of course, all sent instructions via Nicholas to place a fifty guinea wager on their own husbands. And Mr Overbury made four separate bets of twenty-five guineas apiece for reasons which gnawed at the edges of Aristide's temper.

By the time all those wishing to bet had done so, there were bare minutes to spare before the first race. Seeing Genevieve waving back to Cassie, Aristide said, 'You can join her, if you wish. There will be nothing more to do here until after the second heat.'

'Thank you – but I'd rather stay,' she began. And then, lowering her voice, 'Oh dear. Here comes Mr Overbury again. What does he want *now*?'

Another chance to peer down your neckline, thought Aristide irritably. And giving the youthful gentleman a hard, level stare said, 'No further bets at this time, sir.'

'Oh – but surely --'

'I'm afraid not. Perhaps you might enjoy the *race* instead.'

Mr Overbury flushed and took the hint.

'Good,' said Aristide. And to his wife, 'Now ... who would *you* like to wager on?'

Her brows rose. 'Is that allowed?'

'For you, it is. So who shall it be? Sebastian?'

'No. Half the ladies here have put money on Mr Audley. I think ... Lord Nicholas.'

'Write the ticket, then. G. Delacroix wagers A. Delacroix fifty guineas --'

'No. That's far too much! Ten.'

'Forty.'

She shook her head, busy writing their names. 'Twenty.'

'Thirty.'

'Oh – very well. Thirty. If I lose, I'll pay you out of my extravagant allowance.'

'If you lose,' he murmured in the low, seductive voice she'd previously only ever heard in the bedroom, 'I'd be willing to accept payment in kind. What do you think?'

Lord Fleetwood won the first heat by a nose, with Mr Audley – much to the delight of the ladies – coming in a close second. And Rockliffe took the next, a length ahead of Lord Sarre. Since all of these would run in the decider, there was a further round of wagering and more amiable wrangling in the refreshment tent which intensified when the duke let it be known that he was giving his brother the opportunity to bring The Trojan home.

'Is that in the rules?' Philip Vernon asked.

'Why not?' retorted Fleetwood, laughing. 'Certainly, *I* see no reason to argue.'

'Do you think Nicholas can't do it?' enquired Rockliffe lazily.

'I'm not saying he *can't* – just that I'd have a harder time beating you.'

'Ah.' His Grace leaned back in his chair and looked around him. 'Five hundred guineas on The Trojan to win, followed by Warrior. Anyone?'

'Yes,' said Lord Amberley promptly. 'Fleetwood to win, followed by Audley.'

As the two men shook hands, Amberley said quietly, 'Has Nick ever ridden the Trojan?'

'No.' Rockliffe smiled. 'You are thinking your money is safe?'

'Partly. Mostly I was hoping your sacrifice proves worth it.'

In the betting tent, Genevieve gasped, 'Five hundred guineas? *Seriously*?'

'It isn't so unusual. At Sinclairs, gentlemen have been known to wager as much on the turn of a card.' Seeing Mr Overbury approaching, Aristide took a moment to send the gentleman a look which told him to think again. Wisely, Mr Overbury did so. Satisfied, Aristide leaned a little closer to his wife. 'Just to be clear, Nicholas riding now is not covered by your earlier bet. You are still in debt ... and I've some interesting ideas about how you may redeem it.'

She swallowed and said weakly, 'You have? Oh. That is ... well. Good.'

With the last wagers placed, everyone gathered about the track for the final event of the day. Lord Fleetwood looked supremely relaxed; Adrian and Sebastian exchanged a joke of some sort; and Nicholas stared between The Trojan's ears thinking, *I can do this. I can. And if I let Rock down, it won't be for the want of trying.*

Then the handkerchief came down and they were off.

Four horses went thundering along the track to a roar of encouragement from the crowd. Bent low over the horse's neck, Nicholas focussed on the way ahead but was still aware that Sebastian was keeping pace to his right and Fleetwood a fraction ahead to his left. Eating up the ground in long easy strides,

Nicholas could have sworn The Trojan was enjoying himself ... which would account for Rock's only piece of advice.

'Give him his head. He has the speed and the stamina ... and he likes to win. Let him.'

On the first turn, Sebastian nudged Anubis into the lead and Warrior dropped back slightly. Out of the tail of his eye, Nicholas saw Adrian's grey making up ground on the inside. Then they were flying down the straight again and back past the excited spectators, to begin the second and final lap. The air rushed by, taking the ribbon from his hair with it. Utterly without warning, Nicholas found himself laughing with sheer exhilaration.

Although there was little distance between any of the four horses, the turn altered the placing again. Warrior forged ahead, neck and neck with Anubis, leaving Nicholas leading Adrian by half a length.

'Go on!' he yelled to The Trojan. 'Go on – you can do it. Give 'em your dust!'

The great black knew what he was doing. He waited until they were within a couple of furlongs of the finishing post and then – how and from where, Nicholas couldn't imagine – somehow produced an extra burst of speed. They drew level with Fleetwood and Sebastian ... then forged ahead by a nose. Yelling encouragement, Nicholas let The Trojan fly. And fly he did.

The storm of applause as Nicholas and The Trojan passed the post was deafening. They had beaten Lord Fleetwood by less than a head, with Adrian and Sebastian choosing to come in neck and neck behind. Bringing the steaming horse to a standstill, Nicholas dropped from the saddle and leaned his brow against a black neck, slick with sweat. He said unevenly, 'We did it. I can't believe we actually *did* it.'

The Trojan butted against him, blew a long huff and rolled a seemingly sardonic eye.

'Right,' agreed Nicholas. '*You* did it. You think I don't know that?'

Then Rockliffe's grooms rushed up and Nicholas was surrounded with congratulations. Somehow, past the handshakes and back-slapping, he found his brother's eyes.

Thank you, his own said. *Thank you for that.*

And with no more than a very faint smile and a nod, Rockliffe turned away, leaving him to savour his triumph.

* * *

Everyone enjoyed the ball that evening, none more so than Genevieve. Although she danced every dance, her greatest pleasure of the evening was the gavotte she trod with her husband – who, she discovered, moved with a grace few other gentlemen could match. Or perhaps that was her imagination. Love, she was finding, blurred one's perceptions.

As usual, Nicholas didn't dance at all. Although he re-lived the race with various friends, he drank little and played no more than a couple of hands of cards. Later, finding Monsieur Delacroix alone on the edge of the floor watching his wife's progress through a minuet with Mr Audley, he said baldly, 'I'm leaving for London in the morning.'

Aristide was no more surprised by these tidings than Rockliffe had been. He merely sighed, shrugged and said wryly, 'Good luck with that. You'll need it.'

CHAPTER FIFTEEN

In Dorset, the funeral of the late Earl of Sherbourne took place with dignity and without any untoward incident. The contents of the will, however, left the new earl fuming in icy frustration. Grandfather's extensive personal fortune had been handed out piecemeal to even the most distant relatives, to servants and to charitable causes. The only two exclusions were Cedric and Bertram, described in the document as *'a pair of pimples on the arse of humanity'*; while Genevieve, *'of whom the only harm I know was her execrable choice of husband'* received a bequest of ten thousand pounds. As for Ralph himself, he inherited only those things which could not be denied him. The title; the entailed property; and Gardington, along with its contents – of which he couldn't sell so much as a candlestick.

His mood was not improved by the letter he received two days later from Mr Henry Lessing of Chancery Lane. Acting under instructions from Monsieur Delacroix, Mr Lessing asked to be supplied with a detailed accounting and explanation of Madame Delacroix's financial status in respect of the late Lord Westin. The current Lord Westin, said Mr Lessing, was at present reluctant to share information regarding provision made for his cousin's widow. He had, however, provided the figures laid down in the original marriage settlements ... figures which were wholly incompatible with the sums actually received by Lady Westin. Mr Lessing looked forward to Lord Sherbourne clarifying the matter.

Lord Sherbourne handed the letter to his brother.

'This,' he said, in a tone of dangerous softness, 'is your mess. Clean it up.'

Cedric turned pasty white and said, 'I can't. You know I can't. The money's gone.'

'Yes. Thanks to your ineptitude, it is. But you will account for your mistakes. You will list every bad investment; how much, in what and when it failed. You will then sign it and give it to me by the end of today so that I may deliver it to Delacroix's man-of-law when I return to London tomorrow. Is that understood?'

'Yes. But I can't remember *everything*, for God's sake. I --'

'Then you will admit that as well and make your apologies. If you are very lucky, Grandfather's bequest may spare us any further unpleasantness. There is nothing to be done about Genevieve's unfortunate marriage but I refuse to be called to account by a French tradesman.'

'It might not be *such* a disaster,' remarked Bertram. 'He's not short of money. And Ceddie and I were saying only yesterday that membership of his club would --'

'Are you both *entirely* stupid? Aristide Delacroix will not line your pockets. And if you apply for membership of Sinclairs, he will have immense pleasure in refusing you,' said Ralph cuttingly. 'As for you, Bertram, I will repeat my earlier embargo. You will stop selling yourself to elderly women for the price of a coat or a few guineas to squander at the tables. Like Cedric, you will remain here until further notice, doing nothing to antagonise our neighbours. One breath of scandal about either of you and your allowances will be cut off with immediate and permanent effect. I trust I make myself clear?'

* * *

Having no intention of dealing with Delacroix's underlings if he could avoid it, Sherbourne sent a footman to deliver Cedric's confession along with a note of his own to Henry Lessing. Then he set off for Duke Street. Delacroix might have had the unspeakable insolence to tell him he would not be admitted but Ralph had yet to meet the butler he could not make cower with a single look.

Minton neither cowered nor raised his voice. He merely stood his ground and denied the Earl of Sherbourne entry. And since his lordship's numerous faults included neither a lack of intelligence nor a tendency to bluster, he took his rejection with apparent nonchalance and strode round to Sinclairs, inwardly seething.

Mr Edward Hastings was no more helpful than the damned butler had been. He said, 'I'm so sorry, my lord, but Monsieur Delacroix is from town just at present. However, if you will be good enough to leave your card, I will --'

'When is he expected back?'

'Not for some days, though I can't precisely predict --'

'I see.' The earl tossed his card down on the desk. 'In that case, you may inform him that I will expect him to call in Curzon Street immediately upon his return. Good day.'

Edward bowed politely ... and kept the smile off his face until his visitor was safely on the other side of the door.

*** * * ***

In The Bell on Ludgate Hill and not troubling to be polite about it, Cross gave Sir George Braxton an ultimatum.

'Make up your mind or go back to your coal-mines. You've shilly-shallied long enough and I got better uses for my time. I've told you what the choices are. I can send cracksmen to either the club or the ken on Duke Street – though there's no saying how much blunt is kept in either. And since both of 'em are crawling with staff and near as secure as the bleeding Tower, both'd need a small army. Or we can do what I suggested a fortnight since. Delacroix and his bride ain't in town but the sister is and I reckon she'd be an easy snatch.'

'Maybe so ... but *then* what? You say Delacroix's gone away so --'

'That fellow Hastings knows where he is.'

'And if the woman gets hurt --'

'No reason she should. We just tuck her away where nobody's likely to trip over her while we wait for her brother to pay up.' Cross stood up. 'I'll take care of the details. All you have to do is give me the nod and decide how much you want to bleed him for.'

Sir George shook his head. 'I'll think about it.'

'Do that. You got until tomorrow. After that, I walk.'

*** * * ***

Madeleine marked the eighth day of the house-party – the day on which everyone would be gathered at Wynstanton Priors for the race-meeting – with an orgy of shopping which proved marginally distracting while she was doing it but later had her returning nearly everything to the shops.

She had heard nothing from Aristide. In truth, she didn't know why she had thought she might. His silence sent a clear enough message. But she'd thought Genevieve might write; just a brief note, perhaps ... including a word or two about Lord Nicholas's reaction to her own absence which might tell her what to expect if and when she saw him again.

Hindsight suggested that perhaps she had been less than wise in choosing not to go to Kent. Nicholas might eventually accept that they had no future together; what he was less likely to tolerate was her failure to look him in the eye when she told him so.

The dark cloud of misery and the aching emptiness seemed to get worse rather than better. Madeleine knew she had to find some sense of balance; some way of meeting those dark Wynstanton eyes without crumbling. If she didn't, she had the alarming feeling that she was going to humiliate herself beyond bearing.

* * *

Nicholas's journey to London took a lot longer than he had anticipated. Getting away from Wynstanton Priors was the first obstacle followed, a few miles the other side of Sittingbourne, by a lengthy delay when one of his horses cast a shoe. It took an hour to find the smith who had taken his wife to visit her mother in a village four miles away and then far longer than it should have done to get the horse re-shod because the smith's apprentice hadn't kept the furnace up to a workable heat. By the time he was back on the road again with his valet grumbling spasmodically beside him, Nicholas's temper was beginning to fray.

He finally drew up outside his lodgings at around five in the afternoon ... crumpled, dusty and generally out of sorts because he had wanted to go directly to Duke Street in order to confront Madeleine but was in no fit state to do so.

'Your lordship will require a bath and a change of raiment,' observed Brennon.

'My lordship is thoroughly aware of that,' snapped Nicholas. Brennon tested his patience at the best of times and today he'd been a particular trial. 'Just stop talking and see to it, will you?'

This earned him a frigid bow. 'Will your lordship be requiring dinner?'

'No. I'll dine out.' And under his breath, 'If, that is, I ever get through the door.'

Bathing restored his equilibrium to some degree and gave him time to think carefully about what he intended to say to Madeleine – and how he planned to stop her interrupting long enough for him to say it. By the time he left his rooms, hair freshly washed and neatly tied and clad in a new coat of a purple brocade so dark it was nearly black, he had also come to several other conclusions. Although it was still early evening, there was a good chance she was already at Sinclairs and that was no place to hold the conversation he had in mind. Consequently, since his stomach was demanding food, he headed for Whites.

A solitary meal and a single glass of wine later, he strode round to Duke Street where, as he expected, Minton informed him that Mademoiselle was at the club.

Good, thought Nicholas, grimly. *I'll kill an hour at the Hazard table until she's ready to leave and then escort her home. That way she won't be able to avoid me.*

The first person he saw on the club's main gaming-floor was Edward Hastings. Nicholas had heard all about the secret double-wedding from Sebastian Audley – who had made it sound like a Drury Lane farce. Now, since Nicholas vaguely remembered Edward from years ago at Eton, he strolled across to offer his hand, saying, 'I believe congratulations are in order – not least, because Lord Leighton hasn't had you transported.'

'I believe Hetty's mama talked him out of it.' Edward accepted the proffered hand and grinned. 'A pleasure to see you, my lord. It's been a while.'

'Years – and it's Nick to you.'

'Nick, then. I thought you'd still be in Kent with the rest of them.'

'I was until this morning. But I left after yesterday's race-meeting.'

'Ah. I'd like to have seen that. Who won?'

'As a matter of fact,' replied Nicholas, unable to repress a note of pride, 'I did.'

'Did you? Well done! That's impressive – since I daresay the competition was stiff.'

'It was – but I can't take all the credit. I was riding Rock's best horse.' He paused. 'Aristide seems happy. Certainly, the bride was a surprise. Not what I expected at all.'

'Better or worse?'

'Better. A definite improvement on the rest of her family.'

Edward nodded. 'I met the eldest brother yesterday. An unpleasant fellow, isn't he?'

'The other two are worse – trust me.' Nicholas hesitated again. Then, he said, 'Edward, do me a favour, will you? Madeleine and I need to have a conversation but she'll try to avoid it. If I wait to escort her home, can you let me know when she's ready to leave ... preferably without alerting her to the fact that I'm here?'

Edward blinked. 'I *can* ... but the way her temper has been recently, I'm not at all sure I should. In fact, unless what you have to say to her is vital --'

'It is,' cut in Nicholas. 'And long overdue.'

'Oh. Well, in that case, I'll have somebody give you the nod when she leaves the office.'

'I'm obliged to you.' He glanced around. 'Is it always as quiet as this?'

'Just the last week or two. Aristide says it's normal for the time of year.'

'But you're doubtless still turning the odd coin.'

'One or two,' came the cheerful reply. Then, 'Forgive me – duty calls. If you've a fancy for a hand of cards, Lord March is in the smaller salon. He came back to town to escape his mother, he says.'

Nicholas grinned and waved him away. The vagaries of Hazard – all luck and no judgement – would do well enough for tonight.

The clock was just chiming eleven when one of the footmen murmured that Mademoiselle was on her way downstairs. Nodding his thanks, Nicholas shoved his meagre winnings over to the dealer by way of a gratuity and strolled out into the street. Five minutes later, Madeleine stood framed in the doorway and was saying crossly to someone over her shoulder, 'If Dick isn't here in precisely two minutes, he can give me his excuses tomorrow.'

'No need for that,' remarked Nicholas, emerging into the light of the lamp and flicking a coin to the door-keeper. 'I am your escort for this evening.'

Madeleine froze as shock, delight and a wild desire to throw herself on his chest nearly overcame her. Finally, swallowing hard, she said, 'What are you doing here? You are supposed to be in Kent.'

'So are you. I came to find out why you are not.'

Somewhat regretfully, since this sounded as though it might be an interesting conversation, the doorman shut them out and shot the bolt. Grateful for the increased shadow, Madeleine said, 'I had work to do so I chose not to go. I'm sure Aristide told you that.'

'I have seen how much work there is for you here – the answer being virtually none. And what Aristide may or may not have said is wholly immaterial, don't you think?'

'Not at all. Just because the club isn't as busy as usual doesn't mean --'

'Stop. Just stop. You and I had an agreement. I want to know why you broke it.'

'One can't break a promise one hasn't made.' She tried to step past him but found his arm blocking her way. 'And I did *not* promise to go to Kent.'

'Not in so many words. But you *did* promise to give serious consideration to the things I said to you at Richmond. And from where I stand, declining Adrian's invitation looks very much like cowardice.' Nicholas felt the hurt anger creeping up on him again and concentrated on keeping it out of his voice. 'If you've something to say to me – say it. Don't hide behind a mouthful of excuses. I thought you had more backbone.'

That stung every bit as much as he'd probably meant it to. Words of self-justification welled up in her mind. *How much backbone do you think it took* not *to go to Kent? Or how much I need right now to stop myself admitting that I love you almost beyond reason?*

But she swallowed them, shoved his arm aside and moved past him.

'I will not have this conversation here. In fact --'

'Well, *that* I agree with.'

'—I see no need to have it all.'

'But I do. And I really don't give a tinker's damn whether you want to or not. We are going to clear the air once and for all, you and I. So between here and Duke Street, I suggest you think very carefully about what you want to say. Because if you lie to me or say something you don't actually mean, we are both going to have to live with it afterwards.'

There was something in his voice that caused a painful constriction in her throat so she didn't attempt to reply. She merely fell into step and walked, without touching, at his side along Ryder Street – quiet at this time of night before gentlemen started leaving their clubs. At the junction with Bury Street,

Madeleine received a wave from the regular night-time crossing-sweeper who was loitering in the hope of earning a few extra coins from lucky gamesters. She lifted her hand in reply, the gesture purely automatic.

'Friend of yours?' asked Nicholas.

'His name is Billy. This is his patch.'

'And the lad round the corner near your house?'

'Tom. He wishes you called more often.' As soon as the words were out, she saw the trap she'd set for herself and added quickly, 'Nobody else pays him twice.'

'No. I'm a fool in lots of ways.'

Since there was no answer to that, she didn't attempt to make one.

They crossed the black mouth of Ryder Yard. On the other side of the road, a coach stood idle, its lanterns extinguished and its coachman dozing on the box. The night seemed oddly silent.

And then it wasn't.

Without warning, three shapes emerged behind them from the shadows of the yard. There was no time to think. Nicholas reacted purely by instinct, swinging Madeleine behind him with one hand and drawing his sword with the other. It was a light dress-sword, useless against a real blade but better than nothing. It gave him some chance of holding their attackers off long enough for him to offer what he presumed they were after ... because the unpleasant reality was that he hadn't a hope of defeating all three single-handed. And though he didn't think Madeleine would just stand back, wringing her hands, anything she *did* do was likely to result in injury.

Two of the men held cudgels; the third appeared to be empty-handed. Nicholas swept his sword round in a swift arc in front of him and said, 'If it's money you want, there's no need for anyone to get hurt.'

The only reply was a low rumble of laughter. That wasn't encouraging. Clearly, these fellows weren't here to talk. Neither, if they were dismissing his suggestion, was this a simple robbery.

The silent carriage across the street which he didn't dare spare the time to glance at told him something which set alarm bells ringing and made his stomach churn.

If they don't want money and they sure as hell don't want me, that leaves ... well, over my dead body, was his thought. *Though preferably not if I can help it.*

The cudgel-bearers moved closer and a little to his right, requiring his immediate attention and making it difficult to watch all three at once.

From behind him, Madeleine nearly made him jump out of his skin by yelling, 'If you want money, take this!'

And she hurled a handful of coins into the face of the unarmed man at the precise moment he made a grab for her. He flinched and ducked. Madeleine used the second he was off-balance to aim a vicious kick at his knee-cap. His companions used it to move on Nicholas.

Making sure he had the wall at his back, he drove his blade at the attacker nearest to him and managed to scrape a forearm before the fellow danced out of reach. Unfortunately, it gave the second man the opportunity to use his cudgel and deliver a blow to Nicholas's shoulder — which, though it glanced off and wasn't to his sword arm, still hurt like blazes. Sucking in a breath and trying to ignore both the burning agony in his shoulder and the pins-and-needles shooting down his left arm, Nicholas wheeled and made a wild pass. This missed completely but at least made his assailant back off.

So far, mere seconds had passed.

Leaving Nicholas to deal as best he could with the others, Madeleine was using every trick she knew to prevent the third man getting a firm hold on her. She wriggled and twisted; she raked his face with her nails and tried to poke her fingers in his eyes; twice she made him let go of her arm to evade a well-placed knee; and, throughout all of it, she yelled and screamed like a banshee. If Billy could hear her — and she was sure that he could — he would get help from Sinclairs. Mr Jenkins kept a small arsenal of firearms in a room beside the rear door ... and a pistol or two would come in very handy just now.

Nicholas had succeeded in inflicting some small amounts of damage on both of the men attacking him but nothing sufficient to stop them or even to deprive one or the other of their weapons. Inevitably, he'd taken a number of hits himself along the way because there was no time to think or to plan his next move. All he could do was stay on his feet and stop them manoeuvring him into the narrow confines of Ryder Yard where his sword would be of no use at all. In any case, he was beginning to sense that this wasn't going to end well. He could feel desperation edging closer and wished Madeleine's yelling would bear fruit before he made a catastrophic mistake.

A voice from the carriage snapped, 'Shut the bloody bitch up, can't you?'

'Trying,' grunted the man who had been attempting to restrain Madeleine. 'You said not to 'urt 'er but she's like a sodding eel.'

Meanwhile, the pair confronting Nicholas had re-positioned themselves so that one was at either side. There being no way he could defend himself from both of them simultaneously, he lunged at the one closest, felt his point hit home ... and then a blow like Thor's hammer landed on his wrist and sent his sword spinning from his hand. There was another blow to his ribs, followed by a third to his skull. The world went black and Nicholas dropped like a stone.

The fact that he was clearly unconscious didn't deter the two men from slamming their boots into him. If Madeleine had been dangerous before, she now turned feral. The man who had finally managed to imprison her with one arm and slap his free hand over her mouth instantly got her elbow in his stomach while she sank her teeth into the fleshy part of his palm. The second his grip on her relaxed, she was running to Nicholas screeching French curses and ploughing a course through his attackers to drop down at his side and shield his body with her own.

'Leave him alone! Bastards! Have you not done enough?' She was on her knees, dragging off her cloak to put it beneath his head and trying to wipe the blood running freely from somewhere on his scalp to his brow. 'Nicholas ... wake up. *Please* wake up!'

Oddly, though only for a moment, no one touched her. Then, just as one of the men stepped forward with the intention of dragging her to the carriage, the owner of the unseen voice spoke again.

'Leave her.'

'Sir?' asked one of the cudgel-bearers, clearly confused.

'Leave the woman. Bring the beau-trap instead.'

CHAPTER SIXTEEN

Time seemed to freeze. There was a moment of acute silence ... then two things happened at once.

A second voice from the carriage said, 'No! *He's* no use. Bring the girl.'

While in one lithe movement, Madeleine was on her feet having snatched up Nicholas's discarded sword along the way, and was standing guard over his body.

'You will not *touch* him,' she spat fiercely. 'I will kill the first man who tries.'

Still baffled by their new and contradictory orders, the three bullies remained where they were, shuffling their feet and keeping a wary eye on Madeleine.

From inside the carriage, Cross spoke to his companion, a hint of something like amusement threading through his voice. He said, 'Look at her. You want your money? Take *her* and you'll have to wait for a message to be sent to her brother. Take *him* and you'll get it tomorrow.'

Sir George Braxton's face appeared at the carriage window, looking undecided.

Not waiting for him to make up his mind, Madeleine said again, 'Stay back. I meant what I said – and do not for one *moment* think I will hesitate.'

Carelessly waving his men forward, Cross laughed.

'Get that toy off her, bring me the dandy – and be quick about it!'

Two stayed where they were. The third said hopefully, 'Can we hurt her now?'

'Yes – but only as much as you have to.'

'Yes, sir.' He grinned, slapped his cudgel against his palm and swaggered towards Madeleine. 'Drop the sword, if you know what's good for you.'

She didn't reply and her expression did not waver by so much as a hairsbreadth. She waited until he was almost within reach of her sword-point, lunged hard and fast, then retreated just as quickly. The cudgel fell to the cobbles and he lurched back, clutching his shoulder.

'Bitch,' he gasped. 'Bloody bitch.'

She ignored him and fixed her gaze on his associates.

'The next one who tries, dies.'

'The next one who so much as *twitches*,' said Mr Jenkins grimly, appearing silently around the corner behind them, pistol in hand, followed by two other men similarly armed, 'will get a bullet through his skull.' A piercing whistle brought three others running along the street from the other direction. 'You can stand down, Miss Madeleine. We got it now.'

Madeleine heaved in a breath of dizzying relief but wasn't sure she could move.

Finding themselves looking down the muzzles of three pistols, the bullies glanced towards the carriage, startled and unsure ... but if they expected to get either help or orders, they were disappointed. Cross, realising that they were outnumbered, yelled to his coachman to get moving. The carriage lumbered forward and gathered speed.

'Let it go!' shouted Mr Jenkins to those in its path. 'To me!'

Hugging the wall, his men continued running towards where Madeleine still stood, sword in hand. A fourth much smaller shadow fell in behind the carriage, jumped on to the back of it and clung.

'Drop your weapons and get on your knees,' snapped Mr Jenkins to Madeleine's attackers. 'Now!'

Faced with a loaded and cocked firearm, only a stupid man gets heroic. Cross's trio dropped to the cobbles. And that was when Madeleine tossed aside the sword and fell back on her knees beside Nicholas, sobbing his name.

He lay there, still and white except where the blood continued to flow down his cheek and jaw. Trying to rip a frill from her petticoat with hands that were hopelessly unsteady, she moaned, 'Oh please. Wake up, Nicholas. Open your eyes. Please.'

Arriving in the wake of the others, Edward Hastings knelt at her side, dragged off his cravat and pressed it against Nicholas's scalp. He said rapidly, 'He'll be all right. Don't worry. He'll be fine. He's got a hard head.'

Madeleine finally managed to yank the ruffle free and place it on top of Edward's cravat. Through chattering teeth, she said, 'There's so much b-blood. And they kicked him. He was unconscious on the ground and they – they *kicked* him.'

'Did they?' Mr Jenkins, engaged in issuing orders, paused briefly and then resumed. 'Tie them up and lock them in the cellar at Sinclairs. If they give you any trouble – or even if they don't, come to that – give them some of what they gave Lord Nicholas. Nobody'll mind if you hurt them a bit. But right now, I need the rest of you to help me move his lordship. Miss Madeleine, Duke Street's the closest. Can we --?

'Yes,' said Madeleine, still clutching Nicholas's hand. 'Yes, of course. But be careful with him. He might – there might be other injuries.'

'I know. It's all right, Miss.' Jenkins took her arm and drew her gently to her feet. 'Don't you worry. Let's just get his lordship into a bed where he can be looked after proper, shall we?'

She nodded and stepped away. There was blood on her hands and tears on her cheeks. She was aware of neither.

* * *

Minton opened the door and took in the situation at a glance. Within five minutes, he had the entire household racing to do his bidding. In the kitchen, Mrs Constantine set water to heat and searched the still-room for remedies; upstairs in the spare bedchamber, one housemaid lit a fire while another turned down the bed and assembled bandages; Stephen was sent running to fetch the doctor; and with meticulous care, Mr Jenkins and his men carried Nicholas up to lay him fully-clothed upon the bed.

So far, Madeleine hadn't stirred more than half a pace away. Now, however, seeing Minton and Patrick starting to pull off his lordship's boots, Edward drew her from the room, saying quietly, 'They need to remove his clothes. It will make him more comfortable and also enable the doctor to see what other injuries there are apart from the blow to his head.'

'He hasn't woken up,' she whispered. Her face was bone-white, her eyes dark with anguish. 'Why doesn't he wake up?'

'He will when he's ready,' Edward replied, exchanging an uneasy glance with the security manager. 'Meanwhile, Mr Jenkins needs to deal with the men who attacked you and it will help if you can tell him what happened.'

For a second, she looked blank. Then she said, 'They came out of Ryder Yard. The coach was waiting across the street. They meant to take me, I think, but then – then one of the men in the coach told them to t-take Nicholas instead.'

'What else?' prompted Mr Jenkins. 'Did they say anything else?'

'Something about money.' She frowned, forcing herself to concentrate and then, finally understanding what she had heard, 'Oh God. The other man in the coach – it was Braxton. He still wanted them to take me but the first man said to take Nicholas because they would get the money faster.' She pressed the heels of her hands against her eyes. 'All this over a stupid card game! Why couldn't Aristide just buy him off?'

'It has gone way beyond that now,' remarked Edward. 'Braxton is responsible for an attack on the Duke of Rockliffe's brother – which isn't a position any sane person would wish to find themselves in.' He looked at Mr Jenkins. 'Do you know who the other man might be?'

'Yes. I'm waiting for Billy to get back and confirm it – he took a ride on the back of the carriage to see what he could overhear – but I reckon it's Cross. If I'm right, those three we've got locked up at Sinclairs ain't going to talk. They know I'll have to send 'em to Bow Street sooner or later and they'll be more scared of Cross than anything we or the law can do.' He met Edward's enquiring frown, 'Nasty piece of work, Cross is. Those who work for him don't talk because they know what'll happen to 'em if they do. On the other hand, Bow Street will throw a party on the day they get him behind bars on a charge that'll stick. Ah.' This as the bedchamber door opened again. 'Looks like you can go back in now, Miss.'

Madeleine didn't stop to ask questions. As soon as she had disappeared, Edward said, 'I'll stay here tonight. Can you send someone to tell my wife what has happened?'

'Already done that, sir.'

'Thank you. And if you find out anything further …?'

'I'll let you know straight off – though, as I said, it ain't likely.' Mr Jenkins paused, then added grimly, 'We're going to have to send for Monsieur Delacroix, aren't we?'

'Yes. Rockliffe too, if Nicholas's condition looks serious. But I'd as soon wait until we hear what the doctor has to say.'

'Yes. Reckon that'd be best all round.'

Madeleine sat on the side of the bed, holding Nicholas's hand. He was still unconscious, lying motionless beneath the light blanket that covered him up to his throat. The worst of the blood had been cleaned away, though parts of his hair were still sticky with it, and a clean pad had been bound to his head. His skin was sickly white, his breathing laboured and shallow. More frightened than she had ever been in her life, Madeleine looked across at Patrick, waiting by the door in case she needed anything and said, 'Where is the doctor? What is taking him so long? He ought to be here by now.'

'He'll be coming as fast as he can, so he will. It's the middle of the night, ma'am, so he was likely in his bed. And we wouldn't want the poor man running around in his nightshirt, would we?'

As far as Madeleine was concerned, the doctor could turn up wrapped in a sheet. She just wanted Nicholas cared for and to be assured that he would recover. Past experience had taught her that God didn't make deals but she found herself mentally bargaining with Him now in the hope that this time He might make an exception.

Sounds of arrival reached her ears and she sat up. That, at least, was one prayer answered.

Closely followed by Edward, Dr Rayne entered the room, scowling as he always did.

'Well now. What have we here?' he asked, depositing his bag on a table. 'An attack in the street and a blow to the head, I'm told.'

'Amongst other things,' said Madeleine. 'But that is the worst. He hasn't woken up yet.'

'At all?'

'No.'

'Mm.' Lifting one of Nicholas's lids, the doctor looked into a dilated pupil. 'How long has it been?'

'Almost an hour.' It was Edward who answered. 'Is that unusual?'

'Not particularly. It may even be helpful.'

'But the blood,' protested Madeleine. 'He bled and bled. We couldn't stop it.'

'Head wounds always bleed freely, young lady. Now be quiet, if you please, while I locate the source of it.' With deft fingers, he began parting the thick, dark hair strand by strand until he found what he was looking for. 'Ah. Here we are ... and not nearly as bad as the blood made it seem. However, I believe we will stitch it before the gentleman wakes up. If the water in that pitcher is hot, bring it over here.' Opening his bag, he began laying out scissors, slender curved needles and thread on a large white cloth. 'Who is he?'

'Lord Nicholas Wynstanton.' The sight of the needles was making Madeleine feel queasy so she stepped back gratefully, allowing Patrick to place the hot water within reach. 'He is the brother of the Duke of Rockliffe.'

'Is he? Is he indeed? Ah well. As is abundantly plain, his blood is the same colour as yours and mine ... so we will not worry about his family escutcheon just now.' Having threaded three of the needles, he reached for the scissors to begin snipping away long locks of hair and, hearing Madeleine's instinctive sound of protest, said 'It will grow back, young lady. And in the meantime, he has more than enough left to hide the spot.'

She pressed her lips together and said nothing, gathering up the soft strands of night-dark hair to twine them about her fingers. But when the doctor finished cleaning the area around the wound and reached for the first needle she couldn't suppress a tiny mewling sound. Without glancing round, Dr Rayne said curtly, 'If you're going to faint, do it elsewhere. Better yet, leave the room.'

She walked away towards the window and leaned her brow against the cool glass. Edward came to stand beside her and said, 'He won't feel anything.'

'I know. I just can't bear the thought of it.'

'I'm not especially comfortable with it myself.' He fell silent for a moment and then added quietly, 'You should try not to worry. He will be fine, you know.'

Unable to trust her voice, Madeleine merely nodded.

'Done – and a nice, neat job even if I do say so myself,' said the doctor presently, gently cleaning around the wound again in order to apply a dressing. 'A pity no one will ever see it. However, there was mention of other injuries. What were they?'

Briefly and tonelessly, Madeleine explained.

Folding back the blanket back, he took a long look at the bruising which was already becoming evident on Nicholas's rib-cage and chest before beginning a gentle but thorough examination. Finally, he said, 'I don't believe anything is fractured ... but he may have some cracked ribs. It will be easier to be sure of that once he is conscious again.'

'And when will that be?'

'If I could predict that with any accuracy, I could double my fees.' Dr Rayne set about packing away the tools of his trade. 'He is a healthy young man; his pulse is erratic but strong enough not to be a cause for concern; and the skull is intact and feels perfectly normal. He may come round in an hour or two – or it may take longer. This is one of those occasions when we have to trust the body to know its own business best.' He snapped his bag shut. 'I shall call again tomorrow ... or rather, later today. In the meantime, keep him warm and comfortable and be prepared to wait. That is the best I can tell you.'

* * *

Nicholas did not come round in an hour or even two. Dry-eyed and silent, Madeleine sat holding his hand in both of hers as darkness gave way to dawn, then dawn to day. At every chiming of the clock, someone came in with food or drink she didn't want ... or, in Edward's case, merely to lay a hand on her shoulder and take a long look at Nicholas. At some subconscious level, Madeleine was aware that every member of the household was keeping this vigil with her; that they wanted her to know she was not alone. She tried to draw some comfort from that but it was difficult when the man she loved continued to lie, cool and motionless as an effigy, beneath the blankets she had tucked around him.

At around nine in the morning when there was still no change, Edward pulled up a chair and sat beside her. He said, 'We should inform Aristide. And Rockliffe.'

She swallowed hard and nodded. 'Yes. Will you do it? I can't leave him.'

'I'll take care of it, by all means. But you need to sleep.'

'Not yet. Later, perhaps.'

'Then you should at least eat something.'

'I'm not hungry.'

Edward drew a long breath and said carefully, 'Madeleine ... it won't help Nicholas if you make yourself ill. And – God forbid that it does – but if the worst *should* happen --'

'Don't say it! *Don't!* He is *not* going to die. He is *not!*' Suddenly, she dropped her head over the place where her fingers were wrapped around Nicholas's hand, her whole body wracked with great gulping sobs. 'If he dies, how am I to live with myself? Why would I even want to? This is my fault.'

'Your fault? No. Of course it isn't. You couldn't possibly have known --'

'Not that. Don't you see? If I'd gone to Kent as Nicholas expected me t-to, he'd still be there himself. He'd be *safe*. But I was stupid and stubborn and I wouldn't go. And that is the only reason he was in London at *all* last night. B-Because of me. So if he – if he d-dies --'

She stopped, her voice totally suspended by tears. Putting both arms about her and forgetting all the times during the past week when he'd wanted to pour a jug of cold water over her head, Edward pulled her against his chest while the storm broke in earnest. He didn't bother with comforting platitudes; she was crying too hard to hear them and wouldn't have believed him anyway. He just held her until the sobs dwindled to a mere hiccup or two and then, letting his arms slip away, he offered her his handkerchief.

After a little while, she said huskily, 'That was not ... helpful.'

'Perhaps not. But it was certainly necessary.'

'Yes.' She fell silent, turning his damp handkerchief over and over between her hands. Finally she said, 'Thank you, Edward. And – and I'm sorry. I've been unbearable, I know.'

'I can't argue with that. But let's move forward, shall we? Mr Jenkins says Billy's sure the second man in the carriage was this fellow Cross but that finding him now will be a near-impossibility. As expected, the three who attacked you have refused to talk so he's let Bow Street have them; and though Cross will have gone to ground somewhere, Braxton is still at the Bell. Mr Jenkins considered paying him a visit but thought better of it and has left one of his fellows to watch instead.'

'Why?' asked Madeleine. 'Why not confront him?'

'Because he'll run,' said Edward simply. 'Unless he's a total imbecile, mention of Rockliffe's name will have him taking to his heels – which means the duke will be put to the trouble of following him. So we won't alarm Braxton for the time being; though if he shows signs of quitting the Bell, Mr Jenkins will ... let's just say he'll provide him with secure, alternative accommodation.' Rising, he pulled her to her feet and said, 'Go. Eat, rest and change out of that stained gown. I'll stay with Nicholas. And if you send someone with writing materials, I'll draft letters to Aristide and Rockliffe for you to sign.'

* * *

Madeleine washed, put on a fresh gown and allowed her maid to brush her hair. Then she swallowed two cups of coffee and forced herself to eat a slice of bread-and-butter. Resting, however, proved beyond her capabilities and an hour later, she was back at Nicholas's bedside. Knowing better than to argue, Edward merely gave her the letters and then, once she'd signed them, took them to Sinclairs for despatch with the club's courier.

For Madeleine, the hours crawled by with maddening slowness and when fatigue began to take its toll, she kept it at bay first by moistening Nicholas's dry lips with a small, water-soaked sponge and then by talking to him.

'I love you,' she said. Though the words sounded bald, they told him the thing she most wanted him to know. 'I love you. I always have – even before we met, though I daresay you would not believe that. I didn't try to send you away because I didn't want you. I did. Always. But I believed that whatever you felt for me could only be temporary and I wanted ... I wanted you to find someone better. Someone more suited to your world than I am. You should know that it was ... difficult; even when I thought I was only hurting myself, it was a struggle. Later, when I realised that I was hurting you too, I could not bear it. I still can't.' She stopped, dashing a hand across her eyes while she tried to find the rest of the words she needed. 'And now I'm telling you all this when you can't hear me. So you have to wake up, Nicholas. You have to wake up, so I can say it again – all this and more. I'll promise you anything to the end of my life if you'll only open your eyes and give me the chance.'

But he didn't wake. He simply lay there, pale, beautiful and silent. And because she couldn't think of anything else to do, she prayed.

Somewhere out of reach beyond the veils and mists that held Nicholas captive, was a small tangled thread of awareness. There was a hand holding one of his and a voice chanting words he thought he knew. Both were oddly comforting and so, since opening his eyes seemed extraordinarily difficult, he didn't try. He floated, while the voice ebbed and flowed about him, producing random shreds of thought. It was a woman's voice and she was praying.

Ave Maria, gratia plena ... Sancta Maria, Mater Dei, ora pro nobis peccatoriibus

It was Latin. Peculiar him knowing that when there were so many things he *didn't* know ... such as where he was or why so much of him hurt and who was praying. He was still vaguely contemplating these questions when the darkness came again.

The next time he awoke, it was to the sensation of a cheek against the back of his hand and soft hair falling over his wrist. This, he decided, was worth fighting the heaviness of his eyelids so he used every scrap of concentration he could find to prise them apart. For an instant, candlelight dazzled his vision. Then, turning his head a little, he looked at the cloud of pale red hair and the sleeping face of the woman it belonged to. Moving his free arm was even more difficult than opening his eyes had been but he persevered until he was able to touch that glowing hair with his fingertips.

Slight as it was, the movement jerked Madeleine awake. Her eyes flew wide and she sat up, staring at him with an incredulity rapidly shifting into relief. She said, 'You're awake. Oh God – you're awake! I've been so frightened. I thought – I thought --' And then, tears clogging her throat and spilling through her lashes, 'I thought you were going to *die.*'

Nicholas's head was still a sluggish mass of confusion. Frowning, he tried without much success to clear it, aware that tears were dripping on his hand like rain. He swallowed and managed, in a raw, husky voice, to say, 'What happened? Where am I?'

'You're in Duke Street. We were attacked on the way from Sinclairs and you were hurt. You've been unconscious for – for a very long time.' Pulling herself together, Madeleine stood up, poured water and added a few drops of laudanum, then held the glass to his lips.

'Drink this. It will help.'

He swallowed gratefully and then let his head drop back on the pillow. Shards of pain went screaming through his skull, snatching his breath. He lifted a hand to investigate only to have her draw it away before he could do so.

'Don't,' she said. 'You took a bad blow to the head and needed stitches. You should try to stay still.'

This sounded like advice worth following. Since the room was spinning, he closed his eyes and waited for his breathing to settle. Something cool was placed across his brow, bringing relief with it and causing him to murmur groggily, 'Thank you. You're very kind.' And then, even more distantly, 'Who are you?'

The floor shifted beneath Madeleine's feet and she sat down rather abruptly.

'You ... you don't know?'

'I'm sorry. No.' He forced his eyes open to peer at her. 'Should I?'

'Yes.' She hauled in a shaky breath. 'But don't worry about it now. All that matters is that you are awake again. Everything else will come right in time.'

Vaguely aware that his inability to remember a face as beautiful as this one ought to be seriously alarming but somehow wasn't, Nicholas let his lids flutter down again and said, 'You didn't tell me your name.'

'Madeleine.'

'That's pretty.' A yawn crept up and overtook him. 'But not as pretty as you.'

'Thank you.' She could see the laudanum taking effect and, knowing the best thing for him now was rest, said, 'Close your eyes, Nicholas. We can talk later.'

Another piece of good advice, he decided sleepily. And reaching for her hand, drifted back into limbo.

CHAPTER SEVENTEEN

Edward's letters arrived at Sarre Park in the late afternoon on a day when the long spell of warm, sunny weather disintegrated into the all-too-frequent windy drizzle of east Kent.

Fortunately, since this was the day after the earl and countess's village-and-tenants party, no one minded very much. The party had been a huge success under clear, blue skies and, despite a small disagreement over the strawberry jam, no one had seriously fallen out with anybody else. The children's games, the lavish tea and the generous quantities of ale had all been greatly enjoyed. Mr Audley had led his team to victory over Lord Sarre's in the tug-of-war; Aristide had presided over a Hazard table for farthing bets and a rule that no one could lose more than sixpence; and the Duke of Rockliffe astounded everyone with his rowing ability in the boat races, only to lose the final heat to Rob Barnes of the Home Farm. And all of it was followed by an evening of energetic country dancing.

It was therefore not surprising that Caroline's guests were ready for a lazy day of reading or conversation. However, by the time the courier from Sinclairs arrived, most of the gentlemen had gathered for a hand or two of basset while Aristide entertained the ladies with card tricks. Bertrand found Adrian in the library and, handing him two sealed missives, said, 'One of Jenkins' fellows brought them. He says they're urgent.'

Seeing that one was addressed to Aristide and the other to Rockliffe, Adrian suspected that whatever news they brought wasn't good. He said, 'Ask them both to join me here. And be discreet about it.'

Aristide walked in, followed almost immediately by Rockliffe who said, 'I do hope this is important, Adrian. I was holding a rather promising hand.'

Adrian merely passed over the letters. 'These just arrived. From Sinclairs.'

The duke's gaze sharpened but he said nothing. He broke the seal, scanned the brief contents of the sheet and looked across at Aristide who was still reading, a frown creasing his brow. When he finally looked up, Rockliffe said, 'Mine informs me only that Nicholas was attacked in the street last night and that though he remains unconscious due to a blow to the head, the doctor sees no cause for concern. I am hoping that yours offers a little more in the way of detail.'

'Yes.' Since nothing Edward had written needed to be hidden from the duke, Aristide handed him the letter. Then, turning to Adrian, he said, 'Braxton paid men to abduct Madeleine for ransom. He failed and the men who hurt Nicholas are under lock and key in Bow Street. Edward says that he and Jenkins have everything under control and see no reason to fear further attacks but suspect I will wish to return.'

'Which, of course, you do.'

'Yes,' agreed Aristide.

'As do I,' said Rockliffe coolly.

'Then I suggest you both make an early start in the morning, rather than leaving now and travelling in the dark. Also, the fellow who brought the letters is still here if you want to question him.'

'That,' said the duke, 'would be helpful.'

Parted from his supper in the kitchen, Finn gave them such additional information as he had – which, aside from the fact that Miss Madeleine was worried sick, wasn't very much. Then, looking at Aristide, he said, 'Mr Hastings said as I was to bring your reply, sir. And with a fresh horse, I can get back tonight – much faster'n you can do it by carriage.'

Aristide nodded. 'Go, then. Tell Mr Hastings that his Grace and I will be there by mid-day tomorrow.' He handed Finn a guinea, adding, 'And tell him to give you another of those.'

When he had left them, Rockliffe said, 'Adrian ... it will be best if Adeline and Vanessa remain here for the time being, if you have no objection.'

'Do you really need to ask?' And to Aristide, 'Genevieve can also stay, if you wish.'

If she *wishes*, thought Aristide wryly. But said only, 'Thank you.'

* * *

Genevieve most emphatically did *not* wish but, as usual, wasn't sure how much she was permitted to insist. She said, 'I would rather come with you, if you don't mind. It makes more sense since we would have been returning to London in a few days anyway. And if Madeleine has been nursing Lord Nicholas single-handed – which I imagine she has – I may be able to help.'

Although everything she said was true, Aristide knew which part mattered most to her – and he still found it slightly baffling. During the course of the last week, it had become increasingly obvious that whenever there was a choice between this entertainment or that, his wife invariably opted for the one that meant she could be with him. At first, he had put this down to a residual uncertainty of how far the other guests had truly accepted her; but as the days wore by, it became increasingly plain that there was more to it than that. Once or twice, he had even wondered if she might be a little in love with him – but he always dismissed that thought. He knew why she had wanted to marry him, didn't he? And if fondness had grown between them since then, it probably had more to do with the undeniable magic that existed in the bedroom. As for how *he* felt about *her* ... that was a subject he didn't allow himself to probe too deeply.

Now, he said, 'I want to make an early start and travel as fast as possible.'

'Of course. I won't hold you back.'

'*You* won't.' And pointing to the dog in her arms, 'But what about *her*?'

'Blanchette will be good. I promise.'

Although Aristide had a number of names for the dog, Blanchette was not one of them. On the occasion the four-legged pest had begun biting his toes while he and Genevieve had been engaged in a new and rather pleasurable activity, the name that had sprung to mind wasn't socially acceptable even in all-male company.

'She had better be,' he grumbled. 'I didn't save the little beast's life so she could send you into a fit of the giggles at inopportune moments.'

Amongst other things, Genevieve was beginning to learn when not to take her husband seriously. Blushing at the recollection his words conjured up and suppressing a smile, she said, 'She is very sorry about that. So may we come home with you?'

Home. He was startled by how much he liked her calling it that. *Home ... with him.*

'Of course.' Truthfully, had he ever had any intention of leaving her behind? He somehow suspected not. 'Tell me something. What makes you think Madeleine will be nursing Nicholas herself?'

Her eyes widened a little.

'If she loves him, what else would she do? It's what I – what *any* woman would do in circumstances like that.'

Aristide noticed the slip and for the first time came dangerously close to asking the obvious question. Fortunately, Blanchette chose that moment to make Genevieve laugh by trying to chew one of the long curls lying on her shoulder. Distantly, he supposed that the blasted dog sometimes had its uses.

* * *

It had been arranged that Rockliffe would travel with them as far as Wynstanton Priors and then continue the journey in his racing carriage. Thus it was that Genevieve heard George Braxton's name for the first time – Aristide having left her with the impression that the attack on Nicholas and Madeleine had been the sort of thing that frequently happened on London's streets.

'Braxton is proving tediously persistent, is he not?' remarked the duke, before they had even reached the end of Sarre Park's drive. 'He is about to learn, however, that he made a serious error of judgement when he laid hands on my brother.'

'It's unlikely he knew who Nicholas was,' said Aristide, detaching Blanchette from the toe of his boot and placing her in Genevieve's lap. 'Madeleine is usually escorted back to Duke Street by one of Sinclairs' footmen.'

'Oddly enough, it is really of no consequence to me whether he was aware of Nicholas's identity or not. Do you have any plans for dealing with him?'

'Not yet.'

'Excellent. Then you will be good enough to leave Sir George to me. I find I am quite annoyed with him.'

There was a note in that soft, almost lazy voice that caused a tiny chill to run down Genevieve's spine. She rather suspected that *'quite annoyed'* didn't at all describe his Grace's feelings on the matter ... and that Sir George Braxton was going to find himself in more trouble than he'd bargained for.

'If my own apologies are any use,' said Aristide, 'you have them. I am extremely sorry that Nicholas has been caught up in a situation for which I am responsible. For what it's worth, I thought I had put a stop to it. I certainly didn't expect Braxton to go this far.'

'Perhaps not. But he is clearly very sure of his ground.' Rockliffe paused briefly. 'Why *is* that, I wonder?'

'He lost a good deal of money in a short space of time,' shrugged Aristide. 'Afterwards, he decided it could only have happened in one way.'

'Logical as that sounds, I have a distinct feeling there is more to it ... but am able to think of only one scenario that would fit.'

Meeting the astute, dark gaze and knowing there *was* only one possible scenario, Aristide said obscurely, 'It wouldn't have helped when he accused me and it won't now.'

'We shall see.' The duke leaned back in his seat and smiled at Genevieve. 'Forgive me. I am being inexcusably rude, am I not?'

'Not at all. Of *course* you and Aristide need to talk about this ... so please pretend I am not here. Blanchette will keep me company.'

Rockliffe surveyed the small bundle of fur, white but with one comical black ear and a tongue that was currently making determined attempts to lick Genevieve's face. He said, 'I understand she was saved from a watery grave.'

Genevieve beamed at him and nodded. 'It was Aristide who did that.'

'Really?' A faintly amused glance was turned in Aristide's direction. 'I had not realised that you were a dog-lover.'

Aristide's expression very clearly said, *Can we please not have this conversation?*

'I don't think he is,' replied Genevieve seriously. 'Mostly, he finds her annoying. But he bought her for me because he knew how much I wanted her.'

'Ah.' Rockliffe didn't miss the wealth of meaning in her tone. 'That was kind of him.'

'Yes. Yes, it was.'

At Wynstanton Priors and away from Genevieve, Rockliffe said, 'You appear to be uncommonly fortunate, Aristide. In my experience, ladies save that kind of appreciation for diamonds – not mongrel pups. You might want to bear that in mind.'

Back in the carriage and once more on their way, Genevieve said hesitantly, 'Who is this man you and the duke were talking about? And why did he have Nicholas and Madeleine attacked?' Then, when he didn't immediately answer, 'But perhaps I shouldn't ask.'

'No. You've a right to know and if I don't tell you, Madeleine will.' Aristide thought for a moment, wondering how and where to begin. Finally, he said neutrally, 'After Sir Kenneth dismissed me and I was fit enough to work again, I couldn't get steady employment that brought in sufficient to pay the rent and put food on the table.' He paused, seeing the distress in her face and the way she hugged Blanchette closer. 'Don't. It was not your fault. I'm only referring to it because it was the reason for what I did next.'

'And what was that?' she asked, her voice small and unhappy.

'I used the only talent I possessed and started sharping.'

She shook her head. 'I don't know what that is.'

'Cheating at cards.' A hard smile touched his mouth. 'An old man who lived nearby showed me the basics but I refined my skills because the intricacies and possibilities fascinated me. I never expected or even wanted to put those skills into practice ... but there came a point where it was either earn a living at the card-table or starve and let Madeleine starve with me.' He turned his head and met her gaze with an austere one of his own. 'I was very good at it. But it is not something I am proud of. And you should know that I stopped doing it the day I left Paris. When I play these days – which isn't often – I play fair.'

'I don't doubt it.' Genevieve put Blanchette down at her feet and crossed the carriage to sit beside him. Taking his hand in hers, she said, 'Tell me about Braxton.'

Aristide hid his surprise and let his fingers curl around hers.

'A month or so before Adrian and I were about to gamble everything we had on Sinclairs, I needed a substantial sum to equal what Adrian was putting in ... so I went to one of Paris's larger gaming-houses and won it from Sir George Braxton.' He stopped and shrugged. 'Two months ago, purely by chance, he walked into Sinclairs and recognised me. He wants his money back and has tried various ways of getting it. His plan the other evening was to snatch Madeleine and force me to pay for her safe return. Thanks largely to Nicholas, that didn't happen.'

Although she was not quite sure why, Genevieve had the feeling that he had missed something out; something important. She said slowly, 'Does the duke know about ...?' She stopped, not knowing how best to put it.

'My shady past? He didn't until Braxton stood in Sinclairs and called me a cheat.'

'Oh. And Lord Sarre?'

A sudden smile dawned.

'Let us just say that Adrian has skills of his own and that we each keep the other's secrets.'

* * *

In Duke Street, the laudanum gave Nicholas nine hours of unbroken sleep from which he woke slowly. Bit by bit, he became aware of a number of things. He had the devil of a headache; his right wrist and left shoulder throbbed; and when he attempted to move, hot knives lanced sickeningly across his ribs. All in all, he decided that he felt bloody awful.

His hearing, however, was working well enough to enable him to catch fragments of a low-voiced conversation taking place some distance away beyond the bed-curtains.

'How long did he remain awake?'

'Five minutes, perhaps a little more. But I gave him laudanum so …' The voice faded, then came back sounding unsteady. 'He did not know me. He – he asked who I was.'

Did I? thought Nicholas bemusedly. *I don't remember that. Actually, I don't remember much at all. Mainly what the hell happened to me and how I got here.*

'A temporary loss of memory is not unusual in such cases.'

In what *cases, for God's sake?*

'It – it will not last?'

Is she crying? No. That can't be right.

'Most unlikely.'

'You do not sound sure.'

'I am as sure as one may be, young lady. The amnesia may last a few hours or even days, but it will pass. And the fact that he regained consciousness is encouraging. If he wakes again, send for me immediately so that I can make a proper examination of his ribs.'

Ah. Finally something that makes sense and sounds helpful.

'Excuse me,' said Nicholas weakly. 'But if anyone's interested, my ribs feel as if they've been kicked by a horse.'

At the first sound of his voice, Madeleine all but ran to the bedside. Then, hoisting herself up beside him and both looking and sounding frightened, she said, 'Nicholas? You're awake again. That's ... good.'

'I'd call it a – a matter of opinion.'

'Feeling a bit battered, are you?' asked the doctor. 'Hardly surprising.'

'I'll have to take your word for that.' Feeling woozily short of air, Nicholas tried to take a deeper breath and promptly regretted it. 'What happened?'

'You don't remember?'

'Not a thing. I don't remember you either.'

Madeleine felt panic edging close again. She said, 'This is Dr Rayne, Nicholas. You haven't met him before but he's been looking after you since you were hurt.'

'Sooner or later, I hope somebody's going to ... tell me about that.'

'Later,' said Dr Rayne firmly. 'First, I'm going to take a good look at those ribs – and *you*, young lady, can occupy yourself elsewhere while I do it.'

She nodded reluctantly and slid to the floor. 'I'll wait outside.'

When she had gone, the doctor surveyed Nicholas's upper body and said, 'That's an impressive collection of bruising you have there. Take a deep breath for me.'

'I'd rather not, if you don't mind.'

'Ah. Tried that before, did you? Well, let's hope your ribs are cracked rather than broken. Lie still while I find out.' And as an after-thought, 'I'll try not to hurt you but I can't promise I won't.'

What followed sent the breath hissing through Nicholas's teeth and made him swear. Dr Rayne, however, was annoyingly cheerful.

'Two cracked ribs – which we could strap up but won't because it doesn't do a lot of good. Pain will remind you what not to do while they heal. The shoulder is just badly bruised, as is your wrist. Nasty blow that must have been, judging by the swelling. And now ... let's get you raised up a bit so I can take a look at your head.'

Nicholas hadn't believed it was possible to feel worse than he had when he'd woken up but was fast discovering his mistake. Sweat broke out over his skin and nausea stirred in his stomach. But just when he thought he might actually throw up, Dr Rayne stepped back and said, 'Somebody gave you a hell of a beating, young man. You may not think it – but you're lucky to have got off so lightly. However ... a few days in bed should find you on the mend. If the pain gets too bad, don't be afraid to take a little laudanum. Sleep is your friend.' He picked up his bag. 'I'll call again tomorrow. Meanwhile, I'll tell Mademoiselle that she can come back. Be gentle and let her fuss. She needs it.'

Having heard the doctor's verdict, Madeleine returned to Nicholas and, for want of something better, asked cautiously, 'Are you hungry?'

'No.' The mere suggestion of food made his insides recoil. 'Just water, for now.'

She filled a glass and handed it to him.

He drained half of it and then, eyeing her properly for the first time, said, 'You don't look much better than I feel.'

Madeleine knew how she looked. Her eyes were puffy from lack of sleep and pink from crying; her right cheek sported a shadowy bruise she'd presumably got whilst fighting off the fellow trying to drag her to Braxton's carriage; her gown was crushed and her hair needed brushing. Shrugging, she said, 'I was frightened you were going to die.'

Nicholas took his time about replying but a faint glint of humour crept into his eyes. Finally he said, 'That sounds encouraging. Not the dying part so much ... but the possibility you'd mind if I did.'

'*Mind?*' she echoed. And then, realising what he'd said, 'Oh God. You *know* me?'

He blinked, tried to recall exactly what he'd overheard earlier but found it too great an effort. 'Of course I know you. Why wouldn't I?'

Madeleine shook her head and tears threatened again. 'You didn't when you woke up before.'

'I don't remember waking up before. I don't remember a lot of things. But I'm not likely to forget *you*, am I? You're either the light of my life or the bane of my existence. I can never decide which.' He paused and reached out his hand. 'Don't cry.'

'I'm not.' Her fingers closed around his. 'Or perhaps I am. I don't know any more.' She drew a long, bracing breath. 'Do you really not remember what happened?'

'No.' Nicholas shut his eyes for a moment while he searched his memory. Then, opening them again, 'The last thing I remember is talking with Ned Hastings in Sinclairs. I told him ... I think I told him about winning Rock's race. But the rest is a blur and everything after it is completely blank. You'll have to fill it in for me.'

Madeleine nodded and, in as few words as possible, did so. At the end, she said, 'I'm sorry. I'm so, so sorry. It is my fault, all of it. If I had gone to Kent, none of this would have happened.'

'No. Probably not. But I don't think I'm up to having that particular conversation right now.' He paused, pain furrowing his brow and said baldly, 'Did they hurt you?'

'I didn't give them the chance. Don't worry about me. I'm fine and we'll talk later. Now you should rest before your brother gets here.'

Nicholas stared at her. 'You sent for Rock? Why?'

'You were unconscious for *twenty hours*, Nicholas. Of course I had to send for him! He expects to get here around noon and it is nearly ten now ... so try to sleep.'

'Wait.' Without thinking, he tried to sit up and swore as agony stabbed through his midriff. Then, breathing hard, 'Sorry. Madeleine ... how long have I been here?'

'Since the night before last. Why?'

'Has anyone told my valet where I am?' And when she shook her head, 'Christ. He's going to be beside himself, imagining me dead in a gutter. Send someone, will you? Hay Hill ... the house with the bilious green door. His name's Brennon.' Nicholas laid his head back and closed his eyes. 'God. Rock and Brennon. Where's the laudanum?'

* * *

Later, Nicholas was to wish he'd been serious about the laudanum. Brennon arrived at his bedside within the hour and promptly burst into tears.

'Oh *sir* – my *lord!* I feared ... truly I feared the worst. And to find you safe --' He stopped, clinging to one of Nicholas's hands with both of his. 'I b-beg your lordship's pardon. I am overcome.'

'So I see. I mean, I'm sorry you were worried. I was out cold and no one thought to send word – or knew *where* to send it, probably.' Embarrassment at his normally prim and disapproving valet's outpouring of emotion brought the merest tinge of colour back to Nicholas's pallid cheeks. 'All's well that ends well, though. So --'

'But to have no one to care for you, my lord!' Producing a handkerchief, Brennon mopped his eyes and blew his nose. 'You have not even been *shaved*.'

'No.' Nicholas passed a hand over his jaw and then, seeing that Brennon was still visibly shaking, decided he already had enough injuries. 'Later, perhaps.'

'And your lordship's *hair*.'

'Ah. Bad, is it?'

The valet touched it and grimaced. 'Is that *blood*?'

'Probably.' Nicholas made his own investigation and decided that this, at least, could not wait. 'Do what you can with it – but mind the stitches.'

'*Stitches?*' The word was enough to send Brennon off again. 'Oh *sir!*'

Since he hoped to be vaguely presentable by the time his brother turned up, Nicholas summoned Brennon's professional pride.

'Rockliffe's likely to be here at any minute and I'd sooner he didn't find me naked and bloody. I'm depending on you, Brennon.'

The valet straightened his spine, nodded and set to work

Hot water and towels were sent for, along with a list of articles to be fetched from Hay Hill without which Lord Nicholas could not be adequately cared for. His lordship's hair was restored to an acceptable level of cleanliness and the remaining blood was washed from his upper body. Finally, he was helped into a snowy, cambric nightshirt – an excruciating business which nearly caused Nicholas to pass out again.

His Grace of Rockliffe drove directly to Duke Street and, before seeing Nicholas, insisted on speaking to Madeleine, Mr Hastings and Mr Jenkins – from whom, amongst other things, he gained a full and accurate picture of what had happened on the night of the attack.

From Edward, he learned that Madeleine had scarcely left Nicholas's side for a moment; and from Mr Jenkins, news that George Braxton still lingered in Bellsavage Yard, followed by something else that Rockliffe found surprising.

'The original plan had been to take Miss Madeleine. But when that bugger, Cross – begging your Grace's pardon – said to take his lordship instead, she stood over him with his sword in her hand and told Cross's men she'd kill the first one who tried. Damn near *did* kill one of 'em.' He shook his head wonderingly. 'Like a tigress, she was – and not a thought for her own safety. You've got to admire a woman like that.'

Under-slept and brittle, with hands that would not stay still, the tigress looked the duke in the eye, apologised repeatedly and claimed full responsibility for the incident.

'But for me, Nicholas would not have been there. It is my fault, all of it.'

'Forgive my contradicting you,' remarked Rockliffe mildly, 'but the decision to return to London was Nicholas's own, was it not? And I presume you are no more capable of predicting the future than the rest of us.'

'Don't be kind, your Grace. I don't deserve it.' Madeleine dashed a hand angrily over her eyes. 'You don't know how it was. When he arrived at Sinclairs he was so angry – and he was right to be. Then ... then they knocked him down and *kicked* him. After that, all those hours when he didn't wake up, I thought he was going to die. And now he has cracked ribs and is in *such* pain and – and there's nothing I can do about it.'

The duke eyed her meditatively for a moment and then stood up.

'I am sure,' he said, 'that you will think of something if you put your mind to it. And now I believe I will see my brother.'

He found Nicholas bone-white and exhausted. Laying a hand lightly on his shoulder, he said, 'I won't ask how you feel since the question is clearly redundant. Neither will I stay long. Just tell me when you last took something for the pain.'

'I don't know. Last night, I think.'

'Then you'll take more now. No – don't argue, Nicholas. You look like a corpse.' Rockliffe poured water and added some drops of laudanum. 'Drink that. The best thing you can do now is sleep.'

'So the doctor said.' Nicholas took the glass and drained it. 'You needn't have come.'

'Need I not?'

'No. But I ... God, Rock, I'm glad you have. Thank you.'

'Don't be too grateful. There are matters requiring my attention quite aside from assuring myself that the dukedom still has an heir.'

Catching a glint that boded ill for someone in his brother's eyes, Nicholas said, 'What are you going to do?'

'The men responsible for your current condition are being held at Bow Street, so I believe I will have a few words with Sir John Fielding.' Taking an enamelled snuff-box from his pocket,

Rockliffe turned it delicately between his fingers. 'Later, when Aristide gets here – did I mention that he is hard on my heels? – we will pay a call on Sir George Braxton.' A hard smile curled his mouth. 'Do you know ... I am rather looking forward to that.'

CHAPTER EIGHTEEN

Aristide and Genevieve arrived while the duke was in Bow Street. Taking one look at Madeleine's strained face, Genevieve deposited Blanchette in her husband's unsuspecting grasp and went immediately to embrace her sister-in-law, saying, 'How is he?'

'Awake.' Surprised and touched, Madeleine briefly hugged her back before stepping away. 'That is, he's sleeping right now – but he's no longer unconscious and, aside from the assault itself, seems to have his memory back, thank God.' She looked at her brother who was eyeing the squirming puppy with suspicion and, for the first time in two days, she felt a quiver of amusement. 'Rockliffe was here but he's gone to Bow Street. He said he'll return later and asks that you wait for him. Aristide ... what *is* that?'

'That,' he replied, handing Blanchette back to his wife, 'is a small limb of Satan.' And without giving Genevieve time to object, said, 'Where are Edward and Jenkins?'

'They went back to Sinclairs after the duke had spoken with them. What are you going to do about Braxton?'

'I don't think that will be my decision. He may not show it, but Rockliffe is angry and out for blood. Metaphorically speaking, of course.'

'Metaphorically? That's disappointing,' snapped Madeleine. 'Despite the state Nicholas was in, they were going to take him instead of me. Did you know that? If they'd done it, he could have *died*.' She stopped and hauled in a deep breath. 'I'm sorry. You've been travelling for hours and need rest and refreshment. Go up and I'll have Mrs Constantine send a tray. Nicholas is in the room next to mine, if you want to look in on him – though, as I said, he's asleep. His valet is with him.'

'You're the one who needs rest, Madeleine,' said Genevieve firmly. 'If you go on like this, you'll be ill – and that won't help Nicholas. *I'll* see about food for Aristide. You go and lie down for an hour or two, then ring for a bath. It will make you feel better, I promise.'

The ever-present tears filled Madeleine's eyes. 'Yes. Perhaps I will. Rockliffe gave Nicholas laudanum so he shouldn't wake for some hours yet.'

When Madeleine had gone, Genevieve set Blanchette down on a chair with an instruction to be good and started stripping off her gloves, head bent over her task.

'Aristide ... if you're finding Blanchette truly irritating, you must tell me.'

The unpleasant sense that he knew what she was about to say caused a weight to settle in his chest. He said, 'I was teasing. I thought you knew that.'

'Sometimes I'm not sure. Sometimes I wonder if you don't regret giving her --'

'Genevieve, stop. Of course I don't regret it. You love her.'

'Yes. I do.' She glanced round at him, her smile a little sad. 'And that's all it takes for her to love me in return. Dogs are like that. They ask very little and love very easily. She would love you too, if you gave her any encouragement.'

Aristide felt as if he'd stepped off the edge of a cliff and was falling very slowly. Was she saying what he thought she was saying? *Could* she be? He hadn't the faintest idea how to reply but suspected that this wasn't something to get wrong. So he avoided the problem by scooping Blanchette up and sitting down with her on his knee – where she promptly set about attacking one of his cuffs. Sighing a little and putting an end to this absorbing game by tapping her gently on the nose, he said, 'Try one of my fingers instead. This one. I believe I use it less than the others. Now pay attention. We will make a deal, you and I. *I* will provide exciting things which you may chew to your heart's content ... and *you* will leave my boots alone. How does that sound?' He paused, lifting the dog up as if listening to her reply. 'What? The lovely straw hat with the cherries on it? Well, you drive a hard bargain ... but I think it might be arranged.'

Genevieve was laughing and shaking her head.

'You will *not* give her my favourite hat!'

He looked up, his face perfectly grave but for the gleam in his eyes that she still sometimes missed.

'No. Probably not. I would have to buy you another one, wouldn't I?' Absent-mindedly stroking Blanchette who responded with a huge yawn, he said, 'Rockliffe feels I ought to give you diamonds but I believe rubies would suit you better. What do you think?'

'I think you should save your nonsense for Blanchette,' retorted Genevieve. '*She* will believe every word you say. Fortunately, I know better.'

No, chérie, he thought. *Since only a few minutes ago you actually thought I'd ask you to give up your pet to suit my convenience, clearly you do not. There are still times when you misunderstand me. Somehow, I need to mend that.*

* * *

Knowing that his Grace of Rockliffe was likely to come back at any moment and had probably not eaten, Genevieve asked Mrs Constantine for a light repast to be served in the breakfast room. Then, still smiling to herself, she went upstairs to change her gown and tidy her hair. The gentlemen, she decided, would do perfectly well without her.

Aristide spent a little time sifting through the considerable pile of correspondence awaiting him. At the top of it was a note from Mr Jenkins, seeking permission to offer a position to young Billy, the crossing-sweeper, along with an explanation of his reasons. There followed no less than three letters from Henry Lessing which Aristide put aside to read later, a couple of notes from Edward regarding membership applications … and an extremely curt letter from the Earl of Sherbourne demanding to see him at his earliest convenience.

The last one brought a satisfied smile to Aristide's face.

Good, he thought. *Whatever Mr Lessing has been up to is clearly touching a nerve.*

* * *

Returning just as Aristide was sitting down to a meal of cold meat, game pie and pickles, Rockliffe accepted an invitation to join him and, having established that his brother was still sleeping, said, 'I was hoping to see Fielding himself but he is in court today. However, his secretary assures me that the bravos who attacked Nicholas and Madeleine are still in custody and will remain there.'

'And their employer?'

'As anticipated, Cross has taken to the heather. I am told that the chances of finding him are negligible unless someone talks.' Rockliffe took a small bread roll and broke it in half. 'Sadly, thumbscrews and red-hot pincers are no longer in fashion.'

'Madeleine would agree with that. If they were, she'd be insisting on wielding them herself. The notion of Nicholas being abducted in her place did not go down well.'

'That is one way of putting it. I understand the man she wounded can consider himself lucky. Two inches lower and he'd be a corpse.'

'That should please her. She has an intense desire to kill someone.'

'So I've gathered. But I digress. Thus far, the men being held at Bow Street have not been told precisely *who* they attacked. I have asked Henderson to correct that ... and to stress that, in my determination to see heads roll, I have demanded they be charged with attempted murder – a demand which my rank will make it difficult for Sir John to resist. In addition, I have recommended that, when they have had a day or two for the ramifications of that to sink in, Henderson might hint that the charge *could* be reduced to assault should they decide to be ... helpful.' Leaning back in his chair and toying idly with his knife, the duke added, 'Of course they will be spending a long time behind bars no matter what they do. But the possibility of a cart-ride to Tyburn might be sufficient to loosen their tongues.'

Aristide nodded. 'It is worth a try. But Bow Street will need Braxton's evidence which, since it incriminates him equally, he's unlikely to give.'

'I'm sure he can be persuaded otherwise when he learns whose path he has crossed.' A chilly smile dawned. 'You and I will have the pleasure of enlightening him.'

Having expected this, Aristide said merely, 'I am more than happy to face Braxton. In fact, I'm eager to do so. But where your title and influence can be relied upon to frighten him witless, he knows that I am powerless against him.'

'Are you?' asked Rockliffe pleasantly. 'I don't think that is entirely true, is it? Unless I am completely mistaken, you have had ... if not an ace, then at least a court-card ... up your sleeve all along. If you'll forgive the expression.'

Sighing faintly, Aristide considered the various replies he might make and eventually settled for, 'I don't know why you are so convinced of that. But ... supposing I have?'

'If you have, I shall enjoy helping you to play it.'

* * *

At the Bell on Ludgate Hill, Aristide witnessed a new ducal phenomenon. Rockliffe did not use his title or offer a coin or even change his manner in any definable way, yet somehow he had the inn-keeper bowing and scraping as if he had done all three.

'Certainly, m'lord. Sir George is still with us. Been here nigh on two months. He --'

'I did not ask for his biography. I asked where I might find him ... by which I meant you to point me in the direction of his room.'

'Yes, m'lord. Sorry, m'lord. First floor, front. It's one of my best and --'

'Thank you.' Rockliffe took a step in the direction of the stairs.

'Shall I send up some wine, m'lord?' asked the inn-keeper hopefully. 'And Sir George just ordered a meal. If you gentlemen would care to dine with him --'

'We would not.' Pivoting on his heel, the duke subjected him to a cool, level stare. 'You will not send wine and Sir George will take his dinner when my business with him is concluded. I do not desire to be interrupted at *all* and you will see to it that I am not. I trust I make myself clear?'

'Yes. Yes, quite clear, m'lord.'

'Excellent.'

Half-way up the stairs, Aristide said, 'He is expecting food.'

'How convenient.' Pausing, Rockliffe stepped back into the shadows. 'After you. We do not want a vulgar altercation on the landing.'

'You mean we don't want him screaming for help before we get inside the room,' replied Aristide caustically, his hand on the latch. Then, 'Are you sure about this?'

'We wouldn't be here if I were not. Knock.'

Aristide did so and seconds later the door was wrenched open on the words, 'And about bloody time! How long – *Christ!*' This as, taking advantage of his shock, Aristide calmly pushed him back inside with the flat of his hand so the duke could enter behind him.

Sir George Braxton stared at his visitors aghast, his mouth opening and closing.

He had spent two anxious and very depressing days and thought his situation couldn't get any worse. After the debacle in Ryder Street, Cross had lost his temper, demanded the money owing to him and held a knife to George's throat until he got it, before tossing him out of the carriage at the top of Ludgate Hill. It had taken two bottles of claret before George stopped shaking. This entire enterprise, he realised, had been a disaster. Not only had he *not* recovered his money from the damned Frenchman, he had wasted a lot more of it trying. And now here in front of him was another nightmare. Not just the damned Frenchman – who George still hoped to get the better of – but the Duke of bloody Rockliffe who apparently no one *ever* got the better of.

Swallowing hard and with more bravado that he actually felt, he said, 'What the hell are you doing here? Get out.'

Rockliffe closed the door, leaned negligently against it and said, 'Sit down, Sir George.'

'What? No.' He turned a furious yet impotent gaze on Aristide and said, 'I don't know how *you've* got the nerve to face me at all – never mind barging in here like --'

'Sit down,' said Rockliffe again, managing to sound both bored and implacable. 'This conversation may take some time. Fortunately, Monsieur Delacroix and I have no other engagements today.'

'I've nothing to say to *him* – and though I've no idea what tales he's been spinning to you, your Grace, I don't see as I've anything to say to you either.'

'You are mistaken ... but we will come to that presently. I told you to sit. *Do it.*'

Braxton dropped promptly into the nearest chair.

'Good. We progress.' The duke waved a seemingly lazy hand at Aristide. 'Perhaps you would like to begin? I suspect you may be more succinct than I.'

'I will do my best.' Turning an expressionless gaze on Sir George, Aristide said, 'You began by accusing me, publicly and on the floor of my own club, of something that could not be proved. When that didn't take root, you followed it up by trying to blacken my reputation with anyone who would listen and then with an attempt to bribe my employees. You have had me followed and my house watched ... all of it because you lost money at the gaming-table.'

'I *didn't* lose. You damned well *cheated!*'

'That is merely your assertion. But all the things I have just mentioned are facts – and can be proved to be so. However, as far as it was possible, I was prepared to ignore your petty aggravations. Unfortunately, two nights ago you went far beyond the trivial. Aided by a well-known criminal and his assorted cut-throats, you attacked my sister and her escort in the street with the intention of abducting her in order to extort money from me by holding her for ransom.'

Some of Sir George's florid colour leaked away. He said, 'I don't know where you got that idea from but there's not a word of truth in it. It's no fault of mine if somebody tried to snatch your sister. I daresay there's many another innocent man you've fleeced in that club of yours.'

'No. Not even one. But that is beside the point. You were seen and identified, along with the man calling himself Cross, sitting in a carriage on Ryder Street from where you watched the attack take place. When --'

'You're a bloody liar! And who's going to take the word of a Captain Sharp? Nobody – that's who. I wasn't anywhere near Ryder Street and I don't know anybody called Cross.'

'I imagine you *wish* you didn't,' retorted Aristide dryly. 'He wasn't very happy when the pair of you fled the scene, was he? Just out of interest … *did* you pay him?'

'How do you – you can't know --' began Sir George, then stopped abruptly, realising how much he was giving away.

'How do I know? One of my younger employees – the lad responsible for raising the alarm, in fact – travelled on the back of your carriage as far as Charing Cross. He was fairly sure one of the men inside it was Cross but wanted to confirm it. And of course, your own accent is quite … distinctive. I'm sure Billy will know it when he hears it again.'

Braxton heaved himself out of the chair, took a step towards the door, then glanced at the silent presence before it and stopped. He said desperately, 'This is all rubbish and I'm damned if I'll listen to any more of it!'

'Yes. You will.' For the second time and still with no more force than was necessary, Aristide pushed Sir George back until his knees hit the chair and he sat down again. 'We are just getting to the interesting bit. Now … where was I?'

'Your sister and her escort were under attack,' offered Rockliffe helpfully.

'Thank you, your Grace. Yes. Three brawny fellows with cudgels against one man and a woman. The odds probably looked quite good, didn't they? And once my sister's escort was lying unconscious and bleeding on the ground, I daresay you thought you had won. I don't imagine you bargained for help arriving just in time to render this scheme no more successful than your previous ones.' Aristide paused. 'You can continue denying your part in this until Doomsday, Sir George. It will not help you. Cross may have disappeared but the three ruffians who committed the assault are under lock and key at Bow Street. One word from me will see you joining them.' He smiled slowly. 'Ah. Did I say they are facing a charge of attempted murder?'

'*Murder?* What the – what are you talking about? There wasn't any murder.' Sir George was starting to sweat. 'You – you're just trying to frighten me.'

'No.' Almost idly, Rockliffe detached himself from the door and took a couple of steps into the room. 'It is I who am about to do that.'

'Wh-What?'

'Did you think that I am here merely to bear Aristide company?'

If Sir George had been in any condition to think, the duke's use of Aristide's given name would have told him that, between them and despite their differing social status, was something akin to friendship. As it was, he looked completely blank and said, 'I don't know *why* you're here, your Grace. So far as I can see, none of this is anything to do with you and – and there *wasn't* any murder.'

'No. Luckily for you and for the three men currently awaiting trial in Bow Street, there was not. The attack on the gentleman who was escorting Mademoiselle Delacroix home was severe ... and though he did not die, he might easily have done so. The blow to his skull rendered him unconscious for the best part of twenty-four hours, while the subsequent and entirely gratuitous beating meted out by your hirelings caused other injuries.'

'That's not my fault!' Finally recognising that further denial was pointless, Braxton said, 'Look. I never asked them to do it. Blame Cross's men for that – not me.'

'But I *do* blame you ... for although you didn't strike him down yourself, it was through your agency that he was struck at all.' Rockliffe's face was coldly purposeful and there were tiny slivers of ice in his normally smooth tones. 'Despite having encountered the unfortunate gentleman before, you still appear puzzled by my interest in this matter. Allow me to clarify it for you. His name is Lord Nicholas Wynstanton. And he is my brother.'

If Sir George had been pale before, he was now deathly-white. Watching him with a species of clinical detachment, Aristide couldn't decide whether he was going to pass out or throw up. Judging by the look of him, either one was a possibility.

Finally he stammered, 'I d-didn't know. I didn't.'

'Your ignorance is no defence. You didn't know but neither did you care,' said the duke remorselessly. 'While my brother was lying on the ground after that vicious assault, you and Cross discussed abducting him in place of Mademoiselle Delacroix. Can you deny that?'

'It wasn't my idea. I said no. I said to take the woman, like we'd planned. But --'

'But you would have let Cross have his way, had not help arrived in time to prevent it.'

'No – no, I wouldn't. I swear I wouldn't!'

'Of course you would.' For the first time, Rockliffe allowed the full extent of his contempt to show. 'You would have seized the chance to get what you wanted, without a care for who might be hurt in the process. And you would have done it because you are a weak, stupid man, pursuing a vain and foolish vendetta.'

George's nerves were beginning to unravel. He had no idea what these men wanted with him, or where this conversation was going or what they would accuse him of next. Now, not knowing what else to do, he picked on Rockliffe's penultimate word.

'It isn't foolish. He cheated me. I *know* he did.'

'Perhaps. But I suspect that there is rather more to it,' remarked Rockliffe. 'Is there not, Aristide?'

Aristide looked back at him, half-quizzical and half-thoughtful. Then, with a slight shrug and expelling a long breath, he said, 'Yes.'

George looked from one to the other of them and clutched his head.

'What the hell are you talking about now?'

'The night at Belcourt's three years ago that began all this. The night you say I cheated you out of two thousand guineas.'

'And so you did.'

'Yes,' agreed Aristide composedly. 'I did. You have the distinction of being the last man I ever fleeced, Sir George. But you did not realise it at the time, did you? You worked it out later because you couldn't understand how so much money had passed from your side of the table to mine ... unless *you* were not the *only* one cheating.'

This time Braxton looked as if the ground had melted away from beneath his feet. For a moment, his mouth hung open. Then he scowled, shook his fist and tried to put on a show of righteous indignation. 'How dare you? I wasn't cheating! I *don't* cheat!'

'Yes, you do – and very badly, too. Did you honestly suppose I didn't know? You may think yourself clever and skilful but the fact is that you are completely inept.' Aristide shrugged. 'You also cheat purely for the sake of it which is always a mistake. But your *real* misfortune that night was encountering me.' He held up a hand as Braxton would have spoken. 'No – don't interrupt. You want a confession? Here it is.'

Across the room, Rockliffe folded his arms and waited to enjoy the story.

'I rarely played at Belcourt's but I went there that night because I needed a game offering higher than usual stakes,' said Aristide dispassionately. 'I began by playing piquet with a surly Dane. You, Sir George, were playing basset at the adjacent table with three young Englishmen. They were drinking freely, utterly green and happily anticipating a tumble upstairs later on. They had no idea that you were systematically cleaning them out to the point where I doubt they had enough left between them for one of the drabs on the Pont Neuf – never mind one of Belcourt's girls.' A look of pained disapproval crossed his face. 'I watched you. I saw every clumsy, amateur trick; dealing from the bottom, palming cards, marking the aces ... *God*. You were so bad you might as well have had a sign over your head; so bad that I even contemplated alerting the floor-manager. But in the end, what finally made up my mind was the fact that you didn't need to cheat at all. Their play was even more slovenly than your sharping – so you could have won honestly.'

'This,' murmured Rockliffe, 'is quite enthralling. Do go on.'

Suspecting levity, Aristide ignored this and continued to hold Sir George's gaze.

'By the time they left, the contents of their pockets were on the table in front of you and, by coincidence, it was roughly the amount I stood in need of. So I set out to teach you a valuable lesson by giving you a dose of your own medicine ... and you made it ridiculously easy.' He shook his head, almost in disbelief. 'I'll offer you a word of advice. Give up sharping before somebody calls you out and puts a well-deserved bullet through you.'

'And do not imagine,' offered the duke with just a hint of grimness, 'that that is an exaggeration. I can assure you that it is not.'

Snakes were writhing in Sir George's stomach and his hands were shaking. He said, 'What do you want? Just tell me what you want and leave me alone, will you?'

Aristide raised an enquiring brow. 'Your Grace?'

'Yes.' Rockliffe strolled to within two feet of Braxton and watched him recoil in the chair as if anticipating a blow. 'Relax, Sir George. I rarely find the need to resort to physical violence – though, in your case, I am conscious of a certain temptation. However ... this is what you will do. You will write out a detailed account for Bow Street of your dealings with Cross in respect of the attack in Ryder Street, including your own culpability in it.'

'I can't!' said Braxton, horrified. 'If I do that, they'll arrest me – unless Cross kills me first.'

'Oddly enough, the latter possibility does not dismay me in the least. However, you will *certainly* be arrested if you refuse to obey me because I shall insist upon it,' came the cold response. 'But since Sir John Fielding wants Cross more than he wants you, he may be willing to overlook your part in the matter if you give him useful evidence. It can't be guaranteed, of course ... but that is a chance you will have to take. Well?'

Braxton hesitated, still desperately trying to find a loop-hole big enough to crawl through. Eventually, failing, he mumbled, 'I – I don't have much choice, do I?'

'No. Neither do you deserve one. So count your blessings, Sir George. Both Aristide and I would be delighted to see you behind bars. You are fortunate we are giving you an opportunity to avoid that. I suggest you use the string-and-clapper arrangement you call a brain and take what I am offering. Then, if Bow Street turns a blind eye, you should get as far away from me as you can ... and hide. Because if my brother suffers any lasting damage, you will discover that I have a very long and unforgiving arm.'

CHAPTER NINETEEN

Nicholas was awoken by the growling of his stomach at around seven in the evening. Brennon, who had been sitting at his bedside when he'd fallen asleep, had been replaced by Madeleine, now fully-restored but for the shadows under her eyes, to her usual state of flawless elegance. Since her attention was focused on the book in her lap, she did not immediately perceive that Nicholas was awake, thus giving him the opportunity to enjoy a lazy perusal whilst waiting for the drug-induced haze to clear from his skull. He found he didn't like that feeling very much and decided to do without further doses of laudanum if at all possible. When the time came to hold what he thought of as The Conversation with Madeleine, he would need all his wits about him. He was also, he promised himself, not going to do it lying in bed like a damned invalid.

He recalled all too clearly why he'd left Kent early to return to London. He had driven back angry, resentful and determined to have it out with Madeleine – only to have everything unexpectedly turned upside down. Holding on to his anger would have been difficult enough anyway without waking up bruised and battered from an attack he still couldn't remember. And Madeleine was different. There was a warmth and softness to her that hadn't ever been there before ... suggesting that all her barriers were down, if he wished to walk through them. But whether these were genuine changes or something temporary caused by her feelings of guilt, he didn't know.

After a little while, he said, 'How long have you been here?'

The book slipped from her fingers and she looked up.

'Not long. How do you feel?'

'Hungry,' he said truthfully. 'You know that phrase *I could eat a horse*?'

'I do – but you most certainly could not.' She stood up and laid a cool hand on his brow. 'However, you haven't eaten for two days so I would be worried if you *weren't* ravenous. I'll go down and see what Mrs Constantine considers suitable.'

'I don't mind forgoing the horse ... but if you bring me gruel, I'll throw it at you.'

'No.' Madeleine shook her head and smiled. 'If I bring you gruel, you will eat it like a good boy. But I think we can do better than that. Just lie still and I'll send Brennon to you.'

As the door closed behind her, Nicholas became suddenly aware that his body had urgent requirements other than food and hoped Brennon wouldn't be long. Fortunately, he wasn't and, with that problem taken care of, Nicholas took an inventory of his various ills. His head still throbbed but not as ferociously as before and both his shoulder and wrist had subsided into a dull ache. He tried convincing himself that his ribs were also on the mend but it took only one deep breath to prove him wrong ... which naturally left him wondering how long he was going to be bed-bound.

Madeleine came back followed by a large footman bearing a laden tray and Nicholas caught the aroma of fresh bread, along with something hot and homely that made his mouth water. He said, 'Not gruel, then.'

'God save you, no, sir!' grinned Patrick, placing the tray on a side-table. 'It's a good, rich soup to put you back on your feet. Only Mrs Constantine's finest for you, sir – and us all that grateful for you saving Miss Madeleine the way you did.'

'Thank you, Patrick.' Her tone perfectly matter-of-fact, Madeleine set a sturdy bowl and a napkin on his lordship's knees and, having handed him a spoon, put a small basket of bread at his side. 'You can shake Lord Nicholas's hand later. For now, he's hungry.'

The first mouthful of Mrs Constantine's finest made Nicholas forget he'd been about to ask Madeline if *all* her servants were as cheerfully chatty as the Irish footman.

Madeleine sat quietly with her book, leaving him to eat in peace.

Presently, having consumed half of the soup and two soft rolls still warm from the oven, he said, '*Did* I save you? From what you told me earlier, it didn't sound like it.'

'You did all you could – as much as *anyone* could. And you held them off long enough for help to come. If you hadn't fought so hard, they wouldn't have hurt you so badly.'

'Perhaps not.' He dipped a piece of bread in the soup. 'Is Rock still here?'

'Yes. He's downstairs, with Aristide and Genevieve – they arrived earlier while you were sleeping.' A sudden and unexpected smile dawned. 'Aristide has given Genevieve a puppy and is living with the consequences.'

Nicholas glanced up. 'Doesn't he like dogs?'

'He's not sure. But the fact that it chews everything within reach isn't helping.'

Nicholas dipped the spoon in the bowl, looked at it and then laid it down again.

'I'm sorry. This is delicious but I don't think I can finish it. I hope ... Mrs Constantine, is it? ... won't be offended.'

'No. She said this might happen.' Madeleine rose and removed the remains of his meal to the far side of the room so he didn't have to either see or smell it. 'Our respective brothers spent an hour with Sir George Braxton this afternoon. They will doubtless give you all the details themselves ... but the gist is that they frightened him into making a written confession in the hope it will enable Bow Street to put Cross behind bars – assuming they ever find him.'

'Ah. Well, Rock in full ducal mode is enough to frighten anyone.'

'I'm sure that was a large part of it. But the truth about what happened three years ago at Belcourt's also came out.'

'And what did happen?'

'It appears Aristide wasn't the *only* one who was cheating. Braxton had apparently been at it all evening.' She shook her head, laughing a little. 'According to his Grace, Aristide was quite disgusted by how bad he was at it.'

Nicholas also laughed and then wished he hadn't. Seeing him wince, Madeleine stood up, saying, 'Everyone will be up to see you after dinner ... but for now, is there anything else you would like?'

'A bath,' he said promptly, 'though I suppose that should wait until tomorrow. If I pass out in the tub, Brennon hasn't the muscle to pull me out again. But if his hands have stopped shaking, I'll have the shave I refused earlier. And once I'm presentable ... if Genevieve wants to visit me, tell her to bring her dog.'

* * *

Aristide began the following day by reading and absorbing the three detailed letters awaiting him from Henry Lessing – all of which related to funds supposedly owing to Genevieve by way of either her late husband's will or her marriage settlement. It appeared that the current Lord Westin was trying to withhold the monies due to his late cousin's widow by standing on what he thought was the letter of the law - namely, some of the wording of Christopher Westin's will. With undisguised enjoyment, Mr Lessing informed Monsieur Delacroix that battle was now joined and the enemy already in retreat.

The business of the marriage settlements was another matter. The sorry list of catastrophic investments contained in the letter from Cedric Harcourt told its own tale. It might even have been comical had it not left Genevieve virtually destitute. Aristide already had an old score to settle with his three brothers-in-law and he fully intended to do so when the right opportunity presented itself. Meanwhile, their careless treatment of their sister only fuelled his anger.

Having penned a reply to Mr Lessing, he considered writing to Lord Sherbourne and arranging a meeting. Then, deciding the arrogant fellow could wait, he tossed the earl's terse missive aside and set off for Sinclairs. He had intended to spend a few hours at his desk. There were the last fortnight's figures to look at and as well as speaking to Jenkins about Billy, he ought to see the lad himself. But half a dozen yards from the door of the club, he changed direction and headed for the mews to order his carriage.

'Where to, sir?' asked Higgins cheerfully.

'A jeweller's shop. And don't ask me which one because I have no idea.'

'Theed & Pickett, then. Lord Pennington always reckoned they was the best.'

'Fine.'

Hiding a grin, Higgins set the carriage in motion. Monsieur Delacroix not being in the best of moods, coupled with his need to visit a jeweller said he had fences to mend and possibly some grovelling to do as well. Higgins found the idea hugely entertaining.

Inside the carriage, Aristide tried convincing himself that he would have done this anyway – just not today. It didn't work. The truth was that he didn't want to spend another evening like the last one.

Madeleine had joined them partway through dinner, given an account of Nicholas's progress and told Genevieve that he wanted to meet Blanchette. This had somehow led to Genevieve telling his sister exactly how he'd ended up buying the damned dog – which meant that Rockliffe, eyeing him quizzically throughout, heard it all, too. Then, as if *that* wasn't enough, after he and the duke had described their dealings with Braxton to Nicholas, Genevieve arrived with Blanchette in tow and the whole embarrassing story of him saving the demon pup from death by drowning and thus proving what a kind and generous husband he was had to be lived through again for Nicholas's benefit. By the time this was over, both the duke and his brother were looking at him in ways that made Aristide squirm and want to put his own head in a bucket. And so here he was, on his way to visit a jeweller.

Once inside the shop, however, his mood gradually changed. Aristide told young Mr Rundell that he wanted to see rubies – only the best quality and a complete set; necklace, bracelet, earrings and ring. Mr Rundell bowed politely, begged Monsieur Delacroix to take a seat in the private room and, whilst deciding which pieces to show first, mentioned his client's name to Mr Pickett who said promptly, 'He owns Sinclairs – so price won't be an object. Show him that piece Lord Harpenden ordered for his mistress, then couldn't pay for. It's probably just the thing to take his fancy.'

Sending the junior clerk for refreshments, Mr Rundell settled down to business and immediately hit a wall when Monsieur promptly rejected the Harpenden necklace out of hand, followed by three others.

'No. These are too heavy, too ornate and decidedly vulgar. I am buying a gift for my wife, not a courtesan. Show me something less gaudy and more refined.'

Mr Rundell straightened his spine and re-shuffled his ideas. Owning a gaming-club apparently didn't mean that the gentleman's taste ran to flash. He said, 'Certainly, sir. Please give me a moment. I believe we have just the thing.'

An hour later, Aristide left the shop with a flat leather box, the contents of which had cost nearly a week's income from Sinclairs. He considered it money well spent.

Back in his office, he thanked Billy for his quick-thinking of three nights ago and welcomed him to the staff of Sinclairs with a guinea, then gave him a few more coins along with a peculiar shopping list. That done, he tried to find the error in an invoice from the wine-merchant – only to discover that the simple task had become inexplicably herculean. Finally, concluding that he wasn't going to achieve anything useful, he did what he'd wanted to do in the first place and went home, jeweller's box in one hand and a hemp bag containing Billy's acquisitions from the market in the other.

Minton informed him that Madame was sitting with Lord Nicholas while Miss Madeleine agreed the week's menus with Mrs Constantine. Aristide nodded and telling himself that his purchases could wait until later, went upstairs to find a place to hide them. From outside Nicholas's bedchamber, Genevieve's peals of delighted laughter brought an odd feeling he couldn't put a name to but which made it necessary to banish a frown before he set his hand to the latch.

His wife was curled up on the foot of the bed while she and Nicholas teased Blanchette by tossing a ball of wool back and forth between them. The odd feeling turned into a red-hot wire passing through Aristide's chest and acquired a name. However, the second Genevieve saw him she slid to her feet, saying, 'Aristide! This is a nice surprise. I thought you'd be busy at Sinclairs until this evening. Were you looking for me?'

'Not for any particular reason,' he replied neutrally. 'Don't let me interrupt your game.'

Brief though it was, Nicholas hadn't missed the flicker of expression that had touched the ice-blue eyes and he had no trouble at all interpreting it. Fortunately, Blanchette had seized the opportunity to pounce on the wool and settled down to destroy it, so he said easily, 'I think the game is over for today. If Blanchette isn't worn out, I am. But thank you for bringing her to alleviate my boredom, Genevieve. It was kind of you.'

'Nonsense,' she said, finally managing to capture her elusive pet. 'We both had fun and with luck, she'll sleep now, so I'll take her away and leave you in peace.'

Aristide watched her go but made no move to follow.

'How are you today, Nicholas?'

'Better than yesterday and sick of lying in bed. The day seems bloody endless. I'd planned to be up and at least sitting in a chair by now but couldn't because the clothes I was wearing the other night are apparently only fit for burning and Brennon hadn't the wit to bring any others. I've sent him back to fetch some but he's taking his time over it.' He stopped. 'I'm talking too much, aren't I?'

'Yes.' Aristide realised he absolutely did *not* want to hear any excuses about the cosy scene he'd walked in on. He knew it didn't mean anything. What he *didn't* like was the suspicion that Nicholas knew how he'd felt. He said, 'If you're tired, I'll go. If not ... we could play a hand of cards, if you wish.'

Nicholas sat up, winced and grinned. 'Only if we play for pennies and you promise to cheat. This business with Braxton has left me curious.'

Aristide shook his head. 'I *may* cheat. I'm not promising I will. But unless all my old skill has deserted me, you'll never know whether I have or not.'

* * *

Aristide played cards with Nicholas for an hour, relieved him of two shillings and sixpence and finished by demonstrating some of the tricks he had used to do it. Then, when Brennon returned with some of his lordship's clothes, Aristide left him to it and tracked his sister to the little room she used as an office. Shutting the door behind him, he said, 'Nicholas is dressing and intends getting out of bed for an hour or two. At the risk of repeating a conversation we've had before ... have you made peace with him yet?'

'I've no idea what you mean.' Madeleine kept her eyes on the letter in her hand.

'Don't be obtuse. You and I may not have had the opportunity to speak privately but I am quite sure Genevieve must have told you what Nicholas's reaction was when he did not, as he clearly expected, find you at Sarre Park.'

'She mentioned it, yes.'

'And?'

This time she looked up at him.

'And unsurprisingly, given the state of his health, the subject has yet to be discussed. But even if it *had* been, I do not see what right you have to ask what was said. It's not as if you've exactly been very forthcoming yourself, is it?'

'I didn't ask for chapter and verse, Madeleine,' he sighed, 'I merely asked if the matter had been laid to rest. And forthcoming about what?'

'Well, let's see. Your sudden decision to plunge into matrimony, perhaps?' She stood up, her expression distinctly irritable. 'So here is a thought. I'll share my confidences when you share yours. Meanwhile, you can mind your own business.'

And she walked out, being careful not to slam the door behind her.

Alone in her bedchamber, Madeleine paced back and forth, wondering why Nicholas had made no attempt to continue the conversation he'd begun outside the back door of Sinclairs minutes before they had been attacked. Of course, he didn't remember they'd *had* a conversation. But what she was sure he *did* remember was the anger that had brought him to London in the first place ... unless he either no longer felt it or just didn't care.

Throughout all the long hours when he had remained unconscious and she had grappled with the possibility that he might die, she had made endless promises. Promises to God, to herself and to Nicholas. As yet, she hadn't kept any of them; not because she hadn't meant them or didn't want to but because it seemed impossible to look Nicholas in the eye and bare her soul without some hint that he would welcome it. She was prepared to humiliate herself. But if she drenched him in an outpouring of emotion that had come too late, she would simply embarrass him.

The other question was how much longer he would remain in Duke Street. Rockliffe had been content for his brother to be cared for there until the worst was over but Madeleine suspected that as soon as Nicholas was on the mend, the duke would want to remove him to either St James' Square or Wynstanton Priors. If Nicholas didn't provide the cue she needed before that happened, her chance would be lost.

Since it therefore seemed that time might be of the essence, she summoned her nerve and went to see how he did. She found him sitting in a chair by the window, clad in a robe which actually made her blink, while Brennon fussed with shirts and cravats on the other side of the room.

'Aristide told me you were getting up,' she said, 'Are you quite comfortable?'

'Moderately probably describes it best.' Nicholas shifted a little. 'Getting into a shirt proved to be a challenge we decided to leave for another day. But it's progress, I suppose.'

'Doctor Rayne said your ribs would take at least four weeks to heal and it's only been four days. You shouldn't expect too much of yourself.'

'My expectations are fairly low generally so that isn't a problem. I am, however, getting tired of playing the invalid. It's tedious.'

Madeleine heard the faintly sulky note but ignored it.

'You are not *playing* the invalid, you idiotic man. You were *hurt*!'

'Odd as it may seem, I've noticed that.'

She folded her arms and looked at him, deciding that he was definitely feeling sorry for himself. 'Have you never been ill or injured before?'

'Not that I can recall.'

'Consider yourself fortunate, then. Aristide was once so badly beaten he was bed-ridden for over three weeks and could barely walk for twice that. Broken ribs, a broken wrist, a dislocated shoulder and a damaged knee, amongst other things.'

'Why?' asked Nicholas, moodily. 'Did somebody catch him cheating?'

'No. They beat him to a pulp for the coins in his pockets.'

'Oh.' Nicholas looked chastened. 'I'm sorry.'

'Good. Now ... how badly is it hurting?'

'Quite a lot. But I'm not taking any more laudanum. If I'm going to wake up feeling hung over, I'd like the pleasure of getting drunk first.'

* * *

While Madeleine was gently scolding Nicholas, Aristide was trying to decide how best to give Genevieve the rubies. He didn't want her first and strongest reaction to be one of gratitude but had little doubt that it would be unless he could think of a way to prevent it. What he *really* wanted was to give her something he suspected she'd never had – namely, a moment or two of romance. The problem was that he didn't think there was a romantic bone in his body ... which meant he had no idea how to go about it.

He was still considering the matter when he went upstairs to find Genevieve already dressed for dinner, with Madeleine's maid putting the finishing touches to her hair. Aristide sat down and waited. Then, when Becky left the room, he said mildly, 'I thought we agreed you were to have a maid of your own.'

She turned, sliding the silver bangle which was her only piece of jewellery on to her wrist as she did so. 'We did. But there's been scarcely any time – and I don't want just *anyone*. All the servants in this house were in trouble of one sort or another before you and Madeleine gave them the second chance that no one else would – so my maid ought to be another of the same.'

He eyed her curiously. 'Are you sure?'

'Yes. And Mrs Constantine thinks she may know of someone. A young woman recently dismissed without a character because the master of the house couldn't keep his hands off her. Needless to say, through no fault of her own, she's now unemployable.'

'Well, she'll be safe enough in this house.' A faint note of mordant humour crept into his voice. 'The only body *I* can't keep my hands off is yours.'

Turning a little pink, Genevieve bent her head to toy with the bracelet.

'I still ... sometimes I still find that hard to believe.'

'Do I not give you adequate proof?' Rising, he strolled across to pull her to her feet and wrap an arm around her waist. Then, trapping her gaze with his own, he said meditatively, 'Perhaps I should try harder.'

Genevieve's arms slid up around his neck. 'No. Ignore me. I'm just being silly.'

'Yes. You are.' He trailed a series of small kisses from cheek to jaw. 'However, if you are not convinced that I find every inch of you irresistible, I am clearly failing somewhere.'

'You aren't,' she whispered, her fingers straying to his hair. 'Of course you aren't.'

He sighed against her neck. 'And now you are humouring me.'

'No.'

'Yes.' He found a sensitive spot above her collar-bone. 'My self-esteem is suffering.'

The small quiver he felt in her body was one of response but he also detected the warmth of laughter in her voice when she said, 'You are being absurd.'

'Worse and worse.' His tongue dipped into an enticing hollow. 'Clearly, you have no understanding of the fragility of masculine pride when it comes to our prowess as lovers.'

'*Definitely* absurd,' murmured Genevieve, melting against him and adding wickedly, 'since prowess isn't an issue.'

'That might have been better put,' complained Aristide, pausing to kiss her mouth. 'But I'm willing to take it in the spirit in which I hope it's --' He stopped, drew back slightly and looked down. 'My leg is being attacked by a hat.'

Genevieve followed his gaze and promptly dissolved into laughter. Pulling out of his embrace, she said unsteadily, 'Blanchette? But where did she get that dreadful thing? It – it's bigger than she is!'

He dropped on his haunches, grasped a handful of straw brim and pulled. Blanchette gave a little growl and tugged back. Continuing the game, Aristide said, 'I sent Billy to buy a few things she could destroy. There's a long woolly scarf and a pair of hideous slippers as well.' He glanced up, his expression enigmatic. 'I believe in keeping my promises, you see. And I couldn't let her like Nicholas best, now could I?'

He could see her trying to decide if there was an underlying significance in his words. Then, choosing to be equally ambiguous, she said slowly, 'She wouldn't do that. She knows who was there for her when she needed him most. And she certainly knows when she's been given the best gift ever.'

'Are we talking about the hat?' Aristide stood up, leaving the puppy to shake her prize into submission. Then, dusting off his fingers, he added, 'I only ask because I bought something else today ... although that had better wait until later. Did I mention that I ought to spend a couple of hours at Sinclairs this evening?'

Disappointment rose in her chest and was swiftly squashed. 'You know you didn't.'

'True. It is what I was about to say before you distracted me.' He smiled and touched her hair. 'Since I will be out, Rockliffe is dining upstairs with Nicholas – which leaves you alone with Madeleine. If you're lucky, she'll be in a better mood than she was earlier. If not, cheer yourself with the thought that I won't be late. All being well, I'll be back by eleven.'

* * *

Rockliffe took one look at the green and gold swirls shot through with crimson of his brother's robe and shaded his eyes.

'Nicholas ... what exactly *is* that hideous thing you are wearing?' he asked faintly.

'This?' Nicholas extended an arm. 'It isn't hideous. I like it.'

'You like it. Really? I'm not sure whether you have defective eyesight or have completely lost your powers of discernment.'

'If you must know, I enjoy watching Brennon wince every time I put it on – though I suppose I shouldn't tease him. He was completely overset when I disappeared. And when they brought him to me here, he actually cried,' said Nicholas, his tone a mixture of despair and revulsion. 'Honestly, Rock – it was excruciating.'

'Yes. I can see that it would have been.' The duke poured two glasses of claret and handed one to his brother. 'Your taste in dressing-robes apart, I am extremely glad to see you out of bed and looking substantially better than you did a couple of days ago. Are you still having headaches?'

'No. It's just my ribs. I can't laugh, cough or even take a deep breath without feeling as if somebody's driven a blazing poker through me. And I won't *begin* to describe what trying to pull a shirt over my head was like.'

'Ah.' A faint frown crept into Rockliffe's dark eyes. He said, 'In that case, there is no point in my asking if you would like to complete your recovery at the Priors. I imagine a long carriage-ride sounds like extended torture.'

'Yes. But I can't go yet, anyway.' Nicholas met his brother's gaze squarely. 'You know why I left Kent. I came here to settle matters – if that's what you can call it – with Madeleine. Needless to say, I haven't done it yet. And I'm not leaving until I have.'

The duke pulled an enamelled snuff-box from his pocket and surveyed it thoughtfully.

'Until these last few days, my acquaintance with Mademoiselle Delacroix was extremely slight. But my impression now is that she is a little less ... glacial ... than I had thought.'

'I've seen that. She thinks that since she's to blame for my being here, she's also to blame for me getting hurt. Guilt, in other words. But if that's *all* it is, I may as well walk away now.'

'And you think you can?'

'What other choice is there?' Nicholas's jaw was tight and the look in his eyes utterly bleak. 'I've tried, Rock. And before I left for Charlecote I honestly believed she cared for me but was fighting against it because she thought she should. But we know how well that turned out, don't we? And this can't go on. She either wants me or she doesn't. So the next time she slams the door in my face will be the last.'

Still toying idly with the box, Rockliffe said, 'I don't imagine you've had occasion to speak with Mr Jenkins at all, have you?'

'Jenkins? The fellow in charge of security at Sinclairs? No. Why?'

'He arrived on the scene just after you were rendered unconscious and saw what happened next. I think you might find what he has to say … illuminating.' Pausing, he dropped the snuff-box back in his pocket. 'Meanwhile, on another note entirely, Sir John Fielding's fellows gave Braxton a very uncomfortable few hours during which he tried to smear Aristide with an accusation of card-sharping.'

Nicholas's expression relaxed a little. 'Did it stick?'

'No. Bow Street has an unsurprising lack of interest in what may or may not have happened years ago in Paris. I am told that Sir George found this disappointing. He was even unhappier at being tethered like a sacrificial goat in Bellsavage Yard as bait for Cross – since no one found it necessary to tell him that sustained interrogation has already produced information that may eventually lead to that gentleman's whereabouts.' Rockliffe smiled faintly and raised his glass. 'Bow Street, needless to say, is keeping its collective fingers crossed.'

CHAPTER TWENTY

Since Madeleine made it clear that she didn't want to talk, Genevieve picked at her dinner, listened to the chiming of the clock on the mantelpiece and willed the hours to pass a bit quicker. They didn't, of course. But by ten o'clock, she felt able to retire to her own rooms where she could amuse herself playing with Blanchette until her husband came home.

'He said he bought something else,' she told the little dog, while indulging in a tug-of-war with the moth-eaten scarf. 'And he implied he bought it for me. But why? Did he decide that if you had a gift, I must have one too? Doesn't he know that every minute he spends with me is worth more than anything he could buy? Admittedly, I haven't actually *told* him how I feel ... but I haven't tried to hide it, either.' She paused for a moment, thinking it over. 'I *could* say it, I suppose. He's an intelligent man so I doubt he'd feel obliged to respond in kind. I hope not, anyway because I already have far more than I hoped for. *He* is more than I hoped for.' Without warning, she released her end of the scarf and laughed when Blanchette fell over. 'I asked him to marry me because I was desperate, because I remember him being kind when I was young and annoying and because he wasn't like Kit. Not like Kit? He isn't like *anyone*! That cool, business-like façade hides all manner of things ... such as when he's teasing or joking ... and the wickedly seductive Frenchman who knows exactly where to touch me and how and ...' Genevieve stopped, realising that even just *thinking* about that side of Aristide was making bits of her melt with anticipation. Laughing at her own foolishness, she pulled Blanchette on to her lap, saying, 'And that is *quite* enough of that. Such confidences don't belong to ears as young as yours.'

Blanchette yawned and settled down for a nap. Genevieve went back to watching the clock. Time continued to pass at a snail-like pace. Eleven o'clock came, then half-past, but Aristide did not. Sighing, she decided she had better ring for Becky and get ready for bed. She hadn't done so before because Aristide had a variety of ways of removing her clothes that left her breathless with laughter one minute and breathless for quite a different reason the next. The maid's ministrations, though undeniably quicker, were not nearly as enjoyable.

When she apologised for the lateness of the hour, Becky merely grinned and shrugged.

'That's all right, ma'am. Sir said he'd be back early tonight, did he?'

Colouring, Genevieve said, 'He hoped to be – but something must have detained him.'

'Often does, ma'am.' Having handed Genevieve her nightgown, Becky turned away to restore the bronze taffeta to the closet. 'But he spends more time at home now than he ever used to – which ain't no bad fing, if you ask me. All work and no play, as they say.'

When the maid had gone, Genevieve debated waiting up a little longer and then, telling herself not to be silly, climbed into bed. If Aristide was late, it was because it couldn't be helped ... and watching the clock wouldn't make him come home any quicker.

Some considerable time later, she was half-woken by an arm drawing her back against a hard, familiar chest. Not bothering to open her eyes, she said sleepily, 'You're home.'

'Yes. I'm sorry. Sorry I'm so late and sorry I woke you.'

'What time is it?'

'After three. Go back to sleep.'

'Mm.' She laid her hand over the one he'd put around her. 'That's nice.'

'Yes. Sleep, now. You can be angry with me tomorrow.'

Genevieve gave a little gurgle that turned into a yawn.

'Not angry. Just glad you're here.'

Moi aussi, mignonne. Moi aussi.

But knowing she was sliding back into sleep, he did not say it.

* * *

Genevieve propped herself on one elbow and watched her husband sleep. It was a rare pleasure and never lasted as long as she would have liked. A narrow shaft of sunlight from the small gap in the curtains was sufficient for her to see the tumble of straight, pale gold hair he wore rather longer than most gentlemen, the thick sweep of darker gold lashes and the somehow enticing angle of cheekbone and jaw. He looked different when he slept; warmer, younger and less self-contained ... as if the mantle of authority that characterised him by day was discarded along with his clothes.

His eyes opened without warning and Genevieve was trapped in cisterns of winter-sky blue. He said, 'How long have you been watching me?'

'Not long. You came home so late, I didn't want to wake you.'

Aristide passed a hand over his eyes and on through his hair.

'I'm sorry about that.'

'It doesn't matter.'

'It matters to me. I had plans.' He drew her down beside him. 'Stop it. Like most men, I don't feel fit to be seen until I've shaved.'

Genevieve reached out to slide her fingertips along his jaw but said only, 'What happened last night?'

'Lord Seabridge was hosting a small party in the blue dining-room. After a good deal of wine, he and his friend Mr Durand embarked on a competition to see which of them could shoot the most pips out of playing cards.'

'*What?* Inside that lovely room?'

'Exactly. By the time Jenkins' fellows got there a number of shots had already been fired. These smashed a mirror, tore through the wall-hangings and ruined a rather valuable painting. Madeleine,' he finished dryly, 'is going to be incandescent.'

'I don't blame her.'

'Neither do I. Once the damage had been assessed, I told Seabridge to expect a bill for repairs and terminated his and his friends' memberships. They argued. And since I wanted to be home before daylight, I had Jenkins toss them down the steps.' Sighing a little, he tucked a long ebony curl behind her ear. 'And now, much though I'd like to linger here with you, I suppose I'd better get up and face Madeleine.'

※ ※ ※

Having heard the catalogue of destruction in the blue salon, Madeleine said irritably, 'Did you ask Jenkins how pistols got inside the club at *all*?'

'Oddly enough, yes. Seabridge arrived with a domino over his arm, so presumably the box containing the duelling pistols was hidden beneath it. Is there anything *else* you think I may have forgotten?'

Madeleine shrugged and continued moodily pushing egg around her plate.

'Good. Such incidents are rare but, as you know perfectly well, they are a natural hazard of the business. Once you have seen for yourself what repairs are needed --' He stopped as the butler stepped into the room. 'Yes, Minton?'

'I beg your pardon, sir, but Lord Nicholas asks if Mr Jenkins could visit him today.'

'Jenkins?' echoed Aristide, surprised. 'Why?'

'His lordship did not explain, sir. Shall I send a message to Sinclairs?'

'By all means.' And when Minton had gone, 'Does that make any sense to you, Madeleine?'

'None at all.' She stood up and looked across at Genevieve, who had wisely stayed out of the conversation thus far. 'I'll go to Sinclairs in an hour or so. It will still be quiet so if you'd like to look around properly, this would be as good a time as any.'

'Really?' asked Genevieve, eagerly. 'Thank you. I'd love to.'

'In that case,' remarked Aristide, also rising, 'I'll keep Nicholas company for a while. Having still been at the club when I left, I doubt Jenkins will be here before noon, though I suppose --' He stopped again as Minton reappeared and said, 'Now what?

'It's Lord Sherbourne, sir. He is very insistent on seeing you and refusing to leave until he's done so. It did not seem appropriate to leave him on the front steps, so I have had Patrick wait with him in the hall until I have your instructions.'

Aristide sank back into his chair and watched colour ebb from his wife's face.

But before he could answer Minton, Madeleine stood up, saying, 'Use my office, Aristide. It leads off the drawing-room so you can be within call if Sherbourne asks for Genevieve.' And dropping a light hand on Genevieve's shoulder as she passed, 'We can go to Sinclairs another day. Meanwhile, don't let your brother upset you.'

'No. Thank you,' replied Genevieve, surprised. But Madeleine had already gone.

Aristide told Minton to tell the earl he would receive him presently and to show him upstairs in five minutes. Then, when he and Genevieve were alone, he said quietly, 'This has to be done and I had planned to arrange it for tomorrow. Sherbourne will want to complain about the enquiries Henry Lessing has been making with regard to the iniquitous financial position in which you were left before we married. I'd intended to discuss that with you before speaking to Sherbourne but there's no time to do it now. I am more concerned with whether or not you wish to see him. He is bound to ask for you ... but you don't have to do anything you don't want to.'

Genevieve looked up from her tightly clasped fingers.

'No. I don't, do I?' She tilted her head, thinking about it. '*Should* I see him?'

'I think you may feel better for looking him in the eye, secure in the knowledge that he no longer has any power over you. And you don't have to do it alone. I can stay beside you or within earshot from the drawing-room, as Madeleine has suggested. The choice will be yours ... *after* I have spoken to him myself.'

* * *

By the time the Earl of Sherbourne was shown into Madeleine's small office, his patience – which had been limited to begin with – was rapidly diminishing. He strode in and before Minton had closed the door behind him said coldly, 'About time. Did you think to avoid me forever whilst hiding behind your lawyer's insolent communications?'

'*Were* they insolent? Surely *awkward* would have been a more accurate description.' Aristide neither sat down himself nor offered the earl a chair. 'For the rest … no, I have not been avoiding you. Although you may not believe it, I've been awaiting this moment with gentle anticipation.'

'I see.' His lordship's gaze grew scathing. 'Despite the letters I have received from Mr Lessing, I had hoped this might be about more than money. Naïve of me to suppose that marrying the sister of an earl might be enough. I doubt a man like you ever enters any transaction that won't turn a coin or two. Poor Genevieve. Does she know?'

'You shouldn't judge quite *everyone* by your own standards, my lord,' returned Aristide sardonically. 'Yes. Poor Genevieve, indeed … but we'll come to that presently. First allow me to make one thing very clear. My only interest in the money due to her in respect of her previous marriage is in ensuring that she receives that to which she is entitled. God knows, she deserves *something* for five years with the likes of Westin. As for the money itself, it is hers to do with as she will. She can spend it on hats, establish a home for stray dogs or drop the whole lot in the Poor Box for all I care. But until you and the new Lord Westin fulfil your obligations, Mr Lessing will continue to pursue both of you on her behalf.'

There was a short, icy silence.

'Are you *threatening* me?'

'No. I'm making the position plain. Perhaps you might do the same. Because if there is some explanation for the catastrophic list of investments through which your brother lost fifteen thousand pounds which did not belong to him, I'd be delighted to hear it. Well?'

A very faint hint of colour crept across Sherbourne's cheekbones. He said tersely, 'I was out of the country at the time of Genevieve's marriage to Westin and for almost a year after it. Cedric dealt with numerous matters without troubling to keep me informed.'

'And you think that a satisfactory excuse? Not only for leaving your brother free to squander Genevieve's marriage settlements – but for letting her marry Westin at *all*?'

'Had I been in a position to prevent it, she would *not* have married him. But by the time I was made aware of it, it was a *fait accompli* – rather like her marriage to yourself, in fact.'

Aristide couldn't remember ever completely losing his temper but suspected that he was perilously close to it now. He felt a hot tide of fury engulfing him … not because of what this man had done to him seven years ago but because of the way he'd treated Genevieve in the years since. Folding his arms to prevent his hands reaching for the earl's throat, he said, 'Did you *know* what Westin was?'

'I had heard the same rumours as everyone else,' shrugged Sherbourne.

'Despite which, when you came back to England and found your sister married to him, you did absolutely nothing about it.'

'They were *married*. What do you suppose I could have done?'

'Force Westin's father – the man who wanted his child-molesting son given a veneer of respectability – to take a hand? Pin Westin to a wall and threaten him with Armageddon if he didn't treat Genevieve with respect? Visit her from time to time to make sure all was well with her? But you did none of that, did you? She was your sister – and you just washed your hands of her and left her to fend for herself. *Christ*,' finished Aristide disgustedly. 'What sort of man *are* you?'

'I think,' snapped the earl, 'that you have said quite enough.'

'I disagree. The truth is that you can't deny a single thing I have said – though I wouldn't mind hearing you try.'

'This conversation is over, Monsieur Delacroix. As you know, Genevieve's marriage settlements are gone – but the bequest from her grandfather should go some way to making amends and I have already instructed my man of law to make the necessary arrangements with yours. As for your dealings with the current Lord Westin, they are none of my concern. And now I wish to see my sister before taking my leave.'

As far as Aristide was concerned, their conversation was far from over but he decided that the rest of what he had to say could wait. He needed time to control the hard knot of anger in his chest. And he didn't want Genevieve's interview with her brother to be made any more difficult than it had to be.

He said flatly, 'What *you* wish is of absolutely no consequence under my roof, my lord. You will see my wife if *she* wishes it and not otherwise.' And he walked out through the door to the drawing-room.

Genevieve was sitting on the edge of a chair by the windows but she rose as soon as Aristide appeared and said, 'Has he gone?'

'No. He is asking for you.'

Catching the glint of residual temper in his eyes, she said, 'Did he insult you?'

'He tried. But since I had the better ammunition, it didn't work out quite as he'd hoped.' Taking her hands, he smiled encouragingly and said, 'What do you want to do?'

'I'll speak with him and I'll do it alone – though I'll be happier knowing you aren't far away. I've thought about what you said. Ralph has no more importance in my life now than I've ever had in his. It's time he understood that.'

'That's the spirit.' He leaned in and kissed her brow. 'Go to it, *chérie* ... but give me a chance to speak to him before he leaves, please. And remember that I'll come if you call.'

Genevieve nodded, managed a smile ... and walked in to Madeleine's office. Finding her brother lounging in a chair she doubted Aristide had offered, she said, 'Making yourself at home, Ralph?'

'In this house? Hardly.' He looked her up and down, noting the elegant rose-coloured gown and her new air of confidence. 'At least your ill-bred gambler keeps you well-dressed. That must be some comfort for having thrown away any hope you had of being accepted back into society, I suppose.'

'Thanks to Kit, I had no hope of that anyway,' she returned coolly. 'And you would be wise not to belittle my husband in my hearing.'

His brows rose. 'Yes? Well ... you never did have much taste, did you? First Westin and now this. Really, my dear, you must have been desperate.'

'I was.' Quite without warning and somewhat to her brother's discomfiture, she smiled. 'I was – and I thank God for it because if I hadn't been, I wouldn't have Aristide. I am *happy*, Ralph. And there is nothing you can do or say to spoil it.'

'Don't count on that. And you are deluded if you expect it to last.'

'I *know* it will last. And why should that disappoint you? Isn't it enough that I paid for my stupidity in marrying Kit with years of misery? That by the time he died, I hadn't a vestige of self-esteem or pride left?' She shook her head. 'You had no idea what my life was like – neither did you care. You still don't. In fact, I don't know why you wanted to see me. It can't be to check on my well-being since you never did so while I was married to a man whose name decent people spit on.'

'A man *you* chose and who was, at least, born a gentleman.'

'Birth and title don't make a gentleman, Ralph. Character and manners do that and Aristide has both. Also, although you sneer at him from your aristocratic pedestal, he's already achieved more than you will in a lifetime. He started with nothing and made it into something. You started with every advantage – and wasted all of them. In short, he's worth a dozen of you.'

In the adjoining room, Aristide hadn't meant to listen but small snatches of his wife's words teased at the edges of his mind and wouldn't be shut out. He heard Sherbourne say dismissively, 'All that means is that the fellow makes money.' And then, clear as a bell, Genevieve retorting, 'Yes. Aristide *makes* money – whereas you'll have to *marry* it, won't you? If, that is, you can find an heiress who will have you.'

Aristide swallowed a laugh. *Well done, chérie. Hit him again while he's still down.*

Sherbourne uncoiled from his chair.

'You would be wise not to take that tone with me, Genevieve.'

'Why? What can you do about it?' She paused and then said, 'I don't know what you expected this conversation to achieve, but understand this, Ralph. Aristide has my absolute trust and loyalty. He is strong, kind and utterly remarkable ... and I'm a very lucky woman.'

'All of which,' drawled her brother, 'probably boils down to the fact that he is adequate in bed.'

'*Adequate?*' Genevieve turned back to the drawing-room door and pushed it wide. 'Not at all. The word you are looking for is *exceptional*.' And realising from the look in her husband's eyes as he strolled towards her that he had heard, turned extremely pink and said, 'Aristide ... Ralph is leaving. Was there – did you --?'

'Yes.' Putting his arm about her waist whilst wondering why what he was about to say no longer seemed very important, Aristide said, 'I'm going to summon the past. But it includes something I'd hoped to keep from you. If you wish to go --'

'No.' She knew which box he was about to open and had always suspected he hadn't told her everything. 'No. I will stay.'

He nodded and, looking the earl in the eye, said, 'You know my name in connection with Sinclairs. Is it not familiar to you in any other context?'

'No.' Sherbourne picked up his gloves. 'Why would it be?'

'Perhaps because you once had a young man dismissed without a character and sent your brothers to administer a thrashing.' He paused, meditatively. 'Unless you do that kind of thing regularly, I'd have thought you might remember it.'

'I have no idea what you are talking about,' said Sherbourne impatiently. 'If you have something to say, speak plainly. Otherwise I am leaving.'

'Paris; the Hotel Fleurignac, seven years ago. You came to remove your sister from her step-father, Sir Kenneth Forbes-Montague. I presume you recall the occasion?'

The earl was suddenly very still and a frown entered his eyes.

'Of course I recall it. And if I had laid eyes on you at any point or, as you seem to think, heard your name mentioned, I would recall that too. Since I don't, you are going to have to explain what any of it has to do with you.'

'Seven years ago, I was employed by Sir Kenneth as an under-secretary. He also charged me with teaching his step-daughter to speak French,' said Aristide slowly. 'Does that jog your memory at all?'

There was a long silence. Finally Sherbourne said, 'Ah. That was you?'

'Yes.'

'*You* are the poverty-stricken upstart who persuaded Genevieve to run away with him?' His lordship gave a harsh, unamused laugh. 'Well, that certainly explains a few things.'

'It might,' agreed Aristide, 'if it were true.'

'Ah. Let me guess. You were merely the poor, maligned victim of circumstance.'

'Stop it!' said Genevieve furiously. 'I didn't want to go to England with you. I fancied myself in love with Philippe de Chevigny and thought he would help me so I asked Aristide to take a letter to him. That's all he did. Nothing more than a small favour. But you – ' She stopped, breathing hard.

'You blackened my name to Sir Kenneth and sent your vicious siblings to hurt me.' Aristide held his brother-in-law's gaze with clinical detachment. 'It is a pity you didn't spare a thought to discovering the truth. It wouldn't have cost more than a minute of your time. It *would,* however, have made the difference between me lying unconscious in the grounds of the Hotel Fleurignac instead of being at home with my young sister when our mother was dying.' He felt the shudder that ran through Genevieve's body and said, 'I'm sorry. I didn't want you to know.'

'But *he* should.' She drew an unsteady breath. 'He deserves to know what he did.'

Aristide shook his head slightly but his gaze remained fixed on Sherbourne.

His impassive expression not varying by as much as a hair's-breadth, the earl said, 'Although the timing of all this was clearly unfortunate, it is hardly my fault. Also, neither of the sins you've laid at my door are, in fact, mine at all. If you want to talk about truth, try this. I learned that Genevieve's maid was taking a letter to a man with whom she was planning to run away. At the time, I was busy attempting to make Sir Kenneth see sense, so I sent Cedric and Bertram to deal with it. I did *not* tell them to use violence.'

'Since I can't imagine you caring either way, I don't suppose you told them *not* to, either,' returned Aristide. 'I also suppose you're going to deny telling Sir Kenneth I'd been making improper advances to Genevieve and, given half a chance, would have already seduced her.'

'You suppose correctly. To the best of my recollection, Cedric handed Genevieve's letter to Forbes-Montague, saying that it spoke for itself … and I left the man to make up his own mind. *Your* name never featured in the conversation at all. So if the point of dragging all this up now was that you expected me to fall on my sword and offer a grovelling apology for the wrongs done you, I can only say that your nerve outstrips your intelligence. I don't apologise for things I did not do. And I *certainly* don't apologise to the likes of you.'

'What is the *matter* with you?' Genevieve stepped out of the circle of her husband's arm. 'Haven't you understood anything Aristide had just told you?'

'Oh yes. And a good many things he hasn't,' replied Sherbourne. He turned a derisive smile on Aristide, 'They say revenge is a dish best eaten cold and you've certainly waited long enough for yours, haven't you? But this? I'll admit to wondering why you married her.' He put his hands together and applauded lazily. '*Now*, of course, I can only congratulate --'

'Don't you *dare* spill your poison here!' Without any warning and throwing the full weight of her body behind it, Genevieve slammed her fist into her brother's face, barely missing his nose. 'You will *not* cause mischief between Aristide and me – I won't *have* it!'

Lurching backwards, the earl clapped a hand to his throbbing cheekbone, managed to recover his balance and took a step towards her saying furiously, 'Why you damned little --'

Before the words were out of his mouth, Aristide was in his way.

'Raise a hand to her and *I'll* hit you. I'll also make sure that by tomorrow the whole of society knows *why* I did.' He wrenched open the door to the hall and came face to face with his butler and footman, neither of whom should have been there. 'Ah – Minton. And Patrick. How ... fortuitous. Lord Sherbourne is leaving. And in the unlikely event that he calls again, you may leave him on the steps until Doomsday.' And to the earl, 'Now get out of my house.'

Lord Sherbourne gathered what shreds of dignity he could find and achieved a mocking bow. 'In the unlikely event that we meet in public, do not expect me to acknowledge either of you. I shall not.'

'That,' murmured Aristide, as the earl stalked out, 'will suit us admirably.'

The second her brother had gone, Genevieve cradled her injured hand to her chest and said furiously, 'I hope I blackened his eye.'

'There is a fair chance that you may have done so. Let me see your hand.'

She held it out, grimacing. 'It hurts.'

'Yes. I imagine it does,' he agreed a little unsteadily. And glancing through the open door, 'Patrick ... find some ice, please. My wife has – has injured her hand.'

The footman grinned. 'Planted him a facer, did you, ma'am? Well done. Mr Minton and me wished we could've seen it. Nice flush hit, was it, sir?'

Aristide nodded. 'Perfect. But ... the ice, Patrick?'

'To be sure, sir. I'll have it here in a trice.'

'That would be helpful.' Watching him go, Aristide gently closed the door and leant against it. He was struggling with the irrepressible bubble threatening to explode in his chest as well as the mind-shattering revelation the last hour had hurled at him him and with which he had not even begun to become accustomed. Before he could speak, however, Genevieve said suspiciously, 'Are you *laughing*?'

'No.' He turned to face her and gave up the fight. 'That is ... yes, though not at you. It – it was the look on his face. And you ...' He stopped, eyes alight with hilarity and shoulders shaking. 'I'm sorry. It was just so – so unexpected. And very like what I'd been longing to do myself, if the truth be known.'

'I behaved like a fishwife,' she muttered.

'You were magnificent,' he corrected, returning to sit beside her and cradling her injured hand carefully in one of his. 'It's all right to be angry, Genevieve. And it's all right to show it – even with me.'

'I'm never angry with you.'

'No? That's a relief. But if I ever *do* seriously displease you, I'll remember to duck.' He thought for a moment and then added reprehensibly, 'Or I could just rely on my exceptional skills in the bedchamber.'

She shook her head at him, reprovingly. 'You shouldn't have been listening.'

'I wasn't. I just ... heard.' He grinned back. Then, because he needed time to come to terms with this new thing inside him, 'When Patrick brings the ice and your poor hand is less sore, I'll take you for a private tour of my kingdom by way of a celebration. What do you say?'

CHAPTER TWENTY-ONE

Mr Jenkins presented himself in Duke Street at a little after noon and found Lord Nicholas – bored, restless and swathed in a garment the colours of which resembled a travelling show-booth – awaiting him above stairs.

Rising, Nicholas held out his hand and said, 'Thank you for coming – and also for what you and your fellows did on the night of the attack. From what I've been told, your arrival was very timely.'

'As to that, if young Billy hadn't raised the alarm when he did it could have all gone very different.' Mr Jenkins shrugged and grinned wryly. 'But once we got to you and Miss Madeleine there wasn't much Cross's fellows could do – us being armed to the teeth, as we were.'

Nicholas nodded and gestured to a chair.

'Be that as it may, Mademoiselle and I still have a great deal to be grateful for,' he said. 'I've been told some of what happened but have absolutely no memory of it. My brother suggested I speak to you – most especially, about what took place after I was knocked out.'

'That was when we got there, my lord. You was out cold, with Miss Madeleine on the ground beside you, begging you to wake up. And then that bastard Cross told his bullies to take you instead of her.'

Nicholas blinked, then frowned.

'Really? That's the first I've heard of it. And it doesn't make any sense.'

'They reckoned Miss Madeleine would pay any amount to get you back quick. Like I told his Grace, she was up in a flash with your sword in her hand, telling them she'd kill the first man who touched you. And when one of them was daft enough to take a step, she stabbed him good and hard in the shoulder. Didn't hesitate for so much as a second – and with a look on her face that stopped the other pair in their tracks.' Mr Jenkins hesitated and then said, 'I hope you'll forgive me speaking out of turn, my lord ... but there was no mistaking that Miss Madeleine thinks a lot of you. An *awful* lot. Stood over you like the wrath of God, she did, without a thought for what might have happened to her. To be honest, we all know she's got a bit of a temper but what I saw that night was something else again.'

Nicholas's colour rose a little but he merely said, 'I see. And afterwards?'

'Well, it was all over bar the shouting, if you know what I mean. Cross got the hell out of there but we got his men under lock and key ... and brought you and Miss Madeleine back here. Of course, by then she was shaking like a leaf. I reckon the only thing that kept her on her feet was holding your hand every step of the way and telling you over and over again that you wasn't to *dare* die.'

'It's just as well that I didn't then,' said Nicholas with something approaching a grin. 'She might have killed me all over again.'

'Yes, my lord. I think she might, at that.'

'Thank you, Mr Jenkins.' He rose, offering his hand again. 'I'm in your debt.'

As soon as Jenkins had left, Nicholas summoned his valet and issued a *feu de joie* of orders. 'I intend to dress, Brennon – and please do not argue. I want the sapphire brocade suit and the pearl silk embroidered vest. If they're not here, fetch them and be back within the hour. Then I shall require a bath and, regardless of Rayne's damned stitches, thoroughly-washed hair. Is all that quite clear?'

'Yes, my lord. But --'

'Excellent. Then what are you waiting for?'

Wearing a long-suffering expression suggesting there was a great deal he would have liked to say, Brennon departed without a word.

* * *

Having assessed the damage to the blue salon and given instructions for the removal and replacement of the damaged wall-hangings, Madeleine left her brother educating Genevieve in the rules of Hazard and returned to Duke Street where Minton, with a suspiciously paternal air, informed her that Lord Nicholas awaited her in the drawing-room.

'He's left his bedchamber?' she asked, lured into idiocy by shock. 'Yes. Obviously, he must have done. I just ... I didn't think he would be well enough to dress yet.'

'I believe Mr Brennon agrees that it may be a little premature – but his lordship insisted. I was to convey his respects and ask if you would join him at your convenience.'

Her nerves promptly tied themselves into a knot.

'How long has he been waiting?'

'About an hour, Mademoiselle.'

'I see.' Somewhere amongst the jumble in her head was the knowledge that her gown was crushed and dusty and her hair escaping its pins. 'Send Becky up to me and please tell Lord Nicholas that I will be with him as soon as I have changed my dress.' She turned towards the stairs and then stopped, struck by a sudden thought. 'I doubt my brother will come home for some time yet – but if he does, will you ask him ...?'

The words tailed off and, taking pity on her, Minton said helpfully, '*Not* to immediately join yourself and Lord Nicholas?'

'Yes.' Madeleine set her foot on the bottom step. 'Yes. Thank you.'

In the drawing-room and with nothing to occupy him except his thoughts, Nicholas found himself admiring the spare elegance of the décor whilst simultaneously finding it rather soulless. It almost looked as if no one lived there. His own rooms on Hay Hill were cluttered and shabbily comfortable. Even Charlecote had gradually become home to the eclectic bits and pieces he'd collected on his travels, along with years' worth of family gifts. Aside from a few books, this room showed no sign that either Aristide or Madeleine had ever been in it.

When the door finally opened and Madeleine stood on the threshold looking across at him as if unsure what to do next, he rose and managed a slight bow, saying, 'Congratulate me. I have finally managed a shirt and coat.'

'So I see.' Actually, what she saw was an impossibly beautiful man who suddenly looked every inch a duke's brother but who wasn't smiling. Swallowing hard, she closed the door and crossed the room towards him, saying, 'Are you sure this is wise?'

'Brennon doesn't think so ... but then, if I listened to him I'd doubtless still be reclining on a chaise-longue clutching a vinaigrette.' He indicated the chair facing his own, 'If you're staying, perhaps you'd care to sit?'

She nodded and did so, arranging the skirts of her pale green embroidered taffeta around her with more care than was required so that, for a moment at least, she didn't have to meet his eyes.

'I thought,' said Nicholas, resuming his own seat, 'that it was time we talked.'

'Yes. Certainly.'

Despite what Jenkins had told him, every instinct he possessed coupled with the sum of their previous dealings warned Nicholas against making this easy. She might be ready to admit her feelings for him but he suspected there was still a battle to be fought over their joint future.

'As we're both aware, I came back to town because, in spite of the understanding I believed you and I had, I did not find you in Kent. Perhaps you might begin by giving your reasons for that.'

There *had* been reasons. She just was no longer sure quite what they had been or whether they had ever made any sense. She said weakly, 'I thought it was for the best.'

'Best for whom?'

'Both of us, to a certain extent ... but mostly for you.'

The dark Wynstanton eyes contemplated her for what seemed a very long time. Finally, he said, 'If there is the smallest chance of you explaining that without reference either to my title or my brother's title or the fact that, just at present, I'm Rock's heir, I'll be happy to listen. Can you?'

Mutely, Madeleine shook her head.

'So that's it, is it? You were saving me from a relationship which you had decided – regardless of *my* opinions – could only end in disaster?' He leaned back and folded his arms. 'If you expect me to thank you for that, think again. It's bloody insulting.'

'It wasn't meant to be. I just thought that you deserved someone better than me and that if I ... if I stayed away from you, you would find her. Also --'

'Ah. So not only am I fickle – but you know my mind better than I do myself.'

'Also,' she continued as steadily as she was able, 'there would have been a presumption on my part. You've never actually said how you feel about me or what you hope might come of it.'

'No. I held on to that one small shred of pride. But though I may not have put it into words, I think you've known the answers to both of those questions – if that is what they were – for some time now.' He paused for a second to let her digest this and then added, 'But that hardly matters, does it? The plain truth is that, if you wanted to send me on my way, all you ever had to do was to tell me I meant nothing to you. You never quite got around to that ... but here I am, giving you yet another chance to do so. Well?'

'*No!*' Madeleine stood up and whirled away from him. 'Nicholas, can we stop this?'

'And do what? Chat about the weather instead?'

She turned back to face him, hands clenched tight at her waist.

'I don't blame you for making this difficult. God knows I've given you every cause. But if you'll let me, I'd like to start again.'

'Why?'

'Because these last few days have changed everything – or if not *changed* it, than at least made me see things more clearly. I thought you were going to *die*. All those hours when you were unconscious ... when I was terrified that I'd lose you without ever having the chance to ...' She stopped, shaking her head. 'I couldn't bear it. So I talked and talked and talked even though I knew you couldn't hear me. And I promised us both that if only you would wake up, I'd say it all again. I'd like to do that now .... if you'll listen.'

For the first time, Nicholas smiled. He said, 'Do you really need to ask me that?'

'Yes. I've made enough mistaken assumptions to last a lifetime.'

'I won't argue with that. But if what you have to say is going to take some time, perhaps you could sit down?' The smile grew slightly rueful. 'Otherwise, manners dictate that I should be on my feet, too ... and to be honest, I'd just as soon not.'

'Don't even think of it.' Madeleine sank back into her chair and eyed him anxiously. 'Are you sure you're well enough to --'

'Yes. Now stop prevaricating and talk.'

'Very well.' She shut her eyes for a moment, then opened them again to look directly into his. 'I love you. I always have – almost since the first time I saw you on the main floor at Sinclairs. You were with Harry Caversham and you were laughing and I ... well, if anyone had asked me before that night if I believed in love at first sight, I'd have called them an idiot. But I never expected anything to come of it. I didn't even think we would ever *meet*. Only then we did ... and you took my arm to pull me away from the burning rug and I – I just *knew*.' She stopped, shrugging slightly, 'It sounds stupid, doesn't it? But I can't explain it any other way. I wanted you so badly it hurt. And it hurt worse because I told myself nothing could ever – *should* ever – come of it.'

Silence, broken only the ticking of the clock, lapped the edges of the room. Her nerves at full stretch, Madeleine said, 'Please say something.'

'I'm trying. You ... you have rather taken my breath away.'

In truth, the maelstrom inside Nicholas's chest was making it impossible to think, let alone put a coherent sentence together. He didn't need to ask if she meant it. Even before his conversation with Jenkins, there had always been a bone-deep certainty that her attempts to push him away covered something very different ... and so he wasn't sure why he felt so stunned. He did, however, know better than to close the space between them and kiss her until neither of them knew what day it was. Yet, anyway.

He said slowly, 'Madeleine ... there's no denying I was in Ryder Street the other night because of you but what happened thereafter was not your fault. So if any part of what you've just said was born of guilt --'

'It wasn't. Of course, it wasn't! How could you think it?'

'I don't think it. But I don't ever want to wonder if I should have done.'

'Oh. No. I mean, yes. I see that. And you needn't – wonder, that is.'

The disjointed awkwardness of this made him smile again.

'Good. So is this is my cue to make my own declaration or --?'

'No. There's more.' Madeleine sat up very straight and harnessed her courage for what she suspected was going to be the biggest hurdle. 'I once told you that I wouldn't be your mistress and --'

'Stop.' His smile instantly evaporated. 'I will not have this conversation again. I've no intention of asking you to be my mistress – either now or at any time in the future – and I thought I had made that fact indisputably plain.'

'You did. But I had to mention it because of the promise.'

Nicholas eyed her warily. 'Go on.'

'I promised to tell you that, if you still want me, I'll be yours in any way you wish and for as long as you wish it.' She paused, spreading expressive hands. 'No terms and no conditions ... or not on my side, anyway.'

This time, everything inside him gave way before a flood of wild elation, oddly accompanied by an inexplicable desire to weep. He said unevenly, 'That's an extremely generous offer. Tempting, too. But before we discuss it further, perhaps it's time I made a few things clear.'

'You don't have to,' muttered Madeleine weakly.

'Yes, I do.' Rising, he took her hand and drew her to her feet. 'But let's start with this.'

And almost before she knew it, she was in his arms with his mouth devouring hers.

Later, Nicholas would remember that he'd had some idea of teasing and tormenting and cajoling until she was breathless and pliant. He would also recall his ribs making a vigorous protest. As it was, the second he touched her nothing existed except the raw hunger that had been simmering inside him for months. All he knew was the silky heat of her mouth, the exquisite fit of her body against his and the lovely curve of her back beneath his hands. And when she gave a small, involuntary sob and drove her fingers into his hair, the floor tilted beneath his feet.

Somewhere beyond the insistent sizzling of her body, Madeleine was aware that this was not like the kiss in Richmond Park. That, though beautiful, had been a gentle invitation. This was a blaze of sheer passion … coupled with a demand that drew forth an instinctive response. He kissed her brow, her eyelids, her cheeks and her jaw, before returning to her mouth. And throughout it all, her every pulse and breath was saying just one word. *Yes.*

It was when Nicholas's body started making suggestions involving the sofa that a weak voice inside his head suggested it was time to stop. With a reluctant groan, he released Madeleine's mouth and muttered, 'Damn. That was becoming far too enjoyable. Are you going to slap my face this time?'

She traced his cheekbones with light fingers and, with the merest suggestion of a laugh, shook her head.

'Good.' Nicholas stepped back and, taking her hand, drew her down beside him on the sofa. 'Now where were we? Ah yes. I was going to tell you that I love you, wasn't I?'

'Were you?'

She was still smiling wonderingly at him and looking faintly dazed. Since this might well be his best chance, Nicholas said, 'Most definitely. I love you and you love me ... and we are going to be married.'

The smile faded and the green gaze grew troubled. 'Nicholas - '

'No. This isn't open for either argument or negotiation. There will be no *carte blanche*, Madeleine – and that is quite final.' He slid an arm about her and drew her against his shoulder. 'I've never been a rake. The odd affair with a widow now and again ... but the only time I tried setting up a mistress, I didn't like it. It felt sordid.' He dropped a kiss on the tip of her nose. 'And even if that were *not* true, I can't have that relationship with you. I love you ... and it's for always. I want us to have children together – to grow old together. So it's marriage or nothing. And all that matters is whether you want that as much as I do.'

Madeleine found herself blinking sudden tears away.

'I do. Of course I do. But it isn't – oh God. There are things you don't know. The night I told you of when Aristide was so badly beaten was the night our mother died. And afterwards, when he couldn't work and *maman* had to be buried but there wasn't the money to pay for it, I – I did things I'm ashamed of. Not the *worst* thing – never that,' she said quickly, 'but I – I --'

Nicholas silenced her with one fingertip. 'How old were you?'

'Sixteen.'

'Sixteen.' Something curdled in his stomach as he tried to imagine how on earth she'd managed. He said, 'I want you to listen to me. I don't need to know what you did or even what you *didn't*. None of it matters a jot.'

She relaxed against him a little but murmured, 'It matters to me.'

'Enough to let it define the rest of our lives?'

'I ... suppose not. But what about your brother?'

'Do you think us marrying is going to come as any surprise to Rock?' Nicholas grinned. 'Sweetheart ... he knows me better than anyone else alive, so he's always known that – feeling about you as I do – there could only be one outcome.'

'And he doesn't mind?'

'He doesn't mind,' agreed Nicholas. 'Are there any other obstacles you'd like to raise?'

'Your friends?'

'My *friends*?' He laughed. 'Now you really *are* clutching at straws. My friends have in all probability been laying bets between themselves for months – either on the chances of me scraping up the courage to ask you or you accepting me, if I did. So you don't have a leg to stand on there, darling. Anything else?' And when she shook her head, 'Sure?'

'Quite sure.'

'Thank God.' Releasing her, Nicholas slid from the sofa to drop on one knee. 'In that case, Madeleine Delacroix ... the most beautiful, stubborn, impossible, desirable woman in the world ... will you do me the honour of becoming my wife?'

Tears threatened again. He was so warm and sweet and hopelessly, utterly lovable. She reached out to touch his cheek again, as if wanting to make sure he was real. Then she said softly, 'Yes, Nicholas. Yes, please – I will.'

* * *

Arriving back in Duke Street some two hours later, Aristide and Genevieve were greeted with the intelligence that Madeleine and Lord Nicholas were cloistered in the drawing-room and had asked not to be disturbed.

Genevieve removed her hat and smiled at the butler.

'Did Lord Nicholas appear to be feeling better, Minton?'

'That was my impression, ma'am.' Unbending a little, Minton said confidingly, 'And he was dressed in what folk where I grew up would call his "courting clothes".'

'About time,' breathed Aristide. 'Nicholas's patience and persistence do him credit but they're bound to wear thin eventually. So let us hope that, just for once, Madeleine stops behaving like an idiot.' And setting Genevieve's hand on his arm, 'Meanwhile, you and I had better amuse ourselves elsewhere.'

Genevieve nodded but said, 'Where is Blanchette, Minton?'

'In the kitchen, ma'am. Patrick took her out for a romp in the garden a short while ago and Mrs Constantine has fed her.'

'Excellent.' Aristide towed his wife up the stairs. 'We can have an hour's peace.'

Once inside their rooms and watching him pull off his coat, Genevieve eyed him with laughing exasperation.

'Why the sudden hurry? It's not much past five and --'

'I'm not in a hurry,' he replied, immediately contradicting the words by drawing her against him and kissing his way down her neck. 'I'm just not wasting my opportunities. Last night was a disaster.' His teeth grazed her shoulder. 'Did I mention that I'd had plans?'

'Yes.' Genevieve twined her arms about his waist. 'But not what they were.'

'Something like this to begin with, if I'd found you still dressed.' He brushed her mouth with his, pulled her a little closer and started working on the laces of her gown with his free hand. 'Then ... something else. But none of it happened, thanks to Lord Seabridge. And if Madeleine has said yes to Nicholas, I foresee Rockliffe joining us for dinner, followed by a long evening of celebrating and planning and no time at all for being alone with my wife.' Another kiss as the gown slid from her shoulders. 'Please tell me the maid isn't going to walk in at any minute.'

'She won't come until I ring.' Freeing his hair from its ribbon, Genevieve combed her fingers through the thick strands. Desire was already stirring but Aristide's mood had shifted and he was clearly no longer inclined towards haste. 'Thank you for this afternoon. Sinclairs is splendid. You must be very proud of it.'

'Yes.' Aristide considered moving on to her petticoats and stays. Then, contemplating the pretty picture her arms and shoulders made rising above the calyx of white ruffles, he decided against it and began taking her hair down instead.

He pulled out a couple of pins with hands which were no longer entirely steady and a long, curling lock fell free to coil about his wrist. He thought helplessly, *I didn't know. How is it that – despite everything – I still didn't know until this morning? That it took wanting to smash Sherbourne's head into the wall before I could recognise what's been staring me in the face for a fortnight? And now I have to say it and make her believe it and ... and somehow manage to do it all with grace and charm when I haven't the remotest idea where to start.* The last of the pins came free, letting the thick shining hair tumble loose down her back and in a prosaic tone which made him despair of himself, he said, 'Have I told you how very beautiful you are?'

'Once or twice, I believe.' The butterfly-light touches of his fingers here and there against her skin had already made Genevieve's breathing shorten. Sliding her arms around his neck and laying her lips against his jaw, she lifted her head to murmur something trivial and heard herself say instead, 'And have *I* told *you* how very much I love you?'

The floor dissolved beneath Aristide's feet and he felt as if he was falling through aeons of space, wholly unable to breathe.

Equally startled but not unduly dismayed, Genevieve stepped back to look warily at him and said, 'I'm sorry. I had no idea I was going to say that. I hadn't meant to. Perhaps you can pretend I didn't.'

Aristide hauled some air into his lungs and searched for some semblance of coherence.

'I – no. I don't think I can. Did ...' He stopped and cleared his throat. 'Did you mean it?'

Her smile was shy but incredibly sweet. 'Oh yes. I fell in love with you within hours of our wedding. How could I not?' She hesitated, uncertainty creeping into her face. 'Is it such a shock? I thought you might already have guessed.'

'I've sometimes thought that you may have become ... fond of me,' he replied, still struggling to think. 'But love? No. I hadn't – no.'

'Oh.' Reaching out to straighten his cravat, she said matter of-factly, 'Well, it isn't anything you need worry about. I won't say it again if you'd rather I didn't. And you must *not* think that I expect you to feel the same way – or, God forbid, that you ought to say you do even if you don't. I'm not sorry I told you ... but I *will* be if it makes you feel obligated or constrained or --'

'Stop.' The fog inside his head cleared abruptly and he saw the pit yawning at his feet. If he declared his feelings now, she wasn't going to believe him. She was going to think he was doing exactly what she'd just told him *not* to do. And it was entirely his own fault. If, instead of reacting as if she'd hit him over the head with a shovel, he'd immediately said something suave ... something like, *No, you haven't mentioned that. But since I feel exactly that way about you, I'd dared to hope.* Of course, it wouldn't have come out like that – not unless he'd had ten minutes in which to practise it. But now he had no idea what to do and was afraid to contemplate the starburst of euphoria her words had exploded inside him. So he scooped her up in his arms and deposited her, none too gently, on the side of the bed, saying, 'Not another word. Sit there and *do not move*. You hear me?'

Genevieve laughed and reached out to brush his hair back. 'Yes, sir.'

'I mean it. Don't move, don't speak, don't ... do anything.'

She nodded and folded her hands in her lap, still half-inclined to giggle whilst also wondering what he was up to. She heard him leave the room, then return to climb on the bed behind her and crawl across to where she sat, bracketing her with his knees. He said, 'You remember me saying that I had a plan? Well, this is part of it. Close your eyes.'

'What? Why?'

'Because I'd hoped to impress you with a grand, romantic gesture that I probably couldn't have accomplished even if you *hadn't* just cut the ground from beneath my feet. Are your eyes closed?'

She nodded and then gasped in surprise as something cold and smooth settled around her neck. 'Aristide –'

'Hush. I haven't finished yet.' Reaching both arms around her, he clasped the bracelet on to her wrist and then sat back, silently praying. 'You can look now.'

Slowly, she did so. One hand travelled hesitantly to touch the cool stones lying at the base of her throat while her eyes widened at the sight of the perfectly-matched rubies, interspersed with small diamonds on her wrist. Letting go of a long, careful breath, she whispered, 'Oh ... *Aristide.*'

He waited for her to say something else and then, his nerves at full stretch, he waited some more. Finally, her voice very small, she said, 'Can I move now?'

'Yes.' His throat raw, he supposed she would slide off the bed and run to the mirror.

She didn't. She scrambled around, clumsily and in a tangle of petticoats, to bury her face against his neck, saying unevenly, 'Thank you. It – it's beautiful. But you need not have done it ... really, you need not.'

'I know that. I did it because I wanted to.' He waited for a moment and when she neither moved nor spoke, said gently, 'You never ask for anything.'

'I asked you to m-marry me. That's not nothing.'

'True.' Aristide settled her more comfortably in his arms. He wasn't sure exactly *why* she was crying but was less worried than he might have been had she not been clinging to him as if she never wanted to let go. 'I didn't know it meant I wasn't allowed to give you a wedding present. Unless it's just that you don't like rubies --'

'Of *course* I l-like them.'

'Well, if you say so – though you haven't even seen the necklace yet, not to mention the earrings and ring,' he said dubiously. 'And they were supposed to make you happy.'

'I *am* happy,' sobbed Genevieve.

'Of course you are. That's why you're soaking my cravat. Stupid of me.' This won him a watery giggle. 'That's better – though it doesn't solve my dilemma.'

She stirred, lifting her head a little. 'What dilemma?'

'Of whether any bit of my plan is worth saving or whether I should throw it out and start again. There were three parts to it, you see. But the first of them hasn't gone quite as I'd anticipated, so now I'm trying to decide how best to proceed.'

Genevieve detached herself from him and brushed the stupid tears aside.

'I'm sorry. I cried because – though the rubies are beautiful – the most beautiful thing of all was you buying them for me.'

'Yes. I think I knew that. But, very regrettably, my magnificent plan is still hanging by a thread.' He drew her back against his shoulder. 'The general idea was that, after you had finished admiring your gift, I was going to remove everything you're wearing ... except for the rubies, of course and ... yes, your stockings, I think.' He heard her breath catch and paused to let her picture this. 'Then I thought I'd indulge us both with a couple of hours of extremely slow and deliciously wicked love-making. And eventually, when my brain was functioning again, I was going to thank you for asking me to marry you.'

She went rigid with shock. '*What?*'

'Well, by the time *I* got around to proposing you might have already married someone else, mightn't you?' he asked reasonably. 'And it would have been another man – probably one less dense than me – who would have had all the warmth and light and unstinting love that makes me feel that perhaps I'm not quite so hopeless after all. And consequently, I'd never have known that I'd missed my one chance for the kind of happiness I hadn't believed existed ... or lost the one woman without whom a large part of my life would always be empty.' He shrugged. 'I think that's something worth thanking you for, don't you?'

Very slowly, Genevieve moved away so that she could search his face with eyes full of hope and doubt. She said, 'I don't understand what you're saying.'

'In that case, I can't be putting it very well, can I?'

'No. You – you put it beautifully.'

'Ah. That's all right, then. That means you do know what I was saying but you're just not quite ready to believe it yet.' He kissed her with tantalising lightness. 'I'll enjoy helping you with that. And by the time I've worshipped every inch of your body, whilst telling you over and over again that I love you, I'm hoping I'll have made a fairly convincing beginning.'

CHAPTER TWENTY-TWO

The wedding of Nicholas Wynstanton and Madeleine Delacroix was set to take place at Wynstanton Priors four weeks after his lordship had proposed. The bride insisted that the occasion be kept as quiet as possible since, given that she was marrying into a ducal family, a small, private ceremony was out of the question; the groom said that as long as the bride turned up and his brother was at his side, he didn't care if anyone else was there or not. In the end, a list of not quite fifty guests – all of whom accepted their invitations – was considered a reasonable compromise all round.

Having put an extraordinarily fine emerald on the finger of his betrothed, Nicholas departed for Surrey intending to spend the last fortnight before the wedding overseeing the redecoration of the master-suite at Charlecote Park. Madeleine surrendered her domain at Sinclairs to Henrietta Hastings and remained in London until her wedding gown had received its final fitting; then, at the Duchess of Rockliffe's request, she travelled to Kent to pass her last few days as an unmarried woman at Wynstanton Priors. She might – and indeed would – have refused this invitation had it not been for the duchess's extremely forthright letter.

Never having met, wrote Adeline, *it occurs to me that you and I ought to get to know each other a little. At any rate, I would like to know you. And I would also imagine that you need time to understand that Tracy isn't quite as intimidating as you may have supposed. Almost, but not quite. So if you would consider coming here a few days earlier than originally planned, I think we might kill two birds with one stone. On a separate issue, I am reliably informed that Lady Vanessa Jane is also eager to meet her new aunt. I have no first-hand assurance of this as her ladyship's communicative skills are much less advanced with me than appears to be the case with her doting Papa.*

Thus it was that Madeleine learned that it was downright impossible to feel inferior to a duchess who cheerfully admitted having been little more than an unpaid servant in her aunt's house or nervous of a duke whose baby daughter dribbled on his shoulder.

In Surrey, meanwhile, Nicholas had realised that the renovation of the master bedchambers was a much larger project than he had originally envisioned. Having never used the rooms himself, he had forgotten that their furnishings and hangings pre-dated the reign of Good Queen Anne. One look at the heavy Jacobean beds with their gloomy puce velvet hangings and dressing-rooms bereft of any of the usual fittings had him groaning with despair. Madeleine was going to hate it. He already did. And with only two weeks till the wedding, he had no idea how it was all going to be finished in time.

Just when he was about to start tearing his hair out, an unexpected life-line arrived in the form of a letter from the Earl of Sarre.

You may already have plans for after the wedding, Adrian wrote. *If not and you would like to begin married life away from family, friends and servants who have known you since you were six, you are welcome to make use of Devereux House. As you know, it is remotely situated and extremely private. Mrs Clayton will cook, her husband will care for your horses and, if you and Madeleine are content to give your personal servants a holiday, Caroline will supply temporary replacements from Sarre Park. Let me know if the notion appeals.*

Nicholas didn't need to think about it. Devereux House, with no neighbours coming to call or servants taking too-great an interest in his marital goings-on? He wrote back immediately.

Thank you, Adrian. You've just saved my sanity.

* * *

Wedding guests began arriving two days before the ceremony. First came a clutch of Wynstanton relatives. There were uncles and cousins, Aunt Augusta with her aged pug, and Nicholas's sister Kitty with her diplomat husband, taking leave from his posting in Brussels ... while a note from Lucilla, Lady

Grassmere saying that measles in the nursery would prevent her attending added to the general air of festivity. Next to arrive were the Marquis and Marchioness of Amberley, the Earl and Countess of Sarre and Sebastian and Cassandra Audley ... and then, surprising all those who had believed them en route for Italy, Lord Harry and Lady Elinor Caversham, immediately followed by Monsieur and Madame Delacroix.

'But where is Nicholas?' demanded Nell, almost before she had put off her hat.

'He is in Surrey,' replied Madeleine calmly. 'He will be here tomorrow.'

'Cutting it fine, isn't he?' grinned Harry. And holding out his hand to Aristide, 'I understand congratulations are in order. Where is your lady?'

'Upstairs with the duchess,' replied Aristide. 'How was Paris?'

'Expensive. Nell barely stopped shopping from the time we got there. Fortunately, Nick's wedding has spared me the additional cost of Milan.'

'I heard that,' said Lady Elinor. 'And it's only spared you the cost for *now*.' She smiled at Aristide, 'We heard all about your romantic double-wedding from Cassie. I'm so looking forward to meeting your wife.'

Since this provided the excuse he had been waiting for, Aristide bowed slightly and said, 'In that case, if your ladyship will excuse me, I shall go and find her for you.'

Genevieve had descended from the carriage looking pale and been immediately whisked off by Adeline, while Rockliffe had drawn Aristide away to exchange greetings with Adrian. Now, having obtained directions to their chamber, he ran smartly up the stairs to find his wife sitting by the window sipping tea. He said, 'Better?'

Smiling, she set aside her cup. 'It was nothing – just the motion of the carriage, these last few miles. I'm perfectly well.'

'Good.' Aristide strolled across to pull her into his arms and drop a kiss on her brow. 'Since I don't recall you suffering from carriage sickness before, I was a little concerned.'

'I'm sorry. There was no need.'

'No?' He held her gaze, an odd smile lurking behind his own. 'So there's nothing you want to tell me?'

She opened her mouth to agree that there wasn't and then recognised the futility of it. Sighing, she said, 'How did you know?'

'I can count. It's one of the things I'm best at. We've been married for seven weeks and you've yet to be … indisposed.' He gathered her closer and kissed her. 'Also, given the fact that I can't keep my hands off you, it's hardly to be wondered at. Are you pleased?'

'Of course I'm pleased. Are you? Even though it's happened so quickly?'

'*Chérie*, I'm delighted,' he replied gravely. And then, in a huskily seductive tone, 'As for the rest … no man will complain about having his virility proved so speedily.'

* * *

By the time Lord Nicholas arrived, the rest of the party was fully assembled but he ignored them all in favour of dragging Madeleine into the first empty room he could find and proceeding to kiss her until they were both breathless.

'I've missed you,' he groaned at length. 'I'd no idea three weeks could be so long.'

'Nor I.' She looped her arms about his waist and leaned her cheek on his shoulder.

'Two more days. Just two … and then we can escape everybody.'

'Caroline has told me about Devereux House.' A tiny tremor of laughter rippled through her. 'She promised that neither she nor Adrian will visit unless in response to a written invitation.'

'Adrian said the same. Oh – and he's had a couple of horses sent over from Sarre Park. One for my use and the placid little mare on which Caroline had her first lessons – in case you take a fancy to learn to ride.' Nicholas grinned then, sighing slightly, said, 'We should join the others before they start wondering if we're anticipating our wedding vows. What are the plans for this evening?'

'Just a quiet dinner – if one can call a table set for thirty quiet – followed by cards and perhaps a little music. Then a more formal occasion tomorrow, with dancing.' Madeleine looked up at him, her eyes full of laughter. 'And do not think you can escape taking to the floor. Since the ball is in our honour, you and I have to open it.'

'On our own?' he asked, aghast. 'With everyone *watching*? No. Tell me you don't mean it.'

'I do. But if you want to argue about it, go and find your brother.'

* * *

Dinner was a relaxed and cheerful affair and, having left the gentlemen to their port, the ladies gathered in the drawing-room to surprise Madeleine with a succession of small gifts. Fans, lace-edged handkerchiefs, tiny bottles of perfume; and, from the Duchess of Rockliffe, a silver-backed hairbrush. Every single lady produced some trifle ... and all of them laughed when Madeleine was reduced, first to speechlessness, and then to tears.

'You are all so kind,' she mumbled.

'No, we're not,' averred Nell Caversham. 'We're just relieved that Nicholas isn't going to moulder into a reclusive old curmudgeon and grateful you've had the courage to take him on.' She grinned evilly. 'Have you told him about the ball yet?'

In the dining-room, with the decanter embarking on its second circuit, the gentlemen were having a great deal of fun at Nicholas's expense with some merciless teasing. Finally, Nicholas said, 'Rock ... for God's sake, did it *have* to be a ball?'

'I believe tradition dictates it,' returned the duke urbanely. 'And since you are determined to leave for Sandwich directly after the wedding-breakfast, your ... bridal-eve ... would appear to be the only opportunity.'

'After which, Madeleine will probably call off the wedding,' grumbled Nicholas. And when this provoked even more laughter, 'It isn't funny, damn it.'

'That depends on your point of view. However, the first dance will be a gavotte. If you are seriously worried, you have tomorrow in which to master the figures. I'm sure,' finished his Grace, reaching for the port, 'that your friends will rally round to help.'

* * *

After two gruelling hours in the ballroom partnering Caroline and ably, if annoyingly in the latter case, assisted by Cassie and Sebastian, Nicholas thought he might just have conquered the thrice-blasted gavotte. Never one to leave anything to chance, however, Caroline dragged him out for a refresher-course in a deserted part of the garden during the late afternoon, at the end of which she stood on tiptoe to kiss his cheek and said, 'Well done, Nicholas. It will be worth it – you'll see.'

Later still, standing before the mirror in contemplation of the black brocade coat, heavily-laced with gold and worn over a gold-embroidered vest, Nicholas devoutly hoped so. If proof was needed that he loved Madeleine Delacroix beyond reason, today had been it ... and the worst was still to come. If, after all he'd been through, he still managed to make Sebastian howl with laughter by heading off in the wrong direction, he decided he would walk straight down to the lake and throw himself in.

Then he went downstairs, took one look at his bride-to-be, radiant and exquisite in copper-coloured silk, and decided that no sacrifice was too great. He was, without a shadow of a doubt, the luckiest man in England.

Standing beside him in the centre of the ballroom whilst waiting for the music to start, Madeleine smiled up at him and said softly, 'I love you. I'll always love you ... from now until the end of my life. And tomorrow we'll be married. Nothing else matters. Nothing.'

Smiling back, he lifted each of her hands to his lips ... and then the music began.

Afterwards, he didn't know whether it was Caroline's lessons or Madeleine's words that made the biggest difference but, for the first time in his life, he managed an entire dance without making a cake of himself. By the middle of it, Madeleine was looking at him as if he'd slain dragons or crossed oceans and deserts for her; and he found himself laughing and wishing that he could – or at the very least, master the minuet as well so that he could dance with her again.

* * *

The day of the wedding dawned without a cloud in the sky and the promise of heat. Attended by Genevieve, Cassie and Caroline, Madeleine sat in front of the mirror while Adeline's maid did new and clever things with her hair, involving sprays of miniature pale yellow rose-buds.

'That is so pretty,' sighed Cassie when Jeanne curtsied and left to attend the duchess. 'Elegant, too – and perfectly suited to your gown. Nicholas will be entranced.'

'Nicholas already is,' laughed Caroline. 'After what we made him suffer yesterday, it's beyond all doubt. I don't believe I've actually *seen* grim determination before.'

Never having expected to marry, Madeleine hadn't ever allowed herself to dream of what her wedding day might be like. Now, she realised that even if she had, she wouldn't have imagined it like this ... surrounded by laughing, chattering friends and with the sweetest-natured, most lovable gentleman in the world waiting to make her his. Tears stung her eyes, forcing her to blink them away and causing Genevieve to give her a quick hug, saying, 'Don't. It's time for your gown and you absolutely must *not* cry on that silk.'

After that, the minutes flew by. She was laced into the heavy cream silk, lavishly embroidered in varying shades of green and someone fastened the emerald pendant that was Nicholas's wedding-gift around her throat. Then, almost before she knew it, she was descending the great staircase to the place where her brother waited, flanked by Adrian and Sebastian. In something approaching a daze, Madeleine stood quite still while Caroline knelt to adjust the fall of her demi-train and managed to smile when Cassie blew her a kiss. She watched Aristide fold a real kiss in Genevieve's palm before laying her hand on Sebastian's free arm. From somewhere she couldn't see, a string quartet was playing Haydn ... and then she was alone with her brother.

He said, 'You make a lovely bride, *ma soeur*. *Maman* would be proud. Shall we go?'

Madeleine drew a slightly unsteady breath and nodded.

The grandest of the drawing-rooms, its tall double-windows standing open on to the terrace, had been transformed almost into a hot-house with huge tubs of yellow and white roses and trailing greenery. And amidst it all, the cream of the English aristocracy waited to see her marry one of its own.

Standing beside Rockliffe, Nicholas said, 'Thank you.'

The duke's brows rose slightly, 'For what particularly?'

'For all of this. For everything, really. But mostly for being my brother.'

'By and large,' murmured his Grace languidly, 'it has not been a hardship.' Then, as everyone behind them rose, 'I believe your bride is here.'

Her fingers clenched tight on her brother's sleeve and looking neither to right nor left but stomach-churningly aware that fifty pairs of eyes were on her, Madeleine walked slowly to the place where Nicholas turned to smile at her. And in that second, everyone else in the room ceased to exist. Magnificent in dull gold brocade, he looked more handsome than he had ever done; but it was the quality of his smile ... intimate, admiring and meant only for her ... which sent her nerves spinning into oblivion and enabled her to send him a dazzling smile of her own.

Like the final hour before it, the ceremony went by in a blur and, almost without knowing how it had happened, she was wearing a wedding band and being thoroughly kissed by her new husband.

'And now, *finally*,' growled Nicholas softly, 'you are all mine ... as I am wholly yours.'

※ ※ ※

The wedding-breakfast was a happy occasion filled with laughter, congratulations and good wishes. Flushed with pleasure and champagne and holding fast to her husband's arm Madeleine enjoyed it much more than she had expected. But after two hours of celebration in the company of family and friends, she sent Nicholas a look which said, *Will anyone mind if we leave now?* And smiling, he murmured, 'No. And I don't care if they do. Let's go.'

Much of the journey to Sandwich Bay was spent exchanging foolish endearments in between discussing the renovations at Charlecote Park. And later, when they were nearing their destination, Nicholas told Madeleine about his previous visit to Devereux House, when he and Rockliffe had arrived on Adrian's wedding day and a mere hour before Lord Sheringham had tried to murder him. Upon learning that it had been the duke who had dug the bullet from Adrian's shoulder, Madeleine shook her head and said faintly, 'Good God.'

'My thoughts exactly,' agreed Nicholas, glancing out into the late afternoon sunshine. 'And here we are ... the house is just around the next bend.'

The carriage came to a halt and she let him help her down ... but she barely glanced at the house. Instead, she walked a few steps away from it, staring out on miles of empty shingle beach and an endless expanse of blue-grey ocean. Then, arms spread wide in delight, she turned to Nicholas and said, 'I know both you and Caroline told me it was remote – but I never expected anything like this. It's wonderful.'

He laughed at her and shook his head.

'It's wonderful *now*, sweetheart. On days when the easterly wind steals your breath and freezes your bones, it's a touch less lovely.'

Madeleine threw her arms around his neck and laughed back.

'I'm sure,' she whispered, 'that you can think of ways to keep me warm. Can't you?'

'One or two,' said Nicholas, heroically ignoring a spike of pure lust. 'Now – come inside, you hussy. Mrs Clayton is waiting.'

*　*　*

Devereux House was as unpretentiously comfortable as Nicholas remembered – though he could see that Caroline had made a number of small improvements here and there.

A *not*-so-small one was the installation of a large bath-tub in one of the upstairs rooms which immediately conjured up an extremely enjoyable fantasy. Resolutely banishing it, he thought, *Not tonight. Our first time together requires a bed, soft pillows and candlelight. And my very best efforts which I'm going to find difficult unless I stop imagining you naked and wet and smiling at me as you did outside.*

Although Madeleine explored the house and admired the hidden jewel of a walled garden which lay to the rear of it, she was constantly drawn to the windows at the front which overlooked the sea. Standing in the curve of Nicholas's arm and watching the changing colours as the sky darkened, she said dreamily, 'It feels as if the whole world has gone away, leaving just you and me on the edge of it.'

'I'd wondered if you might prefer Venice.'

She shook her head. 'No. I just want you ... all to myself for a little while. This is perfect.'

They dined on trout with minted peas and tiny, succulent pieces of lamb in a delicate cream sauce, followed by a frothy syllabub. Their eyes held as Nicholas fed her choice morsels from his own plate and she drew just the tip of his finger into her mouth, making his groin tighten yet again. Finally, when he wasn't sure he could wait much longer, he said, 'Would you like more wine ... or do you think I might take you to bed?'

Anticipation already accelerating her pulse and fizzing under every inch of her skin, Madeleine rose, held out her hands and said simply, 'Bed, please.'

'Good choice.' The next second Nicholas was on his feet with his arms around her and his mouth on hers. And a long moment later, the words muffled against her hair, '*Very* good choice.'

Once inside the bedchamber, he trapped her body between his and the door for another kiss. Then, stepping back to try and regain a measure of control, he said unevenly, 'Since my lady doesn't have her maid with her ... perhaps she might make do with me?'

And Madeleine said huskily, 'By all means, sir. She has been looking forward to it.'

Just for a second, beset by so many temptations, Nicholas hesitated until the answer became obvious. For months, he had wanted to see her hair in all its flowing glory; so punctuating the task with small kisses, he began removing pins and wedding rose-buds until it cascaded over his hands in a gossamer cloud and he could bury his face in it, inhaling its scent. Somewhat belatedly, he became aware that Madeleine had unbuttoned his vest and was busy unfastening his cravat. Lifting his head, he said, 'Should I --?'

'Yes,' she said rapidly. 'Yes, please.'

Both garments were consigned to the floor, leaving Madeleine's hands free to explore the contours of his shoulders and chest beneath the fine linen of his shirt. It wasn't enough. 'And this.' Her mouth trailed fire up his throat and along his jaw. 'Your shirt. Please.'

Somewhere in a distant corner of Nicholas's mind was the realisation that he was going to have to find enough restraint for both of them; and the discovery that the thicket of thorns had been hiding this eager, passionate woman, was making his head spin. He continued unlacing her gown with hands that weren't working as efficiently as usual. The second it loosened sufficiently, she freed herself from first one sleeve and then the other with a couple of sinuous twists, wrapped her arms about his neck and said again, 'Your shirt. When you were ill I looked and looked ... and I wanted to touch but I didn't have the right. Now I do. Let me.'

Put that way, it sounded reasonable enough. Pulling the shirt over his head, he cast it away and, trying to ignore her sigh of approval or the way her mouth was trailing over his chest, continued the seemingly insurmountable task of getting rid of her gown. When it finally pooled around her feet, he seized her around the waist, lifted her from it and managed to edge a few steps nearer the bed before rewarding himself with a taste of the silky skin of her shoulder. She shuddered.

Corset, petticoats and shift melted magically away, leaving her clad in nothing but her stockings. Nicholas looked at her, his eyes feasting on tempting, pearly-pink curves and his mouth dry with wanting. Trailing his fingertips lightly from clavicle to thigh, he said helplessly, 'Oh God, sweetheart. You are so beautiful.'

Her breathing fast and shallow but emboldened by what she saw in his face, Madeleine lay on the side of the bed and propped her head on one hand. She smiled; a siren, an odalisque, a wicked fantasy made flesh. 'Your turn.'

Every cell in Nicholas's body responded and his arousal spiralled to a degree little short of excruciating. He thought dizzily, *I'm going to die. She's literally going to kill me. And I shan't mind.*

Clinging grimly to his self-control and deliberately taking his time about it, he stripped off the remainder of his clothes, finishing with the ribbon that was still somehow clinging to his hair. Then, without coming a step closer, he said, 'Not that I'm complaining ... but if you keep this up, it will be over in minutes and we'll both be disappointed.'

Madeleine looked back at him, splendid in his nakedness, and felt her bones turn to molten lava. She said simply, '*I won't. I couldn't be. Not ever.*'

Nicholas shook his head, his eyes full of heat and tender amusement.

'Thank you. But a man has his pride, you know ... so perhaps you'll let me set the pace?' He paused, watching a flicker of mingled doubt and curiosity creep into the lovely green eyes. 'There are a few things you've yet to discover ... but you'll have to slow down if we're to get to them.'

'Oh?' She swallowed hard and nodded. 'What things?'

'Well, I think I'll begin,' he said, reaching out with apparent calm to untie her garters, 'with these.'

Her eyes widened and she bit her lower lip. 'Why?'

'Because I can't kiss my way up from your toes if stockings are in the way, can I?'

'Oh. No. I d-don't suppose you can.'

And after that, it was easy. With the stockings gone, Nicholas journeyed slowly from the arch of her instep to the pulse at the base of the throat, stopping frequently to worship everything along the way. When he finally drew the length of her body against his, she gave a sobbing moan. Lightly and without haste, he traced the lines of her shoulders, the curve of her hip; and Madeleine, every sense ablaze, dug her fingers into the thick silkiness of his hair before setting out to learn the texture of his skin and the shape of the muscles beneath it.

There was no room for thought. She had never imagined that an innocent kiss in the crook of her elbow or the inside of her knee could send heat and sensation flooding to quite different parts of her ... or that Nicholas seemed to know exactly what inflamed her most. Nothing existed beyond the swelling vortex of pleasure he was creating as his mouth followed his hands, teasing, touching, caressing ... and bringing the promise of something more; something that came closer and closer until it seemed almost within her grasp.

When the time for delicious torture was past, Nicholas moved over her saying raggedly, 'I'm sorry.' But she shook her head and pulled him against her, aware of nothing except her body's demand for his. And when they were one, she said his name over and over again like a charm, helplessly followed by, 'I love you. I love you so much.'

'And I you, darling,' he gasped. 'And I, you. Always.'

After which there was nothing but sensation and magic ... and eventually bliss.

* * *

Later, lying in the curve of his arm and trailing lazy fingers over his chest, she said dreamily, 'You were right.'

And Nicholas, his brain still enjoying a little holiday somewhere outside his head said, 'I was? Good.'

'I really *didn't* know.'

'Ah. But you do now?'

'Yes.' She stretched languorously against him. 'Is it always like that?'

'Like what?'

'So ... I don't know. There isn't a word that does it justice.'

A few scraps of his missing intellect found their way back, bringing understanding and a flush of triumphant pleasure that he had apparently acquitted himself adequately. He said, 'Love makes it better, I think. But we'll need to try it again – probably several times – before I can be completely certain.'

'Oh.' She hid her smile against his shoulder. 'I shan't mind that.'

'I know you won't. There were a few moments earlier when I wasn't sure you were going to let me get as far as the bed.'

Catching the note of smug masculinity, Madeleine said, 'You didn't fight very hard.'

'I didn't fight at all. Why would I? Your eagerness to get me out of my clothes was --' He stopped when she delivered a stinging slap to his chest and, rolling her beneath him, concluded calmly, ' ... immensely flattering. So I'll strip for you as often as you like, darling – provided, of course, that you return the favour.' He grinned when she blushed whilst somehow also managing to look speculative. 'There are still other discoveries to be made, you see. And fortunately, I'm not short of either stamina or imagination.'

Her brows rose. 'Or conceit, it seems.'

The astringent tone told Nicholas that his love hadn't shed quite *all* of her former prickles; but although it made him want to laugh, he tutted reprovingly.

'It's only conceit if I fail to live up to my promises – which I won't. And I have a number of delicious fantasies in mind.'

'As it happens,' murmured Madeleine, 'so do I. And top of the list is something involving scented soap and that extremely inviting bath-tub in the next room. What do you think?'

Thank you for reading **Hazard**. Reviews are valuable to authors and new readers alike, so if you took a few minutes to post something on Amazon, it would be greatly appreciated.

For all the latest news, offers and Who's Who in the 17th & 18th Centuries – or merely to ask a question or chat – visit Stella at:

http://stellarileybooks.co.uk/

Printed in Poland
by Amazon Fulfillment
Poland Sp. z o.o., Wrocław